13

WHAT READERS ARE SAYING ABOUT
PREVIOUS BOOKS BY DIANNA CRAWFORD

"I loved your book so much that I read it over and over. I thank you for writing such wonderful books that have to do with God, romance, and our nation's history."

› Kim Hanson, Maine ›

"I can't begin to tell you how much I enjoyed your book.
Please keep up the great work."

› Jo An McNiel, Texas ›

"You don't just tell a story; you make it live. I look forward to each evening when, once again, I laugh with true enjoyment and get to know the oh-so-interesting family of characters you have created."

› Deborah Jones, Maryland ›

"I could not put your books down! I have highly recommended them and passed them around to my friends."

› Mary Lou Hess, Illinois ›

"Your stories have been the refreshing oasis that I so often need but can never quite find."

› Kathryn Soulier, Louisiana ›

"So real, exciting, and funny. We have problems every day, and it's so much fun to see how God will help us. Your story shows this in a big and wonderful way."

› Sherrie Sumner, Texas ›

"I used to laugh at my mom whenever I'd see her crying over something that happened in the book she was reading, but now I understand why she does. Now it's her turn to laugh at me, because I have been crying over your books."

› Quimbly Walker, Texas ›

"Definitely the best books I've ever read."

, Jasmine Madson, Minnesota ,

"Your books have turned many a boring night into a wonderful evening
and a trip back in time."

, Stephanie Bastion, Illinois ,

HEART
QUEST®

romance the way it's meant to be

HeartQuest brings you romantic fiction
with a foundation of biblical truth.
Adventure, mystery, intrigue, and suspense
mingle in these heartwarming stories of
men and women of faith striving to build
a love that will last a lifetime.

May HeartQuest books sweep you
into the arms of God, who longs for you
and pursues you always.

a Home in the Valley

DIANNA CRAWFORD

Romance fiction from
Tyndale House Publishers, Inc., Wheaton, Illinois
www.heartquest.com

Visit Tyndale's exciting Web site at www.tyndale.com

Check out the latest about HeartQuest Books at www.heartquest.com

Copyright © 2002 by Dianna Crawford. All rights reserved.

HeartQuest is a registered trademark of Tyndale House Publishers, Inc.

Illustrations © 2002 by Victor Gadino. All rights reserved.

Edited by Susan D. Lerdal

Designed by Ron Kaufmann

Scripture quotations are taken from the *Holy Bible*, King James Version.

Scripture quotations in Note from the Author are taken from the *Holy Bible*, New Living Translation, copyright © 1996. Used by permission of Tyndale House Publishers, Inc., Wheaton, Illinois 60189. All rights reserved.

Library of Congress Cataloging-in-Publication Data

Crawford, Dianna, date.
A home in the valley / Dianna Crawford.
    p. cm. — (HeartQuest) (Reardon Valley ; #1)
ISBN 0-8423-6010-7
1. Women pioneers—Fiction.   2. Shoemakers—Fiction.   3. Tennessee—Fiction.   I. Title.
II. Series.
PS3553.R27884 H66 2002
813'.54—dc21   2002001258

Printed in the United States of America

06 05 04 03 02
5   4   3   2   1

A Home in the Valley *is dedicated to
my grandchildren with all my love
and the hope that they, too, will always be blessed
with a strong and abiding faith
such as Sabina Erhardt has in this novel.*

Acknowledgments

I would like to take this opportunity to thank and acknowledge those who aided me in the completion of A Home in the Valley: Sally Laity and Sue Rich, my faithful and insightful critique partners; my editor, Susan Lerdal; and Louise Cox, librarian in the Nashville Room of that city's beautiful new library. Also, I'd like to thank the librarian in Paris, Kentucky, who was so helpful with information about the "Great Gathering" of 1801 at Cane Ridge, Kentucky.

Chapter One

AUGUST 1801

Mama!" came the frightened wail of a child. "Mama!"

Sabina Erhardt, being pushed along by a noisy throng, stopped at the sound of terror. Bracing herself against the crush of people, she looked quickly around her, searching through the sea of gathered skirts and men's leggings. If a small child fell in this crowd, she might easily be trampled before anyone noticed.

To Sabina's relief, she spotted the little four- or five-year-old youngster fighting her way past swirls of gingham and calico to stumble right into Sabina's waiting arms.

As Sabina pulled her close, the carrottop looked up with wide green eyes and a freckled nose. "I can't find my mama."

Sabina lifted the child up into her arms. Then, hoping to calm the little one, she asked teasingly, "Did that careless mother of yours get herself lost?"

The child stared back, speechless, until the fear in her gaze melted away. She jutted out her frail chin. "Yes, she did. Mama needs a good hard spankin'."

Sabina laughed. "I think mayhap a kiss and a hug is more what she'll be needing. Your mama's probably real scared right about now that she got lost."

The pigtailed redhead frowned, studying on Sabina's words. "Maybe that would be better. Besides, you know how mamas like bein' kissed."

Sabina couldn't help laughing again as she lifted the girl higher. "I surely do. Climb on my shoulders. Perched up there, you'll be able to see into the whole clearing."

Sabina noted that her own mother was being swallowed up by the multitude leaving this afternoon's wondrous session of the great revival meeting at Cane Ridge, Kentucky. Twenty-five thousand people, she'd heard said, twenty-five *thousand*, who'd traveled here from all over Kentucky and Tennessee—more people than Sabina had ever seen in one place. More people than she'd thought even lived in the vales and coves west of the Allegheny Mountains. "Mama! . . . Greta!" she called to her still blonde and slender mother, and was grateful to see the older version of herself stop and wait for her to catch up.

Once Sabina had the child with her blue-plaid skirt collaring her own neck, she worked her way through the human stream to reach her mother.

"I see you've grown a bit taller," Sabina's mother remarked with a curious glance.

"You mean my new friend, here. She's misplaced her mama."

With that gentle way of hers, Greta smiled up at the child. "I see. Mayhap she's gone on to your wagon. Can you point us to where your family is camped?"

The little girl swiveled back and forth. "I think it's—no, it's over yon—no. It's . . . maybe it's—"

The camping sites had been laid out in a series of orderly rows surrounding the meeting area, and to a small child, Sabina reckoned every wagon and makeshift tent looked alike. "Do not worry. All the people will be settled in their own spots soon, fixing supper. We'll just walk down all of the lanes till you find your folks."

Besides, it wasn't as if she and her mother were in any rush to get their own supper on the table—Kurt, Sabina's stepfather, probably wouldn't show up to eat till past midnight. Gamblers preferred playing their games of chance within the cloak of darkness, especially in a holy place such as this. And if Kurt and his cronies got caught luring young farm lads into their dens of iniquity, they'd probably be tarred and feathered and ridden out of camp on a rail.

If only Kurt had joined her and her mother at the meetings this week. It would've been impossible for him to withstand the Holy Spirit's awesome power that had filled the clearing betwixt the seven preaching stands. Seven preachers, all calling out from every direction for the almighty power of God to come down and smite the devil from amongst the people. . . . A shiver raced up Sabina's spine every time she recalled the gloriously electric wind that had swept across the clearing in wave after wave, and of the thousands of "new lights" for Jesus that were being brought forth day after day—new lights in a territory where such a heathen darkness had reigned for so long.

"By the by," her mother said, looking up at the child on Sabina's shoulders, "what's your name?"

The little one leaned down toward Greta. "Lilac. An' my mama's name is Violet, an' Pansy's name is Pansy. Daddy says we're his bouquet of flowers."

The child's innocent bragging touched Sabina. Lilac's fath⸗ sounded like a man who treasured his family. He probably provided a cozy home for them, too—a place where a body could set down roots—unlike her own gypsy existence.

"Lilac! Lilac Wallace!"

Sabina swung toward the sound of the young voice. A half-grown girl came straight for them through the thinning crowd. Pansy, perhaps. But seeing the girl's large doelike eyes and hair as richly brown as a beaver's pelt, Sabina couldn't imagine the two youngsters being sisters.

As the girl reached them, she turned back and hollered. "Papa, over here. I found her. I found Lilac."

A man approached in long strides. He had the older child's expressive eyes, but in contrast to her simple blue-checked gingham, he was dressed in the tailored attire of an Eastern gentleman rather than the coarse linen or deerskin of the usual Tennessee homesteader. Over bronze silk breeches, he wore a waistcoat of gold-and-bronze brocade. And his shoes! The shiny silver buckles were fit for a king.

Sabina curled her own bare toes deeper within the drape of her faded gray linsey-woolsey skirt as she took in the remainder of his features, which were aristocratic, reminding her of the landed gentry of Virginia. To be sure, he was a man of social prominence. But more important, if this fine gentleman brought his family to this great gathering, he had to be a Christian. A Christian father.

The gent swept his tricorn from his head. "Baxter Clay, at your service, ladies."

The lost child's last name was Wallace, Sabina noted. The ndsome man was *not* her father, then.

e are immeasurably grateful to you kind ladies," he contin- oice as pleasing as the rest of him. "I thank you for kindness in taking charge of Lilac. Her mother, frantic."

"And that she should be." Sabina winked at him. "Getting lost like she did. Lilac and me has been searching all over for her. Ain't that right, Lilac?"

"Yes, ma'am. I'm gonna give Mama a good talkin' to when we find her."

A grin lifted the corners of the gentleman's firm mouth. "And I know just where to look." He reached for the child. "Why don't you climb on up here," he said swinging her astride his own strong shoulders. "Delia and I will escort you to your family."

While he settled the child, Sabina quickly straightened her simple shawl collar that had gone askew, then folded her hands as she'd seen so many of the more gently bred women do.

Mr. Clay turned back to Sabina and her mother. "Again, thank you, ladies." After another slight bow, he replaced his braid-trimmed hat and caught his daughter Delia's hand; then the threesome strolled off with the two girls chattering happily away.

The lost child was not his, Sabina knew as she watched them go. Yet the expensively dressed man had not felt he was above joining the search. And neither of the children seemed to fear his wrath in the least. He was undoubtedly a loving father and a good neighbor. The kind of man any woman would count herself blessed to marry.

When he and the girls were swallowed again by the dispersing crowd, Sabina hooked her arm into her mother's. "Rich or not, that is a man after God's own heart. That one shouldn't have no trouble getting into the heavenly kingdom."

Her mother patted her hand as they started walking in step again with the remaining stragglers. "He's the kind of man I pray you'll marry one day. If only we could light in one place long enough to give some good decent fellow the chance to come courting."

Suddenly, the joy was sucked from the day. "We've talked about this so many times before, Mama. Even if we did stay some place long enough and some fine young man actually did want to come calling, how would we explain away Kurt and his gambling ways?"

"My sweet daughter, you are speaking doubt again. Don't forget, 'The salvation of the righteous is of the Lord: he is their strength in the time of trouble. And the Lord shall help them, and deliver them: he shall deliver them from the wicked, and save them, because they trust in him.'"

"Yes, Mama, but nowhere in the Bible does it say I'm guaranteed a godly husband."

"You are 'like a green olive tree in the house of God,' the psalmist says. 'I trust in the mercy of God for ever and ever.'"

"That's well and good, Mama. But I think maybe God has already showed his mercy by turning the curse of my tainted birth into a blessing for us both—the blessing of us always being together, sharing our love for the Lord. It may very well be that my destiny is to never leave your side, what with Kurt carrying you from one gambling den to another. Like Naomi and Ruth in the Bible. 'Whither thou goest, I will go.'"

"You're right. Ruth was faithful to Naomi, just like you are to me. And you've traveled with me now till you're into your twenties. But don't forget, God eventually sent Boaz to Ruth. And my prayer is that you, too, will soon have your Boaz. For years now, my nightly prayer has been that you won't always be burdened with the sins of my youth . . . the shame of your birth."

"Mama, please don't never think I would wish for any other mother. 'Tis true, us living with a loose-footed vagabond such as Kurt is like trying to keep house on a seesaw. But you always been my solid place, my home—you and the Lord—the place I always know I can go to for love and mercy. I really don't need nothing else. Especially not one of them no-accounts Kurt keeps trying to pawn me off on."

"Poor Kurt. He really does do the best he can by us, considering he's abiding in such a dark place. I pray for him day and night."

"I know you do," Sabina sighed wearily.

Greta squeezed her hand. "Don't lose heart. Just keep your eye on the true path, and I know somewhere along the way the Lord has a Boaz waiting just for you. You'll see. Someone fine and upstanding, like that Mr. Clay fellow."

~

"*No!*"

The loud cry brought Sabina from a dead sleep. Was that her mother? She flung off the light flannel sheeting and sprang up from her pallet. Quickly she oriented herself, remembering that she stood in her own small tent, located on the fringes of the great religious gathering. Surely none of these good church people would try to harm her mother. But at any large assembly there were those who lurked around the fringes, waiting to take advantage.

As she rushed toward the canvas opening, she heard the slightly slurred whisper of her stepfather. He'd been drinking again.

"You don't understand, sugar. I didn't have nothin' else to bet with. Ever' cent I had was on the barrelhead. And I had the winning cards. I was sure of it. You gotta believe that, sweetie. I was stone sure. I would'a bet my own mama."

"But you didn't," her mother retorted in a fierce whisper. "You bet *my daughter*."

Stunned, an ominous chill seized Sabina as she slipped out into the mild summer night. But her parents were not within sight. Then she heard Kurt's besotted pleading again, coming from the tent he shared with her mother.

"Now, honey, you know I think of Sabina like she's mine, too. Ain't I raised her since she was just a pup? An' listen—I was thinkin' this over on my way here. If I had to lose her to someone, I couldn't have picked a better sort. Oh, an' by the by, I'm gonna need to sell that brooch I bought you last month. Like I said, I'm plumb busted."

"Who did you lose her to?" Greta's voice sounded angry and as frightened as Sabina now felt.

With her fists knotted as tightly as her stomach, Sabina started for their tent.

"Shockley . . . Tom Shockley." Kurt answered his wife with a hint of hesitation in his voice. Even liquored up, he knew he'd crossed the line. That had to be in her favor.

Sabina paused outside their tent. Her mother would have more luck talking some sense into him if she stayed out of the mix.

"That hulking bully?" Greta charged. "He's got the gambling fever worse than you do."

"Are you sayin' I ain't done right by you and Bina?" His slurring whine had turned stubborn. "When I took you and your fatherless babe on, you was purt' near starved, with nothin' more'n the rags on your back. Since you been with me, you ain't missed hardly a meal. An' I've bought you plenty of purties, like that brooch. An' ain't I been a good an' faithful husband to you? That's more'n I can say fer a lot of them holier-than-thou braggarts I seen struttin' around here this week. I'd take odds, them what ain't tiptoein' off to Curly's tent to visit his girls will be sneakin' upstairs at some dockside tavern come next week."

"Curly and his girls are here, too?" Her mother's shock was laced with disdain. "But that still don't—"

"No more *buts*," he overrode gruffly, outtalking Mama, as usual. "You know Shockley's been wantin' to marry up with Sabina fer years. Ever' time our paths cross he asks about her, sayin' as how he'd sure like to have a sweet cornsilk gal just like I got. Even after she's turned him down. Twice."

"So you just naturally knew he'd be willing to take Sabina as a wager."

"Blast it, woman, Sabina's twenty-two. Practically an old maid. No less'n a dozen of my acquaintances has come askin' for her. An' that uppity gal wouldn't settle on none of 'em."

"Acquaintances? You mean your boozing, brawling, tavern mates?"

"Insult my friends all you want, but what's done is done." A deadly hardness wiped the last slur from his speech. "Sabina belongs to Tom now, and he's got my IOU to prove it. Now shut up and let me get some sleep. Shockley's comin' in the mornin' to take her over to one of them preacher men—you know, them blackbirds what's been yammerin' an' hollerin' round here all week. And as excited as Shockley was about marryin' up with Sabina, he'll probably be here 'fore the sun is halfway—hey, where you goin'?"

"Out," Greta retorted harshly, then softened her voice. "Out behind yon tree to—you know."

The man grunted his acknowledgment as Greta, in a muslin night rail, stepped out into the darkness and almost stumbled into Sabina. Urgently, she motioned for her daughter to follow her into the woods.

Hoping, praying that this was nothing but a bad dream, Sabina trembled as she followed her mother into the deeper shadows of the nearest trees, the only light coming from the flashes of fireflies. This had to be a nightmare—she absolutely couldn't find herself trapped into a godless marriage such as her mother's. Surely the Lord didn't want that, either. Surely he didn't. This could not be her destiny. Gambled away on a losing hand of cards.

Please, Lord, tell me it isn't so.

Pausing for Sabina to catch up, her mother grabbed her hand. "Hurry!" she whispered, moving fast again, heedless of the fact that they walked barefoot across twigs and roots into pitch blackness. "I need to get back before Kurt starts wondering."

With no more than a stubbed toe or two, Sabina and her mother passed enough trees and shrubs to shield them from the outer row of wagons and tents. They stopped behind a thick tree trunk.

Sabina didn't wait for her mother to speak. "I heard everything, Mama. *Everything.*"

"Then you know we have to act fast."

Hope flickered. "What do you mean?"

"As soon as you hear Kurt take up his snoring, I want you to gather up your things. Don't chance putting fire to your lamp. Then I want you to circle around to the other side of the camp and hide out in the woods. With tomorrow morning being the last preaching service, most everybody will be heading out soon as it's over. Maybe even before. Let the Lord direct your steps. He'll find you a safe passage out of here. When he does, promise me you won't hang back like Lot's wife did at Sodom. You just go and keep on going."

"But what if the Almighty doesn't show me where to go? I can't just sit out there forever."

"O ye of little faith," her mother chided. "You trust the Lord just like we always done. He don't want you marrying some no-account gambler no more'n I do."

"But, Mama, what about you? I'd be leaving you here all alone with no one you could talk to or pray with. Won't you be sorrowful lonesome without me?" Even the mere thought of leaving her mother ripped unbearably at Sabina's heart.

"You know I will. But Kurt is determined you're leaving us tomorrow anyway. So it's on your own tonight or with Tom Shockley in the morning."

"Then you come with me. Let God lead us both out of here."

Greta clutched Sabina's shoulders. "I would give anything to go with you. But I can't. Kurt is my husband. I married him of my own free will, for better or for worse till death do us part. I'm bound to that."

"But, Mama, I won't never be able to come back to see you. And the way Kurt keeps moving from place to place, I won't even know where you are or if you're alive and well. I couldn't bear that."

"I know, sweetheart." Her mother expelled a sad breath. When she spoke again, her voice held more promise. "We're headed north of here to a river stop on the Ohio. Cincinnati, I think it's called. Kurt says there's a lot of cash crops being hauled down the river this time of year. And folks laying over for the night. He figures there's lots of money to be made. He says we'll probably hole up for the winter there. As soon as you've found a safe place, you get someone to write a letter for you and send it off to Cincinnati."

"But you can't read any more than I can write."

"Don't you worry about that. I'll find someone I can trust. A local preacher, maybe. And I'll have him write a letter straight back to you. We won't lose each other, I promise."

"Oh, Mama, it all sounds so risky."

Greta pulled Sabina close. "You and me, we're going to pray every night for the good Lord to bring us back together again. You and me. The minute the sun sets—the very minute it drops behind the hills—we'll both start praying. That'll be our pact.

Remember, 'if two of you shall agree on earth as touching any thing that they shall ask, it shall be done for them of my Father which is in heaven.'"

"But, Mama, I still won't know—"

Her mother hushed her with a finger to her lips. "Shh, my sweet. Don't you worry. Just trust that every hair on our heads counts with the Lord. He loves you and me that much. Even when I fell into sin and ruined my life, he saw me through. And you—" she stepped back, holding Sabina at arm's length—"promise me you'll do everything I said. Promise me now, 'cause I'm out of time. I got to get back to the tent."

Sabina's throat began to clog. This was to be their farewell, and the darkness prevented her from seeing the love, the sadness, she knew were in her mother's eyes. "I will. And Mama, *it will happen*. We will find each other again. We will."

Greta sucked in a sob, then ran a motherly thumb along Sabina's cheek. "Fare thee well, my precious gift. Don't you never lose faith." Then Greta whirled around and was gone, running back to the camp.

The tears that had been filling Sabina's eyes spilled down her cheeks, streaking across the place her mother had just touched. It had been difficult enough for just the two of them together to stay true to their Lord among all the gamblers and thieves, but alone . . . ? This would be a purely hard test. For the first time, Sabina understood how Jesus must have felt when he left his family to go into the dangers of the wilderness. Her head bowed with the weighty thought of it.

Finally, gazing up through the trees, she wiped the wetness from her eyes. *Give me the trust of Jesus, Lord. I will go wherever you lead . . . but, please, mark the path big and bold, so I don't make a wrong turn.*

Chapter Two

Sabina sat beneath the low-hanging branches of a beech tree, her two bundles of clothes on either side of her as she rubbed a stone-inflicted bruise on her heel. Charging through the woods at night was definitely not good for naked feet or her clothes. Ever since she'd climbed into this hiding place beyond the sprawling camp, she'd been picking burrs and twigs off her skirt and belongings. And who knew how many eight-legged creatures crawled about?

She couldn't continue to sit here. The sun had been up a good hour. The smell of cook-fire smoke, the rattle of pots, and all the other sounds of folks preparing for the day echoed through the woods. Common sense told her she should catch a ride out of the area before Kurt or her "bridegroom" awakened.

Coming up to her knees, Sabina peered past the leafy branches on the chance that her stepfather was already out looking for her, though she knew he never rose before noon.

"O Lord, I pray Tom Shockley sleeps just as late, that he hasn't rousted Kurt out yet."

"Trust in the Lord," she could hear her mother say. *"Trust in the Lord."* Well, she would try. But how very much she would miss the bosom companionship they shared.

Sabina took a deep, courage-filling breath and crawled out of her haven, dragging her only possessions with her. "All right, Lord," she said, rising to her sore feet. "I'm going to trust."

During the night, she'd crossed to the far side of the stream that watered the camp, but now she headed toward it, staying close to whatever cover the forest's undergrowth provided.

A pair of squirrels quarreled at her from their oak-tree home as she passed, and the birds flying from branch to branch overhead set up a racket, announcing her every move. Even the rustle of the leaves underfoot, every snap of a twig, seemed louder than normal. As she picked her way down to the narrow stream, she was grateful for its steady murmur that muffled most of her own noise.

Upon reaching the water's edge, she glanced up a wide pathway that had been cleared for the campers' convenience. A boy walked along the water, swinging a bucket. Her first instinct was to duck behind a nearby stand of cane. Then reason took hold. Perhaps the presence of this boy wasn't mere coincidence. Perhaps he was part of God's plan.

"Morning to you," she called as she caught up her hem with one of the bundles and started wading across the sandy bottom.

The kid, probably nine or ten, grinned, his grown-up front teeth still too large for the rest of his face. "Howdy. You camped nearby? I ain't seen you around here before."

"I've been here all week."

"Me, too. We was one of the first ones here." The boy's berry-brown face turned sour. "But Papa says we gotta leave early, so's we won't be eatin' ever'body's dust all day. And I promised my friend Barney I'd go fishin' with him this mornin'."

They're leaving early. Thank you, Jesus. "I reckon fishing is a lot of fun. I never been."

He brightened, his dark eyes sparkling gold in the morning sun. "I'd be pleasured to show you how, you bein' such a purty lady and all." His joy collapsed again. "But I can't."

"That is disappointing. Here," she said, setting down her bundles beside him. "Let me fill that bucket for you."

"Oh, I'm plenty strong. I can do it," he said, puffing out his bony chest.

"I'm sure you can. Which way are you and your family headed?" She glanced about her, while trying not to look as jumpy as she felt.

"Back to Tennessee. We're from Reardon Valley," he said, scooping up a bucketful. "Ever hear of it?"

"No, I can't say as I have."

"You ain't no different'n ever'one else. I ain't met a single soul here what knows where it is. An' it's a big valley, plenty bigger'n this puny cove."

The more he talked, the better she liked what he said. Even without her asking, he was telling her exactly what she wanted to hear. A remote valley in the opposite direction of the Ohio. This had to be of God. *Step out in faith*, she reminded herself. *Trust.* "Do you think your folks would have room for me? I can't leave here with the ones I come with."

Surprised, the kid tucked his chin. "Why not?"

Why not? She hated lying. "I'm being asked to do something I don't think God would approve of."

"Like what?" The too-inquisitive boy suddenly sucked in his bottom lip. "Whoops. I done it again. I ain't supposed to be so nosy. Tell you what, you come back to camp with me, an' you can ask Papa if you can come. We got the room, so I don't see why he'd say no. I know my brothers won't, for sure. They likes purty girls a lot."

"I take it they're older than you."

"Aye. And they think they're so smart."

"Lead the way," Sabina said, trying to squelch her amusement. Snagging up her bundles, Sabina followed the youngster up the bank and through the woods.

As the campground came into view she stopped and scanned in both directions again, searching for Kurt or Shockley. But all she saw were people going about their morning chores or eating breakfast. No one paid her any mind at all.

The kid, several yards ahead now, turned back. "We're over yonder," he said pointing toward a site with a fair-sized farm wagon parked in the middle of it. To one side, logs made an L around a blazing cook fire.

Taking one last wary look down the line of campsites, Sabina stepped from the shade of the trees and followed the boy to his family's spot. If she could just manage to slip away undetected . . . the site appeared empty until she saw someone bent low, crawling out from beneath the vehicle. A girl, carrying bedding. Like many families, they must have used their wagon bed for a roof.

The girl, holding blankets piled high, straightened up and swung toward the boy. "It's about time you got back, Sammy. Can't do the dishes without water."

"*Sam*," he corrected fiercely.

"What*ever* you say." Her sarcasm was equally combative. "Just get the water in the kettle and hook it over the fire. Can't do dishes—" Spotting Sabina from behind her wall of bedding, the girl lowered her burden. "Why, it's you. The flaxen-haired miss from yesterday. May we be of service?"

Before Sabina stood the girl from yesterday, the one who came for the lost child. The one with the handsome gent for a father. Sabina stared back at the doelike eyes. Coming to this very camp couldn't have been mere chance. It had been foreknown by God yesterday. Out of the thousands of people, he'd allowed her to meet members of this family, think kindly of them even before she found herself in need.

"Did Lilac leave something with you by mistake?" the girl asked, observing the bundles Sabina carried.

"Forgive my rudeness," Sabina said, unable to stop the smile spreading across her face. "I'm just surprised to see you. Miss Delia, isn't it?"

"That's right." The girl, who was easily as tall as Sabina, shifted the blankets to one arm and smoothed the brunette strands above her night braid.

Making sure the wagon shielded her from the rest of the camp, Sabina dropped her burdens on a flat rock and stepped toward the girl. "Here, let me help you fold those. It's a lot faster with two."

"Sure, if you'd like." Delia stacked all but one blanket on top of Sabina's pile and offered half. "But, why . . ."

"'Cause she can't stay where she was," Sammy yelled from the campfire. "She wants to leave with us."

"Oh," young Delia said, then looked at Sabina more curiously than before as they stretched out the gray wool cover.

"My stepfather has made arrangements for me to marry someone who isn't a Christian man. I can't give myself over to a heathen. It goes against what the Lord teaches."

"And no one should make you—'specially if you don't love him."

Sabina walked toward Delia with two corners of the blanket. "Even if I did—which I don't—it wouldn't be right."

"Yes, I can see why you had to run away. My papa would never make me marry someone I wasn't partial to. . . . Least-ways, I don't think he would." A disturbed look flashed across Delia's expressive brown eyes.

"When I met him yesterday, he seemed like too nice a man to ever deliberately hurt you." Sabina remembered the open kindness that had been in his every word and action.

"He ain't always nice," Sammy chipped in. "He whooped me real good last month for—" He stopped midsentence and got a sheepish look. "Never mind what for. But, for sure, he's nice enough to take you with us. Ain't he, sis?"

"Aye. If we put it to him *just right.*"

"And what about your mother?" Sabina asked. "I wouldn't want—"

"We ain't got no mother," Sammy blustered.

"Oh, I'm so sorry." Sabina saw the children through new eyes.

"I don't even remember her," Sammy barged on. "She died when I was just a baby. But Papa says we need another one now. That's one of the reasons we come here, to get us a stepmother."

"Sammy!" Delia chided. "You make it sound like Papa came here to buy a sack of cornmeal. He loved our mama a lot. But he says it's time we had what he calls a lady's presence. An' he's just visitin' around, seein' if there's anyone of interest. That's all. Nothin' more. He's just lookin', Miss . . . Miss . . . what should I call you?" The girl didn't sound as if she wanted her father to get in any rush to marry, either.

"Sabina will do nicely."

"Sabina?" Sammy interjected. "I ain't never heard nobody called that before."

"It's German. My mother named me after her favorite aunt."

"I'm named after my grandmother." Delia's attention was then diverted by two lads coming with a team of big gray workhorses, their harness jangling, the chains behind dragging in the dirt. "Philip! Howie! Hurry up. I want you to meet someone."

The oldest, a tall gangling lad with the same rich brown hair and eyes as the other Clays, picked up the pace, eying Sabina curiously. The younger, a couple of inches shorter but with the same family coloring, grinned eagerly as they approached with the plodding animals. Both lads were as simply dressed as the other two. Perhaps their father wasn't as rich as Sabina had assumed. However, all four did wear sturdy shoes crafted from fine leather—better than she'd ever owned, whenever she'd actually owned a pair.

The oldest boy, whom Sabina guessed to be sixteen or so, handed the team off to his younger brother and bowed slightly. "At your service, ma'am. Something we can help you with?"

"There sure is," Sammy answered for her. The boy sounded a little big for his britches. "We're takin' her home with us."

"We don't know that," Sabina corrected, while taking another peek past the wagon, searching for her stepfather and Tom Shockley. "I'm looking for a ride away from the camp meeting, if your father is agreeable."

"No reason you can't just come all the way home with us," Sammy proposed. "That way Papa wouldn't have to pay Ma Johnson to come over to bake and wash for us."

"Sounds good to me," agreed the middle brother with a cocky grin. "This one's a whole lot easier on the eye, ain't she, Phil?"

The oldest lad's expression lost its welcome as he continued his slow appraisal. "You're the gal they're lookin' for, ain't you? Cornsilk hair, green eyes, slender."

Sabina's heart stopped, then started again. Hard. Kurt had already discovered she was missing. She darted glances in both directions, then quickly moved between the heads of the two massive horses. "What did you say?" she barely managed to mumble. "Where?"

"At the stock pens. Me'n Howie was—I mean, were—down at the stock pens fetchin' our horses, when these two men come up and start askin' if anyone has seen a purty young lady lookin' for a ride out of camp."

"Stop talkin' so loud," Delia chided. "Or you'll have her caught for sure. Her pa is tryin' to marry her off today to some heathen fella. And that ain't right."

"Yeah, an' they're real serious about it," the middle brother added. "They're even offerin' a reward."

"Well," Delia argued with passion, "I say there ain't no amount of money worth marryin' up with some sinner you don't even love. If Pa tried to do that to me when I come of marryin' age, I'd run away too. And so would you. And you, too, Philip. We all seen how you been chasin' after that prissy Newman gal all week."

"An' he caught her a couple of times," Howie teased.

The nearly grown lad's face burned red. "All right, all right. But if the lady's comin' with us, we best get her hid before them two jaspers come walkin' up this way." He eyed Sabina. "Come here and let me give you a boost up into the wagon." As he hoisted her onto the straw-covered bed, he yelled back at his siblings, "Delia, Howie, grab the blankets and clothes bags quick. Pile 'em over her. Sammy, shovel dirt over that fire."

"But the dishes ain't done," Delia argued as Sabina crawled between a crate and some grain sacks to the spot just behind the driver's seat.

"Pack the dishes dirty," Philip commanded. "We can always wash 'em when we stop at noon."

A body would've thought the lad was an army sergeant, the way his siblings hustled to dump bedding and bundles over

Sabina. He continued to bark orders while he hitched the team, and his siblings hustled to finish loading. Even if she did get caught, she'd be profoundly grateful to these benevolent young people, though she wished she didn't have to involve them in her escape.

At that moment a calming peace settled upon her, and she knew that neither she nor the youngsters had a thing to fear. The Lord had led her to the Clay family as surely as the sun had risen this morning.

~

Baxter Clay caught himself grinning as he strode between two rows of wagons and tents back to his own spot. The farewells he'd shared with Mistress Amanda Atwood, her aunt, and her father, Storekeeper Finch, had been most promising. Attired this morning in his plain working clothes for the dusty trip home, Baxter congratulated himself again for his decision to make the grueling twelve-day trip up here to northern Kentucky. He couldn't have asked for a more fruitful sojourn. Not only had the preaching been the most inspired he'd ever heard, and not only had he received thirty-seven orders for new footwear, but he'd singled out the woman he planned to court. And the young widow was most agreeable to his suit.

Of that he had no doubt.

Both her and her folks' mouths had gaped open when they learned that he was indeed one of the Clays of Virginia, as well as related to the Randolphs. The fact that he was not in line to inherit didn't seem to bother the prosperous storekeeper as long as Baxter's family ties were still intact.

According to Mr. Finch, influential contacts could prove equally profitable. And for the merchant's side, the older man had hinted rather broadly that his daughter would come handsomely endowed when she remarried. His trade was not limited to the needs of Nashville. He'd established lucrative fur-trading posts farther west. The fine carriage in which they'd arrived, along with their two slaves, attested to his wealth.

Yes, it would be a most profitable match all the way around.

And no one would say that Mistress Amanda was not pleasing to the eye. Aside from her fashionable attire, her face and nicely rounded figure needed no improvement. As for love . . . there was no reason to think an affection for her wouldn't blossom in time. Not that Baxter expected to ever love again as much as he had his sweet Sally. Nor did he want to, for that matter. Losing Sally had torn his heart asunder.

He'd defied his uncle to wed the cabinetmaker's daughter. Young and foolish, he hadn't been much older than Philip was now when he forfeited the lucrative future Uncle Grayson had arranged between him and the daughter of a banking associate. But now, for his children's sake, he would pursue the financially and socially wise choice. Return something of their birthright to them.

With Mistress Amanda's dowry, he'd send Philip back East. And later, Howard. Cousin Charles had promised to keep an eye on the lads while they studied at William and Mary for a profession of a more gentlemanly nature than his own shoemaking. Recalling the professors who had been in residence when he had attended, Baxter knew they'd be up to the task of whittling off the boys' woodsy edges.

Equally important, Amanda could teach his dear but ragamuffin daughter the art of being a genteel lady. Delia's opportunity for a promising match depended on it. And if, by chance, he and his family ever did return to Virginia society, they wouldn't be treated as unsophisticated rustics. Baxter shook his head. And maybe now he'd have help curbing their deplorable butchery of the King's English they'd picked up from the other folks in the valley.

"Heard you was leavin' this mornin'," one of his camping neighbors called as Baxter passed the man's outfit.

"Aye, Mr. Snodgrass. It's a full twelve days even with the creek crossings shallow and easy. If I wait till this afternoon, we'll have to camp an extra night."

The callous and scruffy farmer grinned. "The sooner you leave, the sooner you can get started on my boots. Remember, I want 'em oxblood red."

"Don't fret. I have the color written right on your foot pattern."

"Well, then, Godspeed." The farmer extended a work-roughened hand.

Baxter returned a firm shake. "God be with you too."

Returning to his prior thoughts, Baxter felt a shade guilty. It wasn't that he didn't admire men like Farmer Snodgrass, who'd braved the wilderness to carve out an existence for themselves and their families—he just wanted his own children to have the opportunity to reclaim, if they so chose, the life his marriage had robbed from them.

Walking past Snodgrass's wagon, Baxter glanced toward his own site. He stopped. Amazed. Their entire camp was loaded up, the horses hitched, and his kids were already aboard. What had brought on this unprecedented industry?

"Papa, come on," Sammy yelled from the wagon bed. "Time's a-wastin'."

And a mere thirty minutes ago his youngest had been pleading and begging to stay another day.

Baxter stepped alongside the rig. It could have been packed in a more orderly fashion, but . . . "I'm most pleased to see how swiftly you kids prepared for our departure."

"Good," Philip answered from atop the driver's box, the set of reins draped across his palm. "Climb on up here, and let's get goin' before we're eatin' some other outfit's dust."

Another shock. This from the lad who'd asked to be left behind to ride with the Dodds, who lived only a few miles from Reardon Valley, so he could spend more time with the Newman girl. It sounded like Philip's budding romance with the young woman from Greeneville might have come to an abrupt end.

Empathy filled Baxter as he seated himself beside his oldest. First love could be heartrending. "Move 'em out," he said in a casual drawl, not wanting Philip to suspect he'd guessed the reason for the hurry. There'd be plenty of time to talk about it once Philip's loss wasn't quite so raw.

Thank goodness, he himself was older now and wiser about matters of the heart. This time around, his children's future would be his first concern. He'd leave falling in love—desperately, passionately—to the youngsters.

Chapter Three

Sabina, lying hidden against the back of the wagon seat, shifted uncomfortably, hoping to ease the pain in her lower hip. The straw spread beneath her did little to cushion the bumps and jars of the moving wheels, and the two youngsters who used her as a backrest didn't help. But Sabina knew she must remain where she was until they'd traveled many miles from the camp.

"Mr. Clay," someone called out.

Sabina held her breath. Even with all the blankets and sacks covering her, could it be she'd been discovered?

The wagon slowed to a creaking stop.

"Mr. Fleming," the children's father returned in a sociable tone.

"Just wanted to remind you," the other man said, "I'm putting aside all my other tailoring to make that new suit of clothes for you."

Sabina relaxed. Just a tradesman confirming a business deal.

"I do appreciate your special attention."

"Of course, I, too, will appreciate receiving those four pairs of shoes for my youngsters by post before mid-September."

"Actually, I'll be coming to Nashville in a few weeks. We can make the trade then, if that's convenient for you."

"You don't say?" The man's voice took on a knowing lilt. "Well, then, I'll be sure to have your suit ready."

"It's simply that I now require more up-to-date, conservative attire," Mr. Clay explained. "The flamboyance of my current suit of visiting clothes should have been buried with the turn of the century."

"That's true," Mr. Fleming agreed. "Not that anyone out in these backwoods would know the difference. Well, Godspeed to you, Mr. Clay."

"You, too."

Sabina began to breathe normally again as her unwitting host clicked his tongue and the horse team tugged the wagon into motion again. Bracing herself against the jolts, Sabina mulled over the men's exchange and came to the conclusion that she must not know any more about the latest fashions than the other folks on the frontier. To her, Mr. Clay couldn't have looked any handsomer or more prosperous than he had yesterday in the bronze-and-gold silk. And the fact that he was a widower and starting to look for a new wife hadn't slipped past her either. Was there more to God's plan concerning this family than merely her escape? At the intriguing thought, a warm swell of pleasure coursed through her bosom.

Then reason overtook her. A prosperous tradesman like Mr. Clay would never choose to wed an illegitimate child who'd been reared by a gambling man.

Still, the warm feeling didn't go away as Sabina heard both Mr. Clay and his offspring exchange farewells with more people as the wagon wove its way out of the huge sprawling campground. She also heard an occasional rider pass, yet not a single person questioned the Clays about a runaway bride. Perhaps Kurt and Thomas Shockley had already given up the search. A comforting thought, but one she didn't dare count on for some time to come.

"This has been one fine week," Mr. Clay remarked after the last good-byes had dwindled away. "Didn't you think so, kids? I've never heard such great preaching . . . and we've enjoyed some fine fellowship."

Sammy twisted toward the front, carelessly gouging an elbow into Sabina's side. "Yeah. I never played hide-an'-seek with so many kids before. We was practically fallin' over each other, tryin' to find a spot to hide."

"You *were* practically falling over each other," his father corrected.

"That's what I said. I laughed so much, I near split a gut."

Howie, the other lad sitting farther to the back, spoke next. "Me, I liked the footraces and shooting matches best, when we wasn't off visitin' with the pretty young misses."

"Yeah," his older brother up front drawled.

"The only footrace I seen you run," his brother shot back, "was on that path you beat over to Miss Marty's outfit ever' chance you got."

Sammy hooted into laughter along with Howie.

"Boys!" their father reprimanded. "Stop the teasing. Delia, what about you? What did you like the most?"

"Oh, Papa," she said on a dreamy gush. "All them purty day gowns and the fancy parasols and summer bonnets. The ribbons all flutterin', the colors. Like a thousand rainbows. I sure wish I could sew good enough to make me a dress as beautiful as—"

"As the one Marty Newman had on yesterday." Philip's

nearly grown voice dropped low, almost manly. "I sure do wish Marty didn't live all the way over to Greeneville."

"That is a stretch," their father agreed. "Nashville, though, is just downriver from us. And, Delia, I think you will be happy to hear that I've chosen to court Mistress Atwood, the young widow who resides with her father there."

"You have?" Howie called to the front, his tone voicing Sabina's own pang of disappointment. "I thought Miss Fulton was a whole lot prettier. You know, the one with the really light gray eyes."

"Well," Sammy bragged, "I think our own lady is purtier'n all of 'em put together."

Sabina felt Delia shove hard into Sammy.

"Ow!"

"Shut up," the girl whispered fiercely.

"What's going on back there?" their father demanded. "Who are you talking about?"

"The one you picked," Delia spewed in a rush. "Miss Atwood."

"Ah, yes, but it's Mistress Atwood. Well, Delia, I'm sure you'll be pleased to know she makes most of her own clothes. From what her Aunt Charlotte said, she's not only an accomplished seamstress, but she's also quite the fancy baker. Her party cakes are considered the best tasting in all of Nashville."

"How's she at makin' pies?" Sammy asked. "I'm real partial to pies."

"They made no mention of pies, but I have no doubt her talents would extend there as well. And, Delia, my primary reason for selecting Mistress Atwood is that she displays the social graces that would put her in good stead if she visited any home in Virginia."

"What's so good about that?" Howie argued. "We don't live in Virginia." He obviously still preferred the gray-eyed miss.

"That's true. But when you and Philip return East to attend college, we do plan to come visit you as well as our other relatives."

"Philip *and me*? I thought you said you didn't have enough saved to send both of us. You said I didn't have to go."

"After this week, with all my new customers and the possibility of a profitable marriage, I do believe you boys will both be able to attend. Then you'll be prepared for whatever profession you choose. One of you might even become a judge or a senator—or even president, if that's your desire."

And the Lord's, Sabina wanted to add from her hiding place. But, of course, she was not part of the conversation, and from the sound of things, never would be. Not that she'd seriously entertained such a far-fetched notion.

"But it ain't what I want," Howie insisted.

"*Isn't*," his father corrected.

"My grammar won't matter where I'm going," the lad shot back. "Otto Bremmer told me I could go explorin' with him soon as I turn seventeen. That is, if I start callin' him by his middle name, Max. Besides, everyone knows the future lies out West, not back East."

"Your future is where I say it is." The hardness in Mr. Clay's voice brooked no further argument.

Howie fell quiet, as did the other children.

After a moment or so, their father breached the stilted silence with a more cajoling tone. "Howie, what you said about the West is true . . . for those who don't have any other prospects. But you boys do. After you finish with your studies, if you still want to go exploring, the West will always be there waiting."

Philip, who'd kept his peace during the exchange, now spoke. "Greeneville's on the way to Virginia, isn't it?"

His father chuckled. "Aye, that it is."

Sabina felt Sammy and Delia relax against her, and she surmised that the confrontation between Howie and his father was over.

"I'm plumb wore out," Sammy said, sliding down from a sitting position. "All that hard work we did loadin' up. Think I'll take me a nap."

"Me, too," Delia chimed in and did the same, snuggling close to Sabina.

After that, there truly was silence in the wagon. The only sounds Sabina heard above the creaks, clops, and rumbles of the wagon and horses were the occasional caw of a crow or hawk's screech. She'd had precious little rest the night before, and soon she, too, caught herself dozing.

Grateful that she could relax enough to sleep, she thanked her God for spiriting her swiftly and safely away. *And, Lord,* she added on a yawn, *I promise not to worry about anything else . . . not what will happen in an hour or a month from now. Nor will I be disappointed that a total stranger is going courting. I'm in your hands.*

~

The strike of fast-approaching horses' hooves startled Sabina awake. She quelled her instinct to fight free of the shrouding blankets as she heard the horses slow to a walk alongside the wagon. Praying that she was still completely covered, she deftly tucked in her toes.

Delia, lying up against her, sat up and nudged Sammy. "Wake up, squirt. We got company."

"Howdy," came the unmistakable voice of Sabina's stepfather. "We're lookin' for a girl."

Sabina froze except for her heart, which pounded madly.

"Purty little gal," another coarser voice said. Tom Shockley's. "With silky blonde hair. Have you seen anybody like that out on the road?"

"Sorry, no," Mr. Clay replied. "I pray she's come to no harm. How old is the child?"

"She ain't no child—she's my runaway bride. This here's her pa."

"Oh, I see. A reluctant bride. I do sympathize."

"Shucks, I don't mind a gal with some pluck." Shockley's voice rolled into a suggestive chuckle. "I'm up fer a mite o' tamin'."

Sabina cringed. *Please, God.*

"Did y'all come from the camp meetin'?" Kurt asked.

"Aye. And you?"

"Yup." Her stepfather then asked, "How many outfits on out in front of you?"

"I do believe we were the first ones to leave. My youngsters were a big help loading up this morning. Weren't you?"

"That's right," Philip said. "We're hopin' to ford the Kentucky before nightfall."

"The first to leave . . ." By his tone, Kurt seemed to be mulling over Philip's words. "Well, good luck to you on your trip home. Come on, Tom, we best hustle on back to camp. Maybe Sabina headed off toward Louisville."

"Or she's still there at camp. What with thousands of folks millin' about, she pro'bly thinks she can just lie low till we give up a-lookin'. Which I ain't gonna do even if it takes all winter. I got a paper here what says she's mine."

Guilt at hiding from her stepfather, the man who'd kept her and her mother fed and clothed for more than twenty years, warred with Sabina's instinct to run. In the Ten Commandments, not honoring one's father was counted as sin. Perhaps she was wrong to hide from him.

As the two men rode away, she started to rise up and call out to them. Then, remembering some of her mother's parting words, she dropped down again. *"Trust in the Lord. He don't want you marrying some no-account gambler no more'n I do."* That had to be true. She had to allow the Lord to see her through, even if it was just one moment at a time.

Mr. Clay snapped the reins over the horses' rumps, and the outfit started rolling again in the opposite direction of the riders.

Scarcely a minute passed when Sammy nudged Sabina and giggled, obviously pleased that they'd fooled her pursuers.

"Pa, I guess it won't hurt to tell you now," Philip said from up on the seat beside his father, "now that those men have come and gone."

"Tell me what?"

"We fooled 'em," Sammy hooted. "We fooled 'em good."

"Shut up!" Delia scolded.

"Have you kids seen the woman they're looking for?" Mr. Clay asked.

"We sure have," a smug Howie proclaimed. "We know right where she is this very second. Don't we, Phil?"

Panic shot through Sabina. They were about to expose her. And what about Mr. Clay? Would he let her stay with them or insist on taking her back?

"I found her first," Sammy bellowed. "Not you." Feverishly he started ripping the blankets and bundles away from Sabina. "Come on out, purty lady. Show yourself."

Chapter Four

Come on out, lady? Show yourself?

In utter disbelief, Baxter pulled Thunder and Snowflake to a halt, then swung around.

From beneath a disorderly stack of blankets emerged a person brushing straw from her face and silky blonde hair. An untidy night braid lay over one shoulder of a shawl collar that had twisted to the side.

In spite of the fact that she was the perpetrator, the young woman appeared as stunned as he. "I—uh—forgive me for taking advantage. I should have asked your—"

"No, we couldn't do that," Howie said, taking over. "We didn't have time. We had to get you hid an' gone before anyone saw you and told them fellas."

"Even from her own father?" Justifiably irked, Baxter pinned Howie with a glare.

"We was gonna tell you, Papa." Sammy sprang to his feet, adding his twopence worth. "Once we knew it was safe."

"We couldn't take a chance," Delia said, scrambling up to stand beside the kneeling woman in homespun gray linen—a young woman who now seemed familiar. "Her stepfather lost her in a game of chance to that other fellow. Think of it, Papa, gambled away to some heathen gambler. Bein' forced to marry up with him. I knew you wouldn't want that neither."

"Either." Baxter raked a searing gaze across his three children standing in the wagon bed. "If you kids were so sure I'd approve of your actions, why didn't you tell me before now? You've had half the morning."

Philip, sitting beside him, placed a hand on Baxter's shoulder. "Father, we know how you hate lying. By not knowing, you could honestly tell those men you hadn't seen Miss Sabina. And see how well it all worked out?"

Baxter shifted his attention to his oldest, who was trying to sound every bit the grown-up. "I seriously doubt any of you gave my honesty a single thought." He encompassed them all again, his gaze lowering to the young woman. "Do you have anything to add to this mischief?"

She rose to her feet, brushing straw from her lank skirt, then looked at him with serious, sage green eyes. "I–I . . . thank you. You kind people has seen me safe away from this day's trouble. I'm most humbly grateful. I shan't burden you any longer."

"You ain't no burden," Howie stepped close, hovering over her.

"Aren't a burden," Baxter corrected, not yet able to assimilate the damage of their actions.

"See?" Sammy shouted and grabbed the young woman's hand. "I told you Papa wouldn't mind. I found her, Papa. I'm the one what found her and brought her to our camp. Ain't she purty?"

Baxter was beginning to feel as overwhelmed by his children as the woman was. "Aye, but—"

The miss raised a silencing hand. "No need for you good folks to bother yourselves with me no longer. I'll be on my way now." She picked up two large bundles; then, wedging past her protectors, she came to her feet and started for the rear. She stopped, looking back with eyes so haunting, they seemed to reach right into him . . . eyes he was sure he'd seen before.

"Again," she said, "thank you for the ride. All of you. May the good Lord bless you for the kindness you've shown me this day."

Finally it came to him. "You're the woman who found the little Wallace girl yesterday. You and your mother. You've run away from your mother, too? She seemed such a congenial sort."

"Aye, it purely sorrows me, but she's the one who coaxed me to flee. Mama told me to put my trust in the Lord, that he'd see me through this valley of tribulation." Smiling sadly, she stepped past Howie.

Howie glanced from her to Baxter and frowned urgently. "Papa?"

The others were also beseeching him with puppy-dog eyes.

What else could he do, what with the poor thing being gambled away like that? "Miss, wait. Don't climb down just yet. There aren't any settlements for another few miles."

She turned back uncertainly, really just a slip of a miss. "Are you sure I won't be no bother?"

Now he was beginning to feel guilty for making such a fuss. "No, of course not." He quickly changed the subject. "Everyone, sit down. Time's a-wasting."

As soon as they were all settled again, with the young woman sitting between Sammy and Delia and their backs to him, Baxter clucked Thunder and Snowflake into a walk.

"I told you my papa was a nice man," he heard Delia say to the flaxen-haired lass.

Smiling at the offhanded compliment, Baxter wondered where the safest place would be to leave the woman. He looked back at her. "Which way are you headed, miss?"

"Like I said, wherever the Lord leads."

Sammy shot up to his knees and grabbed her shoulder. "I think the Lord is leading you to our house. Papa's always sayin' we need a permanent woman on the place."

Baxter caught his breath. "Aye, but I—"

"An' it looks to me," Howie hollered from the rear, overriding his father's objection, "that the Lord's providin' one for us."

"It really is a good idea, Father," Philip added with his new grown-up tone. "If Miss Sabina stayed with us, you wouldn't have to pay Ma Johnson to come twice a week." He glanced back at their passenger. "If it's agreeable with you, Miss Sabina, you could stay on till Father marries—which could be quite a long spell. It's taken him years to even start talkin' about taking another wife."

Swayed by the persistence of his offspring, Baxter tamped down his reservations. Besides, the idea of the young woman coming home with them really wasn't such a bad one if she'd be willing to work for room and board. This way she wouldn't be left to the perils of man and beast along these wilderness roads. And going to Reardon Valley would take her a good two hundred and fifty miles from the determined gambler. "Well, Miss Sabina, are you interested? Are you willing to work for your keep and maybe a little something extra for necessaries?"

The young woman's large pale green eyes made her face seem all the more fragile as she looked up at him questioningly. "Are you sure?"

"The Bible tells us to care for our brethren in need, and after being showered with such an abundance of God's blessings this week, I can do no less."

"You won't regret your decision, kind sir. To work for a good Christian man such as yourself, that would be like bein' gifted with a treasure chest full of blessings. A treasure chest full."

Her voice held such sincerity, her expression such honesty . . . too much, perhaps. Was this woman really as innocent as she seemed? The children were so convinced that they were literally championing her cause. But would he and his family come to regret giving her sanctuary? He prayed not.

~

"You can stay!" Sammy screamed, assaulting Sabina's eardrum. "You can stay!"

His exuberance was reflected in Howie's and Delia's merry brown eyes and bright smiles—no brighter than her own, Sabina was sure.

"I think this calls for a song," Sabina suggested. "Something lively."

Mr. Clay shot a disturbed look over his shoulder. Did the man think she was going to sing some bawdy tune from the taprooms?

"Do y'all know 'From All That Dwell Below the Skies' by Isaac Watts?"

"Aye," Howie answered with enthusiasm and started digging into a canvas sack.

"I 'specially like the *alleluia* part," Delia said, as Howie pulled out a reed fife.

Sammy didn't wait for the others. "'From all that dwell below the skies,'" he rang out with his little-boy soprano.

Along with Sabina and Delia, Philip joined in on the *alleluia*s as Howie piped the tune. Mr. Clay's smooth baritone joined them on the next phrase. "'Let the Redeemer's name be sung through every land, in every tongue. Alleluia! Alleluia! Alleluia! Alleluia! Alleluia!'"

After that, the rest of the morning flew by in happy song. The melodic Isaac Watts's hymns were mostly favored. But the lyrical "Spacious Firmament on High" by Joseph Addison was the most popular, requested no less than four times as they traveled through the balmy pine-scented morning, the branches overhead their chapel.

The happy swell in Sabina's chest only grew as the sun reached its zenith. What a joy it was to openly and loudly, as a family, sing praises to the Lord. Her mother had been right to send her away. No matter how much Sabina would miss her, this wagon and these dear people already felt like the home for which she'd always yearned.

"Papa," Sammy asked, reaching up to tug on his dad's sleeve, "when are we gonna stop to eat? My stomach is growlin' somethin' awful."

"Mine, too," Howie shouted from the rear.

Though she wouldn't speak up herself, Sabina, too, was hungry. She hadn't had anything to eat since yester's eve.

"There's a grassy spot under that oak over there." Mr. Clay reined the team to the shady side of the wheel-rutted road. "Philip, hop down and take the bucket to yon stream. Fetch the horses some water."

Sabina rose to her knees, remembering the dirty dishes that the youngsters had hastily packed this morning. "If there's another pail, I'll get some to wash the dishes . . . if Howie wouldn't mind getting out the kettle. And Sammy? Would you gather some wood for a fire?" Suddenly she felt the heat of Mr. Clay's eyes on her. "I beg your pardon, sir. I should have asked you first."

Instead of a frown, a slow grin warmed his aristocratic

features. "No, not at all. I appreciate any assistance you can give, particularly since you were the reason for our hasty departure this morning." He glanced at Delia, who was dragging the crate of soiled dishes to the wagon's rear. "Now I know how you kids managed such a swift exit. That oatmeal is going to be stuck on like cement."

Still, there was no anger in his voice, only amusement. The man *was* as kind and gentle to his children as she'd assumed yesterday when she'd watched him walk away, one child on his shoulders and the other holding his hand, all three laughing and talking at once. As Mr. Clay climbed down from the high seat, Sabina glanced to the treetops. "Thank you, Jesus," she mouthed silently. "Thank you for bringing me to these people."

"Here's the pail, Miss Sabina." Sammy thrust the dented metal carrier at her. "Hurry up. I'm so hungry I could eat a horse."

"A whole one? All by yourself?" She burst out laughing and ruffled his shaggy hair. How very much she already loved this dear family.

~

That evening as dusk faded into darkness, Baxter chewed on his thoughts more than he did on his supper of peas and potatoes flavored with salt pork. Thus far he hadn't found any fault in the runaway bride. In the cool of a shady glen, he sat on a fallen log while the kids crowded around Miss Sabina on an old quilt.

He'd listened to her more than watched during the day's ride, and if the young woman was trying to fool him into believing she was a good-hearted Christian, she was doing a bang-up job of it. She'd kept the kids entertained—no, more—enthralled the whole way with riddles and hand games interspersed with Bible-verse bees. She and the children had had such a jolly time, Baxter found himself envying the attention she paid them.

He caught himself staring again at the slender young woman whose coil of rearranged sunny hair set off the simple grace of her neck. He concentrated on forking a potato cube off his wooden plate, but his attention returned to the newcomer. Even with her unschooled ways, the woodsy gal was a joy to have around.

So far, he reminded himself.

It was always best to be cautious when it came to strangers. He'd met many a shirker who, when they first ingratiated themselves into a person's home, couldn't do enough to be congenial and helpful. Then, little by little, their true colors would begin to bleed through. In the case of Miss Sabina, time would surely tell. But for now, she was a welcome help and a pleasant respite during the long and tedious trip.

She must have felt him looking. She glanced up, and the flames from the cook fire turned her pale eyes to fiery gems. "Are you finished, sir?" she asked, rising from the ground and smoothing down her faded calico apron. "I'll fetch you a bowl of them fine sugared peaches and cream."

"Me, too!" Sammy sprang up to his knees.

The other kids echoed his eager request.

"I'll help," Delia offered, scrambling to her feet.

Peaches and cream. What a marvelous bounty he'd had the opportunity to purchase at one of the ferry crossings. Ripe peaches and a crock of butter-rich milk. The perfect dessert to finish off a delightful day. Baxter was tempted to lick his lips just as he watched Howie doing. The lad waited on the quilt with his spoon already at the ready.

Yes, this was turning out to be one fine day. "While you dish the peaches, Miss Sabina, I'll fire up the lantern and fetch my Bible."

From behind the makeshift board-and-barrel worktable, her shimmering gaze lifted up to him. "Oh, yes. That would be a mighty pleasurable thing. It must be purely a blessing to open up your own Bible and be able to read them wondrous teachings any ol' time the fancy strikes." A fierce longing could be heard in her tone and seen on the fragile sculpture of her face.

"Aye, it is a blessing." The knowledge that she couldn't read, something to which he never gave a second thought, tugged at Baxter. Not wanting her to interpret his expression as he had hers, he quickly turned toward the wagon.

And at that moment he knew without a doubt he'd done the right thing by allowing the young woman to accompany them. She truly was a child of God . . . one the Lord had placed under his protective wing.

Fetching his big Bible and removing the soft cloth covering it, he turned back to where she and Delia were dipping peaches into carved-out bowls. "How about I read the story of Ruth in honor of Miss Sabina this evening . . . the account of a brave and loyal young woman leaving all that was dear and familiar to travel to a foreign land."

Sabina's fingers went to her lips. "Thank you." Her voice had turned husky and her eyes sparkled with tears.

It was a good thing that he'd forgotten the lantern and could wheel around to collect it, because his own eyes were starting to water . . . and he certainly couldn't let the girl see that.

Chapter Five

Twelve afternoons later, as the cutoff to Reardon Valley came into view, Baxter heard Sabina erupt into that delightful throaty laugh of hers. Sabina had kept the Bible bee going for the past eleven days, and Sammy had just forgotten to say "he being not a forgetful hearer" in verse twenty-five of the first chapter of James—a new verse they'd chosen to memorize last night during family Bible reading.

"You're such a ninny," Delia chided in her older-sister tone.

"No, he ain't," Sabina said, coming to Sammy's defense. "I think maybe his ears is just a mite dirty."

At that, Sammy let out a yelp that galloped into a giggle.

Glancing back to the wagon bed, Baxter saw that Sabina had snagged his youngest and was trying to capture the boy's ear, laughing all the while.

Baxter turned forward again, a grin crawling across his lips. He hadn't smiled so much in years. Despite her poverty of dress and ladylike decorum, despite her butchery of the King's English, she'd brought unprecedented merriment to the trip south from Kentucky. Time had flown as he'd watched his children warm to this woman who was as loving to them as she was rustic. And she really had proven to be the hard worker she'd professed when he'd first agreed to let her accompany them. The lass had taken over a large portion of the camp chores and had a real knack for organizing the children.

Instead of being all dragged out at the end of this return trip, Baxter actually felt more refreshed than he had since his Sally died. Even in the August heat he was ready, even eager, to get started on the many shoe orders he'd received at the camp meeting.

Yes, the new servant girl would do quite nicely for the time being . . . until he wooed Amanda Atwood into wedding him and coming here to be a more suitable mother for his children.

"Papa! Papa! Save me!" Sammy squealed, giggling.

"When it comes to ears," Philip said, entering the fray as he looked back, grinning, "it's each man for himself."

Even his oldest, who claimed undying love for Miss Marty Newman, adored Sabina as much as the others did. From the moment she'd arrived, Philip had been trying to impress her with the man he was becoming, strutting around with chin up and chest out, volunteering to help her every chance he got. Watching the lad's efforts gave Baxter another reason to keep a smile on his lips.

Without Baxter tugging on a single leather strand, the horses moved as one onto the tree-lined Reardon Valley cutoff and picked up the pace. The grays sensed home, with its familiar sights and smells, and resting at night again in the safety of their barn.

Home! Baxter's grin broadened. With Sabina there, he couldn't imagine it being lonely ever again . . . which would only improve when Amanda came here to live, he quickly reminded himself.

"Sabina," Howie hollered over the rambunctious rough-housing. "This here's the Reardon cutoff. Five more miles and we're home."

"Oh my," Baxter heard her sigh as she and the others in the back settled down. "Will we reach your place before nightfall?"

"Aye," Baxter said, swiveling around to answer. "The boys will see to that." He referred to the big grays who were trotting at an ever faster gait. He turned back and tugged on the reins before they broke into a full gallop.

"It's a long valley," Philip explained, "but our place is only about halfway in."

"Best bottomland in all of Tennessee," Howie boasted, then tempered his tone with, "leastwise that's what everyone here-abouts says."

"An' I know who lives on every farmstead betwixt here and home," Sammy bragged. "My friend Marvin lives at the first one we'll pass. Hope he's around so I can show you off to him. His ma an' sisters ain't near as purty as you."

"Sammy," Sabina chided as the wagon bounced over a tree root, "it's the beauty that comes from within that counts. The other kind is fleeting as the flowers of spring. Nothing to hang your hat on."

"Yeah," Sammy agreed. "But ain't them flowers purty whilst they last?"

Baxter grunted. The boy sure was going to be a handful as he got older.

"I think it's time for a song," Sabina returned. "Celebrate our homecoming to this lush green valley. Howie, get out that fife of yourn."

As they descended into the valley, the words to "Rejoice,

the Lord Is King" bounced and echoed through the forest, drowning out the birds in the branches above. Yessir, they had reasons a-plenty to rejoice.

~

A break in the trees gave Sabina a view of the flat below, and she drank in the sight. Down the length of the long valley, farm after farm spread out with checkerboard fields ready for harvest. They were framed and separated by stands of woods. Bisecting the middle ran the wagon road upon which they traveled. A mile or so down the lane, she saw another team and wagon traveling in the same direction.

Reaching level ground, they neared the first farm clearing, and Sabina caught the pungent aroma from a patch of onions and the scent of freshly mown hay. She breathed in deeply. "Your valley even smells rich."

Delia, beside her on the wagon bed, copied Sabina, taking a whiff. "You're right. I never thought of it like that."

"Specially when it's mixed with cow manure," Howie scoffed.

Sammy leapt to his feet, wobbling till he managed a sure footing in the bumpy wagon. "Marvin! Marvin!" he yelled, waving his arms over his head. "Over here."

A boy about Sammy's age was bent over in his mother's kitchen garden, weeding. Spotting the approaching wagon, he dropped his hoe and came racing toward the road, hollering as he ran. "Ma! Henry! It's the Clays! They're back!"

Folks seemed to spring from every shady spot in the hot afternoon. What Sabina surmised was the mother and two daughters slammed out the cabin door wearing the everyday dress of the backwoods female—a muslin apron over homespun. A man and one lad emerged from the barn while another man came from behind a shed.

"Whoa." Mr. Clay slowed his team to a prancing, reluctant halt. "Steven," he called to the approaching farmer. "How've things been while we were away? Anything of import happen?"

"Could use another good rain, but other than that, not much's been bitin' 'ceptin' the skeeters." The man, whose sunbaked skin seemed stretched over nothing but bone and sinew, pulled off his sweat-stained hat and wiped his brow with a rag.

Sammy's freckle-nosed friend, Marvin, had reached the rig and climbed onto the wheel hub, grinning from ear to stuck-out ear. "Did you get to see any sword swallowers?" he asked, his round blue eyes dancing with excitement.

"Naw, it weren't no fancy fair," Howie answered, sounding superior. "It was mostly just a lotta preachin' and hollerin'."

"Howard," his pa scolded, "you speak respectfully when you talk about the men who have dedicated themselves to bringing the Word of God to us folks out here in this backcountry."

"We did see a fella doin' amazin' tricks with some nutshells and a little ol' pea," Sammy boasted.

Marvin screwed his face into a confused frown, but Sabina knew exactly what Sammy meant. She hoped none of those thimblerig hucksters had gotten any of his money.

Before she could ask, Sammy spread a hand back toward her. "See what we brung home with us? Ain't she purty? Her name's Sabina."

By this time, the rest of the farm family had reached the wagon, and every blue eye was staring straight at her. The wife shaded hers from the sun to get a better look. A body would think they'd never seen another woman before.

The lean farmer glanced from Sabina up to Mr. Clay on the driver's seat and grinned, causing deep creases on either side of his mouth. "All I got to say, Baxter, is when you up and decide somethin', you sure don't let no grass grow 'neath your feet. You said you was goin' wife huntin', but I never 'spected you to bag one this quick."

"No, no," Mr. Clay said in a rush. "The young lady here has hired on to help out till I do take a wife. That's all."

"Oh, is it now?" the wife said as if Mr. Clay were keeping a secret. The woman, as plain-faced as her husband was lean, looked Sabina up and down.

"We'd better get going." Ignoring the woman's insinuation, Mr. Clay snapped the reins over the horses' backs. "Been on the trail twelve days, and we still have a ways to go."

The team didn't take much encouraging. They leapt forward. The wagon bucked into a fast roll behind them.

"See you at church." Tipping his simple wide-brimmed hat, Mr. Clay took his parting from the family as they jumped back from the moving wheels.

From what she'd observed thus far, it wasn't like her employer to be so abrupt with folks. Was his hesitance to answer any more questions about her for her sake—or his? Humble though her attire was, it couldn't be a cause for embarrassment. Those farm folk were clothed no better than she. Most likely it was the circumstance in which she came to be with the Clays that he didn't want to discuss . . . or the fact that she came from a den of gamblers.

An uneasiness crawled over her. Did he now regret that he'd brought her here amongst his friends and neighbors?

For the remainder of the trip down through the lush valley, Mr. Clay never so much as slowed the gait of his eager team of grays. Upon passing several other farmsteads, folks ran forward, calling and waving, but Mr. Clay merely returned their greetings and shouted, "Need to get home before dark. See you Sunday."

Her employer had no intention of introducing her to any more of his obviously curious neighbors.

Only once did he speak again. Speeding through a small settle-ment with a fort on one side of a large parade ground and a town-ship on the other, he yelled to a lad sitting in front of the general store. "No need to come tend the stock tonight. We're home."

The young man stared back as the outfit passed, undoubtedly caught off guard, a hand raised but never quite waving . . . espe-cially once he saw Sabina riding in the rear.

The two youngest Clays chatted away, giving Sabina a multitude of information about every place they passed—infor-mation Sabina felt no need to remember, considering Mr. Clay's sudden change of heart. She nodded and did her best to smile as they rattled on, while she ran through her mind the words she would say once they reached their destination and she could get Mr. Clay alone. She wasn't up to blurting out her intentions to travel on in front of these young'uns. If it were up to them, she'd be welcome till the end of time.

"We're here! We're here!" Sammy shouted, bouncing up on his knees. "See? That's the leaning oak where we turn off." In an area still densely wooded, he pointed to an old giant. "Wait till you see our place. We got the best furniture in the whole valley. Ain't that right, Papa? It shines up slick as glass, huh, Pa?"

Without prompting, the team of workhorses swerved onto a set of wagon tracks, and for the first time since they left that first farm, Mr. Clay directed his attention to the rear. "Son, it's not good manners to brag. But, yes, Miss Sabina, I did receive some well-crafted furniture from my mother. Because of a number of circumstances, it was the whole of what my family could give me when I took a wife."

Was this Mr. Clay's way of warning her not to expect anything more than he originally promised? "I'm sure it's fine furniture," she returned flatly.

"It is," Delia agreed with the enthusiasm Sabina lacked. "But we keep it covered most of the time. We only get to use it when we got company."

"With Miss Sabina here to keep an eye on it," Mr. Clay said, turning to the rear again, "mayhap we'll uncover it more often. Sunday afternoons would be pleasurable."

Sabina wished he hadn't said that. It would make her leaving all the harder for the children.

They broke out of the trees and into a clearing of eight or ten acres with a cabin and a barn built of squared-off logs, along with a chicken coop, a couple of sheds and, across the way, another smaller cabin—most likely Mr. Clay's cobbler's shop. Upon surveying the fields, Sabina surmised that the family's cash money came from his shoe trade since they had only a kitchen garden and fenced meadows. Aside from the work team pulling the wagon, she saw only a milk cow and a spring calf along with hogs in a pen beyond the barn. A flock of some red chickens and some white-speckled ones ran about among an untidy assortment of discarded clutter—old buckets and busted-up crates, horseshoes, broken wheels, rusty tools.

The three younger kids, excited to be home, hopped off the back of the bed. Philip vaulted down from the box seat before Mr. Clay had the team pulled to a stop in front of a two-story house.

"Son," Mr. Clay called to his oldest as the others sprinted up the steps to the covered porch fronting the place, "rub down the boys and put them away, please. I'll be out to help you with the other chores soon as I get Miss Sabina settled."

They needed to get something settled, all right, but not her person. "Mr. Clay, I need to have a private word with you, if you don't mind."

"Aye, I have something to say to you as well."

Fine. Either way, by tomorrow she'd be gone.

Chapter Six

As Mr. Clay climbed from the wagon seat, Sabina rose to her feet and stepped over the blankets and sacks, moving past the boxes of camping gear. By the time she reached the rear, he was waiting to lift her down, a congenial smile adding to his gallant handsomeness. A gentleman, even in his coarse work clothes . . . even when he was on the verge of dismissing her.

"Would you like to try some of our well water?" he asked, lowering her to the ground. "It's quite cool and refreshing even for August."

"That sounds real nice." And that would take them sufficient distance from the house and the children for their private conversation.

He led the way across the clearing to a stone-surrounded well with a pitched roof over it and a bucket hanging from a crossbar. Reaching it, Mr. Clay turned the handle, lowering the water vessel. "I want to apologize for my neighbors today. I didn't realize what an object of curiosity a woman riding in my wagon would be." The bucket splashed into the water below, and he reversed the crank, bringing the bucket upward again. "I'd mentioned to one of my neighbors that I planned to start looking for a wife, and I reckon word got around. It's a small community. They all know everyone else's business. If I had slowed the horses for their questions, I would have been obliged to explain your presence to each and every person we passed. And I'm sure you wouldn't have appreciated that."

Suddenly a half-cocked grin replaced his serious earnestness. "We'll just let 'em stew in their own curiosity for a day or two. I'll introduce you formally at church Sunday."

"You're not having second thoughts about my staying here?"

"No, of course not. I just wish I'd kept my mouth shut about planning to take a wife." His expressive brown eyes looked deeply into hers. "Please, tell me that the neighbors haven't scared you off."

She glanced away under the intensity of his gaze. "Well, Mr. Clay, I—no. This is where the Lord brought me, and here I'll remain until he leads me somewheres else. Ofttimes I forget to pray first and start taking matters into my own hands."

Mr. Clay chuckled with disarming friendliness. "Don't we all?" He unhooked a gourd dipper from the well post and filled it from the dripping bucket, then handed it to her.

Such a gentleman, offering her water first—and her the servant. "Thank you, Mr. Clay."

"Let's dispense with all the formality. Call me Baxter—at least while we're at home. And I'll call you Sabina, if that's agreeable with you."

"That would be simpler," she answered in a casual tone, though she didn't feel at all casual about his proposal. It confirmed that he really did want her here and wanted things to be congenial. She took a long sip of the cold water and glanced around at her new home while swallowing. "You have a fine place here, . . . Baxter. Just needs a little sprucing up. Plenty of good bottomland cleared for your needs and all tucked in cozy-like by the woods. Nobody close enough to be a nuisance. Still, you got neighbors nearby if you have a mind for company. Yessir, Mr.—I mean—Baxter, you picked yourself a fine place to live."

Resting his hand against the well post, he glanced about him, then settled his warm gaze on Sabina again. "A man starts taking things for granted after a while, but, yes, I did select a very nice spot to raise my family. I'd be hard-pressed to go back to Virginia now, even if I did come into a sum of money sufficient to care for them there. The freedoms of Tennessee have a way of growing on you. Not so many societal obligations to get in the way of simple pleasures."

She handed back the gourd. "Yes, I can see how pleasurable living here could be." Beginning to feel shy under his steady gaze, she turned away. "Reckon I best get to unloading the wagon."

"Miss Sabina!" Delia called, running out the front door of the cabin. "Miss Sabina. Come see our house."

"So that's why they were in such a rush to go inside," Baxter mused, stepping up behind Sabina. "I'll bet they've uncovered the furniture. I thought they were just trying to get out of work. Come along." He tucked her hand in the crook of his arm. "Come and see your new home."

Tears threatened. Baxter Clay had no idea how much she treasured the mere idea . . . a home to call her own. And this dear family.

At least for a little while.

~

Sabina felt something move next to her—something warm and breathing.

Then she remembered. She was sharing Delia's bed on the upper floor of the Clay house. She lifted her lashes, and her gaze gravitated to the early light at the open window. On a cool breeze fluttered faded calico curtains . . . a far cry from the elegant red damask draperies that graced the downstairs windows. This family seemed to live in two worlds—one of past glory and one of present practicality.

She surveyed the rest of Delia's bedroom. Except for the finely crafted chest at the foot of the bed, everything in it spoke of the frontier. She had slept in worse. Far worse. The bedstead, closet, and washstand were all simply made of rough wood. Still, a patchwork quilt covered the bed, and rag rugs added splashes of color to the raw furnishings.

With a contented smile, Sabina deftly rose to her feet, careful not to awaken the adolescent girl. She padded to the window and took in the fresh, fragrant dawn air. She looked past the crusty branches of an old oak to the cobbler's shop and beyond to a field of yellow grain ripe for harvest, then farther on to the deep shades of the woods.

Droplets of morning dew glistened like tiny stars on the leaves of the nearby oak. Two orange-breasted birds landed on a limb almost close enough to touch. A lovely summer's day. "Good morning, Mama, wherever you are," she whispered. "And thank you, Lord. Thank you for bringing me to this wonderful place."

To make sure she would remain welcome, she quickly slipped out of her night shift and grabbed a simple but clean brown day gown from off a wall hook, along with a muslin apron. She needed to make herself presentable, then get downstairs and stoke up the fire for breakfast.

The stairs bottomed into the kitchen end of the large common space. Everything about it, from the open cooking hearth to the plain worktables and shelves, was what a body would expect to see in a frontier home. But the rest of the long room held furniture more beautiful than she'd ever seen up close. At the far end stood an actual Franklin stove. Facing it was a carved wood sofa upholstered with red-and-gold-striped fabric and two side chairs of that same deep red. A tea table placed in the center of the grouping was so elegant that its edges were scalloped, and its slender legs dug into a large floral rug so thick that it had practically buried Sabina's toes when she'd walked across it last night.

The writing desk, of the same shiny cherrywood as the other furniture, was a stark contrast to the log-and-chink wall it stood against, as was the china cabinet on the opposite wall. But the contents inside the cabinet's etched-glass doors were even more impressive. The thin, fragile dishes, which had a sparkling white background, were decorated with lovely, deeply hued roses.

Taking up the center of the room, though, was the most important set of furniture—a spacious dining table and six chairs, their legs all footed with carved lions' feet. Handsome yet sturdy, this table was meant for a lifetime of living.

Last night after supper, Mr. Clay—Baxter—had sat at the head and read from the Bible, with Sabina and the young'uns all gathered around in the comfortable cushioned chairs, listening to the wondrous words of God Almighty. What a sublime pleasure that had been.

A tapping sounded.

A woodpecker?

No, it didn't sound quite like that. Then she noticed that the front door stood ajar. Striding to it, she heard the steady tapping again and realized it came from the shop. Baxter was already at work, and without breakfast or even coffee. Poor man, he surely did need a wife.

Sabina scurried about as fast as she could in a strange kitchen and soon had a pot of coffee set to boil on some stoked coals she'd chunked off the back log and shoveled to the apron of the hearth.

By the time she'd returned from taking care of her morning needs at the privy and washstand, steam was coming from the coffee spout. Pulling two everyday crockery cups from the shelf beside the fireplace, she poured portions for herself and Baxter. From a nearby sack, she busted up a goodly chunk of sugar to put in his. He liked his sweet, she'd learned during the trip here.

Hoping none of her silky fine hair had escaped its bun, she shoved the door farther open with her hip and strolled out, taking care not to spill any of the steaming liquid.

It wasn't until she was halfway across the side yard to Baxter's shop that she realized she'd brought both cups, his and hers. She, a servant, presuming to have coffee with her master?

She stopped and started to turn back.

"Where you going?" Baxter's head was poked out an open window.

What could she say? "I brought both our cups by mistake. I was taking mine back."

"What do you say we both walk back and have it on the front porch? It's such a fine morning." Wearing a leather apron with a row of deep pockets, he left the shop behind and joined her, matching his steps to hers.

She handed him his cup as they neared the long covered porch, where she counted five homemade chairs lining it. She wondered, hopefully, if one day soon a sixth one would be placed there for her.

"This sure is nice," he said, dropping onto a large straight-backed chair at the far end. "I usually don't make coffee until I come in to wake the kids. I'm an early riser, so I try to get in a couple of undisturbed hours of work before their day begins."

"La, then I am sorry I interrupted you."

"No, this is a pure treat. Besides, I'll be able to get so much more done with you here to see that the kids are fed and getting their chores done. Then, once school commences again, making sure they get ready on time. It'll all be so much easier, with all the shoe orders I received at the camp meeting." Propping one booted foot over the other, he settled back contentedly and took a sip, then smiled. "Fine coffee. By George, I *am* glad you stowed away in our wagon."

"Me, too, by George." The words came from the open doorway. In it stood Sammy, sun-streaked dark hair mussed, rubbing the sleep from his eyes.

Sabina burst out laughing. "Well, then, by George, so am I."

~

Sunday morning and the whitewashed church at the settlement came into view. Baxter shook his head. He couldn't count a single missing rig in the yard. Everyone in the valley had come to church and come early. In the two days since his return, he had no doubt that news of the strange woman he'd brought home had reached every ear.

Guiding his own wagon toward an empty space, he had to admit that if one of the other men had mentioned being in the market for a wife and then in less than a month returned home with a woman, his own curiosity would've been whetted.

But at this moment he was just glad Howie had forgotten today was the Sabbath. The lad had to be tracked down at the fishing hole, causing them to be late for services, and thereby making it possible for him to introduce Sabina to the whole congregation at once. That would be much easier.

"Hurry, Papa." Sammy stood up behind the box seat, straightening his freshly starched and ironed shirt. "I want to be the one to tell everybody who Sabina is."

"No!" resounded from every quarter of the wagon.

Baxter smiled back at him—and caught sight of Sabina. "In matters such as these . . ." The sun had turned her crown of braids to a silvery gold halo, lending an angelic glow to her face and robbing him of his senses. "In such matters as these," he repeated more firmly as he shifted his gaze steadfastly to his youngest, "the honor falls to the head of the household."

"Or anyone else besides the brat," Howie blustered.

Eyes narrowing, Sammy lunged toward his older brother.

Sabina, sitting on quilt-covered straw beside Delia, caught Sammy in midflight. "Boys, it's the Sabbath. No tomfoolery today. And, Sammy, after church I'm sure you'll get plenty chances to tell your story." She pulled him down beside her.

His lower lip jutted out. "It won't be the same."

"No," she agreed, smoothing his unruly hair. "But you'll make do. I'm sure of that."

Sabina surely was worth her weight in gold. He should have hired a girl like her years ago . . . if indeed there was another quite like her.

Singing came from the open windows of the church as Baxter reined Thunder and Snowflake to a halt. "Behold the Amazing Gift of Love." What an apropos selection. It described exactly what Sabina had become to his family—God's amazing love gift.

"Look," Philip, sitting beside Baxter, said. "Jimmy Johnson is staring out at us."

"And so is Zeke," Howie added.

"Just walk in quietly and sit down as if nothing is out of the ordinary." Baxter wrapped the reins around the brake stick and hopped down, followed immediately by his scrambling youngsters.

Sabina, though, didn't move. "My being here, is it really going to cause such a stir? Mayhap I'd best not go in."

Baxter held out his arms to her. "I wouldn't hear of it. As you pointed out a moment ago, it's the Sabbath, and the day belongs to you as much as anyone else."

A slow trusting smile replaced the apprehension on her lovely face—a face made more delicate-looking in contrast to the coarseness of her homespun dress. She came to her feet and reached down to him.

He noticed she was naked-footed even for church services. The woman needed a pair of shoes.

As always, he was surprised by her lightness when his hands circled her waist and he lifted her to the ground. With her spirit and energy, she always seemed bigger. Capturing her elbow, he escorted her across the beaten-down grass to the steps.

Upon reaching them, Sabina hesitated again, glancing up with uncertain eyes.

"They're all good people," he reassured her, praying all the while that everyone truly would be on his or her best behavior.

Chapter Seven

The coolness of the interior of the high-ceilinged church greeted Baxter, along with the start of a second song.

" 'Blest be the tie that binds . . .' "

His hat in one hand, he held the door open with the other for his household to enter.

Heads turned, the bonneted ones of the women and bare ones of the men. Hushed whispers competed with the singing, "'Our hearts in Christian love . . .' "

As Sabina passed him, Baxter noted that not only did she not have shoes, but she had no covering for her head. And her gown was nothing but faded everyday homespun. The shawl collar, though, was spotless and neatly ironed. *Father,* he prayed silently, *please impress upon these people to show Sabina nothing but the Christian love they're singing about. I know you want special care taken of widows and orphans. And this one should surely qualify.*

"'The fellowship of kindred minds is like to that above.'" The distracted congregation stumbled through the rest of the verse.

Howie led the family toward their pew located halfway down the aisle. Baxter stayed to the rear behind Sabina.

And not a row did they pass that every single person did not gawk.

Charlie Johnson, who led the singing, was every bit as boorish. Long of limb and eyes bulging as big as his Adam's apple, he stared after Sabina and didn't take his eyes off her even after she'd sat down.

As the singing continued, Baxter took the end seat beside her and caught her hand, giving it a supportive squeeze.

"'And perfect love and friendship reign through all eternity,'" ended the hymn, and Brother Bremmer, a blacksmith the other six days of the week and the most massively built man in the valley, lumbered up from an armchair behind the pulpit.

"T'ank you, Brodder Yonson, for da fine singing," he boomed in his German accent. "I t'ink maybe ve better take dis time to haf Baxter Clay introduce his guest. Since *nobody* is going to listen to mine preaching until he does."

At last the moment had come when Baxter could put to rest the laity's curiosity. "It would be my pleasure." He drew Sabina up alongside him. "I would like to introduce to everyone Miss Sabina Erhardt. She also attended the great church meeting at Cane Ridge in Kentucky. She's agreed to come work for me."

"Work for you?" Mistress Jessup, sitting toward the front, asked him while screwing her busybody face into a disbelieving frown. She, no doubt, had expected him to announce an upcoming marriage.

"Aye," he said firmly. "She's taking care of my household. And thus far, she has done a mighty fine job."

"I'll wager she has." The remark came from another woman somewhere behind him.

Anger instantly fired within Baxter. "The house of the Lord is no place for unseemly innuendos."

Brother Bremmer's heavy-jowled face had also reddened. "Baxter is right. *Fräulein* Erhardt, you is most velcome. After da service, I am enjoying very much to hear about all da preaching at Cane Ridge."

Sabina didn't respond. She stood frozen, staring back at the pastor.

Baxter filled the silence. "You're not going to believe all that happened at the camp meeting. It was an amazing sight to see. Over twenty thousand souls arrived there. So many of God's children gathered in one place—I wouldn't have thought it possible this side of the mountains. And the power of the Lord was so strong, it verily filled the air. I'll never forget the experience."

"*Ja*, dat must haf been somet'ing," Brother Bremmer said, nodding, his round blue eyes bright.

"It was," Baxter concurred, pulling Sabina down beside him. "It truly was."

"Now is time for da sermon. . . ."

At long last, the congregation settled down, facing Brother Bremmer for his sermon on—of all topics—Matthew 22:37-40. The pastor concentrated on the "loving thy neighbor as thyself" half of the commandment. But Baxter shouldn't have been surprised by the choice. God knew the message these people—and in particular, the unkind woman behind him—needed to hear on this day. He wished he knew exactly who had spoken so rudely so that he could confront her after church, but he wasn't sure.

After a stirring sermon from their impassioned preacher, a

closing song, and an announcement of a potluck after church the following Sunday, Brother Bremmer gave the benediction. Then, leaving the pulpit, he strode up the aisle to the entrance to greet his departing flock.

Joining the slow-moving stream of people, Baxter walked in front of Sabina, shielding her, and Philip—bless his intuitive heart—moved close in behind her, protecting her from those who followed . . . just to be on the safe side.

When they reached the pastor, Brother Bremmer stretched out his large square hand. "Inga vould like for you and your family to join *mit* us for Sunday dinner. She makes da peach pie dat she knows her Sammy likes."

Baxter drew Sabina next to him. "That sounds delicious, if it's agreeable with Miss Erhardt."

With that welcoming grin lifting the pastor's double chin, how could anyone refuse?

"That would be a real kindness," Sabina murmured softly and dipped into a small curtsy.

Baxter, himself, was twice-glad for the invitation. Aside from Inga's fine German cooking, an easy escape from obtrusive eyes would be only a few steps away. The minister's home sat to one side of the church, and his blacksmith shop and corrals spread out on the other.

~

Sabina felt utterly surrounded as folks crowded toward her, introducing themselves. For the most part, their welcoming seemed genuine, and having Baxter and Philip on either side, with Howie right behind, did give her a measure of comfort. But there were so many names being tossed at her. The only one she was sure to remember was Reardon, for which the valley was called. But still, there was a whole clan of the Reardons whose

Christian names she'd eventually have to get straight, since they were the Clays' nearest neighbors.

And so many questions came flying at her.

"How long have you been overmountain?"

"Where are you from?"

"What does your family do?"

She couldn't bring herself to say that her stepfather earned his living by gambling in any taproom where he hadn't worn out his welcome.

Baxter stepped in and answered that question for her. "Miss Erhardt's family farmed in Pennsylvania."

To the congregation's credit, no snide remarks were made, such as the one uttered by the woman in church. But a number of men did give Baxter knowing grins that he certainly should have done without. As long as Baxter Clay had lived in this valley, a body would think his neighbors would know what a fine and honorable gentleman he was, for gracious sakes.

Then, to Sabina's relief, Sammy and Delia, pretty in her pink Sunday dimity, brought forth a gaggle of young'uns as enthusiastic and welcoming in their compliments as the Clay children had been when she first met them.

After a few moments, Baxter leaned down to her. "It's hot standing out here in the sun. Let's go on over to the Bremmers'." He placed a hand at her elbow and quite expertly guided her past people who were still asking questions.

The kids, seeing them leave, ran to join them, and together they emerged from the crowd to find a large log house shaded by old trees and with a wide, inviting covered porch. On the railings framing the porch, window boxes bloomed with an abundance of flowers. More color-filled boxes adorned the upper windows.

"What a happy house," Sabina remarked.

Walking just ahead, Delia glanced back, her own heart-shaped face pretty as any blossom. "Sabina, can we have lots of flowers like that?"

"If your papa doesn't mind. But I'm afraid it's too late in the season to plant much of anything now."

"Next spring," Baxter agreed in a pleasantly warm baritone.

Sabina took that as a sign that he wanted her to be here next year. A swell of hope filled her as she and her new family reached the light fragrance of petunias.

"Welcome to our valley." Mistress Bremmer stood on the porch step to greet them in a starched white apron—most likely one she saved for company. A fair-skinned blonde who was fading to gray, she was much larger-boned than Sabina. Still the middle-aged woman would be dwarfed by her husband's huge build. Mistress Bremmer extended a work-worn hand.

Sabina shook it, knowing from her own Bavarian mother that it was a German custom for women to shake hands when introduced. "I'm purely pleased to be here."

On the lower step, Sammy crowded next to Sabina and the dull blue of her skirt. He looked up at their hostess. "You don't have to fret about us anymore, *Oma* Inga." He wrapped an arm around Sabina's waist. "Our lady is takin' real good care of us, ain'tcha?"

"I am not da real grandma," Mistress Bremmer explained. "I take care of Sammy before he is old enough to go to da schoolhouse *mit* da ot'er *kinders*. I am pleased to know a voman is on da Clay place now." Her light blue gaze encompassed them all. "Do come up on da porch ver it is cool and sit. I bring out da lemonade."

"Let me help," Sabina offered.

"*Nein*. You are da guest. Delia, you and Howie come help."

As the two charged inside behind the kind woman, Baxter

pointed Sabina to a pillowed rocker and took the chair next to her, while Sammy hopped onto the porch railing.

"Be careful of the flower boxes," his father warned.

"If you don't mind, Pa," Philip said, still on the bottom step, "I'm going to go talk to Benny Thompson a minute before they ride out."

"Sure, go ahead."

"Me, too." Sammy dropped from the railing and took off after his big brother, almost slamming into the minister on the gravel path. Without slowing, the youngster tipped his out-of-shape felt hat in a perfunctory apology.

Paying no mind to the boy, Brother Bremmer trudged up the steps, looking overheated in his black preaching suit. Baxter and the other men in the congregation had sensibly worn no more than their Sunday vests. "Ah, I see you two is alone. Goot. I haf much I vant to ask about da great church meeting. But, first, dere is anot'er matter." He came toward Sabina and Baxter. "Ven Steven Lowe come to services dis morning, he say *Fräulein* Erhardt, here, is not voman you bring home for da vife. She is to be hired vorker only. Dis is true?"

"Aye," Baxter answered in almost a question. Hadn't he already explained that?

"Dis voman, she is sleeping in da house *mit* you?"

Sabina did not appreciate the direction the preacher's questions were taking.

Nor did Baxter. His expression hardened. "Sabina is sleeping in Delia's room with Delia. I thought you knew me better than to think otherwise."

But the pastor showed no remorse. He pressed on. "Da *fräulein* is pretty voman, and you are da lonely vidower. Even if you t'ink you is stronger dan temptation, many in dis valley is not t'inking you are. And I haf to agree *mit* dem. Marriage is da best t'ing."

A gasp escaped from Sabina's lips. She shot a quick glance at Baxter.

His jaw muscles bunched. "Rolf," he grated out, calling the reverend by his given name, "marriage was never our intent. At the camp meeting I met another woman, an accomplished young lady whom I plan to court." He glanced back at Sabina and gave her a pitiful excuse for an encouraging smile. "Sabina's need when I met her was to find employment. She's a hard worker, and she's good with the children. I really don't see what all the fuss is about. Folks hire other people to work for them all the time."

"Name one ot'er household dat has da unchaperoned *fräulein* living *mit* a man and two near-growed lads."

At that instant, Delia walked out the door, carrying two glasses of lemonade.

"Go back inside a minute," her father ordered. "And keep Howie in there with you."

She stared at him, then glanced quickly from Sabina to Brother Bremmer. The girl obviously knew something was amiss.

"*Go!*"

She whirled around, her pink skirts flying, and sped into the house.

Brother Bremmer pulled a chair from beside Baxter and sat in it, facing them. He leaned forward, speaking in a quietly hoarse but serious tone. "Baxter, it seem to me dat you really don't haf a problem here. *Fräulein* Erhardt, she is pretty voman. I see you watching out for her during da service. You care about her. You say yourself, she is hard vorker. And anyone can see da *kinders* love her. No need for you to go courting. Da voman for you is right here."

Baxter rose to his feet, pulling Sabina up beside him.

Was he going to ask her to marry him? Sabina's heart banged against her ribs. Should she say yes? Without praying about it?

He held her hand firmly and inhaled. But he wasn't looking at her. He stared down at the seated minister. "Marriage is not a hole you just happen to fall into. It's serious business. Come along, Sabina." Taking her with him to the steps, he called behind him into the open doorway. "Delia, Howie, come on out. We have to go."

Then he looked back at the openmouthed reverend. "Rolf, please give Inga our regrets. I don't think dinner today is such a good idea."

Chapter Eight

Each of the young'uns complained when they were summoned to the wagon, but Sabina couldn't find any words for them. She could only barely make herself crawl up into the back.

"*Oma* Inga will be real put out," Sammy had argued when Baxter told him they weren't staying for Sunday dinner. "She made a peach pie just for us."

Baxter's demeanor brooked no argument. "I'll explain once we're out of the settlement."

On the ride past the other church attenders and the stores and tradesman shops, the children riding in the back with Sabina looked as distressed as they were puzzled—and rightly so. Yet none of them could have been half as upset as she. Sabina sat at the rear of the wagon, her legs dangling off, distancing herself from the man who had so callously and blatantly rejected the very idea of marriage to her. Whatever Mr. Clay would say to his children could not make up for her humiliation—or her indignation. She would pack her things and leave first thing in the morning. Perhaps someone else in the valley could use an extra pair of hands. If not, so be it. She'd move on.

"Thought you was stayin' in town," a lad in front of the carpentry shop yelled.

Philip, in his usual spot beside his father, shrugged but said nothing. He knew better.

And just this morning everyone had been in such high spirits. The children . . . at the thought of losing them, Sabina fell into a pit of sadness. She would miss them achingly. And whether she wanted to or not, she would miss Baxter, the gentle concern he'd always shown for her comfort before today's calamity, his words of appreciation, his encouragement . . . those searching mahogany eyes, the warmth of his smile. . . .

Sabina's throat tightened. Tears would be next. She took a deep breath. She couldn't let them see how much he'd hurt her.

~

Once Baxter had driven his family out of the settlement and into the woods, he found a wide spot and reined the team of horses to the side. Best to get past the unpleasantness as soon as possible, though he couldn't decide exactly what to say or how, even, to deal with the situation. The kids would be devastated. He was tempted to ignore all the "good" people and just say his family would continue on as it had since they left Cane Ridge.

Cane Ridge . . . he'd left there so inspired, so "on fire" to make a stronger commitment to the Lord. And here it was, the first Sabbath home, and he was tempted never to return to church again.

"All right, Pa, what is it?" Howie demanded, stepping across the fresh straw to the front of the wagon bed. "What happened?"

"Does it have anything to do with Miss Sabina?" Philip added.

Crooking a leg on the seat, Baxter turned to face them.

All their eyes, so distinctly like his own, were trained on him. All except Sabina's. She shifted slightly toward him but did not look up.

"Brother Bremmer feels that it isn't decent for a young miss to live in a house without an older woman there to see that she remains virtuous." He stole a quick glance, but Sabina continued to center all her attention on her folded hands.

"That's ridiculous," Philip blustered. "There ain't no one as virtuous as Sabina."

"Virtuous? What does that mean?" Sammy rose to his knees, his expression as confused as it was disturbed.

Baxter ignored the boy. One difficult subject at a time was more than enough.

"Did Brother Bremmer say she has to go?" Eyes narrowed, Howie stepped closer, practically in Baxter's face.

He leaned back. "Either that, or I wed her."

Sammy swung away. "Is that all right with you, Sabina? Papa's real nice—most of the time. And so am I. Ain't I, Delia?"

Sabina turned away, and her wide jade green eyes swept over to the child, and Baxter knew the pain hidden behind them.

He relieved her from answering the inappropriate question. "Sabina just ran away from one marriage arranged by other people. She didn't come with us to be subjected to more of the same."

"So what are we going to do, Pa?" Philip demanded. "Send her packing? Or defy Brother Bremmer?"

"I vote that we stick together," Howie spewed. "Let 'em think what they want."

"Wait a minute," Sammy shouted. "Pa, how do you know

73

Sabina doesn't want to marry up with you? She might if you was to ask her."

The boy never could leave well enough alone. "Samuel, to begin with, I'm not free to ask her. I told you all before, any marriage I enter into must benefit each of your futures. We've—"

"Mr. Clay, boys," Sabina interrupted, much to his relief. He didn't enjoy saying that she had insufficient breeding. And with absolutely no dowry, how could she be of lasting help to his children?

"I think," Sabina continued, "it would be best if I just pack up and leave. There's bound to be another family in the valley that could use me—one with a wife already on the place."

"I am so very sorry that you were treated like something to be bargained over again today," Baxter said, hoping to erase some of her embarrassment. "I'm going to hate to see you go." And he truly would. He missed her already. "You've brought so much—"

"Singin' an' laughin' an' playin' an' . . ." Sammy's voice trailed off into a whine as he scrambled to her. "Don't go."

"She don't have to," Delia, speaking for the first time, said with surprising authority. "Papa, while you all been talkin', I been prayin'—like Sabina's always tellin' us to do."

Sabina reached over and placed a hand on Delia's shoulder. "How quickly we forget." She exchanged a private look with his daughter.

Delia lifted her doelike gaze to her father. "There's another way to handle this. Build Sabina a cabin of her own so she don't have to stay in the same house. One with a sign on it that says, No Men Allowed." She swung back to Sabina. "I thought of the sign, not God. We'd build the cabin all the way on the other side of the meadow so folks won't say bad things about you. And I could stay there with you so you won't get lonesome." She reached up to Sabina's hand on her shoulder. "Please, say you'll stay."

"I don't know." Sabina's searching gaze moved from Clay to Clay and finally met Baxter's.

"I think it's a good plan," he said, hoping she would agree to stay even after the words he'd been forced to say this day. "Please stay."

Sabina returned her attention to Delia. "Did you say this is an answer to your praying?"

His daughter sat up straighter. "Aye, that it is."

She seemed so grown-up. The thought frightened Baxter. Time was running out so much faster than he ever imagined. He needed to start wooing Amanda Atwood into becoming a mother and instructress for his thirteen-year-old daughter right away. The sooner he went to Nashville, the better.

"Well, Sabina?" Philip urged.

Baxter realized she had yet to answer, her fragile face a mix of emotions, including the pain he'd helped put there.

Then after all three boys started badgering her like a pack of hound dogs, she raised a hand. "Very well, then, if y'all are willing to go to the trouble of building me a cabin."

Sammy flung his arms around her neck, almost knocking her flat.

Philip said, "Won't be no trouble—any trouble," he corrected himself. "We'll fell the trees this week and invite everyone to a cabin raising on Saturday. We'll make a real party of it."

"In the meantime," Baxter said, "you and Howie will be sleeping out in the barn with me. I don't want to give folks any more excuses to talk."

"And, Papa," Delia said, spreading her pastel skirts across the straw, "you need to ride back to the settlement in the mornin' to make amends for bein' so rude to Brother Rolf and Inga."

Baxter stiffened, caught off guard. But for only a second. He reached back and cupped his little lady's chin in his hand. "I'll do that, sugar. And thank you." Yes, his sweet girl was growing up much too fast. Next week the cabin raising, and the week after, he'd get himself to Nashville. Glancing at the other lovely creature in his wagon spurred his urgency. It was a matter that absolutely couldn't wait. As Brother Bremmer had said, Sabina truly was a temptation.

~

"Stop your frettin'," Delia urged as she helped Sabina in the kitchen end of the large common room. She artfully layered strips of crust over a dried apricot cobbler, a special treat for company. "Everybody's gonna love you as much as we do."

The sun had just topped the eastern hills on the morning of the cabin raising, and folks would be arriving any minute. Sabina glanced out the window. She saw no one yet, just Baxter and the boys skinning the bark off the last of the logs that would be part of her house.

Her own home! The thought sent a thrill rushing to her heart. She'd gotten over the foolish dream that she might one day wed Baxter. He was an educated man from an esteemed family. Not only had she been reared by a drifting gambler, but she was an illegitimate child—an even more damning fact, yet one she could never keep from a prospective bridegroom.

But the cabin? It was real. A place to call her own.

And Delia's, she added with a grin. The young darling had been so exuberant about having a place that wouldn't be over-run with mud-tramping boys, she'd cajoled her papa into taking her with him into the settlement for material the day after they'd all left the parsonage so abruptly. Since then she and Sabina had been sewing brightly colored floral-print curtains and making feather pillows to match—pillows for the two rock-ing chairs Baxter had asked the carpenter to make.

"Do you think people will really come, me being a stranger and all?" Sabina asked the young girl, whose straight dark hair had been rag-curled last night. Today Delia looked particularly winsome. Her glossy ringlets were now pulled away from her heart-shaped face and tied up in back with a green bow that matched her checkered day gown.

"They wouldn't miss coming, believe you me." Laughing, Delia wiped her hands on her full apron, placed the latticed cobbler into the cast-iron Dutch oven, and shoved it among the back coals. "Folks didn't get much chance to talk to you Sunday. And 'sides, it's a get-together. We ain't had one here, not since we first come from Virginia and everybody came for our barn raising." Wiping her hands again, she toyed with one of her bouncy ringlets. "I sure hope we got enough tables set up under the trees."

Sabina surveyed the two rows of board-and-barrel tables and benches beneath the honey locusts shading the front of the house. Then, across the way, she noticed she couldn't see water in the long trough in front of the barn. Placing the domed cover on a big pot, she hefted it off the worktable and shoved it among the closest hot hearth embers. "You start cleaning carrots while I go out and fill the trough. If what you say is true, there'll be a lot of thirsty horses here today."

Shooing chickens as she went, Sabina strode across the yard to fetch the bucket hooked beside the barn door. As she did, all four males stopped working on the last two logs and grinned at her. The boys had their father's easy smile and eyes just as expressive. Four princely peas in a pod they were, and so endearing. The thought left her to wonder if the Clay youngsters had inherited any features whatsoever from their mother.

"Almost done," Philip called to her, wiping his evenly tanned brow with his shirtsleeve.

Sabina glanced along the swath that the earlier logs had made when dragged to the site selected for the cabin. They lay on the far side of the kitchen garden, and these last two would soon join the others. The team of grays, rigged with chain, waited just outside the corral, ready for the pull.

At the moment, though, part of the cabin structure already stood tall—the fireplace and chimney. A mason, Mr. Auburn, and his two grown sons had come on Wednesday with a load of rocks and built it in two days for the promise of four pairs of shoes. The married son had been the chatty sort, but the father and other son never spoke. They were quiet by nature, Baxter had said. Still, the unmarried son had stolen glances at her every chance he got. Was he interested in her? He was pleasant in an unobtrusive kind of way. But she supposed that being stared at was to be expected with her being a new maiden woman in the valley.

Snagging the bucket, she turned back to the Clays. "I thank all of you for your hard work on my behalf. I just hope your neighbors are . . ." Sabina chose not to give in to her fears, fears she'd begged the Lord to take from her. "I'm going to go fill the trough."

By the time she reached the well, Baxter had caught up with her, his work clothes carrying the aroma of sawdust. "Let me haul up the water for you."

"No, you have enough to do. 'Sides, I need to keep busy." She set the wooden container on the half wall and reached for the crank to the suspended well bucket.

Baxter already had his hand on the knob. "Sabina." He said her name in his most pleasing voice while unwinding the rope to the bucket. "I know you're uncomfortable about the way you came to be with us. But there's no need to mention the details. When the boys and I rode out to invite folks to the cabin raising, I told everyone you were a hardworking, praying woman with a cheerful disposition. They don't need to know about your stepfather's callous wager."

"But I don't want to speak falsely."

"You don't have to," he said reassuringly, as he reversed the direction of the crank. "Didn't you say your stepfather lost all his money? I'd say that was falling on hard times, as much as when a hailstorm destroys a farmer's cash crop. They're both empty-handed. And telling folks your mother felt it was best for you to find a position with a godly family, that's true as well. So, stop worrying. Be your cheery self, and folks can't help but love you."

The well bucket raised, he transferred water into the one she held steady on the stone wall. The two of them stood much too close. She felt the very warmth coming from him and from his dark, searching eyes.

Abruptly, he took the filled barn bucket from her and swung away. "You boys get back to axing and planing. I'll be with you in a minute."

As he strode away, Sabina took an unguarded moment to watch the most beguiling man in the world walk to the horse trough . . . while she stored his words in her heart: *"Be your cheery self, and folks can't help but love you."* They had been words similar to what his daughter had said, and Delia and the boys were always telling her they loved her. But from him . . .

Catching herself sighing, she stopped gawking and started for the house, reminding herself of what was real. If he loved her the way a man loves a woman, he would have at least taken a second or two to consider marrying her. But, no, he'd already picked out his wife-to-be—the socially accomplished young widow from Nashville. Still, no matter how hard she tried to push the thought of a life with him away, it kept creeping back.

Sabina heard a distant rumble. It grew louder. Her gaze flew to the path between the house and the cobbler shop. A team of horses, a bay and a dun, broke out of the woods, hauling a wagon with several people aboard. The first batch of inquisitors. All the livelong day they would be able to question her.

In the dream she'd always had of living among Christian families, she'd never considered whether or not they would accept her.

"Sabina." Baxter's voice, coming from behind her, was commanding.

She tore her attention from the approaching family. "Yes?"

He smiled reassuringly. "They will love you."

Chapter Nine

Baxter had been correct about the people loving Sabina, or—
more aptly—treating her real friendly-like. When the more than
twenty families arrived, each of the women came up to her with
welcoming greetings and compliments. Their husbands were
also neighborly but in a hurry to join the other men and boys
already at work on the cabin. Whatever Baxter had said to
Brother Bremmer and the folks he'd invited, he must have
satisfied them one and all.

The Bremmers had come in the first group of wagons, and
with Delia's help, Inga had reintroduced the women and their
daughters to Sabina as they arrived. But idleness wasn't the
order of the day for them any more than for the men. Some had
brought a quilting frame, and several women quickly set it up
and stretched the pieced, colorful, wagon-wheel-pattern quilt
across it. Like a mothering hen, Inga handed Sabina a threaded
needle, inviting her to join the quilting bee.

When the Reardon women arrived, the Nordic-looking grandmother and her two daughters-in-law, Sabina made a particular point of putting names to their faces this time, since their property abutted the Clays' at the main road. The two younger women seemed especially friendly.

"You and the Clays must come for Sunday dinner tomorrow," Annie, the honey blonde, said. "That is, if you can put up with our rowdy bunch."

"They ain't so rowdy," Delia said, walking up with another girl her age—one with those same colorless eyes and ebony hair as Jessica Reardon. "This here's Hope. She and her sister Gracie are my best friends in the whole world."

"The whole world?" Sabina couldn't help chuckling as she tugged a needle up through the batting.

In an easy manner that filled Sabina with joy, the other women around the frame joined in her amusement, laughing lightly.

"It's a pure pleasure to meet you, Miss Hope," Sabina said to the fine-boned girl.

Hope, in a lavender-checked gown very similar to Delia's lime green, curtsied politely. "Pleased to meet you, too, Miss Erhardt. Delia says the two of you will be living in the new cabin, and no boys are allowed."

"*Ever*," Delia affirmed.

"Never?" A wide smile splashed across Hope's elfin face . . . as if ridding themselves of the opposite sex was a marvelous treat.

"Not even Sammy," Delia bragged. "Ain't that right, Sabina?"

"Rules is rules," Sabina agreed lightly, though she would have preferred that the subject of their living arrangement hadn't been broached. *Let sleeping dogs lie*, her stepfather Kurt had always said.

"And that goes for any fellas with a mind to come callin',

Mistress Jessup," Delia added, staring pointedly at a woman in her middle years who was working on the other side of the quilting frame. "I seen the way your oldest, Grady, was eyein' Sabina when y'all rode in."

The woman, who looked like she had a permanent frown etched across her wide brow, gasped as Delia barreled on.

"If Grady has a mind to come a-visitin', it'll have to be at the main house with Papa makin' sure he don't try nothin' unseemly."

By this time, Mistress Jessup had swelled into a prickly bristle. "Delia Clay, that is no way to speak to your elders."

The girl didn't back down. "I was just sayin'—"

Sabina stepped in. "Delia, a hostess should never offend her guests, intentional or not. Please apologize."

Her brunette ringlets bouncing, Delia exchanged impatient glances with her friend Hope. Then she propped up a smile. "Our Miss Sabina, bein' the fine Christian lady that she is, is always right. Just the other day, she taught me, 'Wherefore receive ye one another, as Christ also received us to the glory of God.' Romans 15:7. So Mistress Jessup, I really must apologize for any discomfort I caused you."

"Thank you, Delia," Sabina managed while squelching an untimely grin. Today, everything that had come from Delia's mouth had been to promote Sabina's purity. "Now, would you girls be kind enough to fetch a couple of pitchers of ade from the springhouse? One peach and one lemon. I think our guests might be partial to some refreshment about now." She glanced up past the branches of a honey locust to a cloudless sky. "Looks to be another scorcher."

As Delia and Hope strolled away, their arms linked companionably, Sabina stole a glance at the men at work, axing notches, lifting logs, or sawing, and wondered which was

Grady Jessup. But her eyes landed on Baxter hoisting one end of a timber, his muscles straining against his shirt, his brow glistening with perspiration as he gave directions to another man. When he should be working on his shoe orders, here he was, doing all this for her. . . .

"Hope and Gracie and Delia have been quite the trio since the Clays first moved here ten years ago," Jessica Reardon said with a rather timid smile, bringing Sabina's attention back to the circle of women. "Isn't that right, Mother Reardon?"

The older, much taller woman harrumphed on a chuckle. "Aye. They're usually like three chicks in a nest, but poor Gracie had to stay home today with an upset stomach. After Delia's mama died, we sorta took her under our wing when it came to female doin's, her bein' the only girl at the Clays . . . till now, anyway." Mistress Reardon's sharp gray eyes gave Sabina the once-over.

The other daughter-in-law, Annie, entered the conversation from the far corner. "We taught Delia how to lay out patterns and to sew that checked dress she's got on. She cut it out and stitched the whole thing herself."

All this neighborliness touched Sabina. "You're good people. All you've done for her shows. She's such a delightful child." Sabina shot a glance to Mistress Jessup. "Most of the time."

Yes, these were all fine Christians. Inga Bremmer had also pitched in, mothering Sammy when he was small. All because these people were rooted in one spot. It seemed like paradise. Aside from the Lord, she and her mother had been all the female company each other had. . . . And now her mother was gone from her, perhaps forever.

A sadness invaded the pleasant morning. Looking down at the corner of a patchwork piece, she tried to concentrate instead on pushing her needle through it.

"Sabina girl," the gaunt-faced Mistress Reardon said, staring across at her, "we got more peaches this year than we know what to do with. Why don't you and Delia come over next Tuesday and help us preserve 'em? Bring your own jars to take home."

"Why, thank you kindly. But I'll have to ask Mr. Clay first."

"He'll say yes," Annie assured her. "When it comes to sweets, them Clay boys never say no."

"When you and Delia come," the elder Reardon said, her severe features softening as she shot a merry look around the circle of women, "we'll let you in on all the ladies' foibles and the latest gossip."

Surprised gasps escaped a couple of the women.

But Sabina and the others found Mistress Reardon's teasing good fun. She laughed along with her new neighbors at the older lady's droll humor before responding. "The ladies' foibles," she said, trying to sound serious, "I'd find mighty interesting. But as for gossip, I thought me and Mr. Clay was the latest piece being bandied about."

Silence.

Then Mistress Jessup gave the wooden frame a resounding slap. "You are that!" she cried and sputtered into howling laughter, along with every other woman within earshot.

Tears were streaming down some of their cheeks by the time the jolly merriment died away and Mistress Reardon remarked, "I do believe you're gonna fit right in, Sabina girl. Yessiree, right in."

With these simple farm people like herself, maybe. But Sabina knew not to give herself any false hopes concerning Baxter. He was cut from finer cloth . . . and he was a man determined to restore his children to their rightful station in life.

Realizing she should be counting her blessings instead of falling down that pit again, Sabina lifted herself out and looked around at her new friends. Today was not a day for maudlin thoughts.

~

Sabina could hardly believe how quickly her cabin took shape. By noon, the floor had been laid, the walls up and chinked, with the windows and doorway framed. All that remained would be the roof and the layering of shingles.

Inga Bremmer, wearing her usual crown of graying braids, stuck her needle deep into the almost finished quilt and addressed the other women. "Time it is to get food on da tables. Da men ve haf to feed."

The women all scattered to fetch their culinary offerings either from their wagons or from the springhouse where they had stored any food needing to be kept cold.

Sabina walked into her overheated kitchen to collect a kettle of tasty-smelling ham and beans that had been simmering all morning. After delivering it to a serving table, she returned inside for the pot of sliced carrots and the apricot cobbler. These would be her contributions to the potluck.

As she started out the front door with the carrots, Inga Bremmer stepped up onto the porch. "I am t'inking I should say some private vords to you."

The seriousness reflecting in her square Slavic features stopped Sabina. Until now, she'd thought the day was going exceptionally well. Perfectly, in fact. *Lord, please have mercy,* she breathed silently.

The older woman's expression softened. "I chust am vanting to say, Baxter, he tells us about da vay you come to be *mit* him and da *kinders*. You know, da gambling business."

The breath froze in Sabina's lungs. *He'd told them?*

"Rolf and me, ve promise to keep it to ourselves. Sorry I am dat you haf to leave your mama. I know she misses you like I miss mine own *kinders*. Dey is all gone avay," she said sadly. "Better land dey t'ink dey is finding fardder vest. Even Otto, mine baby. Max, he tells me to call him now," she inserted with disgust. "Vat is dis Max business? Vatever." She shrugged. "He is traipsing off *mit* a fur company ven he should be here helping his papa. All of mine *kinders* gone."

"I know all about moving on," Sabina commiserated. "The call of the unknown does get ahold of 'em. My stepfather always thinks he's going to win his fortune in the next settlement downriver, the next trading post. As for myself, I'm sorely tired of moving on. Just for a little while, I'd like to stay put, know where I am when I wake up in the morning." Sabina rested the heavy pot of carrots on the railing. "Just once, I'd like to stay somewheres long enough to harvest a garden I planted."

"*Ja*, I know about dat. I follow my man all da vay from da old country." Inga moved closer and spoke more softly. "Vat I really come to say is, ve are glad dat you is here *mit* da Clays. It is a good t'ing. And anytime you vant to talk, I am villing to listen, chust like your mama."

Just like my mama. Emotion welled up inside Sabina at Inga's offer to be a mother to her. She caught hold of the German woman's work-reddened hand. "God is so good to me. Thank you."

Inga seemed a bit embarrassed by Sabina's outburst. She deftly withdrew her fingers. "You chust take special care of mine Sammy *mit* da puppy-dog eyes."

Sabina smiled. "Those big brown eyes *are* hard to resist. And the whole family has them."

"Even da fadder."

Yes, Sabina wanted to agree, *Baxter, too*. But that was best left unsaid.

~

Baxter paused to observe the men's efforts on the cabin as the others headed toward the bounty laid out on the serving tables. Where once had been meadowland now stood the walls of Sabina and Delia's new cabin. The freshly squared logs glistened gold in the midday sun. And for the first time, his daughter would be sleeping in a room other than the one across the hall from him.

It was strange for them now to be making all these changes when his life and the lives of his children had plodded along predictably for so many years. With the occasional help of their neighbors, he and his brood had managed fairly well up till the present, but now his kids seemed to be growing an inch a day. Especially Delia . . . he just hadn't expected it to happen quite so fast.

"Hey, Clay," one of the men called back to him. "Don't worry. That cabin ain't gonna run off. Come an' eat."

Baxter turned toward the tables set up under the shade trees for nooning. Some of the men and boys already had their wooden trenchers filled and were scrambling onto the keg-and-board benches, while a few of the women and older girls poured glasses of chilled ades of peach or lemon for those already seated.

As he neared, a plethora of delicious-smelling aromas reached his nostrils, and his stomach rolled in anticipation. The women always put out their best efforts when it came to food for these get-togethers.

Among the tables strolled Delia, prettier than ever in summer green and white. She carried a platter of sliced bread, serving the men while laughing and chatting right along with everyone else, having a wonderful time. It was easy to understand why she and the boys couldn't fathom the need for the extra instruction he insisted they should have.

Picking a trencher off a stack and moving down the line to fill his plate, he surveyed the crowd until he found his boys already seated at various tables. Each was in the midst of a lively conversation with one of his friends. They fit in so well with the folks here in the valley, they simply had no perception of how inadequate their limited education would be for life anywhere but on the frontier.

"Here, Papa," Sammy called as Baxter left the food tables with his heaping trencher. His youngest patted the spot next to him. "I saved you a place."

Baxter waved to Sammy while wondering where Sabina was. Heading for his son, he scanned the women standing in clusters talking. He knew they wouldn't take the time to eat until they had the men fed and back to work.

Then he sighted Sabina coming from the direction of the springhouse, bringing more butter. Though she wore the plainest of homespun day gowns, the noonday sun shimmering across her flaxen bun, the straightness of her back and the sureness of her gait gave the rustic girl a regal presence that was hard to resist.

Realizing he'd stopped to stare, Baxter continued on to his son.

Brother Rolf, seated at the next table, tapped a spoon to his glass. "Is time ve bless da meal now."

Baxter remained standing behind his bench. "Rolf, if you don't mind, I'd like to give the blessing today."

The pastor was caught off guard, it being customary when he was present to always perform such rites. "Sure t'ing." He nodded into his double chins. "Is goot."

"Thank you," Baxter said, then raised his voice to be heard all the way to the women. "First, I want to thank you all for coming on such short notice. You are proof of what it is to be a good neighbor. Ever since we came to this valley and tragedy befell us, you've been ready to help whenever a need arose. I will be ever grateful. And I just wanted to add—"

His sleeve was being tugged. Sammy. "Hurry up, Pa, we're hungry."

"Right," he said, with a self-effacing grin. Forks all down the line, including Sammy's, were poised and ready to dig in. "I just wanted to add that I appreciate that same courtesy you are extending to Miss Erhardt." His gaze sought her out.

Placing the butter on the next table, she looked back at him with those achingly sincere eyes.

His heart gave an unexpected jolt. Then remembering to raise his hand, he signaled for the bowing of heads. "Father in heaven, we ask you to bless this food we are about to receive, that it might nourish our bodies as you do our souls. Thank you for blessing my family with so many wonderful brothers and sisters in Christ. And I especially want to thank you for delivering Miss Sabina into our lives. She continues to honor us with her diligent labors and her cheerful spirit. We pray all this in the name of our Lord Jesus. Amen."

"Amen," resounded down the four eating tables as Baxter climbed across the bench and took his place before his food. His stomach growled in anticipation as he eyed the meat-choked dishes swimming in spicy gravies.

Forking into some sausage pie, Baxter noticed Ezra Jessup's grown son across from him, taking a long gander at Sabina. Grady wasn't the only one. Pete and Paul Dagget at the next table also stole glances between bites. Audaciously bold, flirting glances.

And Baxter didn't like it one bit.

Chapter Ten

Biting off a chunk of bread, Baxter took his own long, reassessing look at Sabina as he sat across from curly-headed, flashy-toothed Grady Jessup. She wore nothing but a lank linen dress covered with a plain muslin apron, and no shoes. But since it was a hot summer day most of the other women and all the children had naked feet also. Actually, Sabina fit right in with these homespun folk, and she could easily hold her own when it came to looks.

On second thought, she was distinctly more pleasing to behold than anyone else here. How often did a woman in her twenties still have hair as light and shiny as corn silk and a face that could have posed for a fragile figurine yet could take the sun without burning and freckling? And her eyes were the color of Chinese jade and wonderfully large, the kind a man yearned to have gazing up at him, following his every word, smiling at him. And her infectious laughter . . .

Yes, it was easy to see why the young bucks were interested—something he'd carelessly neglected to consider. One of them, he suddenly realized, might even woo her away before he had a marriage to Amanda Atwood arranged. Hadn't he just sung Sabina's praises to the whole blasted valley?

"Pass the bread," Sammy, beside him, requested around a mouthful of chicken leg.

Baxter complied, his mood turning sour. Here he'd been, taking most of the week off from his shoe orders to build a cabin for a woman who could be gone in a month.

"Miss Sabina," called one of those rawboned twins at the next table. "I'll have some more to drink." Black hair stringing, the impertinent fellow lifted his glass to his mouth and downed its contents as he watched her walk toward him.

Perhaps making that sign that Delia wanted for the cabin wouldn't be such a bad notion: No Men Allowed. One thing was for sure: any courting to take place on his property would be done on his front porch, right where he could keep an eye on these overeager bucks.

"Pass the salt," Baxter barked at Grady. At least that would return one young bounder's attention back to the meal for a moment or two.

～

The next morning, if Baxter could have conjured a plausible excuse for not attending church, he would have. Yester's eve when the neighbors departed the cabin raising, no less than half a dozen fellows had made a point of telling Sabina they'd be looking forward to seeing her today. But breakfast and every chore had been accomplished in short order. The wagon was now hitched, and he and the boys stood beside it, their shoes polished and shining, their felt hats brushed. They all looked as starched and pressed in their white shirts and vests as they had last Sabbath, thanks to Sabina.

"Let me straighten your tie." Baxter reached for the black satin bow at Sammy's throat as he and the boys waited for the girls.

"Why does it always take females so long to get ready?" Sammy asked, pulling at his collar.

"Don't."

"But it's gettin' hot, and the blasted stiff thing is scratchin'."

"Well, don't touch it anyway. You'll smudge it."

"I'd like an answer to Sammy's question," Philip said, twisting his own neck uncomfortably. "Why *does* it take them so blamed long?"

"I don't know, boys. It's one of life's great mysteries."

Howie, perched on the back of the wagon, looked impatiently past the garden to the new cabin. "They didn't even have to get Sunday dinner started since the Reardons have invited us over to their place. Sabina said they'd be just a minute."

"Aye," Baxter replied, fully aware she and Delia had retreated to their new sleeping quarters a good half hour ago. He usually hated waiting almost as much as his lads did, but this morning he'd just as soon they didn't come out at all.

"I forgot my letter." Philip spun around and ran back to the house for the missive he'd written his sweetheart in Greeneville.

Baxter smiled. Young love.

"Here they come," Howie said. "At last."

Turning back toward the new cabin, Baxter saw the two rounding the garden as they came at a fast walk. Sabina wore the same faded blue gown she had worn last Sunday, but this morning she had donned a straw bonnet with a white under-ruffle. It framed her peaches-and-cream complexion most favorably. Most favorably, indeed.

"Don't Sabina look purty in the bonnet *Oma* Inga gave her?" Sammy asked.

"Inga gave her a bonnet?" Baxter himself should have seen that Sabina had one for Sundays. Her running away in the dead of night as she did, she hadn't managed to bring even a mobcap. Or shoes. Before he left for Nashville, he'd see that she had a pair.

And he'd arrange for some adequate chaperoning as well. He certainly couldn't leave her here subject to the whims of the valley's young bucks.

~

The church bell rang out as Sabina and the Clays rolled past the settlement's saddlery.

A family walking to the church house waved cheerily. "Howdy, Miss Sabina," one of the youngsters hollered as the wagon rumbled by him.

"Howdy, John David," she called from her place on the straw, glad she'd remembered the plump-cheeked boy's name. What a joyous thing it was to be greeting passersby on her way to Sunday services. Almost as wonderful as yesterday when these same folk welcomed her as an equal, not like the hired help she was. They'd built her a cabin. And today after services she and the Clays were invited to dinner with the very founders of the valley.

In a burst of exuberance, she caught Delia and Sammy to her. "'My cup runneth over.'"

Delia returned her hug. "Mine, too. We just spent the first night in our own cabin."

"With pretty new curtains." Sabina laughed, remembering that Delia had refused to retire last night until the ruffled floral calico they'd sewn this week hung at the windows.

"I want new curtains for our room, too," Sammy groused.

"Mine, too," Philip said from the bench seat. "Now that I have a room of my own."

"I don't see why Phil should get Delia's room." Howie, bumping along at the rear, glanced back, his brown eyes brittle.

"Whoa." Pulling on the reins, Baxter brought the team to a halt at the end of a line of other rigs and pulled on the brake handle. He then turned around. "Howie, Philip is the oldest. When he leaves home, the room will be yours."

"But you said I had to go away to school too." With a frown marring his slim features, Howie hopped to the ground, then turned back to help the others down.

"Only if Papa marries Mistress Atwood," Philip reminded as he leapt down from a front-wheel hub.

A reminder Sabina could easily have done without on this otherwise perfect morn. Rising, she straightened her pretty straw bonnet and reached out to Howie.

His demeanor brightened as he caught hold of her waist and swung her down. Before releasing her, he whispered, "*If* Pa marries the blamed widow."

Before Sabina could respond, she was fronted by the Smiths, a tall, husky man and his tiny wife.

"Welcome to our valley." Though rather sickly looking, Betsy Smith was one of the sweeter ladies Sabina had met yesterday.

"Thank you. It's my pleasure."

Sabina hadn't taken more than a few more steps when someone from behind spoke softly next to her ear. "Yes, welcome to our valley."

The warmth in Baxter's voice caught her off guard. He took her elbow and despite herself, she couldn't help reveling in his touch or the scent of the bayberry he must have splashed on just before they left. "I'm so pleased to be here," she said. Never having noticed the fragrance on him before, she tantalized herself by wondering if he wore it for her benefit . . . just as they were surrounded by more well-wishers.

What a grand morning.

As Sabina and the Clays walked up the wide church steps, Mistress Jessup, the woman Delia had insulted the day before, came alongside. "Miss Erhardt," she said, a smile softening her permanent frown lines, "we ladies have a surprise for you after church."

A *surprise?* A chill raced up Sabina's spine. Most surprises in Sabina's life had come from the rise or fall of her stepfather's luck—more often the fall. Still, Mistress Jessup had spoken the words with what seemed to be genuine sincerity.

Nonetheless, during the church service, the uncertainty she felt made concentrating on Brother Bremmer's sermon most difficult, especially when one or another of the women looked over at Sabina and smiled with a knowing nod.

After the benediction, Sabina and Baxter were being buffered along by the departing congregation when Delia's friend, Hope Reardon, wedged through with Gracie, her blonde and much taller older sister—the one who favored their Nordic father.

"Don't forget," Hope said, her almost transparent eyes mirrors of delight, "you're coming to our place for Sunday dinner."

"We wouldn't forget that," Delia answered for the Clays.

"I put bouquets of flowers on all the tables," Gracie added. "And on the chance you don't know, the Dagget twins are coming, too. They sort of invited themselves." She and her smaller-boned sister exchanged glances and started giggling.

Sabina had no trouble remembering the Dagget twins. Dark-featured, rangy, with long rather horsey faces, they both had made pests of themselves yesterday, coming up with a host of reasons for her to service their table during the cabin-raising meal. They'd turned it into a brotherly competition. At Baxter's table, Mistress Jessup's son, Grady, had been a bit of a fool himself. She certainly hoped the twins would behave more gentlemanly at the Reardons'.

Emerging from the cool sanctuary, Sabina and the Clays stepped into the glare of a sultry noontime sun playing peekaboo among some high clouds. It would be a sticky afternoon.

"Over there," Baxter said, nodding in the direction of a cluster of women dressed mostly in summer pastels. They stood by one of the wagons.

"Come, Sabina," called Inga Bremmer in more conservative pearl gray. "Come over here."

Still a bit apprehensive, Sabina reached up and checked the tilt of the bonnet the older lady had given her and glanced up at Baxter.

"Go on." His encouraging smile put her at ease.

"Delia, you come, too," the elder Mistress Reardon hollered, looking over the shorter Inga's head. "It's for you, too."

"*Me?*" Dark curls springing, Delia shot forth like a colt. No concerns disturbed her when it came to surprises.

"Go." Baxter gave a gentle shove at the small of Sabina's back.

The ladies were all smiles when she reached them.

"What is it?" Delia's doe eyes fairly danced as they searched the women's hands.

"Settle down, child," Mistress Reardon chided. "We have something to say to Sabina first. Go ahead, Tilly."

Sabina's mouth went dry. Had Inga betrayed her, told Tilly Jessup about her stepfather losing her in a game of cards? Or had the women somehow discovered her deepest, most shameful secret?

Tilly Jessup cleared her throat. "Miss Sabina, in the short time we've known you, we all come to think of you as one of our own. We never seen the Clay place lookin' so neat. Trash all picked up. The garden weeded. The young'uns with their Sunday clothes all starched and ironed. And," she said jerking a nod at Sabina, "you're a pure delight to be around. Any fool can see why them kids think the sun rises and sets on you. But I reckon what really made us all take to you right off is Baxter Clay's praisin' you so high, and him not even havin' no designs on you for hisself."

The woman's last compliment stung. Did every living soul in this valley know Baxter had rejected her as a wife?

"And—"

"Stop your long-winded speechifyin'," one of the other women chided. "Just get on with it."

Mistress Jessup's permanent frown lines deepened. "That's what I was trying to do. Now Sabina and Delia, we was plannin' on rafflin' this off at the harvest fair, but we decided to give it to you for a housewarmin' gift instead. A little somethin' in remembrance of the day we all—"

"You're speechifyin' again," Mistress Reardon broke in.

"Here." Inga Bremmer reached over the sideboard of the vehicle and lifted out the wagon-wheel-patterned quilt made of mostly pinks, reds, and greens. "A new quilt to go *mit* da new curtains." She laid it across Sabina's arms . . . this quilt that every woman in the valley had worked on.

Tears pooled in Sabina's eyes. "Thank you," she said past the blur. "Thank you." Baxter may have rejected her, but these good women were taking her into their circle of love.

Thank you, Jesus.

Chapter Eleven

Baxter couldn't help smiling as he watched Sabina walking with the Reardon women into Ike and Annie's large cabin, happily conversing with them. She chatted with the three Reardon women as if she'd known them for years—one of those endearing qualities of Sabina's. Once she'd learned that every family in the valley was God-fearing and attended church regularly, she'd wrapped herself in the congregation's friendship as if it were the quilt the ladies had given her and Delia.

"The trough's over there." Ike, the older of the tall Reardon brothers, nodded toward a hollowed-out log in front of the barn.

"Aye, I know." Holding the headgear of one of his grays, Baxter left the grassy area framed by the trio of Reardon cabins and walked the horses and wagon toward the water.

"Just makin' sure. The way you was smilin' and gawkin' up at the house, I thought you was plannin' on takin' your rig in with the women."

Baxter glanced over Thunder's and Snowflake's necks at the man who'd inherited his mother's strong Scandinavian features . . . and saw a flash of teeth. Usually serious-minded, Ike was teasing him while he and his brother unhitched their own team of giant chestnuts from the Reardons' much larger wagon. With the eleven children they had between them, they needed the biggest vehicle they could find. As they worked, more than a dozen youngsters ran playing and screaming all the way down to the river that ran alongside the Reardon property.

Noah, the more educated of the two and lawyer for the valley, toted a hefty leather collar toward the barn. He turned back, grinning just as wide as Ike. "You know, Clay, those Dagget boys are going to be riding in here any minute now. You made a serious mistake, thinking you could take your sweet time where Miss Sabina is concerned. It would have been smarter to marry her while you still had a clear field. By now, news about a pretty, marriageable young miss has probably spread from Nashville to Knoxville."

"That's right," Ike contributed. "The postrider came through on Thursday. And you know how he likes to talk along his route."

Baxter tried not to sound irritated as he waited for his horses to drink their fill. "Why is it that no one will believe I have no intention of asking Sabina to marry me?"

"Because," Ike said, pausing from unhooking a chain, "only a blind man couldn't see how you can't keep your eyes off her."

Baxter hiked his chin. "I'm not going to ignore her. She's an admirable person and a joy to have around." Baxter glanced to where his youngsters were playing stickball in the meadow with the older Reardon children, safely out of earshot. "And my kids adore her."

"So why are you draggin' your feet?" Ike asked. "You've needed a wife for years."

"That's true." Frustrated that he would have to explain himself yet again, he turned to the more sophisticated of the two. "Noah, we've talked about this before. When I married beneath my station in life, I robbed my children of their heritage."

"Your young'uns are all happy and healthy, with the whole West about to open up for them," Ike inserted. "I don't think they feel one bit cheated."

"That's because they don't know anything but living out here. They need to spend time in the East, see how people there live, then choose. I've waited this past decade to remarry because, excepting your sister-in-law, Crystabelle, who saw fit to marry your brother Drew instead of me, I haven't found a young woman with the necessary accomplishments and a dowry sufficient to help me restore what I took from them. That is, till now."

"Sabina?" Ike questioned. "But I thought she comes empty-handed."

"No, I'm speaking of a young widow I met at Cane Ridge. She's the daughter of Storekeeper Finch in Nashville."

"Finch. I know him," Ike said. "He's the one who's gotten rich off the beaver trade. Hear he has the finest house on the river."

"Aye, that's the man."

"Well, I'll swan." Ike walked over to Baxter, grinning. "For a man who's had such a long dry spell, ain't you full of surprises?"

Not sharing his brother's amusement, Noah hung the weighty jangle of harness just inside the barn door. "Baxter, I don't mean to preach, but money and social advantages don't necessarily equal happiness. Look to the Lord for guidance."

Baxter didn't appreciate Noah's preaching. "I did ask for guidance. And I feel certain that Amanda Atwood is the Lord's choice for me. She's exactly the kind of woman I prayed for."

"I see." Noah came out the wide barn entrance and walked straight to Baxter. "Well, ponder this, friend. Why, after all these years, when you do settle on someone to marry, has another beautiful, industrious, and blithesome young woman been placed directly in your path? Do you think she's merely a stumbling block? Or, mayhap, God's true choice for you?"

The rumble of racing horses thundering toward them put an abrupt end to the disturbing debate. Leaving a cloud of dust in their wake, the Dagget twins were riding in fast, each whipping his mount to greater speed.

Ike stepped closer to Baxter, that amused grin as smug as ever. "If them lads has anything to say about it, you won't have to fret about Sabina bein' a stumblin' block or anything else."

~

Why did there always have to be more eligible men than women on the frontier? Baxter seethed silently as he looked across the adult Reardon dinner table that had been set up under a big-leafed sycamore. The horse-faced Dagget twins sat there, grinning like a couple of addlepated bookends with Sabina trapped between them.

"Baxter, I hear your trip up to Kentucky was real profitable," Ike, seated at one end of the long oak table said, that bemused smile never quite gone.

"Aye." Baxter laid down his fork and sat back. He had little appetite today. "Far more profitable than I'd expected." His roving glance included the other Reardons. "I received enough shoe orders to keep me busy for weeks. But even if I hadn't, I would have counted the trip as pure profit."

"Because you found Miss Sabina and got her to come here

and work for you," Pete Dagget, the slightly less horsey-looking one, said.

"Yes, of course, that too." Although Baxter didn't want to diminish his good fortune in finding her, he had no intention of making her the topic of conversation again, especially in front of the Daggets. "But what I am speaking about are the blessings I received from attending the camp meeting. Never in my life have I been anyplace where I felt the presence and the power of the Lord so strongly."

"Oh my, yes," Sabina murmured across the table from him, her eyes reflecting the glory of what he said.

Ignoring her loveliness, he charged on. "It was most humbling to experience even a small glimpse of the magnificence of . . ." He caught himself staring at her again. "Wasn't that your impression, Miss Sabina?" he asked hastily, having lost his train of thought.

"Me?" The same person who had no problem teasing and joking with his children or chatting nonstop with the women also seemed at a loss . . . but for only a moment. "Oh yes," she said, the glow returning to her light green eyes. "The wonder of being surrounded by so many of the Lord's children, my eternal brothers and sisters. To an only child, that means so much. There we was, all of us, singing and worshiping and listening to hours and days of God-inspired preaching. Yet even in all that wonderful together time, there was moments when I felt it was just me and Jesus. Him singing with me, him telling me how much he loves me. It was . . ." Sabina glanced about her, suddenly shy again. "I was purely blessed," she finished, her voice trailing off.

"Aye," Baxter agreed, hoping to dispell her discomfort. "I felt that myself. You should all try to go if the ministers hold another big camp meeting next year."

"Sounds wonderful," Annie said, sitting to the side of her husband, Ike. "But that's a mighty long time to go away and leave all our stock."

Paul Dagget leaned around until he was practically in Sabina's face. "If you're goin' again, Miss Erhardt, I'd be pleased to carry you there, be your personal escort."

"Would you, now?" came a woman's authoritative voice from down the table. Louvenia Reardon's.

Relieved that Mistress Reardon had put the clodhopper in his place, Baxter returned to the topic. "Davy Wallace took good care of our stock. But if you don't want to travel so far, a couple of the Tennessee ministers are planning a camp meeting in the Nashville area this autumn."

"Really?" Pete asked. "I got no problem goin' along with Paul and Miss Sabina—" he leaned around the girl sandwiched between him and his brother—"to chaperone or *be* chaperoned, whichever way things work out."

"Speaking of chaperoning," Baxter returned, his ire barely contained, "I'll be leaving for Nashville in a few days, and—"

"That so?" both twins rudely spewed.

"*And,*" Baxter stated with force, then shifted his gaze to Lou Reardon down the table, "I'd appreciate it if Delia and Sabina could spend their nights here. I don't want to leave them at home with just Philip and Howie watching out for them."

"I agree," the older woman said with just as much feeling. She eyed the twins. "That's a wise decision."

"Visitin' here or at the Clays don't make me no never-mind." Paul glanced from Ike to Noah at the other end. "If it's all right with y'all, I'll be droppin' by now an' again."

"Not without me you won't," his twin challenged.

And if Baxter had anything to say about it, they would not be overly welcome. Neither of the unmannerly boors was fit to wipe Sabina's shoes—when he made some for her, he quickly reminded himself.

He glanced across at her. She sat stiffly with her hands tucked safely in her lap, the food on her plate barely touched. Thanks be to God, she wasn't any more pleased with them than he was.

Baxter exhaled a more relaxed breath and picked up his fork. When he returned from visiting Amanda Atwood in Nashville, he'd concentrate on encouraging more suitable young men to come courting Sabina, such as . . . as . . .

With a little thought, he'd surely come up with several who would make her a fine match. One, anyway, who would see beyond her outward loveliness and appreciate the more important beauty within. Her love of the Lord, her generosity of spirit, the way she filled the house with laughter . . . that gift she had for making everyone fall in love with her within moments of meeting her.

Surely somewhere in Tennessee there was a man worthy of her. But he certainly didn't go by the name of Dagget.

One of the oafs elbowed Sabina's ribs, reaching for a gravy bowl.

She winced, her fragile features twisting in pain.

Enough of their reckless abuse. "Sabina, I know you and Delia wanted to finish furnishing your cabin this afternoon. So it would be best if we leave as soon as the dishes are cleared away."

Her brows lifted in puzzlement. Quickly, they resettled into graceful golden wings that flew above her eyes, and a polite smile appeared. "Why, yes. I almost forgot."

The twins, though, looked as if someone had just snatched away their new toy.

Undaunted, Sabina continued as if she and Baxter had actually planned an early departure. "The dinner and the Reardons' hospitality have all been such a delight." Her gaze traveled up and down the table to her hosts, who appeared to understand the situation completely. "But, yes, I can hardly wait to see what the gift quilt will look like on the bed."

"Another time," Jessica said, smiling sweetly. "When you're more settled."

"But you can't go so soon," Paul almost whined.

"Besides," Pete added, "you ain't supposed to work on the Sabbath."

The lad had surely blocked their escape. Sabina would never knowingly break one of the Lord's commandments.

A slow smile curved Sabina's lips, and she favored first Pete then Paul with it.

Did she really want to stay here and be pulled back and forth like a bone between two dogs?

"Decorating our new cabin ain't work," she replied. "It's a pure pleasure."

The relief Baxter felt was profound—a feeling he dared not explore. Quickly he rose from the table. "I'll go tell the kids."

Chapter Twelve

Quietly Sabina pulled the cabin door closed behind her, careful not to awaken Delia. On her walk to the main house to start breakfast, a cool rain-scented breeze filled her lungs, reminding her of the gentle shower that had pattered against the windows during the night. In the first rays of morning, shafts of light found their way across the wooded hill, turning the moist garden and meadows into sparkling fields of magic that rivaled the star-sprinkled sky. The birds, in a cacophony of chirps, caws, and screeches, seemed no less thrilled with the morning.

The wonder of God's glorious creation. *Even the birds see God's glory, Kurt. Why can't you?*

At the thought of her unsaved stepfather, Sabina was suddenly swamped with a wave of longing for her mother. The two of them had prayed for Kurt for as long as she could remember. Sabina glanced at the rising sun. She knew they'd promised to talk to each other with each sunset. "But, Mama, I hope you're listening to me now, too. Dawn is such a perfect time to commune with you. Summer mornings are so lovely. I'll have Baxter write a letter, asking you to meet me then, too."

The chickens, shut up in their coop, heard her talking aloud as she passed and started squawking and crowing. She unlatched the coop door, and as they excitedly ran out of their nighttime sanctuary, flapping their wings and crowing, she walked in to collect eggs from the straw-filled boxes.

"I thank you, ladies," she said to the speckled layers as she came out into the sunlight with her oval bounty in her apron. "I'll come back and feed you soon as I get the biscuits to baking."

Walking in a northerly direction to the house, she was reminded again of her mother up in Cincinnati. Why did the Ohio river port have to be so far away? She needed to talk to Greta face-to-face, needed an answer to a pressing question that she could never put in any letter Baxter might write for her.

Sabina slowed her step as she passed the well. "Mama, I know you always said that my being illegitimate weren't nobody's business but our own. But last night, lying in bed with the gift quilt covering me, I started feeling like I was a fraud. If the women knew the truth, they never would've given it to me. It's like I'm taking advantage of them. Should I give it back?"

No answer came. The only sounds were the birds and the early rustlings of the livestock and the padding of her feet as she mounted the porch steps and crossed to the door.

She sighed and reached for the handle, pressing down. "Father in heaven, are you listening? Sorry to be such a bother all the time, but feelings of guilt is pressing in on me. I need you to tell me what to do."

"Did you say something?" Baxter glanced up at her as she stood in the threshold. He was at the hearth, filling the coffeepot from a water bucket.

"No, I was just talking to the Lord about something."

A smile lifted one side of his generous mouth. "I see."

"Ain't it a lovely day?" she added before he could inquire further.

"Aye." Baxter had already stirred up the coals from the back log and now placed the pot on a small pile of the fiery embers. "I love the fresh smell after a rain."

"The hens are laying good." She spread her apron to show him seven eggs. "Are you partial to bacon and eggs this morning?"

"That would be nice. Can I do something to help?"

"Help?" The man was kindness itself. "I can manage just fine. But if it wouldn't be too much bother, when you got the time, I'd like for you to write down some words for me to my mother. Then when you go to Nashville, mayhap you could send the letter downriver from there. It should get to her faster that way."

"Sure. I'll fetch my writing supplies right now."

Yes, it was going to be a fine day . . . as long as no mention was made of the reason for the Nashville trip. Sabina strolled with her apron of eggs to the worktable by the window and stubbed her toe on a wooden leg. "Ow!"

"What happened?"

"Nothing," she winced, placing the eggs in a bowl while rubbing the injured appendage against the back of her other leg. "Just wasn't watching my step."

"No, it's my fault. I should've make you a pair of shoes a week ago. And I'm not putting it off any longer. Take a seat while I get my patterns to size your feet."

"Now? Before breakfast?"

"It'll just take a minute. I'm not leaving for Nashville till you have a pair of shoes."

I would give up shoes for the rest of my life, she wanted to say as she watched him walk out to his shop, *if you wouldn't go there to visit my replacement.*

No, she conceded, digging into the flour sack with a gourd, Amanda Atwood would be much more than a replacement. She would be Baxter's wife and mother to his dear children.

~

When Baxter returned from his shop, he noticed that Sabina still limped slightly as she scooped lard from its crock and tapped it into a mixing bowl. "Your toe still hurts," he said, dropping a set of wooden patterns on the floor in front of a dining chair.

"It's just throbbing a mite. It won't hinder me in my chores today," she assured.

"Don't push yourself. You already do much more around here than I ever expected." Sitting down to wait for her to finish, Baxter couldn't imagine Amanda, whose hands were as soft as kid gloves, doing nearly so much, especially the outside chores that Sabina had tackled. The garden had never been so free of weeds. All the tools the kids had misplaced had been found and rehung in the toolshed. The yard, no longer scattered with trash, was swept smooth where there was no grass. And, at Delia's urging, Sabina had taken the wheelbarrow to the other side of the fenced pasture and dug up a few flowering plants that the two placed on either side of the front steps. The woman was a treasure. Perhaps he should keep her on for wages after Amanda came. *If* Sabina didn't let one of them upstarts talk her into wedding him instead.

The thought brought the Dagget twins to mind. *Don't let her pick either of them, Lord,* he prayed, unable to muster an ounce of charity for them.

"I know you're frightful busy out in your shop," Sabina said over her shoulder while cutting lard into the flour. "So, while I get the biscuits ready to bake, couldn't I go ahead and tell you what I want in my letter? Then we can measure my feet."

"Sounds good. I do have several shoe orders I need to finish before I leave for Nashville." He rose to gather his writing box from his desk.

"If you're so rushed, please, don't bother with a pair for me. Shoes is just pure vanity in the summer."

Vanity? Despite her exceptional natural beauty, the girl didn't have a vain bone in her body. "Yes, but autumn is coming soon. I'll get you measured, and I'll do my best to get them finished." Returning to the dining table, he opened his ink jar and dipped in the plumed quill. "You want the letter addressed to Greta Erhardt in Cincinnati, don't you?"

"Aye."

He wrote the information on the back side of a sheet of sturdy paper while Sabina cut dough circles with the edge of a water glass. After sprinkling some sand on to dry the ink, he flipped the parchment over. "Dearest Mother," he started while penning the salutation. "What next?"

Sabina turned around, her hands sticky with dough, her expression wistful. "Tell her everything is still fine here. That you and the kids are truly nice to me. And the folks in the valley is just as kind. Good Christian people like we talked about. And—"

"Slow down. Let me get this written before you go on."

"Beg pardon, I do tend to prattle on." Shrugging self-consciously, she turned back to the biscuits.

Baxter didn't consider "prattling" an apt description. Every word that ever came from Sabina's mouth was of greatest interest to him. "Ready for more," he said, finishing her last dictation.

She faced him again, her cheeks flushed from her exertion so near the hearth. "Would you ask Mama to think about me and pray with me at the rising sun each morning, too? Of an evening like we talked about just ain't often enough. Oh, and tell her I miss her and pray for her and, yes, even Kurt, every day. And most of all, tell her to remember to pray about us seeing each other again before the year is out."

Her voice lost its strength toward the end, and Baxter looked up to see a sheen of tears in her eyes just before she swung away. His chest tightened, his own heart aching for her loneliness, this one with so much love to give.

"That's all," she said hoarsely, catching up her apron. Back turned, she wiped her eyes, then put the pan in the cast-iron Dutch oven already heating on the coals.

He finished writing her last words and signed the letter, *Your loving daughter, Sabina*. Laying the quill aside, he picked up the wooden foot patterns and laid out the ones on the floor that he thought might be near her size. "Come over here and place your foot on these till I find a fit."

She walked to within easy reach of where he sat, and he became much too aware of how near she was. How tiny her waist, how round the curve of her hips.

Lifting her skirts, she bent to see her feet, and their heads nearly touched as her long single plait swung forward. It feathered its silken tassle across his lips. Quickly, she caught the braid and tossed it back over her shoulder.

Baxter took a calming breath, then looked down to a delicately turned ankle. He took another breath.

Seemingly unaware of his difficulty, Sabina moved a foot in the air just above the patterns until she found one she liked. She stepped down on the thin wood. "What do you think?"

Thinking was something Baxter was having a hard time doing at the moment. With supreme effort he looked past her slender foot to the amount of board surrounding it. "Aye, you have a good eye."

Suddenly she dropped her skirts and stepped away from him, the color in her cheeks deepened from more than the kitchen heat. In a flash, she whirled away and rushed to the front door. "I promised the chickens I'd feed them as soon as I got the biscuits in."

"Mornin'." Howie stood on the stairs a few steps from the bottom, grinning from ear to impertinent ear.

Baxter felt heat crawling up his own neck. Before this week was out, he really needed to be on his way to Nashville.

~

"But why do I have to go?" Sammy stood beside the horse, arguing with his father.

"We've been through this before." Baxter's frustration was evident in the set of his jaw, the tilt of his head as he sat back in the saddle. "The others have enough to do while I'm gone, without keeping up with you too." He stretched a strong, lean hand down to his youngest. "Now climb on up behind me."

Sabina knew Baxter wouldn't relent. She had both their clothes washed, ironed, and neatly rolled into totes and strapped to Snowflake's back, along with the shoes Baxter had finished these past two weeks.

"I promise, I won't give Sabina no trouble." Sammy peered up at his father with those begging eyes. "I'll work just as hard as everyone else."

"This isn't like you, Sammy. As a rule, you hate being left behind."

"That was before Sabina came."

Standing on the porch watching the exchange, she would rather that neither of them went. But it wasn't up to her.

Philip stepped up behind Sammy. "Don't be a ninny. You and me talked about this. Someone needs to go to represent this generation of Clays. Mistress Atwood should know exactly what she'll be marrying into." He squeezed his younger brother's arm. "Remember?"

"Aye," Sammy groused. "All right." Sammy caught hold of his papa's hand, and Philip helped hoist him onto the giant horse behind Baxter.

"Sabina." Baxter now glanced across to her with that searching, concerned gaze she'd come to relish. "You be sure to have supper and the dishes done well before dark every evening."

"We will," she reassured him as she had not an hour ago.

"And then you and Delia ride Thunder straight over to the Reardons'. No dallying."

"Sir, you can trust me with your daughter. I won't allow no one to waylay us."

"Specially not them Dagget boys," Delia piped. Standing between Philip and Howie, she made an unflattering face.

"And Philip," Baxter continued with his last-minute instructions, "no one is to come calling here during the day either. Only of an evening at the Reardons'."

"I'm sorry to be such a burden," Sabina said, offering whatever apology she could. It had been obvious during the past week that Baxter wasn't pleased with any of the four young men who'd come calling. "I'll do my best to keep everything right and proper."

"The fault doesn't lie with you, Sabina. Let's just hope that someone comes along who is worthy of you. Well," he said, his gaze abandoning her for his children. "Take care. I shouldn't be gone more than a week. Giddyap."

The big gray horse lunged into a fast walk.

Sammy grabbed onto his father more tightly, then swiveled around and waved. "I'll do my best."

Sabina blew him a kiss, missing him and his father already. Too distressed to continue watching Baxter as he set out on his mission to woo the Widow Atwood, she ran back into the house. There were beds to make this morning, furniture to polish— anything to occupy her mind, to keep her from thinking.

She ran for the stairs and up to the first bedroom. Baxter's. The bed where he'd slept stared back at her, the commode where he washed his face and combed his hair. No. She wasn't ready to tidy his private quarters yet. She'd do the boys' rooms first.

As she swung around, a flash of shiny bronze material caught her eye. His satin frock coat. He'd left his dress clothes behind.

Snatching it off a hanger, she raced downstairs and out of the house.

Baxter had already disappeared into the woods.

She shoved the garment at Philip. "Quick! Run after them. Your father forgot his fancy coat."

"Calm down," he said. "Papa didn't forget it. He's picking up his new suit of clothes when he gets to town."

"That's right." What was the matter with her? She knew that. Regaining her breath, she took the satin garment back from Philip, smoothing it with her hand. "But I can't imagine him looking any finer than he does in this. The way it fits across his shoulders and down his back. And the shiny bronze with its creamy silk braid trim sets off his coloring just right and his eyes."

"I know," Delia agreed. "He does cut a mighty fine figure in it. But clothes fashions have changed back East, and, well . . ." She shrugged, then suddenly smiled. "He's buyin' one of them silly tall silk hats, too. Maybe when the widow sees him in it, she won't think he's such a Virginia dandy."

"It really don't matter what he wears." Grinning, Howie

brushed back a hank of dark hair. "Sammy will see to it that she don't never want to be a part of this family."

Sammy's last words came back to Sabina with new meaning. *I'll do my best.* She eyed the two lads. "What do you boys have up your sleeve?"

"Not a thing." Exchanging a merry glance with Philip, Howie threw up his hands in mock innocence.

"Just havin' Sammy underfoot," Philip added, "would send most anyone on the run."

"You haven't seen *me* trying to escape!" Sabina retorted.

"Well, you're not most anyone." Philip wasn't letting her have the last word. "Sammy will do anything for you. He'd jump through fire if you asked."

"And so would the rest of us," Delia said, stepping between the boys. "Don't you know, we want you to keep on stayin' here, not her."

Oh, dear. This was not good at all. "Kids, I love having you say that, but you scarcely met Mistress Atwood. If your father chose her over everyone else he met at the camp meeting, she's bound to be real nice. And she's an educated lady, someone that wouldn't never bring shame to your family."

"Shame?" Philip frowned, looking older and wiser than his nearly seventeen years.

Sabina cringed at her slip of tongue. She prayed he wouldn't guess that a dire secret lurked within her.

"The only *shame* the widow will feel," Philip continued, "is the shame of bein' kin to Sammy when he shows her what a brat he can be."

Sabina gasped. "You boys did cook something up, didn't you?"

Their grins said it all.

And, Lord help her, she was glad. She'd have sore knees tonight, for sure, praying her way out of this.

Chapter Thirteen

Oh, *fiddlesticks!*" From the disgust in Delia's voice, Sabina knew something was amiss as they rode onto the Reardon place at dusk. "There's that Grady Jessup, waitin' for us like some ol' ox at feedin' time."

Sabina stifled her own groan. This courting business was not all that she and her mother had envisioned. This afternoon had been one of those sweaty late-summer days when the air clung hot and heavy, and it had scarcely cooled since the sun had set. She didn't feel the least attractive. And after riding sideways and bareback behind Delia for more than a mile, her brown homespun surely reeked of horse. Mosquitoes, too, were biting. She slapped at one buzzing around her neck.

Delia, sitting astride, turned back to Sabina and spoke for her ears only. "Grady may be a handsome devil, but for all the struttin' and braggin' he does away from his ma, she rules the roost at home. Anyone who marries him, marries her."

Neither Delia nor her brothers had spoken a kind word about any of the fellows who'd come calling this past week. The twins didn't have a lick of sense between them, and John Auburn, the quiet one who'd helped build her chimney, was as sneaky as he was quiet. Perhaps the kids were right. He'd certainly sneaked his share of peeks whenever he thought she wasn't looking. On the other hand, at least he seemed sensible. And he was his own man—not like that Grady Jessup, apparently.

Speaking of which . . . Delia was putting in another twopence worth about the curly-headed blond with the big sparkling smile, who at this very second leapt off Annie's porch to intercept them with the entire Reardon clan watching.

"Here," Grady called, still a dozen yards away, "let me help y'all down."

The adult Reardons called out greetings from the recesses of the porch as did the young'uns who sat under one of the sycamores playing a hand game.

Gracie and Hope hopped up from a spread quilt and also came running.

Delia slid off the tall horse, not waiting for Grady to reach them. "I've got a whole lot to tell you girls. Where can we go private?"

The three skipped off toward Hope's house, giggling and jabbering like magpies. But Sabina didn't have time to concern herself with any secrets Delia might tell. Grady Jessup was flashing that toothy grin of his up at her. She slid down into his outstretched arms.

"Allow me to fetch your tote and escort you up on the porch," he said, twining a powerful arm through hers, taking her over as if they were dear old friends.

Sabina disentangled herself. "I have to put the horse up first."

"You don't need to bother. Jacob!" Grady called. "Come tend Miss Erhardt's horse."

The tall skinny lad leapt up from the grass and came trotting over.

As he did, the older Louvenia Reardon and her daughter-in-law Annie left the porch and strolled toward Sabina.

Mistress Reardon, herself flushed from the heat, carried a clear, sweating glass of lemonade. "We're so pleased you and Delia will be takin' your rest with us this week." She handed Sabina the drink. "Thought you might be thirsty. It sure is muggy this evenin'."

"That it is," Annie agreed, her back braid haphazardly pinned off her neck as she fanned herself with a multifolded broadside. "Ain't no breeze a'tall. Come on up on the porch. We set out a chair for you."

"Bless you," Sabina sighed, taking several swallows of the tart liquid. "It's a pure kindness."

"I've a plump feather bed waitin' for you in my cabin," the rangy older woman said. "No young'uns to pester you there. Just the two of us. We can get better acquainted."

Despite the friendly smile accompanying Mistress Reardon's last statement, Sabina's stomach knotted with anxiety. The matron would no doubt be prying at her for more information. Early to bed this evening and rising even earlier might be her only escape.

"What a supreme pleasure it was," Grady said, his hand now clutching her elbow as he led her up the steps to join the adult Reardons, "when I learned you'd be ridin' in any minute. Here, take this seat."

Sabina was not the least surprised to see the big-boned fellow drop onto the pillow-cushioned chair next to hers.

"I just been tellin' Ike and Noah, here, about my plan," he

said, staring straight at her but loud enough to include the others. "Me and the Reardons is thinkin' on goin' into business together. Could be a bushel'a money in it."

Sabina recognized his telling of his financial prospects as an opening foray, the dangling of the proverbial carrot on a string. "I'm pleased for all of you," she responded politely.

Grady kicked back, crossing his feet comfortably. "Yessir, my pa give me a quarter section of my own when I turned twenty last year. In my spare time, I been clearin' some acreage, an' I been savin' the best logs for my own house."

Sabina reckoned that was his way of letting her know he wouldn't be bringing his wife into his mother's home. Delia's main argument had just lost its teeth.

"Anyways," he said, twirling his thumbs, "I made a real discovery when I was clearin' brush where my land starts climbin' up the hills. All of a sudden, I seen these bats come flyin' up like this great black cloud out of the bushes. And lo and behold, I spread the branches and there it was. A cave. One that goes *way in*."

"That's nice." She kept her expression pleasant while praying he didn't ask her in front of all these people to come explore it with him. That was the kind of ploy one of her stepfather's cronies might've used in hopes of getting her alone.

Abruptly, Grady sat forward, his frown reminding her of his mother's. "It's more'n just nice. The cave's a good six inches deep in bat guano." He must have read her confusion—he leaned even closer. "Half the mixin's for gunpowder is bat guano. And you know how expensive gunpowder is."

"Oh, I see," she said, trying to appear more interested as she noticed the sky had turned to pitch. The only light now came from a lantern hanging in the nearest sycamore with moths already circling it.

"I got the recipe from one of Noah's books. Ain't that right?"

he continued, not waiting for a response. "Charcoal's easy enough to come up with, but I ain't got the money to buy the sulfur I'd need, so the Reardons has agreed to go in with me."

"Don't see how we can lose," Ike said from a dark corner.

"Then," Sabina said politely, "I'll pray you all have a pleasant and profitable partnership."

Grady burst out laughing as if she'd just told a joke. "Miss Sabina, don't you see? We'll make a fortune. There ain't no one else in Tennessee makin' black powder."

"My. I'm mighty pleased for you then. All of you." She lifted her glass and took a sip, hoping Grady's fervent gaze would move elsewhere.

It didn't.

Sabina knew she should be flattered that a handsome bachelor with such a promising future was interested in her, knew she should seriously encourage his courtship. He was the very sort her mother had wanted for her—a good-natured church attender with fertile land and prospects. But instead, her heart ached for another, a displaced aristocrat who found her sorely lacking. Why did she always want what she couldn't have?

"Sabina, dear, would you care for some more lemonade?" Mistress Reardon asked.

"No, thank you." Sabina rose to her feet. "But if you don't mind, this heat has really wore me down. If you could show me where I'm to sleep, I'd be most grateful."

Grady Jessup's stoked expression was doused as he, too, stood up.

Taking pity on him, Sabina put on a smile and extended a hand. "Truly, I am pleased that you allowed me to share in your marvelous news. Perhaps at church Sunday you can tell me more about your new venture."

His blue eyes brightened somewhat. He took her hand and

pressed his lips to the back. "Until Sunday, then. Will you do me the honor of sitting with me during the services?"

Oh dear, she'd given him an opening. "I'm afraid I'll be coming with three youngsters. But I'm sure they'd be pleased to have you share our pew with us." Deftly she reclaimed her hand. "Till the Sabbath."

~

Sunlight shining directly in Sabina's eyes awakened her the next morning. It was well past dawn. She tossed off a thin cotton sheet and sprang off the bed before she realized she stood beneath the pitched roof of Louvenia Reardon's loft bedroom.

Not only had she slept past her prayer time, but breakfast was not on the table in the Clay kitchen—a kitchen that was more than a mile away. Philip and Howie must be worried.

Taking care of her morning needs as fast as possible, she rushed across the shared yard toward Jessica's house to fetch Delia.

The menfolk were already in the midst of their early chores. Jacob, Ike and Annie's oldest son, was pitching hay into the paddocks, and his father already had Thunder out of the barn, slipping a bridle over the big gray's ears.

Surely they must all think her woefully lazy.

If only she'd been able to sleep better last night. But with the heat in the loft, the stir of her thoughts, and her seeking prayers, questions continued to plague her. How could she refuse to consider marriage to any of the four who'd come calling? Surely the Lord had brought her to this valley for a purpose. Perhaps one of them was God's choice for her. Yet she stubbornly refused to look past Baxter to see God's choice.

Then there was the matter of her illegitimacy . . .

Starting up the porch steps, she stopped and closed her eyes.

The cares of the day, that's all she should be dealing with today. Leave tomorrow's worries where they belong.

Sabina walked through the open door into a house filled with the smells of bacon and coffee. The furnishings in the long room were understated but obviously professionally crafted. An ornately framed picture, though, dominated all else—a very large portrait of Jessica when she was several years younger.

Turning to the kitchen end, Sabina saw Delia at a long table that also had simple lines but was made of fine, highly polished wood. The girl was munching on a biscuit while talking in a fast, excited voice to Gracie and Hope. "I know we can do it, if we all—" The second she discovered Sabina, she clamped her mouth around another bite.

The three Reardon women were also in the kitchen to witness Sabina's tardiness. Louvenia was bent over the hearth apron, stirring a kettle of porridge, while, beside her, Jessica turned over sizzling bacon. At a worktable, Annie cracked eggs into a bowl.

The older woman straightened from her chore and caught sight of Sabina. "La, I'm glad you found us. When it's hot we get together and cook breakfast at Jessica's and dinner at Annie's."

"Aye," Annie said, turning toward Sabina with a friendly smile. "After a day like yesterday, I'm determined to get us a summer cookhouse built. If them men won't do it, I'll do it myself."

"And she could." Chuckling, Jessica raised up and mopped her brow with her apron. Standing between the other two, she looked like a half-grown girl. "And good morning, Sabina. I do hope you slept well."

"Much too good." Sabina eyed Delia. "Why didn't you come over and wake me? Philip and Howie will be wondering where we are."

"Oh, I figured you could use the rest. You been workin' so hard since you come to stay with us. Besides, it ain't that late. The younger kids is all still asleep." Her brown eyes suddenly sparked with excitement. She swung to Hope and Gracie's grandmother. "Show Sabina the clothes you're givin' her."

"What?" Sabina jerked her head toward the long-boned older woman. "I can't—"

"Now, dear," Mistress Reardon crooned appeasingly. "They're just some old day gowns I've outgrown in my dotage. But there's plenty of serviceable fabric and lace to make over into a couple of nice outfits for you." She lay her big wooden spoon across a saucer and strode over to Sabina. "You're a handsbreadth taller than Jessica, but not much bigger around. I reckon if we all get to it in our spare time, we could have the first one ready for church tomorrow."

"I'm sure we can." Jessica stepped closer, her transparent eyes catching the colors of the others' enthusiasm. "Delia also mentioned that you desire to learn to read. Between the older kids and me, we'll have you poring over all the books in our library before you know it." She pointed her cooking fork toward the front corner of the parlor end.

Sabina gasped. Two wide sets of shelves rose up above even Mistress Reardon's head, and they were lined with books. There had to be a hundred or more!

"Books," Jessica said with a whimsical smile, "have always been a passion of Noah's and mine. They bring the whole world right here to us."

Sabina closed her mouth and swallowed down her emotion. "I can't believe your generosity. All of you. And Mr. Clay, he promised to make me a pair of shoes."

"They're made," Delia informed Sabina, clapping hands to her cheeks. "I thought I told you. That was the last thing Papa finished before he went to saddle up. They're plain, though. He didn't have time to put on no buckles or nothin'. But he said you wasn't to go one more Sunday without a pair to wear to church."

"He said that?" Sabina's heart melted to mush. Baxter's last thoughts before he left had been of her.

Chapter Fourteen

Now that we're away from my nosy brothers," Delia said, "Tell me why we're riding to the settlement. What you said didn't make much sense."

Sabina sat behind the girl as she had this morning. "I said I needed to see about something at the minister's house. Our chores are done. We can spare an hour or two."

"It must be *real important*," Delia probed further. "Since we'll be coming in again tomorrow."

"Well, at least there's a breeze today." Sidestepping Delia's questions, Sabina glanced past the overhanging branches to the clouds blowing in. Perhaps a cooling rain was on the way.

Delia must have understood Sabina's reluctance to discuss the matter. She spent the remainder of the dusty ride into the settlement talking about another of Mistress Reardon's daughters-in-law—one who had gone west into Indian country with her husband to take the Lord's message to the heathens. It would seem that Crystabelle Reardon had come from a Virginia family as wealthy as the Clays and had attended some exclusive finishing school.

"She was another fancy one such as Missus Atwood. Papa even wanted to marry her once, years ago, before she married Drew Reardon. She was our teacher till last year when she and Drew went west and that awful Mr. Elbridge came to take her place. She even baked us treats. She was real purty too, like you. Now if *she* was here to help us," Delia said at one point, "there'd be nothin' to worry about. But we'll manage."

"Manage what?"

The girl shrugged. "Oh, you know. So none of us look like ignorant woodsies if that uppity Missus Atwood comes to visit."

"Delia, dear," Sabina reminded her yet another time, "your papa hisself said he felt that Mistress Atwood was God's choice for him. And if that's true, you have nothing to fret about." She wrapped both arms around the misguided girl's waist and gave her a hug. "Your heavenly Father loves you even more than your papa does, if you can imagine that."

"But what about you? I don't want you to leave us." Delia's voice conveyed as much emotion as her words. "All them fellas buttin' in, comin' around . . ."

"Take joy from this day, sweet girl. God is watching out for tomorrow."

After leaving Delia at the storekeeper's home behind the general store, Sabina went over their conversation in her mind and concluded that she herself had found it impossible to find the day's joy she'd spoken of. She felt like one of those hypocrites in the Bible as she headed for the Bremmers', praying Inga was at home and alone.

The round cheeks of the thickly built German woman were flushed, and flour dusted her hair, hands, and her stained apron.

Nonetheless, she wore a surprised smile. "Goot afternoon. Is goot to see you. Come in."

"Thank you. Isn't it a mite late to be baking on such a hot September day?"

"Oh, da flour." She rolled her blue eyes good-naturedly. "I vas chasing a mouse, and da flour sack I knock over."

Sabina grinned. "Well, did you catch the little varmint?"

"*Nein.* He get avay again. But one of dese days . . . you go sit in da parlor. Dis mess I clean up; den I fetch us a cool drink."

"Let's both clean it up. That way we'll have more time to visit."

The Bremmer kitchen, a separate room at the back of the house, had half its floor covered with what must have been most of a full sack of the powdered wheat, and a film of white dust coated the furniture and shelved goods.

"Da sack, you hold open," Inga instructed, "and in I scoop da clean flour."

"No," Sabina said, "I'll do the stooping and scooping. I have younger legs."

"You are goot girl." Inga Bremmer patted Sabina's shoulder, then pulled up the fallen bag and spread wide the mouth, while Sabina plucked a gourd scoop from a nearby worktable. "Now," Inga said once they'd commenced work, "vhy it is you come to see me today? Vat is so important it cannot vait till tomorrow?" The woman wasn't fooled by Sabina's sudden appearance.

"You said I could come to you if I had a problem." Sabina dumped a gourdful of flour back into the sack.

"*Ja, ja.*"

"I need advice from someone much wiser than me. I'm hoping you can tell me what to do. I pray, but I still ain't sure what's right."

"I do vat I can. Mine Rolf, maybe you should talk to him instead?"

"No, it'll be hard enough telling you."

Inga reached out and took the scoop from Sabina. "Dis can vait. Come, sit at da table. Some cool spring water I pour you."

Taking a seat at the big table, Sabina tried to think of the best way to start while Inga brought their drinks, but when the older lady sat down across from her, the words "I'm illegitimate" burst unintentionally from Sabina's mouth. A second later, after getting over her own shock, she continued. "My father was killed before he and Mama could marry."

Inga hadn't moved. She stared at Sabina, speechless.

Sabina stared back, wishing she could retrieve the words.

Finally, Inga reached across the red-checked tablecloth and took Sabina's hand. "I am grieved for your loss."

Inga's response caught her off guard. It was completely unexpected. Still, Sabina relaxed a bit. "My mother ran away from home before her family learned about me. She didn't want to burden them with her shame. For a long time she was also too ashamed to pray. Life was very hard for her. When my stepfather was willing to marry her and raise me, she was so grateful to him, she pushed aside the fact that he wasn't a Christian."

"Me and Rolf, every night ve are praying for dem two since Baxter tells us about you."

Sabina's eyes pooled, and she put her free hand over Inga's work-reddened one. "I thank you. It's always just been me and Mama praying for Kurt. We've always trusted that when two or more are gathered in Jesus' name to pray for something, that he's there. And now there's four of us."

"It is goot you are still praying for da stepfadder, even after vat he done, gambling you off like dat."

Sabina smiled sadly. "Oh, he's more to be pitied. Kurt's done the best he could by me and Mama, considering he's got the gambling fever so bad. He's never stopped loving Mama."

"If she's anything like you, I can see why."

Nonplussed by the praise, Sabina glanced away, a bit embarrassed.

Inga patted her hand. "I am glad you come and share dis. Now ve get back to da mess."

"There's more."

"*Ja?*" Inga settled in her seat again.

"Four of your valley's young men have come calling this week. They don't know nothing about who I really am." She lowered her voice. "That my real pa died before he could marry my mama."

Inga studied Sabina for several seconds. "All of us, ve come to dis valley because ve is looking for a better life dan vere ve are coming from. Behind us is da past. Vat you do here *und* now is vat counts."

"But here, now, I feel like I ain't being honest if I don't tell them I was born outside of wedlock. That I am a child of sin."

"Dis sin dat vorries you so much, you did not commit it. It is not your shame."

"But—"

Inga held up a hand. "*Ja*, I know some folks like to make demselves feel better by acting all high and mighty about such t'ings. But ve all make da sins. Nobody is *mit*out sin. *Und* sometimes ve do nut'ing wrong, and ve is branded *mit* da ugly names. Me and Rolf, for seven years ve is bond slaves. Dat is how ve pay for da passage to America. But many in Carolina shunt us like ve is no-goot paupers. But in dis place ve get da new start."

"Are you saying I shouldn't tell folks about myself? What if I wanted to accept an offer of marriage?"

"If da Spirit in you say you must, den tell him. If da man goes avay, he is not da Lord's man for you. And as for da rest of da peoples? You don't see me valking around saying I vas da bond slave. And dis man, whoever he is, he is not coming up to you and telling you all da bad t'ings about his family, is he? You know, you is not de only one *mit* t'ings dey is not vanting to share."

"But—"

Inga put a finger over Sabina's mouth. *"Nein.* Be at peace, mine *kinder."*

The pain that had lain in the dark shadows of Sabina's soul fled in the light of this good woman's words. "Thank you. You purely are God's blessing to me." She touched the woman's flushed face. "God's very own blessing."

Sabina's words caused Inga's cheeks to glow all the brighter. "Goot," the older woman said, rising swiftly to her feet. "Now, you be my blessing and help me get dis flour up."

~

"Sammy, stop pulling at your collar." The boy simply would not leave his new ready-made shirt alone.

"But, Papa, it's sawin' on my neck. For pity's sake, what's it gonna look like if it cuts my head off? Then it'll go rollin' across that widow's floor."

On this unseasonably warm September day, Baxter quickly turned his face away from his son's view. It wouldn't do for the imp to see his unstoppable grin. He pretended to look at some-thing in a shopwindow as they walked up cobblestoned Broad Street, heading for the home where he'd been told Amanda Atwood lived with her father and spinster aunt Charlotte.

After managing to resettle his features, Baxter couldn't resist getting in the last word. "I expect you to act like a gentleman in Storekeeper Finch's home. In particular, whenever a gentleman is visiting, he simply does not allow his head to go rolling."

Sammy's mouth fell open. A second later, he burst out laughing.

Baxter joined him, and the tension he'd been feeling since arriving in the river port yesterday eased. He'd taken care of his other business, shipping several pairs of shoes downriver, then delivered the ones he'd promised to the tailor in exchange for the new suit of clothes he now wore—a coat, vest, and pants of tightly woven wool that fit splendidly, if he did say so himself. The color was complementary, too—a brown somewhere between the hue of his eyes and hair, and a gold-and-tan cravat that added just the right splash.

Plus, of course, the top hat. Walking along the boardwalk past the news office, he glanced in another window for a quick look at its stylish tilt on his head.

Sammy was lagging. Since the moment they'd left Reardon Valley, he'd been trying to convince Baxter not to visit Mistress Atwood.

"Walk a little faster. We need to get out of the sun before we start to perspire."

"You're not even sure they'll be at home," the reluctant boy said.

"They'll be there. When I left the note with Mr. Finch yesterday, saying we wished to call this afternoon, I included the name of the inn where we were staying, in case they needed to send their regrets. And, as you know, none came."

"All this writin' notes, when you was talking right to her pa, sounds mighty queersome to me."

"It's simply the proper way of doing things in polite society."

Following the directions the storekeeper had given Baxter yesterday, they had walked the three city blocks up from his dry-goods store and, crossing the fourth street, they came upon a sweep of lawn made cooler by several shade trees. Set deeply on the lot, a large brick house rose up, trimmed in white with black shutters and a bright red door. A circle drive of crushed brick led them to a stone walk framed by a rose arbor. From there, they got a full view of the front porch, its roof held up by four gleaming white pillars.

"She lives *here?*" Sammy said, his mouth agape again.

"Aye." Baxter allowed himself a slight smile. Impressive as this house might be to the boy, the Clay mansion back home was at least three times its size. His children had no idea of the wealth and the comforts readily available along the Atlantic seaboard.

Sammy caught Baxter's hand as they walked up to gray-painted steps. "You know, Papa, that's the kind of thing Sabina would've said."

"What?"

"About me not lettin' my head go rollin'. You're startin' to sound just like her."

His son was right. Mirth and laughter had abounded since Sabina came into their home, her smile as bright and sunny as her hair. But that was not what he should be thinking about, especially at the door of the woman he hoped to marry.

His tension returned. "Samuel, you are not to speak about Sabina while we're here visiting. I'll say whatever needs to be said about her when the time is right." He straightened the boy's new wide-brimmed hat. "In fact, try not to talk any more than you have to. If they ask you a question, make your answer brief. *And watch your grammar.*"

An older black servant in a crisp white apron and cap answered Baxter's knock. Eyeing him and Sammy with a judging tilt of her head, the slave invited them into a foyer—the first Baxter had stood in since he left Virginia. In the last few years when he'd come here for supplies, he'd noticed some of these larger brick homes being built but hadn't actually ventured this far up from the river until today.

"I goes to git da ladies now. Y'all wait in da parlor." The servant motioned to their left, lowered her gaze, and turned away toward the stairs at the far end of the central hall.

Removing his tall hat, Baxter began to relax again, assured that the family did indeed anticipate their visit. Taking Sammy's hand, he strode across a gem-colored Oriental rug spread over the high shine of hardwood flooring.

"Look, Papa!" Stopping, Sammy gawked up at an actual crystal chandelier suspended from a pearl gray paneled ceiling.

"Your mouth's agape."

Through an archway, they entered a room painted the same light gray—one quite pleasant to the eye, with upholstered pieces of furniture in quiet shades of green. Baxter's gaze was quickly drawn to a large tapestry depicting a hunting scene. It hung over the mantel of a carved wood fireplace. On the floor in front lay another Oriental rug, this one in hues that complemented the tapestry.

"The walls are so smooth," Sammy whispered. "If I had a piece of charcoal, I could draw pictures all over them."

"Don't even think it. Take your hat off and sit over there." He pointed to a Queen Anne chair of warm maple wood. "Keep your hands folded in your lap and both feet on the floor."

"I wasn't gonna do it." Sammy slid a finger under the edge of his collar again. "What do I do with my hat?"

"Just hold on to it till someone offers to take it." He chose a similar seat across from his son. "And I do apologize. Of course you weren't going to do anything destructive."

Sammy shot him a strange glance.

Tall hat sitting on his own lap, Baxter smiled to reassure the boy. "Back East, inside walls are usually painted and smooth.

Sawmills for making boards are plentiful there. Until we came overmountain, I never lived in a house of rough wood and mortar."

"Mister Clay," came a velvety smooth voice from the doorway. There stood Amanda Atwood, wearing a lace-fronted day gown of sheer lawn in a pale green that blended as beautifully with the other colors of the room as did her golden brown hair. Her tresses were swept up in soft swirls above a round, pleasantly supple face.

A smart hostess always decorates to complement her own personal assets, Baxter remembered as he came to his feet, motioning Sammy to do the same. "Mistress Atwood."

"We're so pleased to have you in our humble home." A smile accompanied her words.

"Not as pleased as I am to be here," he said, walking toward her.

Behind Amanda stood her father's sister, of similar medium height and coloring. Her hair, though, was threaded with silver, and her frame a bit thicker. Her lips were slightly drawn down at the corners, as if she were about to see something she might not like.

Amanda stepped aside. "Aunt Charlotte, you remember Mr. Clay, the gentleman we met at Cane Ridge."

The aunt, wearing a darker shade of green, extended a hand sheathed in the thinnest silk. "Charmed to see you again, I'm sure. I do hope you had a pleasant journey." She added a smile that fell short of her hazel eyes as she moved farther into the room. "You and the boy do have a seat. Netty will be in shortly with some cool refreshments."

"Thank you." Baxter remained standing. Decorum dictated he not sit until the ladies did. "Something cool sounds delightful."

Especially in this hot coat, he would have added if he were visiting one of his valley friends.

"Aunt Charlotte," Mistress Atwood said, nodding toward Sammy clutching his new tan hat with both hands. "I don't think you've met Mr. Clay's youngest child. I'd like to introduce you to his cute little Samuel."

"I ain't little," Sammy blustered, his nose wrinkling disdainfully. "I'm ten years old, goin' on eleven."

"Samuel," Baxter reprimanded firmly but quietly, trying to convey his displeasure without disturbing the ladies. "An apology is in order."

"Oh, I forgot. Sorry, Papa, for sayin' *ain't.*"

The boy's wide-eyed expression wasn't all that innocent. Baxter was certain that Sammy was playing with him, assuming he wouldn't make a scene in front of the ladies. "Son, you owe Mistress Atwood, not me, an apology, for speaking so rudely to her."

"It wasn't me!" Belligerence took the place of innocence. "She's the one that done the name-callin'."

What had gotten into his son? Sammy's manners were deplorable. He knew the boy didn't want to come here, but this was outrageous. "Turn around this instant and walk out the door. Don't stop until you reach the inn. We'll discuss this later."

"But what did I do?" His eyes now became big brown saucers reflecting genuine fear. He knew he was in deep trouble.

"You know very well what you did. Go."

Sammy's expression turned sullen as he slapped his hat onto his head and started out. He hadn't expected to be tossed out while his father remained.

Just as Sammy reached the archway, the servant passed him, carrying a silver tray with sweet treats artfully placed on it.

The boy stopped, his gaze following the tasty-looking morsels.

"Go, Sammy."

Not until Baxter heard the front door close behind his son did he turn to the ladies with what must have been a rather lame smile. "I do apologize for his unacceptable behavior. I'm afraid he doesn't approve of our coming to see you."

"Oh?" One of the spinster aunt's brows arched.

Baxter's collar began to scratch again. This visit was not going at all well.

"Please," Amanda said softly with a polite smile, "shall we take our seats?"

The two ladies settled themselves on the sofa in front of the tea table where the servant had placed the tray, and Baxter took the seat he'd vacated moments before. The graying servant, undoubtedly as curious as Amanda's aunt, had yet to leave the room.

"Netty," Miss Finch said, shooing the slave with her hand, "bring the drinks."

Taking a calming breath while the servant walked out, Baxter propped up a hopefully convincing smile before attempting an explanation. "Miss Finch," he began, looking directly at the aunt, "Sammy is afraid that your niece and I will come to enjoy each other's company to the point that the two of you might come to Reardon Valley for a visit."

Miss Finch drew herself up. "And why should that offend the child?"

Baxter glanced at Amanda, who had lost her smile. "I had hoped to speak of more pleasant things today. But . . . we now have a new servant girl. I hired her at Cane Ridge the morning we left. And, it would appear that Sammy has become very fond of her. He fears that if you were to come, say, on a permanent basis, that I would dismiss the girl."

"I see." Mistress Atwood, sitting straight as a board on the

138

couch, looked as if she'd turned to marble. "Do tell me more about her."

The servant must have raced to and from the kitchen, because she was already back with a tray of drinks.

Miss Finch shot her an irritated glance. "Serve the limeade, Netty, then be about your business."

As soon as Baxter had a chilled glass in his hand, the older matron picked up the snack tray. "Do have some, Mr. Clay."

"Perhaps later," he said. Food was the last thing on his mind. He took a draught of the drink, feeling its coolness travel down his throat.

By this time, the young widow had regained her composure. She gazed warmly at him, her smile and demeanor the exact duplicate of the conciliatory belles to whom his uncle had introduced him years ago. "Please be at ease, Mr. Clay. My older brother has sons Samuel's age, and they, too, have more energy than they know how to handle. Isn't it a blessing to know they will all grow wiser with age?"

"Yes, it is." Vastly relieved that she understood youngsters, Baxter settled more comfortably in his own chair. He'd been right about her. This young woman truly would bring to his children all the grace and civility they'd missed.

Chapter Fifteen

"The—fat—cat—ran . . . fast." Sabina sounded out, faltering through the words in the primer Jessica Reardon had given her, yet grateful that the three older Clay kids were taking turns teaching her.

"Excellent," Philip said as they sat side by side on the porch after supper.

She peered up from the page, pleased by his praise, and squeezed his arm. "I was able to sound out the words faster this time. If y'all have enough patience with me, I'm going to learn to read."

With his patrician features maturing, Philip looked more like his father every day, especially when he nodded his agreement. "Sure you will. In no time, you won't even have to sound out the little words. You'll just see 'em and know 'em."

Sabina glanced to the west. The sun had already set behind the distant hills. Not only had she missed her time to commune with her mother, she and Delia should've already left for the Reardons'. There just never seemed to be enough time these days. Closing the book, she stood up and hollered through an open window. "Delia! Are you finished with the dishes yet? We need to go."

"Aye," she called back. "Just gotta throw out the dishwater and get my night things. I left 'em upstairs with the rest of the wash."

Sabina's own tote lay slumped on the porch step, and Thunder waited beneath the nearest tree, munching grass.

"Any of them knotholes comin' to visit you at the Reardons' tonight?" Philip asked with that same disdain all the Clays voiced any time they spoke of the fellows who'd been dropping by.

"None that I know of." She picked up her bundle and strolled down the steps to fetch the horse. Without a saddle and stirrups, Thunder needed to be walked over to the porch for an easy mount.

Four beaus just for her . . . Sabina had eventually discovered the main reason for her instant popularity. Only one other unpromised miss of marriageable age lived in the valley—John Auburn's sister. The quiet, patient man's sister had been sickly most of her life. No wonder she was still unwed, Sabina thought. A farmer in this part of the country needed an able-bodied wife—the very thing Baxter had touted about Sabina that first Sunday.

Sunday.

She would be able to wear her new shoes and day gown again, and another dress would soon be finished.

But were the new clothes, in actuality, accomplices helping her to keep all four suitors under false pretenses? Despite what Inga Bremmer had said about this being a fresh beginning for her, she could not escape the fact that she was a woman without a name. With every beau's visit came the nagging worry—would this one ask for details of her past? If for no other reason, a man should want to know the kind of stock his future children's mother came from.

Delia pounded down the stairs and, pigtails flying, shot out the door at an startlingly wild run. "Papa's back! I seen him comin' out the bedroom window."

Across the clearing, Howie emerged from the barn in long fast strides, carrying the evening's milk. Having a clear view of the path, he waved his free arm back and forth above his head in greeting, his straight teeth flashing in a wide grin. Then he turned to Sabina and Philip on the porch. "Only Snowflake is comin'. Good. Pa didn't bring that woman back with him."

That had not been Baxter's plan, as far as Sabina knew. Nonetheless, she felt her own sense of relief, then gave a second thought to the milk pail. "Howie, did you take the time to strip Daisy's udders before you ran out?"

"Sure," he answered impatiently. "I ain't no dumb kid."

"No, you ain't," she apologized. "The thought shouldn't have crossed my mind."

"No," Philip hooted, traipsing down the porch steps. "Howie would much rather go off an' leave the paddock gate open." He nodded toward the barn.

The ginger-and-white cow came lumbering out, her large, curious eyes rolling this way and that.

Howie dropped the pail onto the ground and ran back to intercept the animal.

Sabina clamped the pail to keep the milk from sloshing over the brim, then started for the springhouse before dust settled on the creamy liquid. She'd let the children greet their father without her getting in the way.

By the time she returned, the family was still in a cluster, with everyone talking at once.

Sammy caught sight of her and broke away from the others. "Sabina!" He ran to her as if she were his very own mother. "You're still here." He grabbed hold of her. "I thought one of them pigheaded Daggets might'a run off with you."

She moved out of his grasp and held him by the shoulders. "No, no. I would never go off and leave you without us saying our farewells." Slipping her arm around Sammy, she walked with him back to the others.

Baxter watched her from over Delia's head. Though he didn't smile, she could see in his intense gaze that he, too, was glad to see her.

Sabina's heart skipped a beat.

"How'd everything go here?" he asked as she and Sammy approached. "Any problems?"

"We missed you and prayed for your safe return every time we took our meals. But other than that, I believe we did all the chores the way you wanted."

"The boys didn't give you any trouble?"

"No, they was perfect gentlemen."

"Good, good. I'm pleased to hear that." His gaze changed to a hard stare as he shifted to his youngest.

Sammy had obviously displeased his father . . . no doubt he'd done whatever his older brothers had put him up to.

Sabina switched to a safer topic. "I'd better ride over to the Reardons' and let 'em know Delia and I won't be spending the night there."

"It's getting dark. Howie'd better do that," Baxter said. "But first, I have presents for everyone."

"You do?" Delia's eyes lit up her heart-shaped face, and she grabbed her father's hand. "Show us."

Baxter untied a bulging bag from a saddle ring. Digging through the uncinched top, he withdrew streams of ribbon and lace. "For you and Sabina. The stores in Nashville had a lot more to choose from than Bailey's does here in the valley."

Greedily, Delia snatched up the notions and spread them across her hands.

Baxter then reached in and hauled out a large velvet bag. "For you, Howie."

In the dying sun, the fifteen-year-old's fingers frantically ripped at the drawstring until he tore the cloth from a shiny violin and bow. "*Papa.* Where did you get it? It must have cost a fortune." He tucked the instrument under his chin and ran the taut horsehair over the strings.

Warmed by Howie's overflowing joy, Sabina smiled along with the lad as the out-of-tune instrument screeched.

"Some trapper traded it for supplies," Baxter said with a fatherly smile. "I know how much you've wanted one. And Mistress Atwood's father gave me a good price." He flinched at a particularly bad squawk. "Sounds to me like you could use a few lessons. Mayhap Zed McKnight can tutor you once the crops are harvested."

Sabina spoke up—for her own ears' sake as well as the Clays'. "If you'd like, I could show Howie how to tune the violin and mayhap play a song or two in the meantime."

The lad, with the winningest smile of all the children, turned his flashing charm her way. "You can play it? Then, by George, we can make us some real music right here at home."

"I ain't that good at it. My stepfather taught me some whenever we had one. The violin was usually the first thing to go if money got scarce."

"Hey, Pa, what about me?" Philip stared at the still half-full tote. "Did you run across something I'd like?"

Baxter clapped a hand on the tall lad just shorter than himself. "Sure did." His face close to the opening, Baxter rummaged all the way to the bottom of the tote, then pulled out another cinched bag, this one much smaller than the violin's. "I know how you've been hankering for whittling tools. I found two. Both made of high-quality steel."

Philip didn't display Howie's exuberance, but from the way he handled the sharp-tipped knife and thin pick, Sabina knew he was mighty pleased.

"Now I can add some fine details, make somethin' real pretty to send to Marty Newman."

"La, that reminds me . . ." His father pulled a letter from the pocket of one of his less-worn linen work shirts. "It's from your young miss. I picked it up at—"

Philip snatched it from Baxter's hand and wheeled away toward the house, breaking the wax seal as he went.

When the smitten lad disappeared inside, Sabina shared a knowing smile with Baxter—one of those rare moments she could openly gaze upon the manly lines of his face, his flared brows, the prominent cheekbones, his strong jaw, regal nose. . . .

She allowed the moment to last too long. He was staring back at her, a thousand questions in his eyes.

Quickly she lowered her lashes. "Howie's having so much fun with his violin. Maybe I'll go on over to the Reardons' and let 'em know we ain't staying."

"No!" Baxter shouted over an unearthly screech. "Howie, you have the rest of your life *and ours*, unfortunately, to play that fiddle. Try to get back from the Reardons' before it's pitch-dark."

The lad grumbled something Sabina couldn't quite hear as he placed the violin and bow in her hands. "I won't be long." He leapt up on the porch and launched himself onto the giant workhorse's back. Collecting the reins, he looked back at

Sabina. "If you got a fella waitin' at the Reardons' for you, is it all right if I tell him to go on home, that you ain't got time for no visitin' tonight? Not if you're gonna teach me to play."

For some unaccountable reason, Sabina would have preferred his not mentioning anything about gentlemen callers in Baxter's presence. "If anyone's there, just tell 'em we can visit at church tomorrow." Grateful for Sammy beside her, Sabina turned to the boy. "And what did you get in Nashville?"

His mouth collapsed into a downward pout. "Nothin'. Pa said I couldn't have nothin' 'cause I was rude to the widow woman. But it was her that was rude to me."

"Samuel," Baxter cut in. "Unload the rest of our things, then feed and water Snowflake."

Baxter didn't seem any more interested in talking about the widow than Sabina was about her suitors.

"Delia." Baxter summoned his pigtailed daughter, who'd wandered several feet away and already had several ribbons tied down her braids. "I have something more for you and Sabina."

The girl's winsome chin came up expectantly. "What? What've you got?"

Baxter slid the bulkiest contents from the bottom of the tote. Fabric. Three pieces of folded material—one a cream-colored cotton with flowers in varying shades of pink; below it, a finely woven linen of yellow; and beneath that, pure white cotton.

"The flowers are for you, Delia," Baxter said, handing the yardage to her. "And the yellow is yours, Sabina. When I saw it, it reminded me of you."

The sincerity in his gaze washed over her. He'd thought of her while he was away. Sunny yellow had reminded him of her.

Suddenly he seemed a bit disconcerted. He glanced down at the white fabric still lying over his hands. "This is for ruffles, and there's some lace trim inside the fold." Still not looking at her, he added, "I thought you might want something a bit nicer for Sundays."

"Me and the Reardons already took care of that," Delia said, smoothing her girlish palm over her own material. "We made over one of Grandma Reardon's dresses for Sabina to wear last Sunday. And me and Sabina is workin' on another one."

"Oh, I see." Baxter's expression deflated.

"Was it wrong of me to accept Mistress Reardon's gifts?" Sabina asked.

"No. It's just—before I left, I should have seen myself that you were properly clothed."

"You took care of the hard part," she assured him. "The shoes you made for me fit just fine. They don't pinch a'tall." She put a hand on his arm. "I've been mightily blessed since I come here. You are kindness itself."

"That ain't all that's been goin' on since you left," Delia said, interrupting another silent exchange between them. "We're teachin' Sabina to read. And she's catchin' on real fast, ain'tcha?"

"*Aren't* you?" Baxter corrected his daughter.

Sabina was reminded of how often she herself said *ain't*—a word that for some unknown reason he never wanted his children to use.

Baxter then returned his attention to Sabina. "I'm so pleased for you. But again, it's another thing I should've thought to do myself. You wouldn't have to store so many Bible verses in your head if you could read."

Along with his apology, his eyes were again engulfing her. Nonplussed, she took the two remaining pieces of fabric from him, then laid them on top of Delia's. "Darling, would you take these over to our cabin whilst I round up something for your papa and Sammy to eat?"

The girl skipped happily away, ribbons streaming, leaving only Sabina and Baxter.

"I made butter pie," she said and started for the house.

He stayed by her side, matching his stride to hers, causing her to wonder again about him and to renew the hope that his meeting with the widow had been a failure. It must have been, particularly since Sammy's punishment was so severe. She knew she shouldn't have any expectations, but she couldn't help herself. Still, she probed as they walked up the porch steps. "I trust all your business went well."

"Aye, that it did. And you'll be pleased to hear I sent your letter with a keelboat going downriver the very day I arrived. It should reach Cincinnati in a week or so."

"That is good news. Thank you."

"Yes," he said as they started into the more brightly lit common room, "there are boats coming and going from there every day now. Nashville is becoming quite the metropolis. I'm sure if I moved there, my shoe business would flourish, too. In fact, it might get so busy, I'd have to hire helpers."

Move to Nashville? Halfway to the hearth, Sabina slowed to a halt and stared up at him.

He stopped too, his gaze gravitating to the nearest window. He peered out at the fading light. "But I would hate to leave my place here. I know it's not much by some standards, but I cut everything I have out of the wilderness with my own hands. Made a home for my family. I did work I never knew I was capable of until I came here." He looked down at his palms and grinned. "And I have the calluses to prove it."

"You done a fine job," she added, preferring the new direction the conversation had taken. "And I'm sure the Lord is pleased, indeed, with the way you've took care of your young'uns."

"Thank you." He gifted her with a tender smile, then continued. "Besides, the Reardons and the Bremmers have been the best friends and neighbors a man could ask for. Especially after Sally died. I would miss these people intolerably if I moved." The man sounded like he was having an argument with himself.

Her uneasy feeling resurfaced. Mayhap she'd been wrong about his visit with the widow? Evidently it had gone very well, and now he was contemplating a move to Nashville. "I'm sure you would miss your neighbors a lot," was all she could manage.

Chapter Sixteen

Devastated by the mere thought of Baxter moving to Nash-ville, Sabina had hoped he would take care of some chores while she put a quick meal together for him and Sammy. But he dropped the almost empty tote with a clunk and walked to the smaller worktable, scooping up a gourdful of water from the bucket.

"Whew, it's hot in here this evening," he observed, taking a swallow from the half gourd. "If you've got victuals left over from earlier, don't bother to stoke up the fire. We can just eat them cold."

The man was as considerate as ever. "I've got fried German sausage. How about some of Annie's cheese to go with it and a plate of fresh vegetables? The garden's still putting out real good."

He pulled a chair out from the cherrywood dining set, turned it toward the hearth, and sat down.

He planned to stay and keep her company. Despite herself, the thought pleased her.

"You know," he said to her back as she sawed off a slice of cheese, "at the Finch household, the cooking is done in a cabin behind their main house. Keeps their living rooms a lot cooler in the summer. If we stay here, I think I'll have the Auburns come over and build us another chimney before next summer."

So Widow Atwood won't get overheated, no doubt.

Before answering Baxter, Sabina had to ask God's forgiveness for her lack of charity. "I'm sure your family would appreciate not having a fire in here through the hot months."

"We could set the summer kitchen close enough so—"

The pounding of Philip's feet running down the stairs was accompanied by his shouting, "Pa, are you down there?"

"Aye. What is it?"

Reaching the bottom, Philip still clutched the letter from his sweetheart. "Miss Marty is asking me to come for a visit before harvesttime. Her pa says it's all right with him. May I go? Please?" Every fiber in the lad's body begged for an affirmative answer.

Sabina glanced at Baxter, hoping he would give his consent.

He looked at her as if he were actually checking with her first, then barked a chuckle. "As long as you're back in time for the harvest. And as long as Howie doesn't mind doing your chores while you're gone."

"He won't," Philip spewed in a rush. "He won't. I'll do his for twice as long when I get back."

"You'll need to be careful on the road," his father warned. "I'll find someone heading east at least as far as Knoxville at—"

Before Baxter could finish, Philip hauled him out of the chair and gave him a big bear hug. "This is the greatest day of my life." His grin was the biggest Sabina had ever seen on the rather serious-natured kid.

Breaking away from Baxter, the exuberant lad stepped to Sabina and thrust her into the air, twirling her around. "I'm going to Greeneville. I'm going to see Marty."

"I know," she laughed, her cutting knife held away from them in one hand and a wedge of cheese in the other. "I know."

Just as swiftly, Philip released her and ran for the stairs. "Better get to carving that figurine. I don't want to go empty-handed."

Sabina had to smother her mouth with the back of her hand to stifle her mirth. She looked over at Baxter, who'd sat down again.

His grinning nod was just as merry as hers as he brushed a strand of dark hair from his brow. "I'll check with the men at church tomorrow. Learn if anyone's heading east."

Then it came to her. For Philip to go visit that particular girl went against all of Baxter's plans for his son. She couldn't help but speak her mind. "If you're set on Philip getting a education back East, and maybe taking up a profession and marrying there, why ain't—aren't—you against his romance with Marty Newman? Her Pa's just an ordinary farmer with an extra trade on the side, like most folks overmountain."

Baxter stretched out his legs and propped his hands behind his head, looking totally at ease. "The lad's just seventeen. Most likely, it'll be years before he thinks of taking a wife. That is, if he's allowed to enjoy his puppy loves. If I were fool enough to forbid this visit, he'd want to see her all the more, and their romance would take on a desperation like in *Romeo and Juliet*. This way, their attraction will simply run its course. Hopefully, well before he leaves for Williamsburg."

"Is that the way it was with you and your wife? You eloped because you were forbidden to see her?"

He grinned. "Something like that. Not by my father but by a cousin who still had his inheritance and arranged a more profitable match for me. My father was not in a position to object. You see, my grandfather had long since fallen from grace, taking my father down with him."

"La, I am sorry." She turned to face Baxter, knowing just how the absence of grace could feel. "I do hope your parents learned to rely on the Lord and each other for their joy."

Baxter said nothing for a moment. He just stared at her with those incredibly expressive eyes. "Actually, even being thrust into poverty, they created a happy home. My mother never once voiced any regret about standing by my father after Grandfather gambled away the family fortune."

"Ah, then you, too, have suffered the pitfalls, the tragedies of gambling." Realizing she was taking their conversation down a sad road, Sabina was grateful to have Sammy walk in with a clothes bag over his shoulder.

"Pa, where do you want this?" His glum expression hadn't improved.

"Upstairs in my room for now. We can unpack after supper."

"Which," Sabina said in a cheery tone as she picked up a cucumber to peel, "will be as soon as you come back down."

The second Sammy left their sight, Baxter bolted to his feet and strode to where he'd left the tote bag. He turned upside down what looked like an empty sack.

A lead soldier on a horse fell in a clunk to the floor. Picking it up, Baxter set the small statue on the table at Sammy's usual place.

"You *do* have a gift for him," Sabina whispered. Thrilled

that Baxter had relented, her first inclination was to kiss him. Instead she said softly, "Bless you. That's a very unhappy boy."

"I know." His gaze followed her as she placed a platter of sausage and cheese on the table, then brought a trencher and utensils for each of them.

If she didn't know better, Sabina would have sworn he watched her with the same admiration John Auburn had at the Reardons' yester's eve.

It didn't last long. He shifted his attention to the lead figure, placing it in the center of Sammy's trencher. "I do have to say, though," he said, looking up again, "the boy was due some punishment. I warned him to be on his best behavior when we visited Mistress Atwood's home. But the first words spouting out of his mouth were belligerent."

"Oh my."

"No harm done, though. Amanda and her aunt were most understanding."

"Then they made friends with Sammy?"

"No, they weren't afforded that opportunity. I immediately sent him back to the inn."

"I see. Well, I'm sure several days on the trail, thinking he wasn't getting a gift, will make him choose his words better next time."

"I do hope so, because Amanda and her Aunt Charlotte are coming for a visit in October. I invited them for the harvest fair."

Sabina sucked in a breath. *The harvest fair.* That was only a few weeks away.

~

Baxter caught the panic in Sabina's eyes. "There's no reason for concern. They're really the most congenial people. In fact, they understood completely when I told them that Sammy's deplorable behavior was due to the fact that he's smitten with you."

The amused smile he'd expect from Sabina didn't appear. Her silence rose up between them and hung there.

Gratefully, Baxter heard Sammy's loud descent. "Supper's on the table," he called up to the boy. "Come sit down, so we can ask the Lord's blessing."

Sammy looked like an old man as he trudged to the table. Then, predictably, he let out a wild whoop. *"George Washington!"* He snatched up the lead horse and rider. "You *did* get him for me." He ran around the table, banging into one of the expensive chairs, and wrapped his arms around Baxter's neck. "Thank you, thank you! You're the best papa in the whole world. Ain't he, Sabina?"

The smile Baxter had hoped to see earlier now sprang wide . . . that smile that filled the room with sunshine.

Sammy let go of Baxter and ran to Sabina. "See him?" He shoved the metal figure up to her face. "See how his cape is blowin' back. And how proud he sits his horse. Just like when he took Trenton and Princeton. And the horse, ain't it magnificent? A real warhorse."

"Aye," she said, ruffling his already mussed hair. "The horse is just as splendid as the rider. Washington will make the perfect leader for your other soldiers."

"Aye," he said with a contented sigh.

"Now, go sit down. Your pa's waiting."

As Sammy turned back to the table, Baxter wondered if his boy would one day run to Amanda in his moments of joy as he now did to Sabina. Once Sammy got to know Amanda for the gentlewoman she was, Baxter could see no reason why not.

Naturally, one couldn't expect his children to warm to

Amanda as quickly as they had to Sabina. As everyone could easily see, Sabina had the warmth of the sun captured within her.

~

Howie was as good as his word. As Baxter and Sammy took their first bites of Sabina's rich butter pie, Baxter heard the lad ride in and head straight for the barn with the horse.

Baxter glanced across the room to where Sabina and Delia had chairs pulled up to the desk and were drawing design ideas for their new clothes.

Sabina looked up at him, and as one they smiled. The violin would be squawking again any minute now.

The very instant Howie charged through the door, his eager gaze swept across the room, settling on Sabina. "I'm back for my lesson. Grady was at the Reardons', waitin' for you. It just plumb broke my heart," he added facetiously, "to have to tell him you wasn't comin'."

"*Howie*," Baxter reprimanded. "That's no way to talk about one of—did you say Grady? Just how many men are courting Sabina?"

"There's four of 'em now." Howie scanned the room until he found the violin bag on the china cabinet. "And Grady thinks he can impress Sabina with a pile of bat droppings."

At Baxter's frown, his daughter explained, "Grady's discovered a cave on the land his pa deeded over to him. A whole bunch of bats live there. Grady says him and the Reardons is going to make gunpowder out of the droppings."

Nodding, Baxter chuckled. "It's called bat guano." Nonetheless, he was impressed. "Depending on how much there is, that could be quite a profitable find." He glanced past Delia to Sabina. "Is Grady Jessup someone you could be interested in?" He tried to sound casual.

Sabina stared at him.

Had his question been too personal? Still, he most fervently wanted an answer. Despite the fact that Grady was easier on the eyes and ears than the twins were, Baxter sorely hoped she wouldn't choose him. A lot of nagging and arguing went on in the Jessup household. And nothing killed sunshine faster than that.

Sabina finally answered, "I'm sure the Lord will let me know who his choice is for me when the time is right. It's not wise to run ahead of the Lord."

The Lord's choice . . . why did the expression sound so familiar to him? What had Noah Reardon said to him that day after the cabin raising—something about the possibility of Sabina being God's true choice for him? Of course, that was just romantic nonsense. Still, there was something in the tone of Sabina's voice that made Baxter think her words were meant more for him than for her. Could it be God's intent that they . . . ? No, it was probably just his own foolish longing. He must remain strong, do what was right for his family . . . and for her. "Never forget that you have a home here as long as you want it. So take all the time you need."

And, Lord, he added silently, *please find a man for her who won't steal her sunshine*.

Chapter Seventeen

Baxter could not fault Sabina. She'd been as good as her word in the following days before Amanda and her Aunt Charlotte were to arrive. As promised, the woman had not rushed ahead of the Lord's leading. She had singled out no suitor. Still, all four men were as interested as ever. They continued to come calling, sometimes two in one evening and always around dessert time. Sammy had started complaining that there were never any second helpings. As for Baxter himself, he yearned for even one quiet evening on the front porch.

Two nights before the Nashville ladies were to arrive, Baxter knew he would need to do something about the excessive company. As Sabina stood on the steps waving good-bye to the Dagget twins, Baxter rose from the corner where he'd sat chaperoning their clumsy attempts at impressing her. "Sabina, I have a request that I hope won't upset you."

"Oh?" She turned to him just as the moon came out from behind a cloud, dusting silver across the lightest strands of her upswept hair.

The sight took the words from his mouth. Had she been born to a prominent Virginia family, she would've had her pick of the most eligible bachelors from every county around, of that he was certain.

"Yes?" she quietly inquired again.

Whispering seemed natural at this time of night . . . at this moment. Baxter cleared his throat. "I hope you won't be offended, but I would appreciate it if you would ask your callers not to come this next week while our company is visiting. I might need to make extra requests of you."

"I already asked 'em not to come. I'll see 'em aplenty at the harvest fair." She reached out and touched his arm, sending a wave of shock up to his heart. "I don't want you to worry about a thing. I've talked to the young'uns. They promised to treat the ladies with the highest regard. Especially Sammy." Her eyes glowed softly in the reflection of an inside lamp.

In them, he saw her own anxiety. "I don't want you to worry, either . . . about your place here with us. Amanda is accustomed to having servants. If we wed, I'm sure she'd appreciate your help."

Sabina stiffened. Her gaze hardened. "If I don't wed first."

"I do apologize. Of course, you're not my slave to be handed over to Amanda. I just meant that you needn't think you have to feel pushed into wedding any of these fellows coming around. Wait for someone who's worthy of you."

"Ah, yes, someone who's worthy . . ." Her voice diminished to a soft breeze as she turned and looked into the night sky. "But how does a body ever know who truly is, this side of heaven?"

Without looking back, she started down the steps. "Tell Delia I've gone on to our cabin."

"*That* went well," he muttered under his breath. He'd managed to insult her coming and going. And that was the last thing he ever wanted to do.

~

Sabina's need drove her to her secret place in the first faint blush of dawn. She'd had a restless night. October was upon them, and tomorrow Amanda Atwood would be stepping her lovely refined foot onto the place. And Sabina knew that from that moment on, nothing would be the same.

Wrapped in her crocheted shawl, she settled on a flat-topped boulder jutting out over the gentle brook and gazed off to the east, willing the sun to gild the hills. At that very moment, her mother should be reaching across the distance to her, as well.

"Mama, I wish with everything in me that you was here at this spot right now. As you know, the Lord has given me Inga Bremmer, and I'm ever so thankful to him for that. But Inga is miles away."

Sabina's sigh joined the unceasing birdcalls as the many hues of feathered creatures flew from branch to branch above her head.

"Mama, our heavenly Father knows how I tossed and turned last night. He knows my deepest thoughts and yearnings, and I know I must trust that he loves me and wants me to be happy. I'm trying so hard to make myself feel good about letting go of this family, when all I want is to hang on all the tighter."

Picking up a twig that had fallen beside her on the rock, she tossed it into the stream, and with tears blurring her vision, she watched it float away.

She wiped at the wetness with the sleeve of her flannel nightgown. "Mama, I've prayed and prayed for the strength and will to love someone else, but like you said that first afternoon when we met Baxter, you said he was the kind of man you wanted for me. And, Lord help me, he's the only one I want. I long to stay with him and this family so much, my chest aches for the wanting. But I know I must step away."

Bright sunlight skimmed the hills, and the first beams shot through the trees. Sabina looked to the north again and raised a hand. "Mama, I've told you about the four young men who come calling. Since the twins always come together and spend more time arguing with each other than anything else, I've never gotten to know either of them as a lone person. Who knows, mayhap they don't even know their lone selves. And there's Grady Jessup. By worldly standards, he's the best prospect. But all he talks about is the money he's going to make and all the things he's going to buy with it. And you know what the Scriptures say: A man's treasure is where his heart is. Never once has he mentioned the Lord, and the church seems to be nothing but a place to meet his friends."

On a branch above, a couple of blue jays started squabbling worse than the Dagget twins. Another twig broke and fell, snagging her old yarn shawl. She plucked the splintery piece off and tossed it away.

John Auburn, though, was another matter. Sabina wasn't sure if she wanted to be totally honest about him, even to herself. As Delia had mentioned, it was true that he did stare at her more than she liked, but so did the others. This one, though, didn't spend his time bragging. He spoke seldom and with measured care. A quiet, serious young man. Despite his thinner frame, he'd proved he was a strong and able worker when he and his pa built her cabin's fireplace, and his face was pleasant enough to look at.

"But, Mama, he never laughs or jokes. I don't think he even knows how."

Sabina glanced heavenward. "Heavenly Father," she prayed, "I know it's possible he's just nervous about all this courting business. I should try to get to know him better. But most of all, Father, I pray that I don't let the coming of the ladies tomorrow put a cloud over today. This may very well be my last Sabbath of having the Clays, this dearest of families, to myself."

Feeling another spate of tears unleashing, she determinedly rose to her feet. "Today *will* be a happy one." She'd start it by using some of those raisins Grady brought the last time he came, mayhap make some scones for breakfast.

Cutting through the woods toward the back side of the main house, Sabina slowed when she reached the clearing. Pausing, she surveyed the grounds as if for the last time. She'd grown to love every inch of the place, especially at this time of day when the early rays brushed the buildings and fields with shimmering gold. She loved the flowers she and Delia had tenderly dug up and transplanted around the front steps—even the pesky weeds that kept springing up in the garden were dear to her this morning.

She began her vocal monologue to her mother again. "Speaking of funny things, Mama, remember when all I wanted was to marry a man who took his family to church on Sunday? My, but ain't—I mean, haven't—I got greedy! I covet this one man, his farm, and every one of his children. I don't sound all that different from Kurt, do I? Both us chasing rainbows."

A sudden overwhelming urge to pray for her stepfather overtook Sabina. She dropped to her knees in the grass. "Lord, forgive my unforgiveness. Take pity on Kurt's weakness and fill him with strength and courage. I beg you, give him the same love for you he has shown Mama all these years." Then breathing in the crisp freshness, she added, "And I thank you with all my heart for today, this glorious day with the Clays."

When Sabina rose to her feet, the joy that came only from being with God lightened her step. Her voice refused to be left behind. "'Rise, my soul, and stretch thy wings,'" she gaily sang, accompanied by the twitter of birds and a woodpecker's tap. "'Thy better portion trace; . . .'" Her feet began to dance along as she skipped across the meadow, the morning dew washing her feet.

Yes, it was a lovely, soul-stretching day. No more room to mope.

~

Baxter's breath caught. His heart skipped a beat. He knew he should have expected it, but even when he'd bought the fabric, he hadn't begun to imagine the beauty of the sight. He stood beside the hitched wagon with Howie and Samuel and watched.

Coming from the distant cabin were two of the loveliest flowers he'd ever seen. When he'd bought yellow fabric for Sabina, he'd thought of the sun. Now he saw nothing but an angel, so glorious was the aura she walked in. And Delia. Delia, the apple of his eye, the joy that brightened his lonely years. On this morning in her pink floral day gown, she was like the first rose of spring.

With the green-and-gold countryside as a backdrop, he didn't think he'd ever seen anything more lovely than his two young misses—not even the ballroom belles of Virginia regaled in their silks and satins.

Their happy chatter reached his ears, adding music to the moment. A number of yards before they reached him, they slowed to a stop, and Sabina retied the hair bow holding back Delia's dark ringlets.

Sabina, helping his motherless daughter primp . . .

The love between the two was almost tangible as Sabina kissed Delia's forehead and said something that caused his darling child to smile shyly.

Lord, Delia and the boys have missed out on so much mothering. I pray that they will share that same depth of affection for Amanda when she comes to live with us. Please, Lord, don't let them reject her.

"Papa, is something wrong?" Sammy asked at Baxter's side. "I think the dresses are downright beautiful. Even Delia looks sorta purty."

"Not just sort of," Baxter said, concentrating on his women-folk again. The white ruffling and lace framed both their slender necks to perfection. "Delia's absolutely breathtaking. Isn't that right, Howard?"

"Personally, I think we should just stay home today." Howie obviously didn't seem to share their enthusiasm.

"That's stupid," Sammy retorted. "We're all dressed up in our Sunday shirts and ties and—"

"But, Pa," Howie continued, "you know we're gonna be spendin' the whole mornin' surrounded by a bunch of lovesick bucks and pups. In that dress of Delia's and with her hair all curled and bouncing like that, it ain't just Sabina we're gonna have to keep an eye on."

"Isn't," Baxter absently corrected in his losing battle with Howie's grammar. "Sorry, but that's the curse of being an older brother. And with Philip off to Greeneville, you're stuck with the duty."

When the two girls reached them, smelling as sweet as they looked, Sabina's gaze played over Baxter and the boys. "My, but you Clay men do clean up right smart."

At the compliment, Baxter caught both boys standing up a bit straighter in their Sunday vests and breeches and dress hats.

Howie removed his gray felt and bowed as if he were some fine plantation gentleman. "May I escort you lovely ladies to the back of the wagon?"

Baxter grinned. It looked as if the lad had decided to bear up under the burden of beautiful women.

Delia tittered and took Howie's arm.

Just as Sabina moved toward them, Baxter stepped toward her. "Milady, with Philip gone, why don't you take his place on the seat? You don't want that bonny skirt to wrinkle." He took her arm and led her to the front of the wagon, all the while assuring himself that he had no other motive for wanting her next to him.

~

Summer had lost its grip in the first days of October, and midmorning was cool and comfortable, adding to Sabina's enjoyment of the day. She caught herself smiling all the way to church, especially with Baxter rendering compliment after compliment—on her sewing ability, her dressing of Delia's hair, on how well the white under-ruffling of her bonnet matched the trim of her dress, the expert starching and ironing job she'd done on his and the boys' shirts . . . for the high spirits she'd brought to his children, his home. The praises continued to flow from him like water from a spring.

But the one that touched Sabina the most was when he said, "I really enjoyed that song you were singing this morning whilst you were coming across the meadow. I didn't see you at first. I reckoned it was an angel who'd come visiting."

All this, and after she'd been feeling so utterly miserable when she first arose . . .

As the settlement buildings came into view, Baxter turned to her. "Howie is concerned we menfolk will be obliged to beat off the fellows today. He figures Delia will also get a rush of lads wanting to sit with her."

Sabina smiled. "Aye, her first glimpse of maidenhood. Well, she *will* be fourteen next month, and with those Clay eyes and hair, she can't help but be a beauty."

"She is a beauty, isn't she?" The man virtually oozed fatherly pride. "But what I was planning to say is, if you haven't already made plans to sit with someone else, I'd be proud if you and the kids would all stay in the family pew today. I'll have the handsomest family at church."

A request she would never consider refusing. "I'll talk to Sammy. He's asked to sit with Marvin Lowe."

"Speaking of Sammy, just what have you been using to tame that cowlick of his?"

Before she could answer, his attention was diverted to guiding the horses past the gathering worshipers.

"Mornin', Clay, Miss Sabina," called the engaging Grady Jessup. He hopped down from his family's wagon, which had just rolled to a stop at the far end of the parked vehicles.

"Good morning," Sabina returned.

Baxter merely tipped his brown felt hat over a grim expression, then steered the team to the opposite side of the parking area.

Reaching Sabina's side of the Clay rig before Baxter had reined the grays to a stop, Grady wasn't put off. His grin was charming as ever. "Miss Sabina, your beauty this morning rivals the flowers of the field."

"Why, thank you, Mr. Jessup. That's real poetic."

Wrapping the reins around the brake handle, Baxter turned their way. "If you plan to ask Sabina to—"

"Grady! Grady Jessup, get yourself back over here this minute!" Mistress Jessup hollered from her perch on the high-box seat. "You know your pa can't help me down."

Grady's ruddy face reddened. "Pa's got a bad back," he sheepishly explained to Sabina. Wheeling away, he hurried across the lot while yelling back, "I'll talk to you later about the harvest fair."

Howie stood and made his way forward on the wagon bed till he reached Sabina and Baxter. He lowered his head between them and spoke softly. "Don't matter how much ol' Grady makes off'n that bat poop, his ma'll still keep him tied to her apron strings."

"Howard, you help your sister down." Baxter hadn't reprimanded his son for gossiping, but neither had he disagreed. He lowered his foot to the wheel hub. "I'll help you off, Sabina."

As he dropped down, she spotted John Auburn dismounting his horse nearby, his ardent gray eyes on her alone, and she wondered if he would beat Baxter to her side of the wagon. In his hurry, the lean young man nearly ran into Baxter. But, thank goodness, Baxter already had his arms raised and waiting.

She reached for his shoulders, feeling his strength as his hands circled her waist. He swung her free of the wagon wheel, his gaze holding hers in a very private moment before he set her feet on the grass . . . this man so full of compliments this morning, so attentive.

"Miss Sabina." Auburn removed his black hat with one hand, while with the other he smoothed down sandy hair that needed a cut. "It's pure pleasure seein' you this mornin'." The large, almond-shaped eyes in his thin face took in the whole of her; then his gaze faltered. "The yellow . . . it's real nice."

"Thank you, Mr. Auburn." She knew if he'd worked up the nerve to pay her a compliment, he meant it.

"Time to go in," Baxter said, placing a hand at her elbow.

John Auburn shot him a panicked glance, then returned to Sabina. "I—uh—" Talking did not come easy for the young man.

She tried to encourage him. "Yes, Mr. Auburn?"

"I—uh—my family wants me to invite you to dinner after church next Sunday. And there's—there's the harvest fair this Thursday. Would you—"

Baxter suddenly pushed between them, unexpectedly, rudely. He took several more steps. Stopped. Stared in the direction of the Bremmer home. His mouth opened and out tumbled, *"Amanda?"*

Chapter Eighteen

Amanda? The widow?

Strolling between Inga and Brother Bremmer came a young woman practically floating on a sea of aqua taffeta. Yards of pleated ruffles and black lace trimmed her gown, bonnet, parasol, and even the fan she carried. Sabina had never seen such elegance. The costume must have cost a pirate's fortune.

Her own yellow linen day gown, the one in which she'd felt so pretty just moments ago, now seemed as drab as sackcloth.

Another richly dressed woman walked on the far side of Inga. Her gown of gray and black stripes blended nicely with the younger lady's. They and the Bremmers headed straight toward Baxter, all wearing smug smiles.

A hush came over the milling congregation as everyone else stopped to stare at the strangers.

Baxter broke out of his frozen state and took a step forward.

"Amanda, Miss Finch. You've arrived." He swept his plantation hat from his head.

"Yes," the lovely widow said, extending a black-gloved hand, her lace fan dangling from her wrist by a silken cord. "We reached the settlement last night at dusk *absolutely exhausted*. Your kind minister and his wife entreated upon us to stay the night with them." The lady's voice flowed from her in little more than a breathy whisper as Baxter bent to kiss her hand.

"Aye," agreed the aunt, stouter and plumper-cheeked than her niece. "They were kind enough to provide us with a room and a most needed bath."

Sabina felt out of place standing just behind Baxter as he turned to Inga. "Thank you for taking such good care of them. I didn't expect them until tomorrow or the next day."

"I could tell by your face," the young widow said, her smile still in place, but her hazel gaze sliding to Sabina. "You looked absolutely surprised. Absolutely."

"Oh, forgive me." Baxter reached back to Sabina and pulled her dowdy self forward. "This is Sabina Erhardt, the woman I told you about. She's been working very hard to ready our place in anticipation of your arrival."

"As any good servant should," the aunt said, an arched brow replacing her prior expression as she eyed Sabina.

"So," the younger one said in that syrupy voice, "you're the one who has completely captured young Samuel's heart. I'm pleased to make your acquaintance." She then moved next to Baxter and threaded her arm through his as if she already owned him.

Decorum dictated that Sabina reply. "I pray I can help make your time in the Clay household an enjoyable one."

"Oh, I'm sure you will." The lady's honey-sweet words dripped from her lips, but underneath, Sabina sensed a steely warning.

Did this affluent belle with a face of angelic proportions

consider Sabina a threat? *No. Impossible. The lady is probably just upset because I was sitting up beside Baxter on the wagon like I had a right to be there.*

The young widow then shifted her attention to John Auburn standing at Sabina's side, although Sabina had forgotten he was there. "And who might you be?"

"One of our neighbors," Baxter said for him. "John Auburn. He and his family are the local masons."

"How do you do." The stylish woman again extended her hand.

Mr. Auburn looked both ways, obviously uneasy, then bowed to kiss it. When he straightened again, his rather narrow face glowed red.

Miffed that he, too, was taken with the lady, Sabina stepped back from the little circle. She certainly didn't want to interfere while they fawned over the winsome widow. "I'll fetch the young'uns."

She didn't have to go far. All three stood no more than a few feet away. "Go welcome your guests," she said, then kept right on walking toward the church steps.

"Is that the woman Baxter Clay went to see in Nashville?" Mistress Hatfield, the squinty-eyed wife of the saddler, asked as Sabina passed a circle of curious women.

From just behind Sabina came the answer. "Aye, 'tis." John Auburn had followed her and spoke *for her* . . . this one who was usually too retiring to speak at all. He moved beside her on the wide steps. "Miss Sabina, I don't mean to be a pest, but you didn't have a chance to say yea or nay about dinner next Sunday."

No, she hadn't. Sabina paused, suddenly grateful that the solemn Galahad had not deserted her for the elegant one.

Wishing it were next Sunday already, she replied, "I thank you. And yes, Mr. Auburn, I'd be pleasured to accept your invite."

"You would?" His eyes widened slightly, and the hint of a smile curled the corners of his mouth. Just as quickly, he glanced away. "We'll plan on it then." He returned quietly, his gaze almost but not quite reaching hers. "One more thing, if I'm not bein' too bold. I was a-wonderin', since the Clay pew is gonna be real crowded today, maybe you'd like to sit in ours with us."

He really was a sweet man. "How thoughtful of you." She took his arm and let him escort her inside, vowing not to look back . . . now or ever.

~

"Girl, the pitcher of buttermilk is empty." The older of Baxter's guests set down the shapely china container that, along with the rest of the floral set and silverware, graced the crocheted table-cloth on special occasions. And, of course, this first meal after the Nashville ladies' arrival was one of those.

Still, Sabina was irritated by the manner in which Miss Finch ordered her about. At the worktable cutting slices of apple pie, Sabina also had no doubt that the spinster knew her name. Biting back a retort, she turned to face those eating the Sabbath meal she'd prepared while she remained standing, ready to serve like the servant she really was.

"Her name's Sabina," Sammy blustered, his manners slipping, though he'd promised they wouldn't.

"And a lovely name it is," the young widow said sweetly from the seat she'd chosen next to Baxter at the head. Her soft pale hand toyed with the black lace at her throat. "I don't think I've heard it before."

"It's German," Howie answered for Sabina. "An old family name."

With her constant smile undiminished, Mistress Amanda tilted her perfectly coiffed head in Howie's direction at the other end. "My mother was a bit of a romantic. She named me after a love poem. 'More perfect than the rose I bring, Amanda is the song I sing . . .'" Then, her gaze turning saucy, the widow's attention sailed back to Baxter. "'Take my hand, you have my heart. Come with me to that place apart.'"

The woman was literally throwing herself at Baxter.

Sabina reached between the older matron and Delia, snatching the pitcher from the table. "I'll go out to the springhouse and see if there's any more buttermilk." She was almost positive there wasn't, but it gave her an excuse to leave, if only for a few minutes. Besides, outside a wispy breeze blew cool autumn air.

Stepping across the threshold, though, did not provide the escape she'd hoped for. The first thing slapping her in the face was the sight of the carriage the women had arrived in. Nothing declared a person's wealth more than ownership of a carriage. And this one had lots of shiny brass and a pair of stylish bays to pull it.

The middle-aged black man who'd driven it sat on a barrelhead he'd placed against the barn door frame. When he saw her, the lanky but muscular older slave came to his feet, his eyes respectfully downcast.

La, she hadn't fixed him a plate of food.

She strode across the barnyard to him. "Forgive me. I forgot about you. Soon as I fill this pitcher, I'll bring your meal."

"I 'preciate dat, ma'am, I surely does."

"And I got apple pie for dessert if that suits you."

"Suits me just fine, ma'am." A hint of anticipation could be seen in his lowered gaze.

Sabina understood how it felt to be an outsider, but to be an outsider *and* a slave? She'd be sure to cut him an extra big slice

175

of pie. "May the Lord be with you," she said and left for the springhouse across the stream.

~

"Took you long enough," the stern, older rendition of Amanda complained when Sabina returned.

"The springhouse is on yon side of the garden, across the stream," Delia muttered, staring down at her half-eaten food.

Another of the children defending Sabina. Despite herself, she was pleased as she set the pitcher on the table beside Miss Finch. "I'm sorry, but there ain't—isn't any more buttermilk." Not that the woman hadn't already downed three glasses. "But since you're partial to it, I'll be sure to churn up a mess of butter tomorrow and pour some more off for you. In the meantime, I brought some fresh apple juice. The kids and I pressed a batch just yesterday."

"If that's all you have," the aunt said, resettling her napkin over her gray-and-black taffeta, "it'll do just fine."

"Good. I'll clear off the table and get your desserts."

"I'll help," Delia offered.

"Me, too." Sammy scooted back his chair.

"No." Sabina gave them an appreciative smile. "You have your good clothes on."

Sammy plopped down in his seat again, looking as if she'd said he couldn't have apple pie.

Baxter, who'd been unusually quiet during dinner, spoke to Sabina for the first time since they arrived at church this morning. "Pie sounds nice, Sabina."

That lifted her spirits. He hadn't actually stood up for her as the children had, but he'd voiced his appreciation.

As soon as everyone at the table had a slice of the golden-crusted dessert smothered in heavy cream, Sabina heaped food on a trencher for the slave, adding the chicken breast she'd saved for herself. With a piece of pie in the other hand, she started for the door.

"Sabina, you're welcome to eat at the table with us." Even as uncomfortable as he'd looked since the ladies had arrived, Baxter hadn't forgotten his manners.

She returned a warm look. "This ai—isn't for me. It's for the carriage driver out at the barn."

"Surely, you're not giving *Bolie* that pie." The aunt certainly liked to put in her twopence worth. "Folks are bound to want a second helping, and there's only one piece left."

Had the ladies given fair warning that they'd be arriving today, Sabina would have baked more, but . . . "I already promised it to him. But you can have my piece, Miss Finch."

The woman stiffened. "I didn't say I wanted it."

"Sabina, dear," the younger one said, joining the fray with her syrupy voice, "Father insists we don't spoil our slaves. It leads to trouble."

"This is the Sabbath," Sabina returned in as gentle a tone of her own as she could muster, "and the Bible says it is a day of rest even for slaves."

"And he *is* resting." Amanda's smile looked strained.

On this, Sabina felt driven to have her own way. "Meaning no disrespect, ma'am, but the Lord said, 'Inasmuch as ye have done it unto one of the least of these my brethren, ye have done it unto me.' And I really want to do this as unto the Lord. It's my piece of pie I'm giving."

Amanda's glance flew to Baxter. Though he tried to hide it, the tension of the moment could be seen behind his own attempt at a smile. And though the youngsters maintained silence, they watched with their own rapt interest.

Perking up her smile, the widow lifted her almost empty glass of buttermilk. "Of course, since you are providing my man's sustenance, serve him whatever you please." She turned back to Baxter as if there'd been no confrontation. "Speaking of slaves, Papa has promised to find me a girl of my own—one who's been trained to take care of my personal needs as well as do household chores. I know highly trained slaves are expensive, but the trading posts Papa has established out in Indian country have proved splendidly profitable. But I suppose he's already told you about his Western ventures." She reached over and placed a hand over his. "Enough about my family—tell me more about your relatives in Virginia."

Sabina couldn't escape fast enough. She may have won the battle of the pie, but Amanda had every intention of winning the war. Not only did she expect to wed Baxter with his family ties, but she planned to replace Sabina with a slave.

～

"Your father has informed us that your education is dreadfully lacking," Amanda's aunt said to Delia the following evening.

Baxter leaned on a porch post, wearing a starched white shirt rather than his normal workday linen, while Delia, her hair caught back in one of the ribbons he'd brought her from Nashville, dutifully sat between the two ladies, tugging her fringed natural wool shawl tighter around her. He prayed his daughter would respond tactfully to the older woman's blunt remark.

Delia shot a glance at him first. "Why, ma'am, I've had a splendid education. The girls in our valley are afforded the same schooling as the boys." For a change, her grammar was faultless.

The spinster's graying brows spiked, and she eyed Baxter. "I see what you mean, Mr. Clay. Nothing but frivolous book learning." She returned her attention to Delia. "But, child, what have you learned about overseeing a gracious home? of your duties as a wife and hostess? how to dress or walk or talk?"

Obviously not comfortable with the line of questioning, Delia again looked at Baxter before answering. "Ma'am, this is the backwoods of Tennessee. There's not much call here for affected niceties."

"Darling . . ." Amanda's smooth voice came into the conversation as she sat with stiff ladylike dignity in her chair, her pink-and-beige-striped gown arranged beautifully around her. "You simply cannot settle for a crude woodsy existence. You're a *Clay*. There are doors waiting to open for you that are not available to most of your neighbors."

"Aye, that's what Papa says. But I have a real fondness for the open doors of this valley. Here, no one is turned away."

Despite his child's stubborn words, Baxter took pride in her politely subdued *and* grammatically correct argument.

In keeping, Amanda's tone maintained its calm. "But, dear, you don't want to be thought lacking in culture when you visit your family in Virginia."

"My hope is," Delia answered, obviously measuring each word, "that my relatives are as thoughtful and truly mannerly as my father. Now, if you'll excuse me—" she stood up—"I'm going inside to help Sabina with the dishes. I don't feel right, leaving all the chores to her."

As his daughter hurried inside, Baxter had a disturbing thought. Would Delia have been so reluctant to accept Amanda and all she offered if he had not brought Sabina here to live? Though the older Miss Finch was tactless, Amanda had been nothing but gracious toward Delia and the boys.

Yet Delia had rushed inside as if dishes were her favorite chore. And the boys? They were nowhere to be seen. The blessing he'd thought Sabina to be might very well have become a monumental mistake.

"Your children," Spinster Finch said, turning to Baxter and lowering her voice to a conspiratorial hush, "have been in the backwoods much too long. You simply must remove them from this dearth of civility." Her disdainful expression matched her sentiment. "Nashville isn't all that much better, but a few of us better families have maintained certain standards. We've created a small but dedicated social circle."

"I suppose you're right." Still, the thought of leaving here to go to Nashville was beginning to tear at Baxter. He'd never had such close friends as he'd found here in this remote valley. He glanced across the garden to the new log house his neighbors had helped build for Sabina and Delia not too many weeks ago. Everyone was always pitching in.

His wayward mind then drifted to Sabina and Delia and how they'd looked leaving the cabin yesterday morning—two lovely flowers of felicity.

"Amanda, didn't I tell you?" her aunt said, congratulating herself. "Mr. Clay is a very sensible man. Once a situation is brought to light, he'll do the right thing. He'll move to Nash-ville."

The woman's voice was beginning to grate on his ears, and that last statement really irritated him. Did she think he'd blithely hop on any suggestion she made as if it were some prized stallion to mount?

He looked from her smug expression to the more pleasant sight of Amanda's round-cheeked smile and mellowed. He needed to keep his sights and thoughts on the generously proportioned young widow. Stay the course. His children's future lay with her, not with the bitter old spinster. "Mistress

Atwood, would you care to take a stroll down by the brook before the sun goes down?"

"I hear someone coming." Her busybody aunt missed nothing.

Baxter walked to the end of the porch and looked up the path leading to the main road.

Jessup. Grady Jessup, riding in on his buckskin pony. Sabina had expressly told him and her other beaus to stay away this week.

"Howdy," Grady called as he rode into the yard, grinning as if he had good sense. He pushed back his hat. "Pardon the intrusion, but I come bearin' a invite."

"For whom?" Baxter kept his tone calm.

"Why, for you, Mr. Clay and—" Grady pulled his wide-brimmed hat from his curly head—"and for you lovely ladies. Schoolmaster Elbridge and his missus asked me to invite you over for tea tomorrow at three."

"Thank you for dropping by with the message," Baxter said, hoping the fellow wouldn't ingratiate himself.

But he was already dismounting. "Thought since I was here anyway, I'd pay my respects to Miss Sabina. Where is she?"

"You go right ahead, young man," the usurping aunt said. "She's in the house, washing dishes."

Grady bounded up the steps and into the house before Baxter could get a word in.

What was done was done, he told himself. No use causing a scene. Returning his attention to Amanda, he noted her pleased expression.

"From the enthusiasm in that gentleman's demeanor," she said, "I'd say you'll be shy a servant girl very soon." Amanda rose from her chair, rearranging her bountiful pink-and-beige skirt, then held out her soft, white hand. "Shall we take that stroll you mentioned?"

Chapter Nineteen

S weetheart, I'm sure there's room for you." Baxter made a last plea to Delia the next afternoon to join him and the Nashville ladies in their fancy carriage.

Sitting on the porch, Sabina discreetly kept her eyes on the bowl of beans she was snapping for supper as Delia again declined his request. "Papa, school commences soon. I'd just as soon not have to listen to Mr. Elbridge expounding and expanding till I have to."

Expounding and expanding? Sabina fought off a grin at the girl's poetic inventiveness as she glanced up to see Baxter's reaction.

Mounting the carriage steps, he looked back at Sabina, and they shared a moment of suppressed humor—the first such since his lady friends had arrived. And Sabina realized how very much she would miss these private snippets of time . . . these moments he would soon be sharing with Amanda Atwood.

Sabina watched the lanky older slave sitting ramrod straight on the jockey seat, wearing his black driving jacket. He cracked the reins over the gleaming bays' backs, and the carriage rumbled around the corner of the house.

As soon as it did, Sammy bounded through the doorway and Howie came swaggering out of the barn.

"Let me help you snap beans," Sammy said. "I love the sound they make."

"Sorry." Sabina lifted the second bowl that had held the whole string beans and turned it upside down. "All through."

"Good," Howie shouted as he trotted toward them, following Delia's ascent to the porch. "You been so busy babyin' them two lazy women, you ain't had no time to teach me any more violin."

"Haven't—not ain't," Sabina corrected. "Remember we all made a pact not to say *ain't* no more."

Howie's merry brown eyes danced as he chuckled. "And after that, I reckon we better start in on them double negatives."

"On what?" Sabina didn't think she'd ever learn all there was to proper speaking.

"That can wait," Delia said, grabbing Sabina's wrist. "You promised to teach us how to do a Scottish reel. And the harvest fair is just two days away."

"I wanna learn, too," Sammy piped in as he took the full bowl of beans from Sabina. "Don't want them Nashville ladies thinkin' we don't got no social graces." Holding out his limp linen shirt as if it were a skirt, the boy twirled around.

"Tell you what. Let me get supper to cooking, and then we'll dance up a storm." Sabina rose to her feet.

"Supper ain't for hours," Howie complained.

"Your pa asked that I cook early enough so the room can cool down before mealtime."

Delia grabbed Sabina's empty bowl and started for the door. "If we all help, it'll get done faster."

184

Sammy put on an impishly impatient face. "If it wasn't for them women, you wouldn't have to cook a big meal for supper. We'd just be havin' what's left over."

Sabina ruffled Sammy's hair. "Folks do things different in different places. For instance, take that geography book of Howie's. Them women in China wear men's trousers, but folks don't think a thing of it, 'cause that's the way things is done there."

"And in Nashville," Howie chipped in, "I reckon folks don't eat leftover vittles."

"Leastwise," Sabina modified as she headed inside, "folks with extra food and the servants to cook for 'em don't."

Coming behind, Sammy plopped the bowl of beans on the worktable. "Maybe movin' to Nashville wouldn't be *all* that bad. If Mistress Amanda will get some slave to do my chores, too."

So their father had spoken to them about going to Nashville to live. Sabina fanned a gaze across these children whom she had grown to love more with each day. *The Lord giveth and the Lord taketh away.* . . .

But for this afternoon they were hers to love and teach. "Sammy, I don't think the good Lord intended for us to sit idly by doing nothing. Remember where St. Paul writes, 'If any would not work, neither should he eat.' So, to stay in good stead with the Lord, go fetch me a bucket of water. And Howie, would you please bring in a load of wood? We got us some some dance lessons to get to."

~

The last time Baxter remembered riding in a fine covered coach to an afternoon tea was during his waning days at college when his father's cousin had arranged for him to pick up Lucinda Weston and her mother and escort them to the Clays' town house in Williamsburg. The day had been enjoyable enough, though at the time his consuming wish had been that his sweet Sally had accompanied him in their stead.

But he was much older and wiser now. Riding in the back-facing seat, he glanced across at the two ladies, one of which would most probably be a significant part of his future days.

As usual, the women were dressed with impeccable taste. Amanda's costume was subdued but elegant—a dusty rose day gown with ruffles and rosettes of the same fabric and sleeve falls of beige lace. Her aunt wore a corresponding gown of beige-on-beige. It was as if they always deliberately, cleverly dressed to complement each other.

"I do believe you'll enjoy the Elbridges," he commented, making conversation. "They've not been in the West overly long. Just for the last school session. They come from New York City and have interesting stories."

"Wonderful." Amanda's cherubic cheeks rounded into a charming smile. "I've been to New York. Without a doubt, it's replacing Boston and Philadelphia as the cultural hub of our nation. The theaters, the lavish parties . . ."

"Aye, that's what they say." Baxter again noted that Amanda had a penchant for everything she'd left behind when her family moved from Pennsylvania. Would she press him to return East? Would he want to go? Aside from considering her request that he move to the more prosperous Nashville, he'd merely thought about what this marriage would bring to his children, not all that Amanda might expect in return. . . . Had he ever prayed specifically about that? Where would this marriage really take him? Thoughts for a later pondering, since the Elbridge cabin was just ahead. Baxter leaned out the window. "Bolie, turn to the left just before you reach the church. It's the cabin that's set back a ways."

Baxter returned to the ladies. "They live in the cabin that goes with the teaching position. It's small, but the Elbridges are childless. Despite the rustic furniture, Georgette—Mistress Elbridge—has added some cozy, homey touches. They've done their best to keep up appearances."

As the carriage turned off on the side path, Miss Finch glanced out at the simple home. "I can't imagine educated people choosing to leave the comforts of New York for such a pitiable situation in this backwater place. There must be more to his coming here." The woman always went straight for the throat.

"There is." Baxter didn't expound, uncomfortable with bandying the Elbridges' personal business.

"Well?" she insisted.

"His people were merchants, too," he said reluctantly, choosing his words carefully, "with their own ships. Unfortunately, they lost every one of them during the Revolution. And the big fire destroyed their warehouses. Family friends kindly saw to it that Harvey had a good education. He took this teaching position because he felt he'd already taken too much charity from his father's associates. I respect him for that."

"Humph." Amanda's aunt didn't hide her disapproval. "If he'd been smart, he would've let his pride go before falling to such a lowly state."

The woman made pleasant conversation impossible. Baxter had to fight to remain calm. "We pray that through the Lord, he'll find success in whatever new venture he pursues."

"Yes, of course." Obviously mollified, the thickset older woman pulled a lace handkerchief from inside her sleeve and brushed at an imaginary spot on her skirt.

The coach rolled to a stop between two tall pines, where the Elbridges stood waiting in front of their single-story cabin.

Short and comfortably round, Georgette stepped forward, carrying a small fluffy dog. "We're most honored that you would gift us with your presence this afternoon," she said in her cheery but rather high-pitched voice.

Harvey, one of those skinny men no amount of feeding would fatten, came alongside his wife; he was dressed in his best dark blue coattails and wore a pin-striped cravat at his neck.

Baxter felt a bit underdressed in merely his starched white shirt and vest with no tie. In the valley, neckwear was usually reserved for church, weddings, and funerals.

Elbridge approached the carriage and opened the half door to help the ladies alight. "'Tis a marvelous treat, having your gentility grace our most humble abode."

After introductions, Baxter followed Harvey with Georgette as their host escorted the two ladies around to the side of the cabin. To Baxter's surprise, a linen-covered table awaited them on a trim lawn surrounded by a crescent of birches. Beneath the trees, plants bloomed in a profusion of pink and white, unusual for this late in the year. Chrysanthemums, as Baxter recalled. "This is all so lovely," he said to Georgette. "I had no idea you'd created such a beautiful little haven."

"Why, thank you, Baxter. It's the small niceties I do believe I miss the most, even more than the hustle and bustle of the city," said Georgette.

"Ah, yes, but the rows and rows of shops are what I miss," Amanda said as Harvey held her chair for her. Her hazel eyes sparkling, she scarcely bothered with settling her skirts before continuing. "After my mother passed on—God rest her soul—Daddy took me on a packet north to New York City. The shop-windows were overflowing with treasures from the farthest ports. So much to choose from." She touched a filigreed heart on a chain at her throat. "The shopkeeper said this came from Siam."

"It is quite lovely," Georgette said, her sincerity evident as she put down her tiny dog and took the seat Baxter held for her.

Baxter suddenly realized how much Georgette reminded him of his own mother, not in her looks but in the uncomplaining loyalty she lived every day, by following her husband to this rustic place and making the most comfortable home she could for him. From what the kids had told him about Harvey, the schoolmaster wasn't adjusting nearly as well. The man seemed to take little pleasure in teaching.

While Georgette poured tea and offered dainty sugar cakes with the finesse of one born to the manor, the women chatted congenially about the latest fashions from Europe.

Baxter regretted not insisting that Delia come with them. She could've seen firsthand some of what she needed to learn. How to pour, whom to serve first, the right questions to ask . . . all done while the ladies sat with demurely perfect posture—a stark contrast to their lively conversation.

And if today was any indication, social graces might soon become as commonplace here in Tennessee as they already were along the seacoast.

"Mistress Elbridge," Amanda said after a time, "you and Mr. Elbridge must come visit us in Nashville at Christmastide. Our church is presenting a pageant this year, and three merchant families that I know of are hosting balls. Of course, it's not New York, but we are trying to carry on some of the traditions." She turned to Baxter. "And it goes without saying, you and your children absolutely must come."

Mistress Finch added a piece of her own mind. "We're trying to convince Baxter to relocate. His cobbler's business would grow tenfold if he were to move to Nashville. And the same goes for you, Mr. Elbridge. From what Baxter said, your family were merchants as mine are. I'm sure with your experience and connections, my brother could find a lucrative place for you in one of his enterprises."

Now the woman was offering positions she had no place to offer.

Still, Elbridge's long face grew more animated than Baxter had ever before seen. "Perhaps we shall come for that visit."

Baxter prayed the man's hope was not in vain.

But there was one thing these past few days had told him: he would have to secure a promise from Amanda. Should they wed, her aunt was never to come live with them. That assurance also would go a long way in winning the children's acceptance of the prospective marriage.

Amanda had shown them nothing but kindness, but as for the old battle-ax? He'd noticed how the children tried to escape every room she entered.

~

Baxter berated himself for his uncharitable thoughts about Spinster Finch most of the way home. He could hardly believe that less than two months ago, he'd vowed to strive as the apostle Paul in the Bible had toward the goal of perfection in Christ. But every time the woman opened her mouth or looked around with those haughty eyes, words like *overbearing witch*, *self-righteous shrew*, and his father's favorite—*old battle-ax*—popped into his mind.

Facing her in the carriage now, he watched the woman's lips relentlessly moving, and he prayed for the self-control not to voice his own thoughts.

"Heavens to Betsy!" The woman's eyes widened as they neared the clearing to his place. She leaned forward. "Look at *that*."

Was there a fire? a bear? or a panther? Baxter swiveled around and poked his head out the window, frantically looking for the source of Miss Finch's alarm. But all he saw were his children and Sabina in the yard, oblivious to any danger. "Where? What?"

"Are you blind, man? Your children and that woman. If I didn't know better, I'd think they were performing some pagan ritual."

"Auntie dear," Amanda said, craning out her own opening, "I'm sure they're merely playing some strange woodsy game."

Although the noise of the horses and carriage drowned out the sound, Baxter saw Sabina sawing on Howie's violin and him piping on his fife as she and his three younger children all wove back and forth, bobbing to the music. Sammy seemed to be clowning as he threw himself around, twirling until he got tangled in his feet and fell. Unaware of the approaching coach, they were undoubtedly have a merry old time.

Baxter couldn't help smiling. Corralling his grin, he returned his attention to the ladies. "Looks like Sabina is teaching them the steps to a reel."

"One more reason to get these children away from these ill-bred backwoods people," the wrath-filled one harped. "Minuets are the only civilized form of dance. Reels are so—so common."

That was the last straw. Baxter couldn't contain the rage that stormed through him. If that woman made one more remark about his—

Staring across at him, Amanda hastily took over. "There's so little amusement in these remote hollows," she said to her aunt in soothing tones. "I think one needs to look upon the children's innocent frolic with compassion and understanding. Besides, Auntie dear, I do believe a stringed quartet would be in short supply in these parts."

Amanda was very good at smoothing things over. Baxter felt the tension inside him starting to uncoil. In her favor, she was not one to be blindly swayed by her aunt. She had opinions of her own . . . opinions not cast in a stone heart. She did have expensive tastes, true, and she did seem to focus overly on earthly treasures; still, Baxter began to feel more comfortable with the idea of entrusting the children to her care and instruction.

But only if the witch were nowhere near. Perhaps a move to Nashville should be rethought.

Glancing out at the happy foursome again, the last of Baxter's anger dissipated. Their laughter now rang as clearly as their lively music. His gaze lingered on Sabina, her smile as sunny as the pigtail bouncing across her back . . . Sabina, his own pied piper.

Chapter Twenty

Sabina saw a scattering of clouds begin to flame in the first rays of dawn. She leapt over the stream, hurrying back from her secret place. This was not a day for dawdling. This was Thursday! The day of the harvest fair!

Yesterday she'd baked, and before she went to bed, she'd placed a number of potatoes in the coals to cook overnight. Aside from her regular chores, chickens still had to be killed, plucked, and fried, and potato salad to be made.

And one more thing. Before the others awakened from their beds, she was determined to speak to Baxter—may the good Lord give her the right words.

Breezing past the well, she saw the manservant walking toward the barn, weighted down by a water bucket in each hand. "Good morning, Bolie," she called, angling off to greet him.

He looked back at her with a cautious smile. "Mornin', missy. Anything yo wants from me?"

"No. From what I hear, you're doing more than your share around here already."

"I likes to keep busy. Helps pass da time till I gets back home to my Netty."

"I reckon it is lonely for you here, stuck out in the barn all to yourself."

"It ain't been so bad. Yo boys has kept me comp'ny quite a lot. Dey's good boys."

"They speak kindly of you too. They told me you rubbed down our horses for Sammy last night. And milked the cow for Howie. Don't let the boys take advantage of you."

"Dey ain't. We just wanted to get da chores done quick. Cuz den dey took me wit' 'em down towards da Carney Fork. We had us a high ol' time frog-giggin'." A rare smile graced his rugged face. "Fried us up a whole mess of dem hoppity legs."

"I'll just bet you did." Sabina chuckled at the picture of the three of them wildly chasing through the marshy backwater that lay just south of the Reardons' land. "Won't be many more chances for that till next year. The leaves are beginning to turn. Well," she said, starting toward the main house, "I best be getting to my own chores."

"Missy."

She turned back. "Yes?"

"I does enjoy jawin' wit' y'all. But just in case yo don' know, when dem ladies is up an' about, I cain't be a-talkin' wit' y'all like dis."

"I understand." And she did. After the pie incident on that first day the visitors had arrived, Sabina had been fully aware of the women's strict rules about not "spoiling" their man. Thank the Lord, they would be leaving for Nashville tomorrow. "Well, I'm on my way to try and make Mr. Clay understand something. Do you know if he's in his house or in the shop?"

Bolie glanced toward the shop. "Dey ain't no lamp lit out dere yet."

Sabina looked back at the house, where the lamps were indeed lit on the lower floor and smoke curled up from the chimney.

The first faint whiff of coffee drifted her way. Baxter had been busy. "Bolie, I'll bring you some coffee first chance I get. Oh, and if you don't mind, pray that I say the right words to Mr. Clay."

Upon entering the cabin, Sabina found Baxter standing by the window with a steaming cup in hand. He must have been watching her and Bolie converse, but he didn't seem disturbed by it.

"Coffee's ready," he greeted with a smile and a nod toward the pot.

"Smells good."

"I got the potatoes out of the coals for you. They're good and done."

Sabina stopped at his words. The man had actually dug around in the smudgy ashes for her. "Thank you. You do amaze me sometimes with your kind deeds."

"Not as often as you surprise me."

His accompanying gaze was the sort that always made her heart leap like those bullfrogs Bolie had spoken of. She wished Baxter wouldn't behold her with such tenderness—not when there was no hope for them to be together. Not when Mistress Atwood was to be his bride.

"I'd like to thank you," he said, taking a sip, "for all your extra efforts on behalf of our guests. Without you here, I know I couldn't have made them nearly so comfortable."

Sabina grabbed a plain crockery cup from the upper shelf above the worktable and poured herself some coffee as she summoned her courage. Replacing the pot on a layer of coals, she turned back to Baxter, who now peacefully gazed out at the morning again. "Mr. Clay, there's something I feel I must say."

"Mister Clay?" His dark brows dipped over his insightful eyes—she certainly had his attention.

She took a swallow of brew too hastily, burning her tongue and throat. "I—" Her courage was failing her already. She stepped closer and lowered her voice. "I need to speak to you about the children."

His expression turned unreadable. "The children?"

For a second, Sabina wondered whether she was speaking out of turn—yet if she remained silent . . . no, she couldn't let the kids down. "Surely you must see that they cannot abide Miss Finch. They do everything they can to avoid her."

Baxter closed his eyes and nodded. "I know."

His admission bolstered her courage. She plunged on. "I don't know what else to say to 'em. Every time the woman is in the same room, she says something to set 'em off again. I see an all-out rebellion in the making when you marry Mistress Atwood."

He returned his gaze to her, a steady sincere one. "I've given the matter a lot of thought myself. Just let me assure you, my children will never live under the same roof with Miss Finch."

"Thanks be to God. I'm purely relieved." Her fingers reached out to him. Quickly she redirected them to her lips. "The young'uns will be too. If you don't mind, I'd like to tell them today. With talk of moving to Nashville and having a new mother to try an' please, along with Miss Finch, well, that's been weighing on them mighty heavy."

Surprisingly, Baxter grinned. "Me, too. And now, after talking with you, I know the decision I've made about all this is the right one."

Had he decided against marrying Amanda? Crazy hope

spiraled through Sabina . . . a growing joy that pushed his voice to the edge of her consciousness.

"I plan to speak to Amanda today. I've decided that when we wed, our first six months must be spent here, with Aunt Charlotte a good fifty miles away."

Sabina's hope plummeted as cold reality set in. She couldn't bear to look at Baxter.

"The children will come to accept Amanda as their mother much more readily," he rattled on, unaware, "if they don't have to adjust to a new house, town living, *and* contend with constant criticism from Miss Finch."

"Thank you for putting your children first," she barely managed around a tightness in her throat.

"No." He placed a hand on her shoulder. "I thank you for caring about them enough to speak up. And don't forget, all I've said to you before still stands. The cabin, your position here, are yours as long as you want them."

How noble of him, she raged inwardly. To offer her the dregs, the crumbs of his life. She stepped out of his hold and walked to the table. "Thank you, but I think it would be best if I'm gone before you wed the widow. Your children might take to her a lot faster if I ain't—if I'm not here."

A sadness clouded his eyes.

But for whom—him or her? Diverting her own eyes, she picked up one of the blackened potatoes and began to pull away the sooty cornhusk wrapping.

He came up behind her. "I suppose you're right. But, please don't marry one of those fellows who keep coming around just so you'll have a place to stay. I can easily find you another situation. You deserve . . ."

She felt his breath feather across the top of her head as he spoke. "I want you to be happy."

His closeness caused Sabina's thoughts to turn to mush. "I—" She took in a lungful of air. She couldn't let him guess that for her, happiness was being here with him. "I won't wed anyone until I'm sure he's the Lord's choice for me. Only God knows what is truly in a person's heart."

"Aye," he said softly, "only God knows." He stepped back. "Well, I'd better get busy. I have a pair of shoes to finish before we leave for the fair."

"Aye," she repeated. "And before I start breakfast, I need to go outside and get a tub of water a-heating and kill a couple of chickens to pluck."

"I'll kill the chickens for you. Just let me know when the water's ready for the dipping. And the boys can do the plucking. I'll run up and roust them out."

Before she could thank him for yet another kindness, he was already on his way up the stairs, stepping quietly, of course, careful not to disturb the late-rising ladies . . . a solid reminder that she wasn't the only recipient of this man's kindness.

Or was he, in truth, wary of waking the formidable Miss Finch? Turning back to the potatoes, Sabina gave in to a grin beginning to crawl across her lips. It helped keep the tears inside, where they belonged.

~

After spending several days with Amanda, Baxter had gotten a pretty good idea that inviting her and her aunt here for the fair had been a mistake. He'd lived in this isolated valley for so long— with no slaves, no bond servants, no families of wealth or position—that he'd forgotten about the many layers of society, the lines that were not so easily crossed.

But he had invited the ladies to the festivities, and he was going to make the best of it. Sitting across from them, he knew the carriage would be coming into the clearing any second.

Amanda, of course, was attired far more grandly than any other female at the fair would be. She wore sheer floral silk of peaches and beiges layered over bronze satin. Her gracefully slanting bonnet had matching flowers and a flowing feather. No doubt she would be the envy of every woman present. Her aunt wore the same beige costume she'd worn to the Elbridges' tea, but again, it acted as a background to set off Amanda's finery. It all seemed so incredibly calculating, women's fashion, but who was he to try to understand such things?

Loosening the cravat he'd been obliged to wear with the vest and pants of his new suit, he attempted a friendly smile. "Just a little farther. And please let me say, I realize country pleasures may not amuse you, so the moment you two wish to leave, it will be my pleasure to see you home."

"At least," Miss Finch said, fanning herself, "we waited to come until the sun lost most of its bite."

And light, Baxter groused silently. It was already past three o'clock. "We're experiencing a touch of Indian summer."

Sabina and the kids had left for the fair before noon, not wanting to miss a minute of the games and contests, the feasting. Baxter wished he'd been with them to watch every footrace and horse race, every shooting match, to judge the pie contest, to . . .

"Whoa!" Bolie cried from up top, and the horses and carriage began creaking to a stop at the edge of the parade ground.

Baxter reined in his wandering thoughts and drew a slow breath to bolster himself for the duties that lay ahead.

Festivities filled the large area between the row of public buildings and the sturdy timber fort that, thank the Lord, had never weathered an Indian siege. Folks from all over the county milled among the contest tables that held prize produce, preserves, whittled pieces, quilts, or tatting. Across from them were booths with sale items from apples to ax blades. More tables and benches for eating and visiting were set up under the trees beside the church.

"Would you prefer to find a comfortable spot to sit or browse past the tables first?" he asked as he helped Amanda and her aunt from the carriage, then collected a quilt for sitting.

"A shady spot," the aunt ordered, as bossy as ever. "Then I trust you'll be wanting to check on your youngsters. That servant with whom you sent them is not the most prudent person I've ever met."

Baxter locked his jaws to prevent his own venom from spewing forth. Strange how a person like Spinster Finch, who'd had so much instruction in the social arts, could have so little tact.

"Yes, Auntie," Amanda said, her voice calm as always, "let's do find a spot where you can refresh yourself while Baxter and I check on the children."

Avoiding the crowd, Baxter escorted the ladies to the outer edge of the festivities. Cheering broke out near the stockade, and he saw two fleet-footed steeds racing along that side of the parade ground. He didn't recognize the animals or the riders. "The competitors must be from some of the other settlements. Folks who live twenty, twenty-five miles away come for our fair."

"It would seem so," Miss Finch said with her usual disdain.

Finding a shady place to rid himself of the shrew became Baxter's primary interest. As late as they were, the good spots were all taken. Beneath every tree lay a number of blankets.

"Baxter, over here," came a woman's call.

He sighted Louvenia Reardon beckoning him. "Come, ladies; it would seem Mistress Reardon is inviting us to join her."

The Reardon matriarch sat alone beneath the shade of a beech on one of several old quilts that had been spread for her large family. "Do sit with me. Keep me company. As you can see, I've been deserted," the rather gaunt woman said with a smile. "I have a jug of cider. Would you ladies care for some?"

"That would be delightful." Mistress Finch didn't wait for Baxter to spread his blanket. She melted down beside her hostess into a billow of her heavy skirts.

Small wonder the woman complained so much. She was weighted down by far too many clothes. That would make anyone irritable. Baxter tugged at the suffocating cravat at his throat. "Louvenia," he asked, "do you happen to know where my family is?"

"Their quilt is here with ours."

The older woman pointed a long bony finger to a spread he recognized. It was cluttered with baskets and shoes, along with a variety of homemade music makers and Howie's new violin. Together, his kids and the Reardons must have made quite a racket.

"And the last I heard," Mistress Reardon continued, "Jacob and Ike Junior, along with your boys, was gettin' in a corn-eatin' contest. Delia, Gracie, and Hope went with 'em. And of course where them giggly gals go, a whole passel of boys is taggin' along." She shook her head. "Three young gals just comin' into bloom, and with Sabina in full flower . . . my, my, what a stir they're makin' here today with young lads from all over the county."

Baxter should have been here to keep a close watch over his pretty daughter. He scanned the parade ground. "Sabina has kept Delia with her, hasn't she?"

"La, yes. Her and Jessica is keepin' a eagle eye on them flouncy gals."

Amanda wound her arm through Baxter's. "If Delia's with Sabina, I'd say she's among the crowd over there." Amanda pointed a sheer-gloved finger to a group near the food tables. "No one could miss that yellow gown of Sabina's. It's so bright, one would think she deliberately set out to be noticed."

Not sure whether to be insulted or embarrassed, Baxter shot a glance to Louvenia. The woman knew very well the yellow linen was a gift from him.

The elder Reardon looked back at him and shrugged but said nothing.

He, too, chose to ignore the remark. He tipped his hat to the seated women. "If you ladies will excuse us . . ."

Strolling across the beaten-down grass with the fashionable Amanda, they wove through the merrymaking throng. Baxter witnessed person after person turning to admire Amanda's expensive ensemble . . . ample proof that the remark she'd made about Sabina could more easily refer to herself. Her bonnet alone looked ready to take flight.

He glanced several yards away to Sabina, who had her back to him. The slanting rays of sunshine glowed over her lithe form, giving Baxter a rush of pleasure. But then he caught sight of the Dagget twins flanking her on each side. He turned back to Amanda, who was also staring at Sabina, and he noticed that the lady's customary smile was absent from her lips.

Baxter suddenly realized something. *Amanda is jealous—jealous of Sabina.* Had one of the children led Amanda to believe that his affections lay with her instead? No. If that were so, Amanda's outspoken aunt certainly would have addressed the issue.

What about Sabina? Had she done anything to give Amanda that impression? If anything, Sabina had avoided conversing with the ladies more diligently than the children

had. And she'd also kept her distance from him in their presence.

So why was she jealous?

As he and Amanda neared the corn-eating event, he caught
only glimpses of Delia and the Reardon girls. Sabina stood just
behind them, blocking his view of them. Her flaxen hair was
pulled up in a chignon, baring her slender neck and giving her
a stately yet oddly vulnerable quality he couldn't help admiring.
She intently watched the contest from over the girls' heads.
"Go, Sammy, go!" she rooted.

Because of the crowd, Baxter couldn't see his youngest son,
who most likely was sitting at a table, but he had no trouble at
all spotting one of those fresh Daggets curling his fingers around
Sabina's waist.

Not missing a syllable of another "Go, Sammy, go!" Sabina
nonchalantly removed the bounder's hand.

Someone squeezed his own arm. Amanda. "Is something
amiss?" she asked, looking from him to Sabina.

Heat exploded up his neck as if his guest had been privy to his
thoughts. "No," he lied, "I was just trying to see through to my
boys."

The smile Amanda propped into place didn't play any truer
than his words.

At an instant realization, the heat burning his neck and
cheeks turned to ice. Neither Sabina nor the kids had given
Amanda any cause to be jealous. The blame was all his.

Chapter Twenty-One

Seconds before reaching the contest where they would encounter Sabina, Baxter grasped Amanda's arm more tightly and escorted her in the opposite direction. "If you don't mind, I'd like to speak with you alone. We can join the others in a few minutes."

Amanda's large hazel eyes searched his face, her expression understandably apprehensive. "Of course. As you wish."

He led her from the parade ground to a grassy place beneath an old oak that stood between the church and Bremmer's blacksmith shop. The lower branches provided a modicum of privacy.

Unable to deny that he was responsible for the sadness in her childlike face, he gathered her sheerly gloved hands into his own. "Amanda, I owe you an apology. When you and I spoke at the Cane Ridge camp meeting, I told you that my children and I were on our own and in great need of a genteel wife and mother. And that was all true. But the very hour we left for home, Sabina came to be with us."

Amanda withdrew her hands. "You need not speak further. I just wish you hadn't waited so long to speak, prolonging this embarrassing situation." She started to whirl away.

He caught her shoulders. "You misunderstand. If you'll have me, I am as intent as ever on marrying you. But from the moment Sammy found Sabina, the children have championed her cause, and—"

"What do you mean by 'found' her?" Amanda's words were controlled but demanding.

Baxter hadn't planned to tell Amanda the details of Sabina's coming to stay with them, but perhaps the knowledge would give her more understanding and, hopefully, sympathy. "I'll gladly explain, but this must be for your ears only. Your aunt lacks, shall we say, a gentle spirit."

A quicksilver smile brightened Amanda's rounded features. "Of course. You can always trust me to keep a confidence."

He relaxed. Perhaps telling her was best, after all. At the very least, it would bring the two of them closer. "Sammy found Sabina hiding from her stepfather and the man he'd just lost her to in a game of cards."

"Lost her? I don't understand. She was the wager?"

"It would seem so. This fellow had been wanting to marry Sabina for some time, but she had refused him."

"What manner of people must this wench come from? Certainly not the sort you'd want your children mixing with."

"Exactly. Sabina feels the same. She's opposed to marrying a gambler or anyone who doesn't follow the Lord. She's a fine Christian."

"Oh, really." Amanda didn't seem all that convinced.

Knowing he was probably handling the situation badly,

Baxter pressed on. "To sum it up, while I was saying farewell to you and your father, the children took it upon themselves to hide her on our wagon. Near noon, her stepfather and the other gambler stopped us on the road, asking if we'd seen a runaway girl. Not until after they'd gone on their way did I learn that Sabina was with us."

"You should have sent her packing, then and there."

"We were miles from a settlement by then. Besides, the children were so adamant about wanting her to stay with us that eventually I conceded. And she has done a really fine job. The place is in much better order since she arrived."

Amanda looked at him as if he were just making excuses, as if he hadn't done what any decent Christian in that situation would have done. "I see," she finally said. "But, still . . ." She cocked her head to the side. "You seem as taken with the wench as the children are."

Was he that obvious? The ring of disdain had been unmistakable in Amanda's voice . . . an arrogance in her he'd never noticed before. Still, Baxter knew better than to allow even his gaze to waver. "That's true, I'm quite fond of Sabina. She's a cheery, hardworking woman. But the cabin I built for her should be ample proof of my intentions concerning her."

"Her cabin?" A puzzled frown etched Amanda's brow.

"Aye. When Brother Bremmer learned she was living in the main house with us, he said that for decency's sake, we couldn't stay under the same roof without the bonds of marriage. So I chose to put her under another roof."

Amanda's slow smile testified to her full understanding of what he was telling her. "And a fine-looking cabin it is."

Hopefully that would be Amanda's last question about Sabina. He could not afford for her to probe too deeply into his feelings about the sunshine that had consumed so many of his thoughts

. . . thoughts that again were stealing his attention. "There is one more item we need to discuss. It concerns your Aunt Charlotte."

"Oh?" Amanda's hat feather shimmied as her head tilted to one side.

"If you agree to my proposal of marriage, it shall be with the understanding that she will never live with us."

Her questioning expression collapsed into one of humor as she chuckled. "Have no fear. I readily concede that."

"Thank heavens." He sighed with relief, their greatest hurdle accomplished. But there was still another. "One other thing. Something you might not find as palatable."

Her merriment fled. "Are you saying my aunt is banished, but Sabina stays?"

Baxter caught her hands again. "Nothing of the sort. Fact is, Sabina herself said that the children would warm to you much more readily if she were gone."

Amanda's rosebud mouth opened in surprise. "She did, did she?"

"Aye," he reassured. "And because of the children, I feel we should marry first, let them get used to you being with us, then move to Nashville at a later time."

"Me, live here?" She glanced around uneasily. "But I thought—"

"Only for a few months. The children and I could come to Nashville at Christmastide for the wedding—if that's agreeable with you—then bring you back here until the worst of the spring rains are past. That would also give me time to find a buyer for my place and have a home built for us in Nashville."

"If we locate near Daddy," she encouraged with a wooing expression, "I'm sure he'd be most generous financially." Her expression then flashed into a childlike pout. "But what about that trip to Virginia you promised me?"

"Of course, once we're resettled, we'll take that trip to

Williamsburg. Visit my family and some old friends and see about enrolling Philip in college. He'll be eighteen by then. You remember my oldest son, don't you? He's away, visiting a young lady he's rather fond of. But he should be returning for harvest any day now."

In a burst of exuberance, she flung her arms around him and kissed his cheek. "A trip to Virginia—I can hardly wait! You will take me to some plays and to visit your rich cousin, won't you?"

This moment of absolute joy was the first unbridled emotion he'd ever seen her express. Glad that he could make his betrothed happy, he smiled. "Now that all is as it should be, shall we rejoin the others?"

But as they strolled back toward the parade ground with her arm tucked in the crook of his, he realized Amanda's blithesome spirit had been induced not by their upcoming union, but by the prospective trip. . . . She no more loved him than he did her.

She, too, had been inspired by the preaching at Cane Ridge. She must be following the Lord's lead as he was, trusting that affection would come in time for them both. The important thing for now was that Amanda's dowry would provide tuition for Philip at William and Mary College, and Delia would become an acceptable young lady. Besides, romantic love was a luxury of the young and unencumbered.

And as for what God's will for them all was . . . passing the church, he remembered belatedly to include God in the plan. *And may the good Lord bless this union.*

~

Sabina had tried not to care, but from the instant Baxter had driven into the settlement for the harvest fair, she'd been aware of exactly where he was. When she'd known he was coming to join her at the eating competition, she'd been purely—foolishly—pleased, even though he had Amanda Atwood in tow.

But he'd retreated abruptly, taking Amanda away to be by themselves . . . the very second after Pete Dagget put his hand around her waist.

Now the judge of the corn-eating contest had called a halt, with neither Sammy nor Howie winning. One of the Thomas boys had gobbled down thirteen ears of corn in five minutes. A little disappointed that her boys' frantic efforts had gone for naught, Sabina watched as the judge pinned a blue ribbon onto the chunky boy's shirt spattered down the front with kernels and juice.

Sabina and the overly attentive twins stood a few feet from Jessica and Annie Reardon. The women, along with their kids, burst out laughing as two of the Reardon boys and the two Clay boys pushed away from the table, their eyes bulging as much as their bellies. Disappointed, the competitive lads struggled to their feet, wiping corn mess from their own faces and shirts.

"The footrace for twelve-year-olds and older is next," called a young boy from out of the valley who'd been buzzing around Delia and the Reardon girls all afternoon. "Howie, Jake, are you game?"

"Sure." Tall and blond-headed Jacob took off at a run with some other boys.

Grimacing, Howie glanced over at Sabina and shrugged. Grabbing his distended belly, he chased after them, not one to be left behind. The trio of giggling girls picked up their colorful skirts and followed at a slightly slower pace. And, of course, Sabina and the Reardon mothers tagged along, with the Dagget twins taking up the rear and arguing over who could've eaten the most corn had the judge let them participate.

Surrounded by so many friends, Sabina tried to concentrate

on what should have been a wonderful day. It was hard to take the twins too seriously, but she did enjoy the quiet attention of John Auburn when he was around. Yet she could not help being aware of every second Baxter and Amanda had remained under that tree. She had actually seen the alluring Amanda throw her arms around Baxter's neck and kiss him on the cheek, right there in public. Even now as Sammy edged one of the twins aside to grab Sabina's hand, she glanced toward the blacksmith shop.

Arm in arm, Baxter and Amanda were strolling from that direction to where Amanda's aunt sat with Mistress Reardon. From the gay smile on the young widow's face, Sabina knew without a doubt that Baxter had said the dreaded words. He'd formally asked Amanda to be his bride. Sabina's chest felt as if lead were being poured into it.

"Sabina." Sammy pulled on her hand.

"What?"

"I asked if you think Howie has a chance to win any race after eating all that corn? I know I sure feel queasy."

"If you're gonna throw up," Paul, the twin who'd been edged out by Sammy, said, "do it somewheres else."

"I ain't gonna throw up." Giving Paul a defiant glare, Sammy held on to Sabina all the tighter. Of the four who'd come courting Sabina, Sammy particularly didn't care for the twins or for the attention they paid her. "I just said I felt like it. Why don't you and Pete get in on the greased-hog contest?"

As Sammy tried the latest of many ploys to rid them of the Daggets, Sabina's gaze again took the torturous journey to Baxter. He and Amanda had reached Miss Finch.

With Baxter's aid, the stouter, usually sour version of Amanda rose from the ground, wearing the first full smile Sabina had seen on her. Miss Finch gave her niece a big hug, then opened her arms to Baxter. She was undoubtedly giving her blessing to their betrothal.

Any last fragment of Sabina's hope was dashed. If not for Sammy pulling her along, she would not have had the presence of mind to put one foot in front of the other. She'd never felt such a terrible urge to weep.

Oh, Lord in heaven, she prayed, *please give me the grace to be glad for them. And please, God, please help me to accept your decision if one of these four men must be your choice for me. I think I know what I want, but the heart is deceitful above all things, and I don't trust my own anymore. I must move on. You know my heart has had no room for anyone but Baxter. Only Baxter.*

"The egg toss is after the race," Delia announced. "Is it all right if I partner with Benjamin?"

"And, Sabina, you do it with me," Sammy blurted out fast before either twin had a chance to ask her.

"Aye," she answered woodenly, "on both requests."

The Dagget twins exchanged disgruntled glances as they both sent Sammy a menacing stare.

Grown men threatening a little boy. Sabina could not imagine God would saddle her with either of them. *Please, Lord, not them.*

The hundred-yard dash ended quickly with neither of the corn-eating contestants winning. Clutching their bellies, Howie and Jacob practically crawled back to Sabina and the Reardon women.

Annie caught hold of her splotchy-faced son's shoulder. "I think your stomach needs a chance to settle. Go sit with your pa and the other men. Learn something about them newfangled boats Dan Johnson saw back East. They go upstream without a sail or any polin'."

"He's seen a steamboat?" Forgetting his belly, Jacob sprinted toward the general store's covered porch, where most of the men had congregated, with Howie, Junior, and Sammy chasing after him.

Then Sammy stopped short and ran back. "I almost forgot. We gotta get ready for the egg toss." He shot a glance up at the Daggets and snatched Sabina's hand again. "Let's go. They're doin' it in front of the church."

As Sabina and the remaining group headed for the church-yard, Annie winked at her, then turned to her sister-in-law. "Jessica, since we don't have partners, you take Pete, and I'll take Paul." Annie eyed the two long-limbed brothers jockeying for the one remaining spot next to Sabina. "You fellas can catch, can't you?"

"I can beat Paul any day of the week," Pete bragged.

"Sabina and me can beat you both," Sammy piped in. "Ain't that right?" He looked up at her for support.

"I reckon." But her attention and her floundering heart were elsewhere. Baxter and Amanda were leaving Miss Finch on the Reardon quilt and coming in her direction. Amanda sashayed along, looking like she'd just been offered a shipload of treasure.

After each pairing received their raw egg from Mistress Smith, the twins stationed themselves on each side of Sammy, both grinning straight across at Sabina, and both tossing their eggs from hand to hand. This could get real messy if she didn't forget about Baxter and pay attention.

"You better be as good as you claim," Jessica, standing next to Sabina, shouted to her partner. "I need a ribbon for my collar."

"Me and Bobby are gonna beat you and Mama!" Gracie shouted from down the line. "Aren't we, Robert?"

"You bet!" With big eyes and ears to match, Bobby Bailey had been Gracie's shadow the livelong day.

Good-natured bragging and challenges took up along the

opposing lines, but all Sabina noticed was Baxter and Amanda coming closer, coming with their news.

And in that moment, she knew. She knew that somehow she must make herself pretend to be glad for them, to congratulate them. Sabina's hands began to sweat. Never could she let them or any of these good people surrounding her know how much she loved Baxter and how desperately she wanted him as her own husband . . . more desperately than even she had known. Had God revealed his choice for her after all? Did she trust this feeling enough to believe that God might want the same thing for her that she wanted? Her heart and soul felt as if they were being torn asunder with confusion and . . . longing.

"Listen up!" Betsy Smith, the contest judge, called out. "Everyone take four steps backward and toss your eggs."

Once she and Sammy had counted off the right number, he ever so gently lobbed the fragile orb into the air in a high arc, sending it in Sabina's direction; then he yelled, "Howdy, Pa!"

"Howdy."

Baxter's voice. Directly behind her.

Sabina swung around.

Splat.

The egg hit Amanda's peach floral overskirt.

The widow gasped as yellow and shiny, white slime oozed down the sheer silk material along with bits of shell that clung to the fabric. Her chin jerked up, and sparks of outrage flew from her glittering hazel eyes.

Chapter Twenty-Two

Baxter watched as the broken egg drizzled down Amanda's gown. Absolutely nothing between her and the children seemed to go right. He whipped a kerchief from his vest pocket.

"Everyone take two steps back!" Betsy Smith shouted at the head of the lines, directing the contestants.

Handing Amanda the kerchief, Baxter pulled the flabbergasted woman back from the players.

Standing in front of Amanda, Sabina looked equally stunned. Baxter caught her hand and brought her with them.

Sabina regained her senses first and whisked the square of cloth from Amanda. "Allow me." She stooped and in quick strokes captured most of the excess into the kerchief. "I humbly beg your pardon. I took my eye off the egg." She then removed a smaller handkerchief from a hidden skirt pocket and continued to wipe.

The sight of Sabina in all her yellow radiance dabbing at the remaining mess at Amanda's feet suddenly brought another picture to Baxter's mind—that of Jesus, the very Son of God, as he knelt before one of his disciples, washing the man's dirty feet. Jesus, too, had given no thought to himself as he performed the demeaning task.

Amanda said nothing. She just stood there, staring down at the stubborn stain that had seeped past the silk onto the satin.

Eventually, Sabina rose from the ground. "We need water and maybe some flour to absorb the rest." She glanced about her, then brought her distressed gaze back to Baxter. "Do you know where Inga Bremmer is? I'm sure she has something at her house that would take care of this."

Baxter spotted the older woman at the quilt table.

As he did, Sammy reached them after circumventing the contest still in progress. His expression was hard. "Sabina! How could you look away? The egg was comin' straight to you. And we didn't just lose—you made us be the first ones out!"

"Oh, Sammy, I am sorry. I—"

"It was my fault," Baxter said, taking the blame from Sabina. "I shouldn't have shouted directly behind her."

"That's right," Sammy agreed, his eyes suddenly beaming with new light. "Papa, you go tell that to Missus Smith." He looked back at the game leader, who was motioning for the lines to be made wider for the next toss.

"I can try," Baxter said doubtfully.

"*Excuse me.*" Amanda had finally found her voice. "We have a much more pressing matter here."

"Yes, of course. Samuel, I'm sorry, but the stain on Amanda's gown must be addressed immediately."

"But, Pa, I could've won a blue ribbon. I know it."

"I'll see if Betsy will hold a second game," Sabina volunteered, "while you deliver Mistress Atwood to Inga."

"Thank you." What was he going to do without Sabina when she left them? There she stood with a soiled cloth in each hand, trying to make everything right again. "Come this way, Amanda," he said, taking his betrothed's elbow.

"Baxter," Amanda said as they headed toward the row of display tables, a hint of irritation still in her tone, "I appreciate your affection for your children. But I do believe that your giving way to your youngest, as you have a habit of doing, is spoiling him."

Baxter glanced back at Sammy and Sabina. They walked around the expanding lines of the egg toss, the boy almost as tall as the woman. At ten—going on eleven—he really wasn't such a baby anymore. "I suppose I am too easy on him."

Amanda looked up at Baxter and smiled. "From now on there will be two of us seeing that your children receive the proper guidance they need. That girl you hired spoils all of them shamelessly, lets them do anything they want."

He knew that wasn't true, but to defend Sabina would only add to the already prickly situation. "Well, let's take care of first things first." He nodded down to her egg-stained skirt.

"Quite. The fabric for this gown cost a small fortune. The materials came all the way from Paris." She picked up the skirts for a closer examination. "Oh, I do wish Papa had allowed me to bring Netty. Our house slave would know exactly what to do about the stain."

"Don't fret. I'm sure Inga Bremmer will too."

"I do hope so. This is one of the gowns I plan to wear when we go visiting in Virginia."

Virginia again.

Baxter was grateful that they reached Inga just then, saving him from further discussion.

"*Ja*, I see," Inga said, coming from behind the quilt table after

Baxter described the egg incident. "Ve must do somet'ing fast. You come *mit* me, *Frau*." Taking Amanda's hand, she hurried toward her house.

"I'll see you in a few minutes," he called after them, more glad for the respite than he cared to admit. Turning back, he searched the area beside the church until he caught sight of sunshine yellow.

Sabina had kept her promise to Sammy. The two were in line opposite each other for a second game. About five yards apart, Sammy was gently lobbing an egg to her.

She successfully caught it, her hands cushioning the fragile missile as it reached her. The egg being tossed next to her splatted in the receiver's hand—Delia's, Baxter now noted.

Sammy jumped up and down, crowing at his sister.

Not wanting to distract anyone, Baxter approached the competitors, especially Sammy and Sabina, with more caution than last time. The boy didn't have a single blue ribbon pinned to his chest—only two red ones. And winning had obviously reached paramount importance for him.

With each new toss, more eggs broke. But not Sammy and Sabina's.

Delia spotted Baxter and walked over to stand beside him, along with some lad he didn't know. "Howdy," she prudently whispered. "Where's the widow?"

"Getting the rest of the mess off her gown."

Another toss, and Annie Reardon, along with one of the twins, joined Baxter and the other losers. On the next toss, Gracie, Hope, and their mother, Jessica, all failed, along with others down the line, to catch their delicate orbs. Eggs splatted, mostly short of the catchers.

But not Sammy's. Sabina had thrown overhanded, and the egg sailed past the others and right into the boy's ready hands.

Holding the only unbroken missile, he hooted and ran across the field toward Sabina. "We won! We won!"

Baxter scanned the losers' faces and had a pretty good idea that some of them may have fumbled on purpose. He really did have fine neighbors.

Just before the exuberant Sammy reached Sabina, he tripped over a half-hidden rock and went sprawling, crushing the egg in his hand.

Instantly regaining his feet, he shot a frantic glance to Betsy Smith. "We still won, didn't we?"

"Aye," the sweet-natured woman shouted back. "Come get your ribbons."

Sabina threw an arm around the boy, laughing as they went.

Baxter followed after them and watched as Betsy pinned the folded ribbon on Sammy's dirty shirt. "Congratulations!" Baxter said, patting his son on the head.

Sabina whirled around, as startled as she'd been when he approached during the prior game.

"You, too, Sabina." He gave her an encouraging smile that came as easily to him as water flowing downhill. "You two make a great team. Where's Howie? I'd like to speak with the kids before Amanda returns."

"Oh, yes, I was expecting that." The last trace of Sabina's smile vanished. "Howie was over with the men a few minutes ago. I'll go with you. Maybe I can help."

Once Sabina's ribbon was pinned, they went to collect Delia. The lad who'd been his daughter's partner in the game was still beside her, telling her something with lots of facial expressions and hand movements while she listened, her large brown eyes raptly following his every gesture.

"Young man," he said to his daughter's admirer, "will you excuse Delia for a few minutes? We need to have a family discussion." Baxter then turned to Sammy. "Run ahead and fetch Howie. We'll meet you at that empty table over there." He pointed to the rows of eating tables.

When Howie and Sammy returned, not a smile could be seen on their faces or on the faces of those already seated at the long table. They all knew something was brewing; foreboding haunted all their eyes.

Baxter inhaled. Best to say it quickly and be done with it. "Amanda and I have come to an understanding. Our wedding will be in Nashville at Christmastide, and then Amanda—*without her aunt*—will live here with us till spring. Then we'll all move to Nashville. Once we're resettled, we'll take a trip back to Virginia to visit our family."

No one uttered a word.

Delia fiddled with a ringlet.

Sammy rubbed a finger across his satin ribbons.

Howie stared at Sabina, who sat across from him and Baxter. "What about you?" he asked. "I reckon you'll be marrying one of them Dagget twins straightaway."

"No, not them." Her lips parted. "I take that back. If one of them is the Lord's choice for me, then I will. But far as I can tell, they ain't—aren't—for me."

"What about them other two jaspers?" Sammy asked. "Are you gonna leave us for one of them? We built you that house, you know. You don't have to go nowhere. You could just stay on with us forever."

Delia grabbed her arm. "Please, Sabina. Don't go."

Sabina looked across at Baxter, her eyes a pale sea of sorrow. Then she held the boys in her gaze. "I will promise you this—if the Lord's willing, I shall stay until y'all leave for the wedding in Nashville."

"In the meantime," Baxter ordered, "you kids will all treat

Amanda with the utmost respect. It wouldn't hurt, either, if you could come up with some kind word for her."

"Yes," Sabina agreed. "Make a point to do it this evening. She leaves in the morning. Remember, a kind word turns away wrath."

"Wrath?" Sammy cried. "You mean she's gonna be yellin' at us?"

"No," Baxter answered for Sabina. "That is *not* what she meant. She meant, if you don't want trouble, don't cause it." A very liberal interpretation at best, but it fit the moment. "And I, for one," he added, placing his hand over Sabina's, "am very happy you're staying on until Christmas."

"Me too." Sammy slapped his own hand over Baxter's and Sabina's.

"Me too," Howie and Delia chorused, their own hands stacking atop the others.

Sabina's head jerked up, her gaze shooting above Baxter's head. She quickly withdrew her hand from the bottom of the pile.

Baxter swiveled around. *Amanda.*

At that moment, the church bell rang. Suppertime. *Thank you, God.*

Baxter disentangled himself from the others and his feet from the bench. Standing up, he caught hold of his betrothed's arm. His other hand, though, still tingled from the feel of Sabina's fingers beneath his. "Shall we go eat?"

"You jest." Amanda glared up at him as if he'd suggested they go to the gallows.

Had she seen his head together with Sabina's and again felt slighted?

"Surely you've noticed my attire."

Taking a second look, he realized her distress was caused by her appearance rather than their little conference. She no longer wore her own day gown, but an ill-fitting black linen with a simple shawl collar. Against the somber clothing, her elegant bonnet and gloves looked rather silly.

"Mistress Bremmer loaned this to me. She will need to keep my gown overnight. Needless to say, I shan't allow myself to be seen in this ridiculous costume."

"Of course. I'll see you home immediately." He glanced back at Sabina and the children.

"You don't expect us to go too, do you?" Howie asked as Sabina contemplated one of her hands—the one Baxter had covered with his own.

"Howie brought his fife," Sammy said, taking up the argument, "and the violin for Sabina. And me an' Delia brought the drums and whisks she made us. After lunch, we practiced 'Greensleeves' with Jake and the other kids, and we're set to play it for everyone right after supper."

Baxter studied Sabina again. When exactly had she made the music makers for the younger children? He'd been so occupied with Amanda and her aunt, he hadn't noticed another of her many acts of kindness to his children. Tearing his gaze away, he returned his attention to his children. "Of course you may stay. Have a good time."

Turning away, he took Amanda's elbow. "I'll take you to the carriage, then fetch your aunt."

But all the while he escorted her to the carriage, he wished he could stay.

Chapter Twenty-Three

Sabina sat at the table with such mixed feelings, her mind was in a whirl as she watched Baxter walking away from the harvest fair with his betrothed.

"La," Delia said, "the widow's managed to take Papa from us again."

"Well," Howie argued, "'tis better than all of us having to go home."

"And leave all that good food over there." Sammy jumped up and took off toward the line forming at the three long tables loaded with the dishes the womenfolk had contributed.

Howie started to follow.

Sabina caught his arm. "Wait. What about your pa and his guests?"

After a moment of convincing, the three of them rushed madly to the head of the food line, made their excuses to those they displaced, and filled plates for Baxter, the two ladies, and their slave before the carriage departed.

With their offerings in hand, they raced across the grassy field and past the sprawl of parked vehicles, reaching the fancy rig just as Baxter was helping Miss Finch up to her cushioned leather seat.

"We didn't want you to leave without something to eat," Delia said, handing a plain wooden trencher to the older woman.

Miss Finch glanced down at it, then eyed not Delia but Sabina. "I see. So, this is how you plan to slide around your duty to us."

"Ma'am?" Sabina wasn't prepared for hostility.

Baxter stepped between them and took the two trenchers Sabina held. "Thank you for your thoughtfulness. Do enjoy the rest of the evening, you and the kids." The words were pleasant, but his expression was grim.

Sabina turned back toward the large gathering, knowing she had been dismissed. Her confusion lingered as she walked away. Had Baxter been angry with her or protecting her?

Delia and Howie caught up with her almost immediately, their own faces hard-set.

"At least Bolie was glad to get his supper," Howie remarked once they were a fair distance from the departing carriage.

"Why on earth does Papa want to marry her?" Delia bemoaned. "Can't he see how miserable we're all going to be?"

Sabina caught the girl's hand and squeezed it. "Dear heart, you must keep in mind Mistress Atwood's aunt will *not* be living with you. And in the meantime, if this is the Lord's will for your family, pray every day that the Lord will give you a love over-flowing for your new mother. With a love that will 'passeth all understanding.'"

Delia shot her a withering look. "It passeth my understanding, that's for sure."

"More trouble's comin'," Howie grumbled.

Sabina looked up and saw the Dagget twins waiting for her return. They were now joined by Grady Jessup and John Auburn.

"Oh, dear," came out of Sabina's mouth before she could stop it. As she and the kids approached the men, she wondered if God would give her a love overflowing for one of them—a love that could match what she felt for Baxter. She turned to the youngsters. "You two run along to your friends. I'll see you after supper."

The four men came walking out to intercept her: the tall, dark, and long-bodied twins; the ever-smiling one who had as many big plans in his head as curls on his head; and the leaner built, quiet one.

"You said you'd spend time with Pete and me till *after* supper; then them two could have you." Paul jerked a nod in Jessup and Auburn's direction.

Sabina cringed at the thought that these men had been arguing over her, especially in such a public place. "I don't recall saying that."

Grady, his eyes narrowing, brushed past Paul. "I thought not. You nooned with the Daggets, Miss Sabina. It's only fair you sup with me and John."

"Aye, that does seem only fair." Sabina prayed that the Daggets would back off graciously. She turned to the twins. "This afternoon has been most enjoyable," she fibbed politely. "Thank you for the time you spent with me."

"All right," Pete Dagget muttered begrudgingly, his black brows dipping as he eyed the other two suitors. "We'll go. For now."

"Sabina," came a call from a central eating table. Annie

waved an arm above her head from where she sat with the other adults of her family. "Get your food and join us."

The Reardons had saved most of a bench for her and her beaus. Smiling, Sabina waved back, thanking God for the Reardons' care and understanding.

Supper with these two suitors on either side wasn't nearly as crowded as lunch had been with the Daggets. Grady did most of the talking during the meal but didn't get directly in her face. Out of politeness and even a little sympathy for the less confident but more appealing John Auburn, Sabina made a point of including him in the conversations.

Yet, she again felt as if she were performing a juggling act. As a young girl, the thought of having several beaus vying for her attention had seemed titillating, but the reality sorely tried her patience.

Of course, if she'd just make a decision, a choice, her life would be much simpler. The idea of ending the men's competition, especially on a day like this one, was very tempting. But a hasty decision would live with her the rest of her life. Pestered as she was, she knew she had to be sure she heard the Lord correctly, that the choice was his—and not just her own unguided decision. She must fight against her feelings for Baxter and listen to the Lord. Was he gently leading her to John Auburn?

". . . and I insist on the first dance," Grady said, abruptly changing the subject after several minutes of droning on about some book on explosives and fireworks he'd just read. "What do you say, Miss Sabina?"

"I reckon that'll be fine," she agreed, expecting nothing less from him.

"Then I reckon I should put in for the last dance," John said quietly.

She turned to him and smiled. "It shall be yours." If she had to pick one of the four at this very minute, John would be her choice. He wasn't so bad, really. If she put her mind to it, mayhap she could muster sufficient feelings for him. She would probably never feel about him the way she felt about Baxter, but John, at least, wouldn't be in her face pressing her for something all the livelong day.

But selecting the least bothersome was insufficient reason to wed anyone for life. Still, she really should start to seriously consider John Auburn. She couldn't imagine the Lord saddling her with one of the others. Especially one of the twins.

Supper was almost over. Would the Daggets try to bully their way close again during the dancing?

She glanced down the rows of crowded tables until she came across them. The sight sent a wave of relief through her. For a change, they had some other unfortunate young miss cornered. Never having seen the lass before, Sabina surmised that she was from another settlement. Her own spirits rose at the prospect of an evening without the Daggets.

"Sabina." Sitting across from her, Jessica nodded toward the head table, where Brother Bremmer presided. "I believe they're waiting for you."

The Clay kids and several of the Reardons had gathered next to the pastor—the boys and Delia with their homemade music makers, along with Gracie and Hope, the singers of their little band.

"If you'll excuse me," Sabina said.

Her escorts readily leapt to their feet, giving her space to dislodge herself from the bench.

Straightening the gathers of her buttercup yellow skirt, she explained, "The Clay and Reardon young'uns has a bit of enter-tainment they been practicing to give."

She started toward the front, walking past numerous staring

227

eyes, and she became more than a little nervous. She should have checked the condition of her hair. Was the back of her skirt too wrinkled? Putting herself forward like this, would folks think she was too full of herself? Or would they laugh at her, think her a fool? How on earth had she let the children talk her into performing with them? She'd been so preoccupied, she simply hadn't given it serious thought.

Her hands were trembling by the time she reached Howie, who held out the violin and bow to her. Her fingers quivered like willow leaves in the wind.

The other musicians—except for the singers—didn't seem to have her problem. They stood there, grinning or giggling. But Gracie's blue eyes and Hope's colorless ones had the same scared-rabbit look that churned within hers.

"Your voices are a beautiful blend," she said, wishing to take away their fright. "You'll do just fine."

"Play loud," Gracie pleaded.

The last thing Sabina wanted to do was attract undue attention. "We all will," she heard herself saying.

"We're ready," Jacob Reardon said to Brother Bremmer, a washboard and splayed stick at the ready position.

The pastor's double chins tripled as he grinned and stood. "Friends and neighbors, some of da *kinders* haf a special treat for us to go *mit* da dessert. Dey is performing da old Englander song 'Greensleeves.'"

Standing to one side of the mostly kitchen band of skin-stretched pots, sticks, and spoons, Sabina inhaled a deep breath, then raised Howie's violin to her chin. "One, two, three." And she swept her bow up to start the ancient melody.

During the first few strands, the young people played hesitantly, and the girls sang almost without sound. Sabina was obliged to play louder to give them more courage.

Then, blessedly, the performers and the tempo came together, and though amateurish, they rendered a tuneful and airy piece. Sabina forgot herself and swelled with pride for them all. She glanced out at the audience and saw friendly, encouraging smiles.

Her only regret . . . Baxter was not here to see his children perform. A stringed quartet they may not be, but she had no doubt he, too, would have been as proud of them as she was.

~

"'Greensleeves was all my joy . . .'"

A raucous rendition of the old tune came to Baxter through the night. At long last, Sabina and the youngsters were nearing home.

"'Greensleeves was my delight . . .'"

Baxter had been sitting on the porch, drinking hot cider to ward off the autumn chill. The two ladies had since retired to their beds. He'd been waiting in the dark for the return of his family, wishing he'd been able to enjoy more of the fair with them. And from the enthusiasm in their singing, they'd surely had a grand time.

Rising from his chair, he walked to the end of the porch to catch sight of them. An approaching lantern light jostled and flickered through the trees, accompanied by the sound of happy singing, the clomp of the weary horses, and the jingling of chain and harness.

As the noise increased, Baxter hopped down from the porch and strode up the path to meet them. The last thing he wanted was to awaken Amanda's crabby aunt.

"Quiet down, now," he heard Sabina say, still a distance away, "or we'll wake the house."

The singing ceased, replaced by loud whispers.

"But I want to tell Papa."

"And take a chance on waking the old witch?"

"Boys, you promised to be respectful." That whisper was no doubt Sabina's.

"Besides," a thinner whisper added, "they're leaving in the morning, and we don't have to worry about them again until Christmas." Delia.

"Hallelujah!" Howie whisper-shouted.

"Hallelujah!" Sammy repeated even louder.

The children really were going to have a problem with his marriage.

The horses clopped much closer now. The lantern light was almost upon Baxter. "Good evening," he said.

"Papa?"

"Aye. 'Tis I."

Thunder and Snowflake passed by, and the wagon drew alongside Baxter. All four were huddled up on the bench seat, sharing the quilt.

The children started talking all at once as he walked along with the wagon.

"Shh," he warned. "You don't want to wake the ladies."

"We had the best time," Delia whispered. "Artie Hall and Tim Matthews both wanted to dance every reel with me. And Tim said I was the prettiest girl at the fair. He came from the other side of the Nashville road. Artie—his family lives just over the hills—he says I have the most beautiful brown eyes he's ever seen."

"So?" Howie, driving the team from the far side of the bench, dismissed his sister's words. "The kid ain't seen all that many. Just about everybody else in Tennessee has blue eyes. On the other hand, Betty Jane thinks that all of me is just plain good-lookin'."

Sitting closest to Baxter, Sabina burst out laughing, which she instantly muffled with her hands.

Baxter, too, had trouble keeping a lid on his mirth.

"Papa." Sammy was deadly serious now. "You should've stayed there with us. Sent them fussy women home by theyselves. You missed our performance."

"That you did," Delia further reprimanded.

"Ever'body clapped real loud," Sammy continued, "and said they'd never heard 'Greensleeves' done so purty."

"Folks over on Clear Creek has asked us to come and play at their pumpkin-growing contest next month." Howie's pride was obvious as he reined the horses to a stop in front of the barn.

"You don't say." Baxter felt even worse that he hadn't been there for such an important moment. "That's the truest kind of compliment." Reaching up, he lifted Sabina from the box seat.

As she came into his arms all warm and fragrant, he whispered "Thank you" next to her ear.

Her eyes caught the lantern light as she looked into his. "You were sorely missed." The words were for him only.

His heart jolted crazily as he held this miracle that had come into their lives. He never felt this way with Amanda. Regaining his composure, he set her feet on the ground, then quickly reached up for Delia. Still, he was wholly aware that Sabina continued to stand exactly where he'd set her, unmoving. Had she been as struck by their private moment as he?

Abruptly she went into action, pulling down the quilt and folding it. "Howie," she called up to him, "you and Sammy put the horses away right. Rub 'em down and give 'em some extra oats."

"It's late," Sammy whined. "I'm tired."

"Aye," she retorted, "and so are the animals that the good Lord has placed in your care."

Sammy stopped complaining and climbed down behind Howie.

As always, Baxter was amazed at how readily the youngsters did Sabina's bidding. They'd become so attached to her. Her leaving would be very hard on them.

On him.

Then he remembered what he'd overheard Delia say. *It's a long time until Christmas.* Yes, she'd be with them for at least another six or seven weeks. Time to get used to the idea of her leaving.

"Boys," he said, "let me help you with the animals. Together we'll have them bedded down in no time."

Chapter Twenty-Four

Sabina woke with a start.

The sun shone directly into her eyes! It must be eight o'clock. Or even nine!

"Delia, get up! Quick." She gave the girl beside her a shake, then leapt from the bed.

"Huh? What?" The words spilled groggily from Delia's lips.

"Quick. Get dressed. We overslept, and the ladies are leaving this morning."

"Good." She rolled over. "Wake me when they're gone."

"Don't be ridiculous." Sabina ripped the blankets and colorful gift quilt from Delia. "That is no way to treat company."

Ignoring any further complaints, Sabina rushed through her morning toilet and ran out the door, tying her apron strings as she went. Ignoring the cold dampness beneath her bare feet, she sped along beside the last of the corn, fully aware that breakfast should have been on the table an hour ago. *What a dreadful send-off.*

Rounding the chicken coop, she spotted the carriage, with trunks tied at the rear and the horses hitched. The ladies' things were loaded and ready to go. Realizing she was much too tardy to make a difference, Sabina slowed to catch her breath.

As she did, Delia caught up, stepping directly in front of her, the child's hair hanging down in tangles. "Oh, la, we are late. Lace the back of my dress, please."

Sabina did so and also ran fingers through the girl's dark hair just as the ladies walked out of the main house and down the porch steps, followed by Baxter and the boys. The women wore durable dark velvet traveling costumes with feathered bonnets to match, looking as prosperous as ever. They came to a stop beside the open coach door.

Sabina hesitated to go any farther. She'd failed in her duty so miserably.

Delia grabbed her hand. "Come on. I ain't facin' 'em alone."

For some odd reason, Baxter didn't seem the least perturbed when he spotted Sabina and Delia. He smiled warmly. "Good, you're up just in time. Delia, come say Godspeed to our guests."

Lagging behind, Sabina noted a steady plume of smoke rising from the chimney of the main house, which gave her hope that the women had been fed, but she lacked the courage to ask.

"Farewell, children," Miss Finch said, her chin tucked, her expression stern. "We will meet again at Christmastide." She put out a hand to Baxter for assistance and mounted the lower step of the coach. Then, in that obviously disdainful way of hers, she looked back, pinning Sabina with a withering glare. After what seemed like an eternity, she shifted her narrowed gaze on Baxter. "We expect that matter we spoke of to be resolved by then, too."

The words were loud and distinct, and Sabina guessed that she was the 'matter' to which the older woman alluded. Her own chin hiked. She would not let the spinster know the hurt those words caused.

"Children—I mean—young lady and gentlemen," Amanda Atwood said in her perfectly modulated tones, "we have enjoyed our stay here and look forward to your visit. But in the meantime, I'd like to show our appreciation by sending each of you a gift."

Their interest definitely piqued, all three riveted their attention on the young widow.

"What would you boys like?"

Howie didn't hesitate. "I'd like one of them sideways metal flutes like the schoolmaster has."

"That's much too expensive," his father said as he handed the young widow into the carriage. "Pick something else."

Mistress Atwood placed a hand on his arm. "Baxter, dear, don't fret about the expense. Your days of pinching pennies are over. Dear boy, if there's a flute to be found in Nashville, I'll see that you have it."

"Why, thank you, ma'am." With enthusiasm in his voice, the lad ducked his head in an abbreviated bow.

Sammy pushed ahead of his older brother. "If Howie gets a real flute, then I want one of them big drums like drummer boys in the Revolution had."

"My lands," the young widow exclaimed on a light, airy laugh, "you could create quite a racket with one of those."

"I know," Sammy agreed with a devilish lilt in his voice.

"Well, if your father doesn't mind . . ." She then gazed past the boys to Delia. "I already know what you'll want. I'll be sending you a fur-trimmed cloak with a matching bonnet and muff, so you'll be stylish as well as warm on your winter trip to Nashville. What color of cloak would please you?"

Delia's surprised expression spread into a delighted smile. "Color? I don't know. What do you think?"

Mistress Atwood's smile relaxed into a more natural one. "With your hair and those remarkable eyes? I think a ruby russet would be simply stunning."

"You do?"

Delia's eager expression told Sabina that the rich widow had won her affection. She could watch no more. Swinging away in her drab homespun and aproned simplicity, Sabina headed for the main house. Even if breakfast had already been cooked, there'd be dishes to do.

And two days hence, she'd be going to Sunday dinner at John Auburn's. If the Clays were ready to cast her off, she had several other places she could go.

Her conscience edged in, reminding her that the widow was to be the kids' mother and Baxter's wife. Loving Amanda Atwood was the right and proper thing for them to do. Hadn't Baxter himself told her that the woman was the Lord's choice for him?

∼

On the Sabbath, Sabina wore to church the indigo gabardine day gown that Mistress Reardon had made over for her. A pure white, lace-trimmed shawl collar went particularly well over it. Unlike the prior Sunday, today she felt confident that her clothing was adequate. She knew she fit right in—hand in glove— with the folks here in this woodsy valley.

At the close of the service, she took a last look at Baxter standing on the church step. His face was unreadable as he watched her walk away with John Auburn.

Sammy stood beside his father, frowning as he waved only

once. At least he wasn't averse to showing his disapproval of her leaving for dinner at the home of the masons.

"I thought you'd prefer riding double with me." The lean young man pointed toward his sorrel pony with white stockings. It was tied at the back of a rig. "Gets kinda noisy in the wagon."

"That's fine," Sabina said, though happy noise never bothered her in the least. She'd noticed that the quiet fellow didn't do well around crowds. He'd escorted her away from the particularly talkative congregation as quickly as possible, although she would have enjoyed hearing a retelling of the great time they'd all had at the harvest fair.

John hadn't even introduced her to the rest of his family. She'd seen him sitting with two women, their ages not that different from hers. The tall, much sturdier-built one with black hair had helped the day they all worked on the quilt and had been a real talker. Sabina reckoned her to be a sister-in-law, since the men were sandy-headed and whipcord thin. The other woman's face was hidden within a large-billed bonnet, and Sabina didn't recall seeing her at church before. Most likely she was the sickly maiden sister she'd heard the kids mention.

When Sabina and John reached his pony, he had no problem lifting her onto his saddle, despite his slight build. She knew he did more than his share of hoisting and hefting as a man who worked with stone. His hesitant gray eyes, more than his mouth, smiled as he ventured to look directly at her before he mounted behind her.

Riding in the circle of John's arms as he guided the horse was the closest Sabina had ever been to him. This man had never attempted so much as to hold her hand. Although he'd asked her to dance at the harvest fair, that last reel had been out of the question for him. He'd brought her a cup of punch and cookies instead. Even now, she could feel the tension in his arms. Poor fellow, he was so terribly shy.

Along the wooded lane leading north from the settlement, they traveled in silence, while others they passed going home from church sang hymns or chatted with one another. Upon seeing Sabina and John, folks waved and shouted greetings. She waved back, but John merely nodded.

Finally, Sabina could be still no longer. "The weather's starting to cool off fast," she said, testing a safe topic. "When do you think we'll get our first frost?"

He said nothing for a moment; then after a long pause, he spoke quietly. "Sometime before November, I 'spect."

"The trees turn such beautiful colors then. I always love this time of year."

Hoping he'd contribute something as they rode past fields and woods, she smoothed her hand over his mare's flaming mane and waited . . . and waited.

Until finally he spoke. "That's our place over yonder."

Glancing off to the right, she saw that the land had been cleared from the road all the way to the Auburn home place. With the fields mostly harvested, the farm looked like the others in the valley except for the structures. The upper part of both homes was of milled boards and painted, one pink— an odd but cheery color—the other a somber gray. Their lower halves were of stone, and they had massive chimneys at each end. Several of the outbuildings were also built of stone—a testament to the family trade.

John reined the pony onto the Auburns' track. Sabina remembered that she and John had left the church before the rest of his family, giving her more time to spend with a man who had nothing to say. He'd never been much of a talker, but today he was practically mute.

He brought the pony to a halt in front of what looked like the older of the two homes, the gray one. Swinging a long leg over the horse's rump, he lowered himself to the ground, then reached up and brought her down.

As he did, Sabina realized she was experiencing none of the thrilling feelings she felt when Baxter put his hands to her waist. None whatsoever.

A wagon turned with the usual clomp and rattle onto the Auburn path. But it was the sound of voices that Sabina appreciated, and that did send a sensation through her—one of relief. People were coming. People who talked.

"Howdy," shouted the young woman Sabina had noticed not only in the Auburns' church pew several times but also at the cabin raising. Black-headed and large-boned, with a wide generous mouth, she sat between father and son. In her arms lay a sleeping infant. "The name's Esther, Newcomb's wife. We ain't had much chance to meet, the way my two little brothers has taken you plumb over."

"Your brothers?"

"You know, them rascally twins."

Amazed that no one had mentioned that John's sister-in-law was a Dagget, Sabina turned and stared at him.

He was busy as usual, studying the ground.

It occurred to her that if he wouldn't discuss the weather, he certainly wouldn't discuss a relationship to the Daggets.

As their rather haggard-looking father drew the wagon team to a halt, Sabina stepped forward. "My name's Sabina Erhardt, and I'm real pleased to meet y'all."

"You already know me, from when we built your chimney," John's older brother said with a friendly smile. "I'm Newcomb, the handsome one of the family." A bit more filled out than John, his friendly grin and manner lent an almost prankish buoyancy to his thin face. He hopped down, then reached up to assist his wife and baby.

John strode to the back of the wagon to help down the girl Sabina had never seen before today. Painfully thin, she looked to be not much younger than Sabina. Yet, even now Sabina had a hard time seeing the girl's face, it was recessed so deeply within her dark gray bonnet.

"'Course, you know Pa," Newcomb continued as he swung his wife to the ground.

The older, weathered, and graying man merely gave a quick jerk of his chin and grunted as he snapped the reins over scruffy brown geldings and drove them toward the barn.

"Come on in," Esther said with a commanding smile. "Everything's cooked. We just got to heat it up. Meg, you come and help."

Sabina glanced over at John.

He merely shrugged. Even among his own people he wasn't speaking.

For the life of her, Sabina couldn't figure out why he'd even bothered to invite her to dinner.

As she followed Esther and the slump-shouldered girl inside to a pleasing aroma of fresh-baked bread, Esther turned back to her again. "I reckon you ain't met Meggie, neither. She don't feel up to comin' to church services all that often."

"I'm very pleased to meet you, Meg." She wished she could've added that John had spoken warmly of her, but that simply wasn't so.

Meg glanced out from beneath her bonnet with those same mournful gray eyes as her brother's. "How do," she mumbled, then looked away again.

"Take off your bonnet, Meg," her sister-in-law ordered while laying her sleeping baby in a cradle at the other end of the simply furnished room. "Then stoke the fire up under the black-eyed peas."

With three sets of hands working on a hearty meal of ham and peas, squash, potatoes, and corn, it was soon on the bare oak table along with a pitcher of cold milk and a loaf of warm bread. Esther walked outside and rang the triangle hanging from the eaves, and within seconds the three men tromped in, neatly washed up with their light brown hair combed.

Newcomb brought an extra chair from a back room, and the others took their places. Stony-faced Mr. Auburn sat at one end with affable Newcomb at the other. Sabina was seated next to John. Across from her sat a third set of opposites—smiling, bustling Esther and the wraithlike Meg. There was no way Sabina could feel comfortable. She had no idea what was or was not acceptable at this table of contradictions.

"Lord," Mr. Auburn began without warning, "bless this food we planted and harvested with our own sweat and muscle. We leave it to you to see that it nourishes our bodies. Amen. Pass the bread, Esther."

Sabina realized her mouth was agape. She quickly shut it and accepted the bowl of squash John held before her. Scooping a helping into her wooden trencher, she stole a glance around the table. No one seemed the least disturbed by the arrogance of the older man's prayer; their attentions were solely upon filling their wooden plates.

Weren't these supposed to be God-fearing Christians?

Silence prevailed until everyone had taken several bites of the simple but tasty pork-flavored fare.

Then, buttering a thick slice of bread, Esther glanced up at Sabina. "Miss Erhardt, John says your folks hail from the Pennsylvania Dutch. That right?"

"Aye." Did the conversation have to start with a personal question about her?

"I'm surprised you don't say *ja* and *da* like the Bremmers do," Newcomb said with a grin.

"I wasn't born there, myself."

"Inga Bremmer said your folks has fallen on hard times," Esther continued with a directness Sabina could have done without. "That you had to hire out."

"Aye."

The prying woman shifted her attention to her milk and took a swallow, then continued, "If you don't mind my askin', what sort of wages is Mr. Clay payin' you? For all his airs, he ain't never seemed no better fixed than the rest of us."

Airs? Sabina did not appreciate Esther Auburn's inference. But she was a guest at their table. "Our arrangement is one of mutual need."

"Ha! I thought so. He ain't payin' much of anything, is he?" She leaned forward, her spoon in hand. "A lass needs to think of her future. The more you can bring to a marriage, the better match you'll make."

John, Meg, and their father didn't even look up from their trenchers during this exchange. It was as if they'd left the room. But Newcomb chuckled. "I wouldn't say she has much to worry about, Esther. She sure don't lack for beaus. I seen her dancin' with every young buck at the fair—" he slid a glance to John— "'ceptin' you, little brother."

Sabina avoided looking at John but noticed that the knuckles holding his fork had turned white. As backward as he already was, his older brother shouldn't tease him about it.

"Brother Bremmer don't hold with dancin'." At the other end of the table, Mr. Auburn startled Sabina with his abrupt statement.

"La, I do wish I'd known that." Sabina reddened slightly. Had she behaved unseemly? The pastor and Inga had always treated her with pure kindness.

"No need to take on over it," Newcomb said. "Rolf is a Baptist, but he decided a long time ago not to make a fuss less'n someone brings a jug of hard cider or corn likker. He just sits there, keepin' a eye on all of us."

"He ain't the only one," Mr. Auburn growled, his deep-set eyes narrowing.

After that, little was said at the table, just pass this or that. Sabina was vastly relieved when the older Mr. Auburn scooted back his chair.

"Best get on out and see how ol' Minnie's doin'."

As he strode out the door, Esther settled back in her chair, visibly more relaxed. "His milk cow's been off her feed the last couple of days."

At the far end of the room, the baby started making gurgling sounds.

"Newy, dear," Esther said, her voice changing into a sweet pleading tone. "Would you run over to the house and get Baby Jim's sugar rag? I need to clean up here before I go feed him."

Newcomb didn't hesitate. "Sure thing, darlin'. I'll take him on over with me." Leaving his seat, he went to fetch the babe. Smiling tenderly down at his wee son, he gathered up the bundle and walked out the door, cooing closely at the infant's face as he went.

"We live over to the other house," Esther explained. "We only eat here on Sundays, thank goodness. I don't think I could put up with that sour old man more'n once a week. Newcomb says he's been an ol' grudger ever since his wife passed on. But that's been a dozen years or more." She pushed back her chair. "Come on, Meg. Let's get these dishes done before the ol' goat comes back in."

John, who hadn't said a single word from the moment he'd sat down to eat, finally spoke, but only to excuse himself from the table. Then without another utterance, he walked out the door.

Rising from her chair, Sabina stared after him, amazed, as she shook out her indigo skirt folds.

Esther snorted. "I know how you feel. I'm surprised he worked up the gumption a'tall to ask you to come for dinner. Like Meg here, he keeps to himself, for the most part. But I'll tell you one thing: as bashful as he is, he must want you real bad to try an' go up against the likes of Grady Jessup and my brothers to court you."

Sabina glanced out the window and saw that John had knelt down to pet an orange tomcat that was rubbing arch-backed against his leg. She saw his lips moving. Why, he was talking to the cat! A tenderness for him filled her. The fellow did have love to give—he just didn't feel free to express it to the people around him.

And neither did his sister. Sabina wanted to cry for both of them. Instead, she stepped close to Meg and smiled at the frail girl. "Let me help you clear the table."

When the dishes were finished, Sabina walked outside and found John standing beside his white-stockinged pony, holding onto the reins. She reckoned that it was his way of telling her it was time to go without his actually saying the words.

The trip home would be much longer than merely a return ride to the church, since the Clays lived far beyond it in the opposite direction. Sabina dreaded what she expected to be another long-drawn silence.

Yet why had he asked her here? This visit made no sense. Not only had he not talked to her, he'd scarcely even looked at her. It was as if the entire experience had been a painful chore for him. Very strange . . . particularly since he'd been the suitor she'd been favoring.

Chapter Twenty-Five

As Sabina had expected, John Auburn uttered nary a single word on the ride from his family's farm to the Clays'. She felt the tension in his surrounding arms even more tautly than before. Upon seeing the leaning oak that signaled the turnoff to the Clays', a wave of grateful relief washed over Sabina, but she schooled her breathing so he wouldn't suspect. The last thing she wanted was to make him feel worse than he probably already did.

Suddenly Auburn jerked on the pony's reins and halted the animal. "I–uh—" he stammered. "Please, I–I wanted you to see my family, to see what they're like at home. I didn't want to play you false. To . . . to . . ."

"Yes?" She could feel him trembling behind her. She turned to look back at him. "It's just me here. Say what's on your mind."

"I–I kept quiet today 'cause I didn't want to get in the way, have you think things is any different. But I ain't no slacker. I work hard . . ."

"I know you do. I saw how fast you and your menfolk built the chimney for my cabin."

"Thing is, I ain't got nothin' of my own, 'ceptin' this pony, my rifle, and my clothes. That is, till Pa dies."

"I see."

"He says that then half of everything on the place will be mine."

Sabina wasn't exactly sure how to respond. He was so rigid that she could see a vein on his forehead bulging.

"It ain't like we're so poor we don't have spendin' money from time to time. And we always have plenty to eat."

"I can see that," she said gently, hoping to calm him. "The meal today was real tasty."

He pulled himself up with a deep breath. "I reckon what I'm tryin' to say is, I know my family's kinda hard to take."

"You don't feel so at home there with your folks, do you?"

He exhaled in a rush, and she felt the tension begin to leave him. "No. I don't reckon I do. But if you'd be willin' to marry me, I'd build us a house far enough away so's we wouldn't be bothered less'n we wanted to be. The far side of the fields, if that'd suit you." His words picked up speed as he continued. "I know you'd be a pleasure to live with, 'cause I seen how the Clay young'uns took to you right off. And I'd be a good husband to you. I wouldn't never lay a hand to you, like some men I seen."

She placed her own hand over his, which had a clenched hold on the pony's reins. "I know you wouldn't. And I think your offer of marriage is a fine, honest one." Viewing the desperation and, yes, the sincerity in his dove gray eyes, she did not doubt that he was the sort of man a woman would never be ashamed to call husband. As shy as he was, he'd shown how much he wanted a life with her by not letting the other three suitors shove him aside with their bragging and strutting ways. Steady and utterly courageous he'd been, all things considered.

But was he the Lord's choice for her? Could she love him enough?

"Mr. Auburn, before I can give you an answer, I must search the Lord's heart—and mine. I won't marry anyone unless I know I'm following the will of God."

He sat back. "I don't—how—when will you know?"

"I'm not sure. God has a way of picking his own time." Then she looked up at John with resolute determination. "I want you to be praying right along with me for the Lord's guidance in this matter. I could never wed a man who didn't court the Lord's favor with the same perseverance that he did mine."

For once, John's gaze didn't falter—he returned her steady stare. "I'm ashamed to say, I ain't thought to pray about this a'tall. I know I should have. I will. I surely will."

Unable to keep from smiling at his guileless candor, she squeezed his hand. Many a man would've lied about it to put himself in a better light. "With both of us praying, we're sure to get us an answer real soon."

∼

Sabina had another of her restless nights in prayer, seeking the will of God. Rising to a chilly, misty morning, she bundled herself within an old quilt and hurried to her secret place by the stream. Not taking her usual spot on the flat stone, she remained standing, gazing above the trees to the north.

"Mama, I purely hope my letter found its way to you and that you're looking back at me this very second." She reached forth a hand. "Are you there? I like to imagine you're right here in front of me when I talk." She gave a little nod and continued. "John Auburn, the quiet one I told you about, he asked me to marry him yesterday. He seems to be a good man—except that in this most important decision of his life, he didn't seek the Lord. I don't know if it's a sign I should turn down his offer or not. John did say real definitely that he would pray about it now. I think mayhap because his pa hasn't set a good example, he just didn't think to. But Mama, I can't make any sure sense of what I'm supposed to tell him, 'cause so far the Lord's keeping real closemouthed about it."

Weary before the day had even begun, Sabina pulled the quilt tighter to ward off the dampness and slumped down on her sitting stone. With a disheartened sigh she watched the water tumble over the rocks here in this place the Lord of the universe had created for her.

She lifted her chin again. "La, Mama, that's not exactly everything. The truth is, the Lord's not answering is probably just my not wanting to hear what he has to say. You see, I think John Auburn is a nice man, and I feel sorry that he don't feel comfortable around folks. The poor fella don't even feel as much at home with them as I do with the Clays. Ain't—isn't that sad? But I don't have deep loving feelings for him like I do for you and the Clays. Even after Kurt went and gambled me away to that horrible man, I still have more affection for him than I do for John Auburn."

"Speaking of Kurt," she said as new thoughts began to take over, "I do want you to know, Mama, I pray for him every day, even if he is too thickheaded to ever learn he needs God."

"Oh, dear." Sabina pressed a hand to her lips. "Forgive me for saying that, Mama. I know better than to do the Lord's judging for him." She'd as much as declared her stepfather eternally dead.

Her gaze ran along the length of what looked like a thin piece of pine. Reaching down, she picked up the stick and slowly, awkwardly wrote in the damp sand the words of one of the commandments she'd learned from the children: Thou shalt not kill.

With her bare foot, she then wiped away the words, sensing she needed to write others. Her gaze drifted into the misty distance. "Heavenly Father, if you do want me to wed John Auburn, you know I'll need to be as honest with him as he's been with me. I need to tell him about my shameful birth."

Painstakingly, she scratched out Help me tel him . . . She couldn't figure out the spelling of *about*. She changed it to *of me*.

Standing, she smoothed more of the sand with her foot, then lowered the stick again. Giv me a love for him like I hav for . . . After a couple of marks, she again stopped. She wasn't sure how to spell *Baxter*.

Deciding that was for the best, she smeared across the attempt and replaced it with the Clays. Baxter was, after all, bespoken to another woman. No point in reminding herself of someone she could not have.

Sabina heaved a shuddering sigh, tears threatening to fill her eyes. If she could love John Auburn even half as much as she did Baxter and the kids, she'd gladly fly to him on those "wings of the morning" Baxter had spoken of in the nightly Bible reading he'd taken to including Sabina in . . . the very wings of morning.

~

In his cobbler shop, Baxter set aside an awl he'd been using to mark holes in a piece of black-stained leather and rubbed his tired eyes. To make up for the time he lost when Amanda and her aunt visited, he'd been working since before dawn this morning, and now it was near noon.

Scanning the outside surroundings through the closest window, he saw that the sun had burned off the morning fog. Near the well, he spotted Sabina and Delia doing the week's laundry at two washtubs set over low flames. The boys, though, were not out plowing under the cornfield as he'd told them to do.

Perhaps he'd stretch his kinks out by checking on them.

At the threshold, he lingered a moment, gazing at his womenfolk. Both were a pure pleasure to watch. Unaware of anything but their scrubbing and wringing, the two performed their tasks with similar grace. Sabina had a natural elegance about her, a loveliness of movement that now seemed to be expressed in Delia as well. Because of Sabina's influence, Amanda would have much less of a chore turning Delia into a lady. If Amanda could keep herself from speaking ill of Sabina, that is. The thought was starting to grate on him.

Sabina's blonde braid and Delia's brunette one slid delicately across their backs as the two held a sheet at opposite ends, wringing out the excess water. They smiled and chatted amiably, two dear companions. Despite having to contend with Amanda's jealousy of Sabina, he could never be sorry that the pretty young woman before him had brought her sunshine to this family.

Speaking of family . . . Baxter stepped out the door and took a second look around for the boys. Not seeing them, he cut across the clearing to the girls. "Howdy," he called.

They turned at the sound of his greeting, just as Sabina was gathering the sheet from Delia. "Is it time for nooning already?" she asked, looking up at the sky.

"Soon, I reckon. But I came to see what the boys are up to."

"Sammy said some of the chestnut trees in the woods is

droppin','" Delia informed him, drawing his gaze to the sweetness of her heart-shaped face. "They went a-tree shakin'."

"How long have they been gone? They're supposed to be plowing under the corn."

"They don't see no need—"

"Delia," he reprimanded, "I know you're capable of speaking correctly."

The imp rolled her eyes disrespectfully. "If we're moving to Nashville next spring, they don't see *any* need to bother."

"They *don't*, do they?"

A grin sparked across Sabina's lips, and she wagged her head. "I told 'em you wouldn't approve."

Her smile took the edge off his ire. Sabina had been so somber yester's eve after her visit with the Auburns, it had worried him. "Delia, to which trees did they go?"

"The ones across the stream behind the springhouse."

"Good. I'll have 'em back in short order."

Determined to set those boys on a righteous path, he strode past the chicken coop and leapt across the brook, heading toward the two mature chestnuts. The plan to move next spring didn't mean they could let the place go to ruin in the meantime. Everything needed to be kept in good order for any prospective buyers.

Reaching the nut trees, Baxter saw that the boys weren't there. From the disturbed earth beneath, he knew they'd finished and left. He headed for the tree that grew upstream a few hundred yards away.

Following the animal trace along the brush-crowded bank, he came to the loveliest spot on his property, a small glen. Here he saw evidence that they'd come this way. Some writing was scrawled on the sandy bank.

Help me tel him of me.

Hmm, *tell* was misspelled. Even Sammy should know better. Fortunately, school would commence again next Monday.

Giv me a love for him like I hav for the Clays.

More misspelled words. Perhaps Sammy's punishment for not plowing should be to write each of them a hundred—

The realization suddenly hit Baxter. None of his children had written these particular words. They wouldn't refer to themselves as the Clays. Only Sabina could have scratched out that sentiment. And after only a short period of tutoring . . . she was doing splendidly with her letters. Plus, he thought with unabashed pleasure, it was exceedingly gratifying to know for a certainty that she loved the children.

But who was the *him* she'd mentioned? Most likely John Auburn, the fellow with whom she'd had dinner yesterday.

And here she was, asking God to give her a love for him. Auburn must have asked her to marry him. That's why she was so quiet last night.

Baxter's heart pounded uncomfortably in his chest, and his throat tightened. He swallowed stiffly and studied the first sentence again. Help me to tel him of me.

Not only did she not love John, but she felt compelled to tell him a secret about herself. About her stepfather gambling her away, mayhap? Didn't she understand by now that it was Kurt Erhardt's shame, not hers?

He smeared his shoe across that first sentence, seeing no reason for her to divulge anything of the sort to anyone. It certainly had no bearing on her character. There wasn't a dishonorable bone in her whole beautiful body.

A chilly breeze came up, a reminder that winter would soon be upon them. He'd be marrying Amanda, and Sabina . . . would she marry John Auburn?

The thought disturbed him more than he was prepared to

admit. Shaking it off, he suddenly recalled that Sabina had no cloak to keep her warm. After all she'd done for his family, he certainly wouldn't send her to the Auburns or to anyone else without one. He might have no other rights concerning her, but this he could do. She needed a proper winter outfit for church, too. And another pair of shoes. Pretty ones this time, dyed to match the new day gown. With silver buckles.

Aye, right after lunch, he'd ride into the settlement and buy Sabina some of Bailey's best cloth.

In the meantime, he'd better round up those wayward boys.

Chapter Twenty-Six

Baxter rode into the settlement with a letter in his pocket whose presence nagged at him—a letter Sabina had written to her mother with not his but Delia's assistance. He couldn't help wondering if there was something in the message she didn't want him to know.

Though he told himself Sabina's private matters were none of his affair, a thought kept rolling through his mind. No doubt she'd informed her mother that by Christmas she would be going elsewhere to live. But would that place be to the Auburn farm?

As far as he was concerned, that would be almost as bad as her marrying one of the Daggets. John was too much like his dour father. For a cheery lass like Sabina, the existence he'd provide would drain the very life from her.

In comparison, from the moment she'd stepped inside his door, she'd thrived on and provided much of the laughter that had filled his home.

"Lord," he prayed, "please don't let us forget to laugh once she's gone."

Realizing he was speaking aloud as he brought Snowflake to the front of Bailey's store, he sheepishly glanced around to see if anyone had heard. Fortunately, the chill of the day didn't allow for loitering on the store porch. He did note, however, that the horse of the very man he'd been thinking about was tethered at one of the hitching posts. John Auburn's roan pony. The last person he wanted to see today.

Setting his jaw, Baxter swung down from his much larger draft animal, tied the reins, and started up the porch steps.

Just before he reached the door, it swung open, and John Auburn strode out, a sack of sugar under one arm and a letter held up with the other, hiding the lower half of his thin face. So engrossed in the letter was the young man, he didn't even look up as he brushed by.

Relieved, Baxter walked inside to the pungent smells of the pickle barrel and dried herbs, and the fire crackling in the hearth.

"Howdy," George Bailey said from behind the counter. The short, square-featured redhead always had a smile for the customers.

"Afternoon." Baxter tipped his wide-brimmed everyday hat. "I take it the postrider's already come and gone."

"Aye." George pointed to a box on a shelf behind him where he kept the incoming mail. "He left here a couple hours ago."

"That's a shame." Baxter walked past the stacked crates and sacks and barrels, making his way to the proprietor. "I have a letter to send out." He handed it over.

"Harry said he'd try to get back by in a week or so. In the meantime he left some mail for you folks." George fetched the wooden box and placed it on a cleared space of the cluttered counter. "And if you got the time for a little extra readin', Harry left some broadsides from back East. They're on the chair by the fire." Sorting through the mail, he lifted out several pieces for Baxter. "You folks sure do get your share."

The top letter was from a settlement in Kentucky, probably a shoe order. "That trip up to Cane Ridge has proved to be mighty good for my cobbler business."

The next—from Cincinnati—was addressed to Sabina. Great! She'd be happy to know her mother received at least one of her missives. The next two had return names and addresses he didn't recognize. Most likely more shoe orders.

The last piece of mail was from Philip. That disturbed him since he'd been expecting his son—not some letter—home any day now. Harvesttime was upon them. Baxter broke the wax seal and unfolded the thick paper.

> *Dear Father,*
>
> *I hope this missive finds you all in good health. I am fine. I am writing to tell you that Marty's pa has been teaching me how to fashion copper. We have not finished this very large tub for bathing yet. And I know how you do not like for me to leave work unfinished. I will start for home in a week or two.*
>
> *Your obedient son,*
>
> *Philip*

∾

The anger building in Baxter erupted into laughter at Philip's closing. "Your *obedient* son, my eye." Not one of his boys had shown a shred of obedience this day.

"What's so funny?" George asked, his own ready smile joining in.

"Oh, just my Philip." He waved the letter. "He won't be home from Greeneville for another couple of weeks."

"The winter rains should be comin' on real regular by then."

"Aye, I know. It'll be a good lesson for him, having to travel through the muck and mire." One thing for sure: if the lad didn't show up by then, Baxter would be going after Philip. He wasn't marrying Amanda Atwood to then have his son become a common tradesman like himself.

Shaking off the disturbing thought, Baxter moved down the counter to where the bolts of cloth were stacked. "Speaking of cold weather, do you have any fabric that's sturdy enough for a winter cloak?"

"I just received a shipment the other day." On the other side of the counter, the storekeeper also strode to the material. "I got one bolt here that will go real good with your daughter's colorin'."

"A cloak's already being made for Delia. This would be for Miss Erhardt."

The entry door opened behind Baxter, followed by a gust of cold air.

"Ah," George called, with his famous smile. "Brother Rolf. I have mail for you."

"Afternoon, Rolf," Baxter greeted as George turned back to him.

"Your Miss Sabina would look lovely in just about any color." George lifted several bolts off the top of one pile and laid them aside. "These four on the bottom will all make fine warm cloaks."

"Goot to see you, Baxter," Rolf, still in his blackened leather apron, boomed and walked up beside him. "So, you are buying da fabric for Sabina."

For some reason, Baxter was reluctant to confirm that, but he had no choice; the storekeeper had already said it for him. "It is turning cold, you know." Regardless of his rational explanation, he felt an uncomfortable warmth around his neck.

"*Ja*, 'tis. And you are picking da color for her?"

Again, Baxter hesitated. Still, it wasn't as if he didn't have every right to be making the purchase. She was in *his* care, after all. "Aye."

He made a project of fanning the bolts of wool cloth, hoping Rolf would occupy himself elsewhere. A charcoal gray, a deep red, a forest green, and a light dusty blue lay before him, and he pictured how each would go with her coloring. Because Sabina herself was an array of pastels, he preferred the more subtle hue. He could already see her corn-silk hair cupped in the hood as the soft blue framed the peaches and cream of her complexion. Yes, the perfect choice.

"I say," Rolf said, moving beside him and pointing with one of his thick, sooty fingers, "blue is da color for her. Da *fräuleins* vat come from da old country alvays look best in da blue."

Baxter wished he'd spoken the words out loud first, told the storekeeper he wanted yardage from that particular piece before Rolf opened his mouth. But . . . "I know. George, cut me off enough for a generous cloak."

"Our Sabina," Rolf said, still beside him, "she is da jewel to be prized no matter how she is dressed. She is da kind King Solomon writes about. Houses and riches are da inheritance of da fadders, and da prudent vife is from da Lord. Da riches Sabina vill bring to her husband is much more precious. Dey come from da Lord. Dat kind of riches cannot be bought or sold or stole."

No doubt the man was referring to Baxter's betrothal to Amanda. Sigh. Rolf and Inga came from peasant stock and simply had no understanding of the realities of the society from which Baxter came.

Once the pastor's disapproval was voiced in not so subtle a manner, he turned to the storekeeper with a big toothy grin.

"Mine Inga, she sends me over for some gingerroot. You got some?"

Baxter moved to the corner near the hearth, pretending interest in an ax handle until Brother Rolf completed his business and walked out the door. The fabric and trims for Sabina's winter day gown—the last he would ever purchase for her— would be his choice. His alone.

~

Sabina heard the beat of a horse's hooves. Baxter? Home so soon? She looked over the clothesline as she unpinned a dry tablecloth; she quickly folded it and put it in the basket.

No, a white-stockinged roan. John Auburn.

Panic gripped her. He was back already. It had been less than a day since he'd proposed marriage. And the Lord had given her no answer concerning it. *Or, Father, am I just refusing to listen?*

As John rode closer, he waved. There was a lightness in his demeanor, even a bit of a grin.

Pulling her shawl tighter around her, she walked from behind the gently flapping laundry, trying to force a smile of her own.

~

Riding home from the settlement store, Baxter heard the pound of racing hooves coming toward him before horse and man broke into view from behind a tree-edged curve.

Auburn's pony! The man had not gone directly home from the store but had ridden south. To Baxter's place? Had Auburn purposefully gone to visit Sabina, knowing he would not be present?

The thin young fellow shot past, not slowing one iota to give Baxter a chance to question him. And the upstart had the nerve to grin at him like a daft child as he waved.

John Auburn grinning? An uneasy feeling crawled up Baxter's spine. Sabina must have agreed to marry him.

A heaviness weighting upon his chest, Baxter watched until horse and rider disappeared around the next bend. John might be filled with glee today, but how long would he keep it up? In the long run, that morose spirit of his would come creeping back in and suck all the joy out of Sabina. It just wasn't right. *Please, Lord, if my suspicions are correct, protect her from this marriage.*

No sooner was the prayer out of his mouth than Baxter felt a stab of conscience. Had he spoken from a true concern for her, or was it just plain jealousy? *Father, you must take away this deep affection I have for her. I, too, am to wed, and I mustn't carry these feelings with me into my own marriage.*

Yet the very proof of his love for Sabina was bundled just behind his saddle. He hadn't even bothered to ask the price of the fabrics or buttons and trims until the moment came to pay the storekeeper. He'd spent far too much, yet he'd been glad to do it. The look on her face when she unwrapped the brown paper would more than compensate him.

Baxter allowed that imagined vision to play across his mind as he reined Snowflake onto his farm's cutoff—and spotted Sammy running his way. His youngest should be out in the fields, working. "Where are you going?" he yelled and nudged his big gelding into a faster pace to intercept the boy.

"Thank Providence, you're back!" Sammy sputtered, out of breath. He grabbed hold of a stirrup for support. "It's Sabina and that John Auburn. They was huggin' and laughin'," he added, his cheeks flushed. Then he gritted his teeth. "The bushwhacker run off before me an' Howie had a chance at him—all 'cause we was way out in that blasted cornfield."

Sammy had just confirmed everything Baxter feared.

"I was comin' to get you," the boy rattled on, "so's we can go give him what for." He slammed a fist into his other palm. The boy seemed even more jealous than Baxter and ready for battle.

Baxter felt defeated. "Climb up behind me." He extended a helping hand to Sammy. "Before we race off half-cocked, I think we'd better speak to Sabina."

Riding into the clearing, Baxter sighted Delia and Howie by the well, talking with their heads close together. But he didn't see Sabina anywhere. He guided the horse to a stop just short of their stricken faces.

"You shoulda been here, Pa," Delia railed. "That John Auburn hooted and threw his hat in the air, then him and Sabina hugged." His daughter's voice turned even more venomous. "And then Sabina kissed him. Smack on the cheek. It was awful, just awful."

As Baxter dismounted, feeling just as betrayed, Howie grabbed Snowflake's bridle. "I woulda done something, but the bounder galloped away before I had a chance. And Sabina, she skipped off to the house like someone had just baked her a birthday cake."

Baxter glanced both ways. "Which house?"

"Ours."

He started for it, then took a pulse-slowing breath and swung back to his kids. For all their sakes, he had to remain calm. Rational. "It's been no secret that she was being courted," he reminded them, as much for himself as for them. "Fellows have been coming around ever since she arrived. You had to know this would happen someday. So I want y'all to come inside with me and congratulate her on her choice. At least it's not one of those strutting Daggets."

"But, Pa," Sammy whined, "she promised she wouldn't leave us till Christmas."

Baxter wrapped an arm around him. "And I expect she'll keep her word. She always does."

With the kids at his heels, Baxter headed for the house. Opening the door, he heard singing coming from within.

"'The higher up the cherry tree, the sweeter grows the cherry. . . .'" Her lilting alto voice came in a bouncy rendition of "Weevily Wheat."

"'The more you hug and kiss a gal, the more she wants to marry,'" she continued.

Stooped at the hearth, Sabina heard them and swiveled on her heel. "Wonderful. You're back." She almost bubbled with enthusiasm. "Come in." Returning to her chore, she flipped something in the big iron skillet. "I have the happiest news to pass on, so I'm making raisin scones and tea. I know it's only midafternoon, but I thought we could have us a little treat whilst I tell you. Take a seat, boys. And, Delia, honey," she tossed over her shoulder, "would you get out the good china? Makes it a little more festive. Oh, and pour hot water into the teapot."

As merry as Sabina was, neither Baxter nor the youngsters managed a lone smile between them as they did her bidding.

A moment or so later, she brought a platter of the spicy-smelling fried cakes to the table, removed her spattered apron, and sat down next to Delia. She grabbed his daughter's hand. "I'd like to ask the blessing, if y'all don't mind." Bowing her head, her long braid fell across her shoulder. "My dearest heavenly Father, you never cease to amaze me with your goodness. Thank you, and bless this treat we are about to share. In the precious name of our Lord Jesus, amen."

Baxter certainly couldn't recall that he had announced his own betrothal with such enthusiasm. As the scones were passed around the table, he waited impatiently for her to say the words, all the while dreading the fateful moment.

Finally, Sabina glanced around, virtually beaming. "I reckon

I better start from the beginning. Yesterday, Mr. Auburn asked me to marry him. I wasn't sure if I was supposed to say yea or nay, so I told him I would ask God for the right answer. I also asked him to pray for the Lord's decision. And bless him, he did."

"Who? What?" Howie asked before Baxter could. "John Auburn or God?"

"Why, John, of course," she said, directing her smile to Howie. "He prayed, and can you imagine? God's answer to him came today—the very next day. And in writing, plain as can be."

"God wrote it down for Mr. Auburn?" Sammy asked, his eyes doubling in size.

Sabina laughed. "Not exactly. Still, it's the most amazing thing. Purely amazing. John got this letter from his old sweetheart. He said she and her family had moved farther west four years ago. The Witakers. Do you remember them?"

"Aye," Howie answered. "Patsy was the only girl John ever got up the gumption to even look at. Till you came. They was always makin' moon eyes at each other in church. It was enough to make a fella gag."

"Go on." Baxter held himself in check, not daring to let himself begin to hope . . . yet.

"I'm sad to say," she continued, her expression serious for the first time, "Patsy's pa was killed. Got between a she-bear and her cub. May God rest his soul. Anyway, John said he didn't have no sons, just daughters."

"Aye, that's right," Baxter said, reminded that the man would have no one to carry on the Witaker name.

"Well, Patsy and her ma have asked John to come take her pa's place. And, naturally, though she didn't put the words down on paper, that's as good as her saying she'd like to marry up with him. Leastwise, that's what John is counting on."

Praise be! Sabina wouldn't be John's wife after all. A wave of profound relief swept through Baxter.

Delia, still unsure, asked, "Are you sayin' John is leavin' here to go marry Patsy Witaker?"

"Aye. John told me she was the only one he could ever talk to, and he's been awful sad ever since she left. And with Patsy being shy like he is, she never got up the nerve to write till now, so he didn't even know where she'd ended up. He figured by now she'd married somebody else." Sabina sat back in her chair. "Didn't I tell you? Ain't God just the best? All he was waiting on was for John to come to him and ask him for guidance. 'Ask, and it shall be given you; seek, and ye shall find.'"

"You're right, Sabina," Sammy practically yelled. Grinning from ear to ear, he picked up his scone. "This is the best news I ever heard."

Baxter wished he had the right to say those same words. But knowing he didn't, he reined in his soaring spirit and pulled Sabina's letter from his pocket. "I do hope this is more good news."

Chapter Twenty-Seven

Eagerly, Sabina took the letter from Baxter as the whole family remained around the table. Her mother had actually received at least one letter from her and was responding. She recognized her own name on the front and slowly sounded out the words below it . . . the name of the valley and a long word that had to be *Tennessee*.

Breaking the seal, she unfolded the paper and found line after line of writing. *So many words.* "Please." She handed it back to Baxter. "Read it for me. Figuring it all out will take me too long."

"My pleasure." He spread the parchment paper before him.

"Is it from her mama?" Sammy asked, sounding almost as thrilled as Sabina herself.

Baxter glanced up at him and smiled. "It starts 'My dearest daughter.'" Emotion swelled within him when he read the touching salutation.

"Go on," Sabina pleaded.

He cleared his throat and began again:

My dearest daughter,
I got your letter yesterday, and when I read it, my heart nearly
burst, it was so full of the oil of joy. To know you are safe and happy
with a fine Christian family and that they treat you good is all I been
praying for these long empty weeks. I put you in God's hands, and he
has not failed us. I tried to always remember his promises, but I could
not keep this deep and wide sadness from filling me top to bottom.

"Poor Mama." Sabina wrapped her fingers around her fragile
teacup. "I prayed she wouldn't mourn me too much."

"But even in sadness," Baxter said, "the Lord has provided.
Listen." He continued reading:

Kurt became so distraught over the unhappiness he brung on me
by his gambling, he vowed never to do it again. He has took a job
down at the river dock, loading and unloading. And behold God's
mercy on us sinners. Kurt went to church services with me last
sabbath.

Sabina's chin jerked up. *"He did?* Please, read that last part
again."

Baxter did.

She hadn't been mistaken. "Kurt has always loved Mama very
much."

"Aye," Baxter agreed, "I can see that. If she's anything like
you, that wouldn't be hard to do." A muscle flexed in his jaw as
his gaze held hers.

Sabina saw what looked like love in Baxter's eyes. But she
couldn't—wouldn't—allow herself to believe it. He was to
marry Amanda Atwood. "Do go on."

I, too, am earning money. I bake bread to sell to the river men. Both of us are saving to buy back the paper Shockley holds on you. As soon as we have enough, we are bent on tracking Tom down and getting it back. Then we will come to you. The Lord willing, we shall be there by Christmas. Easter, at the latest. Until then, sunrise and sunset, I am with you.

> *Your loving mother,*
> *Greta*

"Oh my." Sabina's eyes flooded with tears. "Oh my."

Delia, next to her, wrapped both arms around Sabina and laid a cheek against hers. Chairs scraped back, and Sammy and Howie hurried around to join in a family hug.

And through a blur of tears, Sabina saw Baxter reach across the table to her.

He squeezed her shoulder. "This is wonderful."

"I know. The oil of my own gladness runneth over."

"And now," Sammy said, "you don't have to marry any of them ugly ol' fellas."

Swallowing down her mirth, Sabina reached up and pressed her hand over Baxter's. Yes, on this day her gladness did run over. Let tomorrow take care of itself.

~

If there'd been even the slightest hint of a doubt that Sabina wasn't the pure and lovely person she purported to be, it vanished as Baxter watched her caress the letter she now pored over as they finished their afternoon treat. The sight was enough to bring tears to a man's eyes. He took a breath, then another bite of scone.

Reaching for a second fried cake, Delia looked past Sabina to him. "They sure are good, aren't they? The scones. And fast to make." She turned to Sabina. "I'll have to learn this recipe."

Sabina made no indication that she'd even heard, so intent was she on deciphering her letter.

"Pa," Howie singsonged, a smug grin curling one side of his mouth, "looks like we ain't the only ones who forget to do things around here. You forgot about Snowflake. He's starin' in the window at you right now."

Baxter swung around. Sure enough, since the lamps were lit on this overcast day, the big gray had a clear view to the inside.

"Soon as we're through here," Howie offered, "I'll put him away for you."

"That's mighty nice of you, son." Baxter flipped up his own smile—it was his turn to tease. "Then you and Sammy have another horse to tend. The one you left out in the cornfield, hitched to the wagon. Thunder is waiting for you to go finish your chore."

The bottom lip that had been so confidently smiling was now being chewed. "I plumb forgot."

Glancing out at Snowflake, Baxter remembered that he had left the fabric tied behind the saddle. He had another, much more pleasant chore awaiting him. He turned his attention to Sabina.

An amused grin graced her delicate features as her gaze left Howie for his. "Speaking of chores . . ." she said, neatly folding her coveted letter. "Delia, honey, would you clean up here? I need to bring in any laundry that's managed to dry today. The clouds outside are getting darker by the minute."

Baxter rose before Sabina had a chance to move and pulled out her chair for her, interested in taking care of that one particular 'chore.'

Sabina looked up, surprised, and he realized he hadn't until now made a practice of helping her from her seat. And that was the sort of thing gentlemen did for their special ladies.

Now aware of his every move, he walked to the door and vacillated on whether or not to hold it open for her . . . then decided he would have rendered that courtesy naturally, without a second thought.

The slightly confused expression on her face as she passed him conveyed that he probably didn't usually wait to let her go first. Or was she reading something different in his own countenance?

Going out behind her, he did, however, have the pleasure of watching her walk toward the lines of clothes with that unaffected yet graceful swing to her gait.

Once she disappeared behind a gently flapping tablecloth, he hurried to fetch the paper-wrapped bundle. With chores awaiting the kids, he assured himself they would linger inside over their treat. Give him the chance to present his purchase without them in the middle of everything.

After removing the bundle from the saddle rings, he headed for Sabina. He was followed by the sound of a low impatient whinnying from the horse. Then he stepped within the seclusion of two lines of sheets and found Sabina folding a tablecloth.

"I have something for you." Taking the linen covering from her and dropping it in the basket on the ground, he placed the package in her hands.

"It feels like fabric." She nodded. "Good. The boys were asking to have some new shirts made for school, and—"

"No. It's not for them. With winter coming on, you are in far greater need."

She searched his eyes.

Not wanting her to see his true feelings—his love for her—reflected there, he glanced down at the package. "Open it. See if the fabrics are to your liking."

"I'm sure they will be." Her gentle voice flowed over him like warm honey.

He watched her slender fingers pull loose the bow-tied string securing the brown paper, then spread it open to expose the plaid wool of blue, green, and gray. Her hand smoothed across it with the same tenderness with which she had touched her mother's letter.

"It's a fine tight weave," she murmured, checking the thickness. "And the colors. I couldn't have picked anything I'd favor more."

She didn't look up. Now, when he wanted to behold her eyes, to see if she was truly pleased by his choice, she kept her head down.

"There's more," he said in the stillness. "For a cloak."

"More?" she whispered huskily. Slowly, she folded back the layers of plaid, pausing to fondle every trim tucked in between as she went.

Finally she reached the heavier dusty blue. Her head still bowed, she stared at it a full twenty seconds without moving. Then, abruptly, "I have to go." Without looking up, she whirled away.

He caught her arm. "You hate it, don't you? We can take it back, and you can choose whatever you like."

Her face jerked up. "*No.*" Tears filled her eyes and streamed down her cheeks. "I love it—all of it."

"Then why are you crying?" The sight ripped at his insides.

"Because I love it too much. Everything. Because," she said with a shuddering sigh, "today has all been too perfect."

She does love my gift. Relieved and utterly touched, he pulled his kerchief from his pocket. "Well, then, you don't mind if I wipe away some of that perfection, do you?"

As he reached for her cheek, her lips started trembling, and a whole new rash of tears spilled down.

His own chest flooded with overwhelming emotions, tensions long suppressed. And he knew. If he so much as wiped away a single tear, he would not be able to stop until he'd kissed the rest of them away . . . kissed her eyes, her mouth, held her close . . .

As if his kerchief were on fire, he dropped it on the stack of materials and backed away from her. "I just remembered. I have to–to–go unsaddle Snowflake."

~

Baxter turned a pair of shoes back and forth. In the lantern light, the highly polished black leather shone like a mirror. The soles were thicker for winter wear, but the uppers were cut stylishly low to make a woman's feet seem all the smaller. The silver buckles, too, were of a dainty shape. A pair any woman on either side of the mountains would find attractive, if he did say so himself.

Shoes Sabina could be proud to wear to church and visiting. As for that first pair he'd made her, she could use them for workdays.

He took a rag and polished off a thumbprint. These, he'd present to Miss Sunshine this evening at the supper table. He knew better than to give them to her in private as he had the bundle of winter fabrics. Too dangerous.

He glanced out the window. The overcast dawn caused the fall colors to be all the more welcome, as cheery as the windows of the main house that glowed bright this morning. With the sun rising later now, every lamp and candle was lit while the children finished getting ready for their first school day, which in Reardon Valley always followed the harvest. Always an exciting morning for them. But for the first time in years, Baxter wasn't required in the house to hustle them along. With Sabina doing the chores, he'd been allowed to keep to his prior work schedule.

Thunder stood beside the porch, bridled, blanketed, and hitched to a post, waiting patiently for the kids to emerge. The gentle giant had been carrying them to school for the past five years. And with Philip still away and not available to man the wagon, the youngsters would have to make do with just the one mount.

But shouldn't they be on their way to the settlement by now? Baxter pulled his timepiece from his fob pocket: 7:05. Yes, they were late.

Stuffing the watch back into its slot, he strode out of the shop and headed for the house. He'd reached halfway when the front door swung open.

"If you don't come now," Howie shouted over his shoulder, walking out in a heavy shirt and vest, "me an' Sammy are gonna go off and leave you." Carrying a lunch basket, he set it on the edge of the porch beside Thunder.

Sammy charged out behind Howie, his hat on crooked. "Let's just leave her."

"You boys ready to go?" Baxter called out.

"Yep," Howie replied. "But that Delia. You'd think she was off to see the queen, the way she's got Sabina fussin' with her hair in there. And it's all gonna bounce loose on the ride in. So what does it matter?"

Baxter chuckled. "When it comes to females and their toilet, ours is not to reason why. You'd better start getting used to it, because the older they get, the longer they take."

"I'm comin', I'm comin'," Delia cried from inside, then swept out the door, a knit shawl wrapping her striped, red-and-black gabardine dress. Black pleats had been added to the bottom, which Baxter presumed were meant to add style as well as length to his sprouting daughter's skirt. The girl must have grown half a foot since last spring. The same pleating ruffled the inside of her straw bonnet. She and Sabina had been very busy turning her into a fashionable young lady for this school term.

His beautiful daughter. *Don't rush growing up*, he wanted to say. *Don't leave me behind before I'm ready to let go.*

She ran off the porch to where he stood admiring her. Rising on tiptoe, she pecked his cheek, then took a step back. "Do I look all right, Papa?" Her big brown eyes searched his face.

"Actually, you look too good, sugar. Maybe I'd better get some ash and smudge your face, or the boys at school won't get their lessons done today."

"Oh, Papa." With a coy smile, she traipsed up to the porch again to mount Thunder behind Howie and Sammy.

"Here." Sabina rushed out into the cold, heedless of her bare feet. "Don't forget your books." She placed them on Delia's lap, then trailed her fingers along the threesome's cheeks. "You all look out for each other, you hear?"

"We will," Howie assured, heeling the big gray into a walk.

"Bye, Sabina. Bye, Papa." Sammy looked back, waving.

"Take care," Sabina called. From the stricken expression on her face, a body would think the kids were riding off into the wilds of winter instead of a day at school.

"They'll be fine. The road will be overrun with all the other youngsters on their way to school."

"I know." Sabina stopped watching their departure long enough to gift him with a smile. "It's just that this is the first time they've all been away from home at the same time. And, well, the schoolmaster doesn't strike me as someone with a tender spirit."

"No, not that much," he said, more aware than ever how much she cared for his children. "Elbridge can be a bit quick with the hickory stick. But . . ."

Baxter lost his train of thought as the realization that all the children would be away from home hit him. He and Sabina would be here—alone—most of the day. No one would be around to interrupt any moment they might have together.

"But what?" she asked, waiting for him to finish.

"Uh—nothing. The kids already know not to give Elbridge any trouble." He took a prudent step back.

"Baxter." She stopped him.

"Yes?"

"I've been meaning to ask, the next time you're at the store, could you buy a bag of wool? I need to spin some thread for knitting. You're all in need of stockings."

"Stockings . . . yes." They were the last thing on his mind. "I'll have Howie bring some home tomorrow. Well," he said, retreating another step, "I'd better get back to work. With shoe orders coming in like they are, I have plenty to keep me busy till Christmas."

"Aye, Christmas . . ." Her features lost all expression. Turning on her heel, she hurried inside.

It was for the best, he told his wrenching heart. For the best.

Still, he had a hard time concentrating on leather cutting, gluing, and stitching—with him in the shop and her in the house . . . all alone.

An hour or so later, a knock on the door startled him—he hadn't heard anyone ride in. When he opened it, Sabina stood, waiting.

"Why didn't you merely walk in?" he asked.

"I—I wasn't sure. I've never been in here before. I usually send one of the young'uns for you." Her gaze darted away.

Heaven help him, he must have been staring at her. "What can I do for you?"

After a second, her eyes of pale green came back to his. "I was wondering if you would mind if I cooked the big meal at suppertime when we'll all be here to eat. This noon I could make you a fine meal out of leftover vituals."

"Sure. Whatever works best for you."

Hesitating but a instant, she turned around and sped back to the house.

Sabina seemed as uncomfortable at being alone with him as he was with her. But was it for the same reason? Did her heart burn for him like his did for her? Or did he merely wish it were so? And why on earth was he entertaining such bold thoughts in the first place?

Getting back to the business at hand, he hooked a half-finished boot over a wooden form and began tapping tacks into the sole to hold it temporarily in place.

But his mind refused to stay on his work. Grady Jessup and the Daggets were still showing up a couple evenings a week. And now that the nights had turned nippy, they spent their time dawdling on his good furniture, finishing off any dessert the girls made. Bottomless pits, they were.

"Ow!" His thumb. He'd struck it with the mallet.

And that's the way his morning continued . . . jabbing a thick needle into his thumb . . . clumsily spilling a pot of glue. . . . He heard the clang of the dinner triangle with utmost relief and removed his apron.

After washing his hands and throbbing thumbs at the outside stand, he ran a comb through his hair—something he realized he rarely did this time of day.

"Enough of this schoolboy nonsense," he muttered to himself, dropping the comb in his shirt pocket. "We're having dinner like we do every day at this time."

Walking inside to the smell of fresh coffee and stew, he saw that the big table was covered by some of the day-gown fabric he'd bought Sabina—the blue, green, and gray plaid wool.

"I've cleared off the small worktable for us." Standing by it, Sabina pulled out one of the cushioned chairs she'd placed there. "I hope you don't mind."

"I thought you'd finished cutting out your dress."

"Aye, and I have enough material left over to make Sammy a shirt."

"Are you sure? I don't want you skimping on your own."

"Skirts that are too full just get in the way." She sat down across from him and started dipping out last night's wild-turkey stew from a footed pot.

"And," he added knowingly, "I did hear Sammy say that plaid would make him a fine-looking shirt. You do too much for him."

Shrugging, she grinned. "Have some bread."

He took a slice. "You spoil him, you know. Terribly."

"What's it hurt," she asked, handing him the butter, "to give him a little extra mothering? He didn't have his mother as long as the others did."

Sabina had hit Baxter's tender spot. "All right. But don't let the scamp take too much advantage of you."

She chuckled softly. "I won't. But one thing I know. I have to get my gown and his shirt finished before the apple-peeling party next week. It's real important to him that we go dressed alike."

Baxter grinned and relaxed a notch. "Trying to get one up on your other beaus, is he?" If Baxter had his way, he'd put the entire Clay clan in her tartan. But that was just childish dreaming—like Sammy thinking Sabina would marry him when he grew up. "Shall we bow our heads for grace?"

With just the two of them at the small table, he was very aware of her every breath and stumbled over his first words before he could wholly concentrate on the prayer.

Before he completely regained his senses, they'd both taken several bites, and she was speaking to him. "What exactly is a frolic?" she asked out of the blue. "I ain't never—I mean—I have never been to one."

"A frolic? When it's just the valley folk, we don't usually hold a dancing party. No jigs or shuffles. Instead, at a frolic the fellows march around in a circle with their ladies on their arms. Brother Rolf feels that's more dignified. There's some bowing and skipping and such, depending on the song."

A smile spread across her pink lips. "Then there is music. The young'uns do love music."

"Aye. 'Green grow the rushes, O,'" he sang to demonstrate. "'Kiss her quick and—'" He stopped midphrase and shrugged. Kissing was not something he should bring up in a song or otherwise, considering how close her lips were to his. He picked up his spoon and filled his mouth with stew, giving himself something else to think about. "This turkey Howie shot doesn't taste gamey at all. What did you put in it?"

"La, I almost forgot. Everything was in such a rush this morning, what with it being the first day of school and all. Delia wanted me to ask you to make her a pair of dancing slippers. She said you was making some for Gracie and Hope and—" Sabina's voice took on a dramatic affectation—"she'll *simply die* if she has to show up in her clunky old shoes."

Baxter sat back in the chair and grinned. "She will, will she? Then I reckon I'd better see she has a pair. And you, too, of course. What sort of cobbler would I be if I don't have my own household properly fitted for a Reardon Valley frolic?"

"Nay, the shoes I have are just fine. Truly they are."

"Think of it as advertising. Pretty soon, every young miss between here and Knoxville will have to have a pair."

"But with three to make already . . ."

"Slippers don't take much time. I can finish all four pairs in a morning." Amused by her concern, he wondered what she'd think if she knew he'd just finished a pair of shoes for her that altogether had taken ten or twelve hours to make.

"What's so funny about making dance slippers?" she asked, taking a bite of bread.

"Nothing. But Delia and the Reardon girls are, them trying to act so grown up all of a sudden."

"I know. They are cute together, swishing their skirts around, stealing glances at the boys." She picked up her cup and took a sip of coffee. "I do hope Philip gets home in time to go with us."

Baxter grimaced. "If he doesn't, I reckon I'll have to go to Greeneville and fetch him."

"Yes, he's too young to stay gone this long."

Taking a sip of his own coffee, a bittersweet thought drifted across Baxter's mind. If Sally had lived, they probably would've been sitting here on this chilly day, warmed by the cook fire and having this very same conversation. Husband and wife discussing their children.

And that was when he stripped away all pretense.

Sabina's leaving was going to hurt almost as much as when he lost his wife.

Chapter Twenty-Eight

Baxter ran his fingertips across the soft kid of one of the blue-dyed dancing slippers, then made one last adjustment to the bow he'd stiffened, a bow he'd fashioned from the plaid of Sabina's new day gown. The white rosette he'd glued to each center added that perfect extra touch and would repeat the white ruffling at the gown's square neckline and the belled cuffs.

Beautiful shoes for a beautiful lady.

Finished with his daily cobbler's work, he slid the slippers into a tote to take to the house, along with the pairs he'd made for Delia and the Reardon girls. He grinned. Theirs, of course, were an identical shade of cream, set apart only by different-colored velvet bows selected to complement the party gowns they each would wear. He'd have Howie deliver Hope's and Gracie's as soon as his kids rode in from school. The apple-peeling frolic would be held at the Wallaces' barn tomorrow.

The aroma of baked bread and spices teased his nostrils as he closed the shop door behind him and stepped out into the crisp afternoon air. Long shadows that were streaked from trees aflame with autumn stretched across the clearing, and he realized Thunder would be plodding home with the kids any minute now.

Walking up the porch steps, he saw Sabina inside, kneading another lump of dough for the loaves of nut bread she was taking to the party. He paused to take an unguarded look at her, still unable to believe what beauty and blessing her presence had brought to their lives, even if only for a short while.

Remembering the tote of shoes he carried, he made a sudden, rash decision. He would not wait to give Sabina her dancing slippers at the supper table, along with Delia's, but would present them to her right now, while they were alone. He knew it was flirting with temptation, but he couldn't resist the thought of bathing in the expression on her face when she saw them.

The pound of horse hooves came from the west.

Blast. That special moment was not to be. He walked down the steps to greet the children. As he did, he heard the front door open.

Sabina, wiping her hands on her apron as she walked out, followed him as far as the edge of the porch, her expression reflecting anticipation such as he'd hoped she would show him. She did love his kids.

Abruptly, her face changed.

Baxter turned and looked up the road.

Hat dipped low, a man came riding on a blaze-faced brown horse that Baxter didn't recognize. Only a sun-bleached beard caught the light. Slowly the fellow lifted his head, leaned forward, and stared. Then, abruptly, he kneed his mount into a trot.

Sabina gasped. "Shockley."

It couldn't be. But it was. The same broad-chested, square-faced brute who'd stopped Baxter and his family on the road, looking for his runaway bride. How on earth had he found Sabina here, so far off the main trails and river traffic and hundreds of miles from Cane Ridge? Had her stepfather lied to her mother about his coming to the Lord, gained Greta's confidence, and betrayed Sabina again?

The powerful man rode straight for the porch—and Sabina—yanking his gelding to a halt directly in front of her.

Baxter had never seen her look so frightened. He ate up the distance separating them.

"Get your things," the man on the horse said in a gravelly voice. "And I don't want no argument. You cost me too much time already."

Mounting the steps, Baxter went to Sabina's side. "She's not going anywhere she doesn't want to."

The block of a man sat up straighter, his wiry brows flaring. "I don't want no trouble, but this ain't your affair. I got a legal paper here what says she's mine." He pulled a wrinkled and smudged folded scrap from inside his heavy coat. "She's been given to me for the purpose of matrimony. And I'm here to—"

In the blink of an eye, Shockley whipped around toward the road. Just as fast, his knotted shoulder muscles relaxed, and he turned forward again. "Just some young'uns a-comin'."

"They're mine," Baxter explained, taking note that the gambler was not only on guard for trouble but was quick, despite his bulk. "Let me see your paper." Baxter held out a hand. "Let's see just how legal it is."

Shockley reared back, eyeing Baxter warily. Unfolding the frayed paper, he held it up but out of Baxter's reach. "I ain't fool enough to just give it over to you. You can see from there that it's signed by both her pa and me *and* two witnesses."

"Aye, that it is," Baxter said, noticing how tightly Sabina gripped the porch post. Her knuckles had turned as white as her face. "But I'm still not sure if you can legally force her to marry you."

"It says so *right here*." He slapped the paper emphatically.

"Hey!" The yell came from up the road. From Sammy, who rode behind Howie and Delia. "Ain't that the fellow who's chasing after Sabina? Well, you can't have her," he railed as the three rode up next to the still mounted intruder.

"In our valley," Delia added, "folks can't be bought and sold."

The big man swung his attention back to Sabina. "You an' me both know you belong to me, don't we?"

"I, uh—" Sabina clung to the post, staring back at him, her face frozen in fear.

Baxter wrapped an arm around her shoulder. "Delia, Sammy, get off the horse. Howie, ride over to the Reardons'. Get Noah. Our lawyer," he added, eyeing Shockley. Then, remembering the bag he still held, he pulled out Sabina's and Delia's slippers, then tossed the tote to Howie. "Give these to Hope and Gracie." He stuffed the other pairs in his vest pockets.

"Pa." Howie's tone was brittle. "Don't you let that man take her before I get back."

Baxter pulled Sabina close again. "I won't."

"Neither will I." Sammy, who'd been on the horse mere seconds ago, now stood in the doorway with Baxter's musket pointed at Shockley. He stepped to Sabina's other side with a weapon longer than he was tall.

The gambler spread his blocklike hands. "Ain't no call for guns."

"No, there isn't." Baxter crossed behind Sabina and whisked the Brown Bess from his youngest. "Sammy, go do the barn chores. Delia, feed the chickens. Then . . ." What else? He needed to keep them both occupied. "Then go help your brother with the livestock."

"But—"

"Do as I say. *Now*." He added a glower that brooked no back talk. Then he turned to his interloping guest. "Mr. Shockley, do come in out of the cold to wait. My son should be back shortly— with our lawyer."

~

If Baxter's arm hadn't been around Sabina, pulling her along, she wouldn't have been able to move. She felt as if she were in one of those nightmares where she was being chased by a bear and she couldn't make her feet run or any sound come from her mouth. This had to be one of those terrifying dreams . . . except that the clomp of boots on the plank floor, the smell of bread baking in the Dutch oven were all too real, along with Baxter's warm breath upon her ear.

"Don't worry," he whispered. "You're not going with him."

That did little to ease her panic. Mayhap Baxter had a musket in hand, but Tom Shockley was known along the rivers for being a real bone-breaking brawler.

Baxter walked with her to the hearth. Shoving aside the chair Sammy must have climbed on to reach the musket, he replaced the firearm on the rack above.

He replaced the only weapon capable of stopping Shockley. Sabina stood there, staring at it. *Heavenly Father, I beg you, no matter what happens here today, please keep Baxter safe.*

He again bent to her ear. "Please pour us all some coffee." Leaving her standing at the hearth, he strode toward Shockley. "Let me take your coat. Have a seat."

Shucking off the heavy homespun garment, the man stood in the middle of the floor, his feet apart, scanning the room. In stark contrast to his fierce countenance, he wore a fancy ruffled shirt, as if he'd been invited to the frolic. "You two have yourself a real cozy place here." His words dripped with carnal insinuation.

"Sabina sleeps in the cabin by the stream." Baxter defended her in a fierce tone, his back and shoulder muscles rippling.

Stunned by Baxter's boldness, Sabina feared he might strike the much larger man. If he did, that would be the end of him.

Instead, Baxter took the blackguard's coat, slammed it down on a hook near the door so hard she was surprised it didn't rip, then joined Shockley at the dining table, sitting directly across from their unwelcome guest.

The tension in the room escalated until she felt she would choke. Why did the Lord see fit to allow this man to disrupt their lives in this way, to allow him to heap danger on those she loved? On Baxter.

"Sabina. The coffee, please."

Baxter's command broke her out of her paralyzed panic. With shaky hands, she retrieved two everyday cups from a shelf beside the hearth and stole another glance upward at the musket. Was it even loaded? or primed? Grabbing a thick, quilted pad, she swung the hinged rod to the front of the fireplace and unhooked the coffeepot, all the while feeling Shockley's small, piercing eyes on her.

An uncontrolled tremor raced up her spine. *Why, God? Why now, when Mama and Kurt are earning the money to buy back the IOU? And Kurt has finally seen the light—your light. Why now, when we could all be living a life—together—for you? Is this part of your plan for me, that I be cast off to this man? You said you loved me. In your Bible, you say it over and over. . . .*

"Sabina, the coffee."

"Oh, yes." She saw that she'd already filled the cups with steaming brew and even rehooked the pot. Straightening on unsteady legs, she carried the coffee to the men, avoiding both sets of eyes. She set Baxter's before him first, then walked around to the other side.

"Why, thanks, my li'l purty." Shockley grinned up at her as if he already possessed her. "I been waitin' a real long spell for you." He patted the seat beside him. "Sit here, beside me."

Quickly she backed out of reach and pulled out a chair at the far end.

"Yessir," he said, undaunted. He settled back, both hands around his cup, as if he were a welcome guest. "I spent these past months goin' up and down the rivers—the Ohio, the Tennessee, the Cumberland—askin' everyone I met if they'd laid eyes on the purtiest gal this side of Ol' Smoky. I been pinin' away this whole time." He straightened. "What's that smell? It sure is makin' my stomach growl."

"The nut bread!" Sabina sprang from her seat and, passing by on Baxter's side of the table, hurried to rescue the loaves she'd placed in the cast-iron oven.

"She's baking for a frolic the valley's having tomorrow," Baxter explained in a casual tone. "But there's plenty. Sabina, when you finish there, cut our guest a slice."

What? He didn't usually order her about without so much as a please. Only a few moments ago, he'd seemed to be kindness itself. But now he was treating her as if she were property . . . the same as Tom Shockley did. Like she had no say-so over her own person.

And the awful truth was, she wasn't sure she did.

Stifling a sigh, she sliced the hot bread.

"You know, missy, every meal I et since I won you from Kurt has been a pure disappointment. Just think, eatin' all that greasy slop them taverns put out when I coulda been eatin' your tasty cookin'. But everything's gonna be better now. Yessiree. I just won me a good-sized poke, so anywheres you want to go, I'll take you. You might want to go on up to Cincinnati. Last I seen Kurt and your purty ma, they was still there."

Sabina hurried to set an oversized chunk of nut bread and fork in front of him. She wanted to shut him up as much as anything else.

But it didn't. While Baxter merely sat there showing no expression, Shockley droned on, in between bites, about how he'd been wanting to marry her for years, hanging around, waiting his chance, all the places he'd searched for her. . . .

Finally he switched the topic to her stepfather. "You know, Kurt was real down on his luck when I left the Ohio. You ain't gonna believe this, missy, but he was actually down on the dock doin' hard labor. First time I ever seen him work up a sweat. An' his palms had blisters on 'em the size of quarters, turnin' to calluses. Not good for a gambler's hands." Shockley then removed his intense gaze from Sabina and spoke to Baxter. "Once I laid eyes on Sabina and her ma, I set my mind on it not to settle for no less than what ol' Kurt's got. I stayed close. An' one night, it all came my way. Yessiree."

Though her throat was too tight to swallow, Sabina poured herself some coffee—anything to spend more time away from the table and his leering eyes.

And Baxter's. No longer was his expression contained. The anger in his stare was as potent as Tom's glee.

Lord, she prayed, *please keep Baxter from exploding before Noah gets here. And please give us a miracle. Please.*

Sabina had never heard anything more beautiful than the sound of horses' hooves. *Thank you, Lord.* She left her cup on the mantel and started for the door.

But the moment she opened it and saw Noah and Howie riding up on winded animals—the very instant her eyes locked with Noah's—she was struck with the thought that he and his family would now learn that she had been gambled away. More humiliation to bear. Her chest became so tight, she could scarcely breathe.

Fear and humiliation aside, would Noah be able to find a way—a legal argument—that could save her? If so, would Shockley abide by it?

Chapter Twenty-Nine

Noah Reardon tipped his hat over a grim Nordic mouth, then walked past Sabina into the house.

On his heels strode in Howie, seeming older than his fifteen years, his face hard-set, his breathing labored—a testament to the hasty trip he had just made to fetch the only lawyer within many miles.

"Noah." Baxter had come to his feet as had her determined pursuer. "This is Mr. Tom Shockley. He's come here with—"

"No need to explain," Noah cut in. He shot a glance back at Sabina. "Howie gave me the details." She cringed as the tall man strode to Tom Shockley and extended a hand.

Obviously leery, Tom gave him a sideways glance, then reluctantly shook Noah's hand.

"May I examine the document now?"

Tom's square features went flat. "That's no lawyerin' coat you got on. You look like you been out in a field plowin' all day."

"I have," Noah said, barking a chuckle. "I'd starve if I counted on the meager legal fees I garner out here in the wilds."

Tom set his jaw, still unconvinced. "This better not be some trick to get my paper offen me."

Eyes narrowing, Baxter gripped the table separating him from Shockley. "Are you accusing us of being dishonest?"

"I'm sure that wasn't his intent," Noah said in an obvious attempt to defuse Baxter's rage. "Open the document out on the table. We won't put a hand on it."

Unwilling as he was, Tom did as Noah instructed, and the lawyer leaned over it, reading.

With his back to Sabina, she couldn't see Noah's face, his reaction. Baxter, though, stood as rigidly grim as before. Desperately trying not to panic, she shifted to Howie, wishing the lad was out in the barn with Delia and Sammy. He was too young to be witnessing such shameful business.

"I realize the document wasn't drawn up by a lawyer," Noah said, straightening. "But, I'm sorry to say, it appears to be quite legal." He turned to Baxter. "It even has the signatures of two witnesses."

"I've seen," Baxter remarked, his face set hard.

Sabina felt herself beginning to sink. She grabbed the back of a chair for support.

"And," Noah continued, "with Howie telling me how Mr. Shockley and Sabina's stepfather rode up to your wagon outside Cane Ridge looking for her—that's further proof of the marriage agreement's validity."

Baxter shot a withering glance to Howie—one that Sabina felt should have been directed at her.

Before Howie could respond, Shockley bellowed, "So that's why y'all look familiar!" His deadly eyes narrowed onto Baxter.

"You're some of the people we questioned the day Sabina took off. You *lied* to us."

"No, he didn't." Howie stepped forward, fists clenched in his father's defense. "Pa didn't know we had her hid in the wagon. We didn't tell him until later."

"That's of no consequence now," Noah said, the only calm voice in the room, "unless the debt is paid, Sabina is forfeited to him for the purpose of marriage."

"That's not good enough," Baxter said and stared around the table. "File an appeal. We received a letter from Sabina's mother last week. She wrote that they would have the money to pay this debt by Christmas. That's only two months away."

Tom Shockley burst out laughing.

The sound tore into Sabina like the blast from a long rifle.

"That'll never happen," he scoffed. "Erhardt won't save enough by then, not loadin' riverboats. Not now that the fool has seen the light and give up gamblin'. He won't earn enough in a year, if ever." Puffing out his barrel-like chest, Tom folded the hated paper and stuffed it inside his fancy shirt.

He then turned his smug expression to Sabina. "Yessir, this is my lucky week all the way around."

Baxter, his fists knotted, rounded Noah to reach Tom.

Sabina started to cry out, but Noah caught Baxter's shoulder, halting him. "Steady, now," Noah said with a low urgency.

Tom Shockley grinned, baiting the smaller man before turning his attention to Sabina, who stood behind them. "Would you believe, girly, I won almost two hundred dollars in some hovel ol' tavern down on Nashville's waterfront. Two hundred dollars, *cash* money. Then, to top it off, when I went up to the dry-goods store to buy me a new shirt—by the way, how do you like my weddin' shirt?"

Sabina sucked in a breath as he proudly ran his beefy hand

down the lace-lined front. He'd come dressed and ready to marry her.

Baxter took a step forward, dragging Noah with him.

"Anyway," Shockley continued, mockingly unaware, "I asked the kindly miss behind the counter iff'n she'd seen you, just like I been askin' everybody everywhere I went. And lo and behold, not only did she tell me where you was, she drawed me a map."

Wrenching free from Noah's grip, Baxter grabbed Tom's much larger arm and swung him around. "This woman, was she young or old?"

Tom shot him a queer look, then jerked loose. "Don't know what difference it makes, but she was young. Cute little thing with a honey of a smile. Daughter of ol' Finch who's been gettin' rich off'n the trappers."

Amanda Atwood. She'd been betrayed by Amanda.

Howie rammed between Baxter and Tom, his face dark with anger. "Pa, I knew that mealymouthed betrothal of yours couldn't be trusted. Underneath all that sweet talk, she's just as mean-spirited as her aunt."

"We'll discuss this later," Baxter ordered gruffly, stepping around the lad. He eyed Tom. "We have more pressing business here."

Showing no concern whatsoever, the vile fellow burst out laughing again. "That woman—she's your betrothed? No wonder she was so happy to help. With a comely wench like Sabina livin' right here with y'all . . ." His sneer suddenly turned deadly. "Or does she have cause to worry? What's really been goin' on around here?"

Baxter lunged, grabbing Tom by his fancy shirt. "Don't you dare drag Sabina down in the mud with you."

Frantically Sabina glanced toward the musket above the mantel.

Noah, acting fast, pushed between Baxter and the much sturdier man. "Now fellas, simmer down. No need to—"

"No need to fight," Sabina hurled, her heart pounding wildly. The two men were poised, knuckles bared for battle . . . her Baxter and the gouging, biting bone-breaker.

"Please!" She tugged at Tom's sleeve until she pulled his attention away from the impending battle. She would not have one of Baxter's dear eyes gouged out on her account, his body broken and bleeding. "Please, Tom, go outside and wait. I'll get my things from my cabin and be right with you." She started for the door.

Baxter caught her arm. "You're not going anywhere." He swung back to Tom. "I'll pay the debt myself. Noah, that is correct, isn't it? If the debt is covered, she's free of him."

Sabina's gaze flew to Noah.

"Aye." He nodded in agreement.

"No! No slick lawyer is gonna cheat me." Tom shoved past Baxter and Howie to reach Noah. His powerful hands shot to their neighbor's throat, slamming him up against the table. "I'm not leavin' here without her."

"Shockley."

The man's face went blank, and he released Noah.

Sabina followed his wary gaze to Baxter, who now stood near the hearth, musket in hand, its barrel pointed directly at Tom. "You'll take the money and leave . . . one way or the other."

"It'd be a shame to have to resort to violence," Noah said, rubbing his neck. "But the law will be upheld here, the same as if we were in the capital. Baxter, go get your money."

His aim steady, Baxter remained where he was. "Howie, run upstairs. Get my money pouch. It's at the bottom of my big chest."

As the lad took the steps two at a time, Sabina felt sick to her stomach. What trouble she'd brought down on this family. She turned back to a room wrought with tension. Baxter's flintlike gaze and musket were both aimed at the middle of Tom's wedding shirt.

While the two men glared at each other, Noah unbuttoned his overcoat and pulled out a pistol he had stuffed in his belt. Removing a pouch from his shirt pocket, he poured a bit of the black powder into the pistol's flashpan, then cocked the weapon, adding his own threat to the deadly mix.

Prudently, Tom spread his hands while backing up a couple of steps. "Now, take it easy, boys."

Sabina's legs threatened to give way again. She caught hold of the nearest chair.

All the while, Howie's every footstep could be heard as he rummaged in the room above, then the pounding of his shoes as he raced back down the stairs. Howie stopped at the bottom, eyeing the added weapon now trained on Tom.

"Come here, Howie," Baxter summoned. "Hold the musket on our *guest* while I count out the money." Exchanging the weapon for the pouch, he strode to the table and dumped the contents onto the white linen, then started counting the coinage.

Tom Shockley moved in for a closer look.

Sabina stepped aside, not wanting to be within his reach.

"That's only ninety-two dollars," Shockley said, sounding relieved. "You're short eight dollars."

It isn't enough. Sabina felt her chest banding tighter than a barrel's. She could scarcely breathe. Either she went willingly with him or there would be bloodshed.

"I'll make up the difference," Noah abruptly offered.

"Now wait a minute, boys." Worry was back in Tom's beefy face. "Y'all gotta be crazy." He turned to Baxter. "Are you tellin' me a upstandin' citizen like yourself would spend your last pence, plus eight owin', on Sabina? Did you forget, man, you're set to marry that rich trader's daughter? Purty l'il thing she is, too. You gonna risk throwin' all that away—on Sabina?" He pointed a vile finger at her. "You're actin' like she's some hoity-toity heiress or somethin'. Don't you know? Why, she ain't nothin' but illegitimate trash."

"*No! Stop!*" Sabina stumbled back.

But he didn't listen. "She ain't even got a name of her own. She has to borrow her stepfather's."

Baxter, Howie, Noah . . . they'd all heard. Her secret was out—she'd been stripped bare.

With a sob ripping from her throat, she fled out the door.

～

Nearly blind with rage, Baxter ripped the musket from Howie's hands and jammed it into the miscreant's miserable belly.

"Hold on! Hold on!" Shockley stumbled backward.

Baxter himself was being pulled away.

"Calm down." Noah stepped between him and Shockley. "This worm isn't worth the ball and powder to blow him away."

"Pa! Look out!"

Baxter sidestepped Noah to see Shockley holding one of the hardwood chairs above his head, ready to wield it. With two firearms pointed at him, the culprit slowly lowered it.

"Now let's all sit down and cool our tempers," Noah suggested, "while I pull out my purse." He tucked his pistol in his belt.

"It don't matter what you do," Shockley growled as he perched on the edge of the seat he'd just lowered to the floor. "I ain't takin' your money."

"Yes, you are." Shifting the musket to one hand, Baxter shoved his every last cent down the table toward the man.

"That's right," Howie concurred, snatching up the fireplace poker. "The only choice you got is whether you're leavin' here with or without your head." The boy's eyes were as deadly as Baxter's own resolve.

"Take it easy, Howie." Noah spoke in a cautious tone, saying the words Baxter knew he should have—would have—if he could just get control of his own rage. His desire to fill the gambler's belly with lead was so strong, his finger trembled against the trigger.

Shockley must have noticed. Fear sparked in his eyes, just before he turned his head and looked away. The man was finally beginning to understand just how close to dying he really was.

Once Noah had added his eight dollars to the other coins, he retrieved his weapon. "Baxter," he ordered firmly, "get some ink and a quill. It's vital that this transaction is legal."

As Baxter lowered his weapon, the fear in Shockley's eyes was replaced by pure hatred.

But Baxter had no intention of being intimidated by the menacing tavern prowler as he moved to the desk to retrieve the needed items. Too much was at stake. Sabina.

"Bring forth the IOU, Mr. Shockley," Noah ordered as Baxter placed the writing materials on the table. His neighbor was again trying to maintain some semblance of order. "You need to sign your name after I write down that you've received payment in full. Then I'll witness it."

Like an angry bull, Shockley lowered his head. "I said, I don't want his stinkin' money. Or yours."

Catching up the musket, Baxter aimed it at Shockley's temple. "It's the money or nothing. Let's get it over with. Now."

"I say we blow his head off," Howie threatened recklessly. He reared back the poker.

"All right, all right." The man threw his hands up. "No female's worth gettin' kilt over."

Once the legal work was done, Noah handed the paper to Baxter with a reassuring nod. "Mr. Shockley's business is finished here. So it would be my pleasure to see him on his way for you. Out of the valley."

"I won't forget this." Baxter extended a hand to Noah. "I couldn't ask for a better neighbor."

Shockley lunged to his feet, shoving past them and out the door.

"Wait! He's got a rifle on his saddle." Baxter charged after the man. "Hold it right there, Shockley." He didn't know if the gambler would've gone for his weapon or not, but Baxter wouldn't risk it.

Removing the firearm from its holster, Baxter handed it to Noah. "I'd better go along with you." He collected Thunder's reins as the other two mounted.

At that moment, Delia came running toward the house—not from the barn but from the opposite direction. "Papa. It's Sabina. She ran off into the woods, cryin' somethin' awful." Delia spied Shockley. She whirled toward him, grabbing his gelding's bridle. "What did you do to her?"

Shockley rolled his eyes. "I give up. You win. Just get me outta here, Reardon."

"Delia," Noah ordered, "let go of the horse's bridle. Mr. Shockley and I will be leaving now. And Baxter, you better go see about Sabina. The two of us will do just fine on our own, won't we?" he said, shifting his Nordic gaze to the other man.

"Like I said," the blustering hulk repeated, "just get me outta here. The whole blasted family's crazy."

Now that Shockley appeared to be accepting his loss, Baxter trusted that Noah, a war veteran like himself, could handle the man's departure without help. He shifted his attention to Delia. "Which way did Sabina go?"

"Past our cabin. Sammy ran after her."

"You and Howie stay here in case she comes back." Baxter didn't think she would, though, not after the horror and devastation he'd seen on her face just before she ran out. He tossed the musket to the lad. "Fire a signal shot if she returns."

Chapter Thirty

Baxter slammed into Sabina's cabin and searched every corner to make sure she hadn't returned. No sign of her. He ran out the door, leapt across the brook, and followed it upstream, traveling the path to the glen. If she did stop, it would be at her private praying spot, where he'd found the written words in the sand.

About halfway along the trail covered now by colorful autumn leaves, he came upon Sammy. Moving slowly, the boy's attention was on the ground. He spun around. "Pa! I think Sabina went up the trace here, but I ain't sure." Sammy stooped and brushed aside some leaves and studied the multiple tracks that lay beneath, then pointed up a sparsely wooded rise. "She could'a gone thataway."

"You go up the hill. I'll keep to the path." Grateful for another pair of eyes to help him search, Baxter took off at a jog. Sabina had been so distraught when she ran out, there was no telling what she might do. Like some horses he'd heard stories about, she might not stop running until her heart burst.

Nearing the glen, Baxter heard strange sounds. Sobbing. Wrenching sobs.

He stopped to catch his breath, giving thanks to God that she hadn't run up the hills and into the wilderness that surrounded the valley—into the vast stretches of primeval forest where bears and wolves still reigned. It felt good to pray again. He hadn't done enough of that lately.

Sabina's low wails traveled through the branches to him, sounding almost animal-like in their raw pain; they dug into his stomach, his heart.

Quietly now, he moved toward her, fearful lest he startle her into bolting again.

"I thought you loved me, God," he heard her cry out, her voice broken with her sorrow. "Yet you've let this happen. I–I don't think I can do this, what you're asking of me. . . ."

Looking through the branches of an almost leafless willow, he saw her near the sitting rock . . . on her knees in the dying grass, her hands outstretched, her drenched face turned upward.

"Is it all a lie?" she asked in a plaintive lament. "Everything I thought I knew about you?" Her hands fell to her sides, and she clutched herself, looking utterly defeated.

Baxter couldn't bear to see her this way, her faith in God shattered, weeping over this worst of losses.

She raised a hand again. "Or is it just me, Lord, that you have no use for?"

"*No,*" Baxter rasped, his own voice coming out in a croak. "*Never.*" He reached for her.

∾

Tom Shockley! Blinded by tears, Sabina swung wildly at the figure beside her. "I'll *die* before I go with you."

He pulled her up, trapping her arms against his chest. "Sabina! It's me, Baxter. You're safe. I paid Shockley off. He's gone."

Baxter. An instant of joy, then her spirit dove to the depths as she remembered. He knew the shameful truth about her. "Please, go away. I can't bear for you to look at me. To see the true me." She wrenched from him.

But his arms banded around her even tighter. "Please," he begged, "don't run away. You have nothing to be ashamed of."

"How can you say that?" She buried her tear-ravaged face against his vest, away from his searching eyes. Away from her ugliness.

"Don't you know?" he said in a feathery whisper, his lips against her ear. "You are the angel God sent into our lives. No circumstance of your birth could ever take away your beauty. You are the sunshine that warms us . . . our very own oil of over-flowing joy."

His unbelievable words poured over her. They were her own balm, warm and fragrant and healing.

Gently, he lifted her face from against him, his gaze tender upon her . . . wiping her tears with his thumbs . . . lulling her. . . .

Regaining her senses, she turned her head away and stepped back. "Those are things you may have thought about me before, but now you know this disgrace on top of knowin' I was raised among gamblers and thieves. I'm not forgettin' that up 'til the very minute Tom Shockley walked in the door, you had every notion of dismissing me from your service once you married

303

Mistress Atwood. She's the kind you could take home to Virginia, a lady you would be proud to present to your family. Not someone like me. And Howie, he knows about me, too, and—" tears choked her again—"and so does Noah Reardon."

Baxter caught hold of her again.

"Don't you see?" She thrust away from him. "Soon everyone will know my shameful secret. The Reardons—everyone in the whole valley—will find out. Look down on me. With pity, maybe, but still . . ." She shook her head. "I can't stay here."

Catching her chin, Baxter lifted her face up to his. "If you feel you must go, I accept that. But whither thou goest, *I* will go, Sabina Erhardt. I love you. My children love you. I can't imagine life without you ever again."

His words staggered her. He loved her. He would go anywhere with her, just to keep her. But . . . "What about Mistress Atwood?"

"After she betrayed you like that to Tom Shockley? No amount of dowry could ever make me marry her now. The betrothal is severed." He gathered her close again. "Besides, I've been an utter fool, thinking my children needed money and position to have a good life. I can't believe I was willing to throw away my happiness—and theirs—by rejecting the very bride that God himself brought to us. I blindly forged ahead, making my own wrong-headed decisions about what God's will was for me. *I* decided what I thought I needed, then arrogantly thanked God when I met someone who fit *my* criteria. Not once did I listen to him, seek his wisdom, his pleasure. I couldn't see the treasure he laid right before me. Everyone tried to tell me. And now, because of my stubbornness, I've caused you untold suffering—those tears in your eyes, the ache in your heart. I blame myself for giving you a reason to doubt the Lord." His fingers dug into her arms. "Please, please, can you ever forgive me?"

She was hearing everything she'd ever dreamed of, but could

he really, truly, mean all he was saying? Or was he merely caught up in the high drama of Shockley's arrival? She looked into Baxter's eyes.

His gaze faltered . . . but for only a second. "I reckon what I'm trying to say is I'd be honored if you'd allow me to come courting. For the purpose of matrimony."

He'd be *honored* if she'd allow him? He a Virginia Clay, and she less than a nobody. *But not in God's eyes*, she reminded herself . . . or in those eyes beholding her this very moment. All his love poured from them, reaching out to her, willing her to say yes. More tears spilled down her cheeks, tears of undescribable joy.

Abruptly, he released her. "La, I do apologize. I've overstepped myself and caused you more suffering. I thought . . . I hoped you had affection for me too. A little, anyway."

How could he doubt it? She flung her arms around his neck. "Oh, I do. I do. I just can't believe you love me too."

He caught her to him in a rib-crushing embrace. Then his lips came down on hers, jolting her as if she'd been struck by lightning, melting her every thought into a wondrous, thrilling oneness with him.

When at last he dragged his mouth away from hers, his eyes glistened with tears. Swiping at them, he laughed. "Forget the courtship. After that kiss, you have no choice but to marry me right away. But first—" he unbuttoned his big-pocketed work vest—"put this on; you're freezing."

She hadn't noticed her chill, but he had. The dear, dear man. As she allowed her shoulders to be draped within the garment that still held his warmth, she knew that every word uttered from his glorious mouth had been everything she'd ever wished to hear from the man she loved.

But what if he were only caught up in the excitement of the

moment? A gentleman saving the fair damsel? There were still Howie and Noah—and what they knew about her—to consider. The scandal of her past.

She stepped back. "Mayhap we should speak of this later. I had a chicken potpie simmering on the back coals, and—" she took an anxious breath—"there's Howie and Noah. They might not be so understanding, so willing to accept me."

~

"Pa found her! They're comin'!" Sammy jumped up and down beside the plowed-under garden, then ran toward the main house. "They're comin'!"

Cautiously happy, Sabina felt drained and not a little apprehensive. She and Baxter laughed nervously at the lad as they strolled home, his hand determinedly keeping hold of hers.

"That boy's a corker." Baxter's own chuckle was much more relaxed. "I never saw a youngster with so much energy."

By the time they reached the water well, Sammy had climbed the porch, and all three kids waited there, watching. But Sammy remained for no more than a few seconds. Leaping off the steps, he ran toward Baxter and Sabina.

"Sabina," Sammy jabbered loudly, "you should'a stayed. You missed the best part." Reaching her, he grabbed her free hand. Then dancing backwards, he pulled her toward the house. "Howie said Papa was gonna shoot the gambler. *Twice*. He ain't scared'a nothin' when it comes right down to it. Are ya, Pa?"

Alarmed, Sabina halted and looked up at this normally calm and composed man. "It came to *that*? You didn't tell me that part."

He reddened, a guilty grin spreading across his mouth. "I—he—I lost my temper. I guess I'm not the perfect gentleman you took me for."

"A man's supposed to protect his family," Howie interjected, walking out to join them, his adolescent face man-hard. "And as far as us kids is concerned, Sabina's family."

His words touched her deeply. They held no condemnation. He still wanted her to stay as much as before. Sabina moved to him and brushed her hand along a cheek that was showing the first signs of peach fuzz. "And a woman's job is to feed her household food that's not all burned up."

Picking up her skirts, she ran for the house. She passed Delia and slowed just long enough to give the puzzled girl a hug, then hurried on to check the potpie.

A blast of heat stung her face as she walked in, the aromas of spicy bread and chicken stew welcoming her into this house she thought she'd left forever, this home that now surrounded her in the same warm comfort as Baxter's vest.

Remembering her purpose, she removed the bulky vest and tossed it over a chair on her way to the large fire opening. She grabbed a poker and pulled a legged pot from the blackened rear. With quilted pad in hand, she lifted the lid. To her amazement, there was no smell of char wafting up on the steam, and the top crust of the pie was a marvelous golden brown. Not a hint of burning. It had seemed like an eternity since she'd shoved the pot into the fire and gone outside to greet the kids and instead discovered Tom Shockley; but it couldn't have been more than an hour.

The thundering rumble of footsteps brought her to her feet. Delia came in, followed by the menfolk, all grinning just like it was Christmas morning.

"Delia, dear, help me set the table."

"We'll all help," Baxter jubilantly offered. "Let's use the best napkins and dishes. I feel like celebrating tonight."

"Me, too." Sammy ran for the china cabinet.

Instead of moving into action like the others, Howie's expression took on a seriousness, and he sidled up to Sabina. "I just want you to know," he said for her ears only, "Pa and Noah paid off Shockley, and—"

"*Noah* paid too? Even after he heard about me?"

"Sure." Howie stepped closer. "Do you think any of us gives two hoots about what that snake said? Nobody who loves you will ever care, and it just ain't no one else's business."

For all his mischievous ways, he was such a dear boy. "Thank you."

"For what?"

She pulled the lad into a hug. "Just for being you." Then pushing him away, she said, "Get the butter whilst I cut some corn bread."

As she stacked the yellow meal squares onto a plate, she noticed that all had suddenly gone silent. No one spoke. No one moved. Turning around, she saw the Clays all standing behind their chairs and looking at her with their big brown eyes, grinning mighty suspiciously. "What is it?"

"Look at your plate," Sammy blurted, followed by Delia's slap across the top of his head. He'd obviously spoken out of turn.

Still, Sabina did as he bade. And on the dish lay a pair of dancing slippers. Not just any slippers, but beautiful blue ones with plaid bows and white rosettes to match her new winter gown.

She thought she'd shed all the tears possible for one day, yet more stung the back of her eyes as she looked beyond them to Baxter. Even before he'd thought to propose marriage to her, he'd made these for his lowly servant girl . . . these shoes fit for a queen. "They're so elegant. And you made them for no one else, just for me."

"Aye, that I did. Beautiful shoes for a beautiful lady."

Moving to the table, she picked up one of the slippers and turned the wondrously soft leather over in her hand. This was the final proof she needed. The Lord truly had brought her to this family and to the one man chosen just for her. She gazed up at the love in his rich mahogany eyes. "I'll wear these to dance at our wedding."

"*Wedding!*" Baxter banged into two chairs to reach her. He grabbed her in a fierce hug, not caring that the kids were watching.

"What's goin' on?" she heard Sammy ask.

"They're gettin' married," Howie informed him. "She's stayin' with us forever."

"Truly?" Delia squealed and ran to Sabina and Baxter, wrapping her girlish arms around them both.

Baxter pulled his daughter into their circle.

Then Howie and Sammy piled on, everyone laughing and hugging at once.

The door burst open.

Sabina froze. *Tom Shockley?*

In strode Philip. "I know I'm real late gettin' home and I'm real sorry I missed out on the harvesting." Before he lost his nerve, he blurted in a rush, "But before you say anything, I've got somethin' to say. I refuse to go to college in Virginia. I don't want to go back East or back anywhere else. I want to go forward with Marty Newman."

Baxter looked at the rebellious lad from over Delia's head. "Well, son, it gladdens me to hear that."

Philip's mouth fell open. "It gladdens you?" With a confused frown, he took stock of his family, standing close, their arms around each other. "Hey, what's goin' on here? Did I miss something?"

Epilogue

The dishes are done, Sabina," Delia said, hanging her towel and those of the Reardon girls on hooks beneath the cup shelf. "May we start making the pew bows now?"

Sabina glanced up from sewing at the dining table, taking in their fresh young faces. "Aye, and thank you, girls. I know you had a mountain of dishes with both our families here for Sunday dinner."

The trio ran to the parlor end of the room and dropped down on the floral carpet, scooting close to the tea table. Across the polished cherrywood top lay wide pastel blue ribbons and thinner white lengths for roses.

"Do a good job, now," Mistress Reardon instructed from where she sat with Sabina and her daughters-in-law. "Make them the same size as the sample I made for you."

The elderly matron returned her attention to the task before the women—Sabina's wedding gown. "No, Annie, add the second ruffle, starting with just the tiniest bit showing, then gradually make it wider. That's right." She patted her golden-haired daughter-in-law's hand. Annie was always more adept in the cheese-making shed or out with her bees than trying to master any of the arts of homemaking.

Sitting beside Jessica, Sabina worked on a triple row of sleeve ruffles, concentrating on making as minuscule stitches as possible, lest she too be reprimanded. But even if she were, she was certain she wouldn't mind. Bossy as Mother Louvenia was, she merely wanted Sabina to have the prettiest wedding gown possible.

And what a gorgeous one it would be.

Spread out before them were yards and yards of two complementary shades of light blue satin—Baxter's favorite color for her. The fabric had been taken from gowns donated by Jessica and Betsy Smith. And scarcely a woman in the valley had passed up the opportunity to contribute some lace or glass beads for the gown. Everyone seemed especially pleased, not merely because Sabina and Baxter would wed but because the two would remain in the valley.

So many cut pieces to sew together and so much decoration to add. And Mother Louvenia knew where every scrap and bead would go. Such wonderful neighbors Sabina had.

"I want to thank you ladies again," she couldn't help repeating, "for all you're doing to help with the wedding. You've been so good and patient with me ever since I first arrived."

"My patience will end if you don't keep your mind on your stitches." Mother Louvenia pointed at Sabina with her needle. "There ain't no time for dillydallying. Everything has to be ready by next Sunday. Only one week left."

Annie leaned forward as she pulled the thread through the fabric. "It will be ready if the whole valley has to pitch in. We're all that glad Baxter ain't marryin' up with that snooty Nashville gal. We all spent a lot of time prayin' he'd come to his senses and ask you instead."

Sabina glanced up from a stitch. "I had no idea y'all was praying for us. More reason to thank you. My only concern is the sacrifice Baxter made. Not only did he forfeit a sizable dowry to wed me, but paying off my debt took every cent he had. Now none of the boys can go east to college—not that any of 'em wants to, not right now anyway."

"That ain't nothin' to fret about," the bony older woman scolded. "I heard Baxter tell Ike that his shoe business has tripled since he come back from the Cane Ridge revival. It won't take no time for him to fill his poke again. 'Sides, if any of the lads in the valley purely wanted to go back East to college, we'd all see he got there."

"Yes," Sabina mused, more grateful to God than ever for leading her to this very special valley. "All the folks pitching in, like with cabin raisings and corn shuckings and everything else." Yes, a purely wonderful place.

She glanced out the window at the men and kids warming themselves against the December chill around a bonfire that had been growing larger by the minute. The younger children delighted in feeding it every stick and sap-frosted pinecone they could find.

While untangling a strand of lace, ebony-haired Jessica turned to Sabina beside her. "Even if Baxter has relinquished his opportunity to live with the extra luxuries Miss Atwood could provide, don't let that bother you. Some of the saddest people I ever met were exceedingly wealthy. I never once regretted choosing happiness with Noah over a privileged life with them. Happiness is found in following where the Lord takes us, not in the accumulation of wealth and prestige or power."

"And you had the entire Clay family pick you over that prissy gal and her money," Annie said, looking up. Her gold-flecked eyes sparkled in the lamplight as she grinned. "But I sure do wish I'd been here to see Howie and Sammy when that gambler showed up. Noah said them skinny boys of yours bristled up like a couple'a banty roosters. Howie stood right up to the scoundrel."

Able to see the humor in the aftermath, Sabina nodded. "They surely did." Her gaze slipped outside again. She found Howie with a long stick, sword fighting with Annie's Jacob, and Baxter, standing with Ike and Noah. Her betrothed had what seemed to be a permanent grin on his face . . . one he'd worn almost constantly these past few weeks.

Abruptly, though, the smile vanished as Sammy ran up to him, excitedly jabbering about something Sabina couldn't hear because the windows were closed against the cold.

The tousle-headed boy pointed toward the road.

Curious, Sabina rose from her chair and walked past the girls to the window at the far end. Two riders and three horses were coming out of the woods. She recognized the horses.

She whirled away from the window, her Sunday blue-and-green plaid sweeping clean the tea table full of ribbons and pew bows as she ran for the door. "It's my mother and Kurt!" She'd written to her parents last month with the faint hope that the letter would reach them in time for them to come for the wedding. "Praise the Lord!" Picking up her skirts, she flew past the men and youngsters. "Mama! Mama!"

By the time she reached her parents, Greta had slid down from her mount. They grabbed each other, hugging and kissing and crying.

"Hey, save some of that for me." Surprisingly tanned and fit looking, Kurt had also dismounted. He pulled her into his arms—this man who was the only father she'd ever known—squeezed her tight and patted her back. "I'm so sorry, Sabina, for what I done to you. I don't ever expect you to completely forgive me, but maybe just a little?"

With the puffiness gone from his face and the red from his sky blue eyes, Kurt looked quite handsome—even the gray at his temples added to his pleasing appearance. He truly was a new man. "Your giving yourself to the Lord makes everything right." Sabina drew her mother close again. "So many years Mama and I prayed for you. I wanted to give up, but Mama wouldn't hear of it. She just wouldn't hear of it."

"Tell them who I am." Sammy had come right behind them and was tugging on Sabina's plaid sleeve. "I'm the one what found Sabina and hid her. I'm the one who saved her."

Greta turned toward him, her smile as glowing as her mature face. She took Sammy's shoulders. "And such a stalwart young man you are."

Sammy reddened slightly, and his wide gaze faltered. But just for a second. "You're real purty, too. Like Sabina, just a lot older."

Her mother chuckled. "Why—thank you."

Baxter and the older boys had reached them, but they hung back, not putting themselves forward as Sammy had.

Sabina beckoned them to come closer, then started by introducing the boys and saving Baxter for last. "Mama, Kurt, with the purest pleasure, I want you to meet the rest of the Clay menfolk." She caught the nearest hand. "This here is Philip. At the moment he wants to be a coppersmith. But he's real good with book learning, so if he decides to go ahead and study medicine or read for the law, he won't have no problem a'tall."

Next she turned to Howie. "And this here is Howard. He hasn't settled on a trade yet. What he loves most is making music. He plays the fife good as anyone, and he's learning the violin."

"We'll have to get together then," Kurt said, shaking the lad's hand. "I play a mean fiddle myself."

Howie's umber eyes brightened. "That's what Sabina said."

"And Hope and Gracie sing real pretty," a feminine voice chimed in. Delia had come from the house and joined them unnoticed.

Sabina reached out and pulled her to the fore, proud of how delightful she looked in her new winter-red Sunday dress. "And this is my new daughter, my bosom companion, Delia. She's as lovely inside as she is to look at."

Delia's cheeks turned almost as red as her day gown. "Sabina always says things like that."

"And my girl don't lie," Greta said, taking Delia's hands into her own. "It will be a pure treat, getting to know you. All of you."

"And this," Sabina said, intertwining her arm with Baxter's, "is the man I wrote you about. Mama, he's everything we ever prayed for. And more. So much more."

Baxter's coloring heightened a bit, too, as he extended a hand to Kurt. "We couldn't be more pleased to see you. Your being here for our wedding means the world to Sabina."

"And to us," Greta said, wiping away a stray tear.

Sabina wrapped an arm around her mother. "Come inside out of the cold. I'll fix you a hot cup of spiced cider. And, Mama, I want you to meet some of the neighbor ladies. I have so many friends. Wonderful Christian friends . . ."

Once her mother was ensconced in working on the elaborate wedding gown with the Reardon women and glowing with more contentment than she had ever seen, Sabina poured a second cup of spiced cider and took it outside for Kurt.

He and Baxter stood several feet apart from the other menfolk in what appeared to be a serious but congenial conversation.

Sabina paused. *Oh Lord, I pray they do get along, that Baxter can see the redeemed man in Kurt, not the man who gambled me away.*

Then she headed across the yard to them. "Here, Kurt. I brought you some hot cider. And I'm warming some food. It'll be ready in a few minutes."

"Thank you, Bina girl. I was just telling Baxter here how much I 'preciate the good care he's taken of you."

She exchanged a tender glance with Baxter, then turned back to her stepfather. "And I thank you and Mama for coming so quick." She gave him another hug. "Reckon I better get on back to the women." She turned to leave.

Baxter caught her hand and drew her back. "You never told me Kurt had apprenticed as a saddler with his father. That he knows how to work with leather."

She looked from Baxter to Kurt. "As long as I can remember, he mostly just kept our own tack in good repair."

"Well, we've been talking," Baxter said. "With our getting married, you and Delia will be moving back into the main house, leaving the cabin empty. Since I have more shoe orders than I can handle and since your stepfather is determined to pay back what I spent on his debt, he's agreed to stay in your cabin and work with me, learn the cobbler trade—if that's agreeable with you."

"Agreeable? Oh my . . ." Her whole family here in one place, to visit with anytime she pleased, to go to church together . . . "You and Mama staying? For truth?"

With that infectious grin of his, Kurt stuck out his foot, which sported a scuffed and worn boot. "When times was good, I owned enough pairs of fine boots to know what they should look like."

At the mention of footwear, Sabina recalled her everyday shoes and dancing slippers lined beneath her bed as well as the stylish Sunday ones she wore right now, knowing that neither she nor any of her family would have to go naked-footed again. Or hungry. Or unloved. And her mother at long last would have four walls to call her very own.

To think, just a few short weeks ago, Sabina had accused her heavenly Father of not loving her. How fickle her faith had been, how meager her love. Yet God in his infinite and wondrous wisdom had brought everything together. Far better than she could have ever imagined.

Slipping her arm around Baxter's waist, she rose up on her toes and whispered what henceforth would be the song of her life. "My oil of gladness runneth over."

"Aye, and so do my riches." Caressing her with his eyes, Baxter wrapped her in a hug. "Milady comes to me with treasure beyond treasure."

A Note from the Author

While initially researching the late 1790s Tennessee, I learned that drinking, bragging, and brawling were commonplace in a mostly godless, lawless land, where whiskey was taken in trade as often as money. Even the entertainment was violent: bearbaitings, cockfights, and gander pulls.

Then came a man who was "on fire" for the Lord—George McGready. He convinced three small congregations to pray in faith and in the spirit of their own repentance for the conversion of their fellowmen. He asked each person to sign a covenant, agreeing to pray every Saturday evening and Sunday morning and to devote the third Saturday of each month to prayer and fasting.

From that small beginning came the "weeping with shame of some of the boldest and most daring sinners." This *holy fire* rapidly spread to other ministers and congregations, and the following summer, 500 people traveled from "far and wide" to come to a quarterly communion service to be part of the "floods of salvation." By the next summer, 10,000 attended a camp meeting; the next summer saw an astounding 25,000 in attendance . . . all coming together for yet another great outpouring of the Holy Spirit.

I traveled to Tennessee this fall and was blessed to see the fruit of those first few people's prayers and fasting. So many of their descendants are still faithfully attending the numerous churches that dot the landscape along with Christian colleges and hospitals.

As wonderful as it was to witness the lasting results of God's power and grace in Tennessee, during this past year I have been thrilled, humbled, and gratified to be one of the multitudes to witness another of God's great outpourings. Last August when eight Christian aid workers were arrested in Afghanistan along with sixteen of the local boys they had witnessed to, I feared they would all be executed—the Islamic regime that held them was known for deadly suppression of any beliefs differing from their own. While praying for the prisoners, I felt defeated, thinking there was no hope for them this side of heaven.

Then 1 Chronicles 29:11 came to mind: "Yours, O Lord, is the greatness, the power, the glory, the victory, and the majesty. Everything in the heavens and on earth is yours, O Lord." I realized how puny my faith was. I wrote in my prayer journal: "You, God, are more powerful than any evil." Fiercely I underlined the words several times. Each day thereafter I would reread that truth as a reprimand to my own doubtful faith. Through the Christian media I learned that people all over the Christian world were also praying for the prisoners, that thousands upon thousands of us were bombarding heaven with our petitions.

But the situation soon turned even more impossible following the September 11 tragedy. I of little faith wavered again, thinking the captives were doomed for sure. But God not only took hold of the Taliban and miraculously shook the captives free of their clutches, he also gave those lovely, humble saints the opportunity to give God the praise and glory before the entire world.

In the wake of this, I am at long last learning that no effort I expend in service to the Lord will ever match "the earnest prayer of a righteous person. [It] has great power and wonderful results" (James 5:16). First and foremost, I've learned God wants me to commune with him without ceasing while truly believing in *his power and his majesty* as much as I do in his love and mercy.

I wish the same for you . . . as did Paul two thousand years ago when he wrote: "I pray that you will begin to understand the incredible greatness of his power for us who believe him. This is the same mighty power that raised Christ from the dead and seated him in the place of honor at God's right hand in the heavenly realms. Now he is far above any ruler or authority or power or leader or anything else in this world or in the world to come" (Ephesians 1:19-21).

Dianna Crawford

About the Author

DIANNA CRAWFORD lives in southern California with her husband, Byron, and the youngest of their four daughters. Although she loves writing historical fiction, her most gratifying blessings are her husband of forty years, her daughters, and her grandchildren. Aside from writing, Dianna is active in her church's children's ministries.

Dianna's first novel was published in 1992 under the pen name Elaine Crawford. Written for the general market, the book became a best-seller and was nominated for Best First Book by the Romance Writers of America. Three more novels and several novellas followed under that pen name.

Dianna much prefers writing Christian historical fiction, because she feels that our wonderful Christian heritage is commonly diluted or distorted—if not completely deleted—from most historical fiction, nonfiction, and textbooks. She felt very blessed when she and Sally Laity were given the opportunity to coauthor the Freedom's Holy Light series for Tyndale House. The books center on fictional characters who are woven into many of the real-life adventures and miracles that took place during the American Revolution.

The Freedom's Holy Light series consists of *The Gathering Dawn*, *The Kindled Flame*, *The Tempering Blaze*, *The Fires of Freedom*, *The Embers of Hope*, and *The Torch of Triumph*. Dianna has also authored two HeartQuest novellas, which appear in the anthologies *A Victorian Christmas Tea* and *With This Ring*. She is the coauthor with Rachel Druten of the novel *Out of the Darkness* (Heartsong Presents). Her HeartQuest series, The Reardon Brothers, consists of *Freedom's Promise*, *Freedom's Hope*, and *Freedom's Belle*.

Dianna welcomes letters from readers written to her at P.O. Box 80176, Bakersfield, CA 93380.

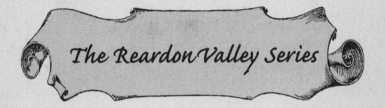

The Reardon Valley Series

Turn the page for an exciting preview
from book #2 in the Reardon Valley series
by Dianna Crawford.

(ISBN 0-8423-6011-5)

~

**Available spring 2003
from Tyndale House Publishers**

JUNE 1804

The hair prickled at the back of Belinda Gregg's neck, despite the sticky noonday heat. She was being watched.

Hiking her chin, she refused to show concern as she picked up her olive plaid skirt and mounted the steps to Bailey's General Store. Her mother needed more ginseng and figwort, or some other herb that might begin to soothe the tormented woman's soul. Without delay.

Still, Belinda kept her head down, making sure her own eyes could not be viewed from beneath the floppy brim of her sunbonnet.

But it was hard to be inconspicuous with the soles of her shoes flapping like drumsticks as she strode across the porch planks to reach the open doorway. As she stepped inside, cooler air brushed her cheeks, giving her an instant of relief—before she spotted those who had been watching her. Two young misses stood gawking out the front window. Obviously a couple of busybodies.

Instead of turning to face Belinda, they continued to stare at the dusty street outside. Someone else must have captured their attention.

Glad for the reprieve, Belinda started past the sacks and barrels for the counter at the other side of the store, where the short, stocky proprietor leaned over a ledger. Gripping a quill in his stubby fingers, he seemed unaware that she'd entered his establishment. Belinda had felt a special affinity for the middle-aged store-keeper the few times she'd been in the store during the three years since she and her parents had moved downriver of this settlement. Mr. Bailey always had a ready smile, and, though graying like her father, he had the same shade of red hair as the Greggs.

"From the way Max is a-hobblin'," one of the girls at the window said to her companion, "I cain't imagine how he got hisself this far from his house. Nursin' a broke arm whilst hoppin' along on that crutch."

Her own interest piqued, Belinda couldn't resist turning back to look, but the two calico-clad misses blocked her view.

"Why don't ya'll run out there and help him, Sissy?" the one with long, sandy hair urged, giggling. She elbowed her taller friend.

"Not *me.*" The neatly bunned brunette stiffened. "He thought he was too good to settle down with one of the valley girls when he run off to go explorin'—near broke poor Sally Sue's heart." She tilted her head. "Now, the way I see it, we're too good for what's come draggin' back. His ma told mine that his leg is so busted up that only a miracle of God's mercy will put it to rights again."

"You gotta admit, though," the smaller one said, "he's still one big hunk of a man. Even all busted up."

"Liza, I swan. You'd take on over a stinkin' ol' polecat iffen he wore pants."

"I would *not!*" The smaller one whirled around, her hair sailing out from her back as she stalked to the door. The dark-haired one chased after, leaving Belinda with a clear view of the subject of their conversation.

Even hunched over his crutch, he appeared to be an exceptionally tall, broad-chested man. Hatless, his thick thatch of blond hair shone like ripened flax in the noonday sun, especially against the deep tan of his squarely etched face. He truly must have cut quite the stalwart figure before he suffered his injuries.

A wave of compassion washed through Belinda. Poor man. As usual, town hypocrites were circling for the kill like the vultures they were. Belinda glanced up the street to the white spire of the community's church. Those heedless girls were given the privilege of hearing the love of God preached every Sabbath, yet they apparently never bothered to listen.

"Miss, can I be of help?" She swung back to see Mr. Bailey looking up from his ledger, his round blue eyes crinkling with a ready smile.

"Yes, sir. I have my list right here." Pulling a scrap of paper from her skirt pocket, she handed it to him, then took a last peek at the injured man. He'd turned off the road onto a narrow path that trailed into a thicket of trees tangled in vines and brush. It probably led to some bluff overlooking the river. If the fellow was smart, he'd go down to the dock instead, get in a canoe and paddle as far from this town as he could . . . just as she would be doing as soon as the storekeeper filled her order.

∿

Grunting with pain, Max Bremmer lowered himself onto a sheared-off boulder above a smooth stretch of the Caney Fork. Sweat beaded his brow, and not merely from the heat. It had taken all his strength—what there was left of it—to reach this hidden spot. But here for a little while, maybe, he'd be allowed to relax and breathe a bit of unused air. Get away from his mother's smothering concern and the solicitous pity of the neighbors.

A sharp pain shot through his throbbing leg as he eased his heel onto the ground. Sighing, he adjusted the sling holding his splintered arm. Resettling it upon his linen hunting shirt, he absently massaged his dangling fingers. What a broken-up mess he was. Helpless as a newborn pup.

How much longer was the healing going to take? Five weeks had already passed since the attack. Five wrenching weeks, with the first spent laid out in a canoe, half unconscious with fever, as his friends brought him up from St. Louis way.

Max focused on the dark, shadowy depths along the far bank, where the sun even at its zenith couldn't reach. A twig broke free from a skimming branch. Caught in the current, it swept out to the center of the wide fork.

His gaze followed its journey downstream; he was aware that within a day or two, the flow would reach the Cumberland, then travel on till that river fed into the mighty Mississippi. Farther upriver from where the Cumberland joined the Big Muddy, the Missouri merged. The Missouri . . . the river that came from the far west, cutting through vast reaches of virgin land. Open prairies as far as the eye could see, mountains so high their peaks floated above the clouds. And beyond? No white man knew for sure what lay on the other side. Only rumors of great wealth in furs and land so fertile that, if planted, even a broomstick would sprout leaves.

Ah, but this was the year the mystery was destined to unfold. President Jefferson had assigned that task to the Lewis and Clark Expedition. At this very minute, the surveying party was on its way west, up the Missouri . . . while he sat here in a broken heap, left behind.

Noticing that his teeth were clenched, he relaxed his jaw. No sense getting all hot over lost chances. Or much of anything else, for that matter. From what the Widow Smith said when she examined him, too much of his thigh muscle was damaged for him to ever do much trekking off into the wilderness again.

He sucked in a breath. "No, I'll be stuck here the rest of my life, pounding iron for Papa. Sweating away in his smithy, just like him and Mama always wanted."

Max's eyes fell shut at the throat-clogging thought. *Lord, will you please tell me, what did I ever do that was so bad you'd let me fall into this state?*

Loud cawing shattered the stillness. Max snapped his head around, taking in his surroundings. War parties imitated ravens when signaling to one another.

A pair of ravens swooped high above the river in a playful dance. *War party?* Feeling foolish, he relaxed. There weren't any tribes within a hundred miles of here. Never had been. Black Bear was the closest thing to an Indian he'd ever seen step foot in Reardon Valley. And he was only Shawnee by adoption.

Max then caught another flash of movement upstream. A birch-bark canoe came sliding out from behind a bend. As it floated into full view, he saw a lone woman down on her knees, paddling from inside the sliver of a craft. She glanced behind her as if she were being followed, then settled back and pulled the oar from the water. She laid it inside the canoe, letting the slender boat glide with the current.

Max guessed that her wariness had been unfounded, and she now felt safe to rest a bit. From a distance, he couldn't place her, especially with a sunbonnet covering her hair and most of her face.

As if she'd read his mind, she reached up, ripping loose the ties and tearing the bonnet from her head. And tumbling down in a mass of curls came the brightest red hair he'd ever seen. Redder than fiery flames. Not a single young woman in the valley could he recall who had wildfire for hair. She must have moved here after he'd left to join Drew Reardon at that Shawnee village north of the Missouri.

The woman shook her head, and the blaze flew about her like a spreading forest fire.

Breathtaking.

She retrieved the paddle and redirected the drifting canoe downriver again. Max hoped she'd look his way. If her face held even a hint of the beauty of her hair, she'd purely be a sight to behold.

The black birds swept down toward the canoe, cawing loudly, then spiraled up and swerved in his direction.

The woman's attention followed their lead, and she turned toward the high bank where he sat. Though more than a long stone's throw away, he could easily see the saintly perfection of her face, made blessedly human by a sprinkling of freckles. Then he realized she had caught sight of him.

Startled, she quickly recovered and gifted him with a smile, hesitant at first, then more friendly.

Gorgeous.

She lifted a hand and waved.

Before he could think to return the greeting, she'd sliced past, heading away . . . to where, he knew not.

Max squeezed his eyes shut for a second to clear away any blur of his vision, any distortion. When he opened them again, he caught naught but a last glimpse of the flame-haired lady as the current swept her from his sight.

He shook his head to clear it. Was this merely his imagination? He must be coming down with another fever. She was far too radiant to be real.

But what if she was?

Grabbing his crutch, Max hauled himself up on his one good leg and started to hop-skip toward home. If anyone would know about the mysterious redhead, his father would. Brother Rolf was pastor to everyone in Reardon Valley, as well as to anyone living in the surrounding hills and coves. He'd know if she existed.

Max slowed to a stop. Then again, why bother? No woman would ever look twice at a man with a game leg.

But this one might. She just might. Hadn't he seen it in her smile?

The corners of his mouth curled with his own meandering grin.

Visit www.HeartQuest.com for lots of info on
HeartQuest books and authors and more!

www.HeartQuest.com

CURRENT HEARTQUEST RELEASES

- *Magnolia,* Ginny Aiken
- *Lark,* Ginny Aiken
- *Camellia,* Ginny Aiken

- *Letters of the Heart,* Lisa Tawn Bergren, Maureen Pratt, and Lyn Cote

- *Sweet Delights,* Terri Blackstock, Elizabeth White, and Ranee McCollum

- *Awakening Mercy,* Angela Benson
- *Abiding Hope,* Angela Benson

- *Roses Will Bloom Again,* Lori Copeland
- *Faith,* Lori Copeland
- *Hope,* Lori Copeland
- *June,* Lori Copeland
- *Glory,* Lori Copeland

- *Winter's Secret,* Lyn Cote

- *Freedom's Promise,* Dianna Crawford
- *Freedom's Hope,* Dianna Crawford
- *Freedom's Belle,* Dianna Crawford
- *A Home in the Valley,* Dianna Crawford

- *Prairie Rose,* Catherine Palmer
- *Prairie Fire,* Catherine Palmer
- *Prairie Storm,* Catherine Palmer

- *Prairie Christmas,* Catherine Palmer, Elizabeth White, and Peggy Stoks
- *Finders Keepers,* Catherine Palmer
- *Hide & Seek,* Catherine Palmer
- *English Ivy,* Catherine Palmer
- *A Kiss of Adventure,* Catherine Palmer (original title: *The Treasure of Timbuktu*)
- *A Whisper of Danger,* Catherine Palmer (original title: *The Treasure of Zanzibar*)
- *A Touch of Betrayal,* Catherine Palmer
- *A Victorian Christmas Keepsake,* Catherine Palmer, Kristin Billerbeck, and Ginny Aiken
- *A Victorian Christmas Cottage,* Catherine Palmer, Debra White Smith, Jeri Odell, and Peggy Stoks
- *A Victorian Christmas Quilt,* Catherine Palmer, Peggy Stoks, Debra White Smith, and Ginny Aiken
- *A Victorian Christmas Tea,* Catherine Palmer, Dianna Crawford, Peggy Stoks, and Katherine Chute

- *Olivia's Touch,* Peggy Stoks
- *Romy's Walk,* Peggy Stoks
- *Elena's Song,* Peggy Stoks

HEART
QUEST®

COMING SOON (FALL 2002)

- *Ruth* (Brides of the West #5), Lori Copeland

- *A Victorian Christmas Collection,* Peggy Stoks

HEART
QUEST.

HEARTQUEST BOOKS BY DIANNA CRAWFORD

Freedom's Promise—For the first time in Annie McGregor's life, she's free. Free! Her years of servitude drawing to a close, Annie hears there's a man in town looking for settlers to accompany him across the mountains into Tennessee country. Could this be the answer to her prayers?

Isaac Reardon is on a mission to claim his betrothed—along with a preacher and a small group of settlers—and return to the beautiful home he has carved from the rugged wilderness. He is devastated to learn of his intended wife's betrayal. And now to make matters worse, he's confronted with a hardheaded, irresistible young woman who is determined to accompany his wagon train—without a man of her own to protect her!

Together, Annie and Ike fight perilous mountain passages, menacing outlaws, and a rebellious companion. And as they do, both are shocked to discover their growing attraction, which threatens to destroy the dream of freedom for which they have risked their very lives. Book 1 in The Reardon Brothers series.

Freedom's Hope—Jessica Whitman lives for one hope: Reaching her mother's family, the distinguished Hargraves of Baltimore, far from the clutches of her drunken father.

Noah Reardon, bitter over a broken betrothal, wants nothing to do with people. So why is he captivated by the intriguing Jessica? Despite himself, Noah reluctantly offers his protection to this feisty young woman.

Together Noah and Jessica discover a shared passion for truth, for integrity, for the very ideals upon which their new nation was founded. Noah is tempted to make the biggest mistake of his life—giving his heart to a woman who doesn't share his faith. Then a shocking discovery about Jessica's family threatens to shatter her hope. As they struggle to understand God's plan, both Noah and Jessica learn who truly offers hope for each tomorrow. Book 2 in The Reardon Brothers series.

Freedom's Belle —Desperate to escape the cruel man her parents insist she marry, Crystabelle grasps at the chance of a teaching position in a remote settlement beyond the mountains. Surely neither her betrothed nor her father will be able to find her there! And she will be free to pursue the independent life of which she has always dreamed.

A beautiful, refined heiress is the last person Drew would expect to be seeking passage overmountain to Tennessee Territory. But the lovely miss seems determined to procure the position of schoolmistress to Reardon Valley's youngsters. Dubious but intrigued, Drew finds himself helping her achieve her goal. Once he gets her safely to the valley, though, he'll be off again. Not even the growing threat to Crystabelle's safety can dissuade him from exploring his beloved wilderness . . . or can it?

As the two join forces, they learn the true meaning of adventure and freedom—but a shocking betrayal threatens to tear it away from them forever. Book 3 in The Reardon Brothers series.

A Daddy for Christmas—One stormy Christmas Eve on the coast of Maine, the prayers of a young widow's child are answered in a most unusual manner. This novella by Dianna Crawford appears in the anthology *A Victorian Christmas Tea*.

OTHER GREAT TYNDALE HOUSE FICTION